PRAISE FOR PAULE

The Artist of Blackberry Grange

"A bold, fresh story about the ghosts that haunt us and the ones we overcome. Paulette Kennedy explores loss and humility through the eyes of a saucy flapper who may bend the rules but not her sense of morality. This book will linger in your heart like the fond memory of a loved one."

—Mansi Shah, bestselling author of *The Direction of the Wind*

"Paulette Kennedy has once again proven herself to be a true master of gothic fiction. *The Artist of Blackberry Grange* is unsettling, atmospheric, and deeply moving, a haunting and heartfelt exploration of love and letting go. Perfect for readers who appreciate both the beauty and darkness of the human experience."

—Molly Greeley, author of *Marvelous*

"With *The Artist of Blackberry Grange*, Paulette Kennedy continues her streak of writing brilliant gothics. Part *Dorian Gray* and part exploration of the dark legacy of family trauma, I adored every twisty, gorgeously written page. Don't miss this one!"

—Kris Waldherr, author of *The Lost History of Dreams* and *Unnatural Creatures: A Novel of the Frankenstein Women*

The Devil and Mrs. Davenport

"An original, fun, and fascinating read from start to finish, *The Devil and Mrs. Davenport* is a must for fans of gothic fiction, magic realism, and historical thrillers. Author Paulette Kennedy reveals a genuine literary flair for creating memorable characters, as well as the kind of narrative-driven storytelling style that fully engages the reader's attention from cover to cover."

—*Midwest Book Review*

"There is a bit of romance, and a theme of embracing one's true self. This is a satisfying mix of historical mystery and paranormal fiction that fans of those genres will enjoy. Highly recommended."

—*Historical Novels Review*

"Taut with suspense, haunting, and unapologetically feminist, in *The Devil and Mrs. Davenport* Kennedy masterfully nods to gothic greats such as Shirley Jackson and Daphne du Maurier while cementing her own voice as one of the strongest in the genre today. A true masterpiece."

—Hester Fox, author of *The Last Heir to Blackwood Library*

"Paulette Kennedy is the rare species of author who somehow manages to outdo herself with each new book. It seems like a cliché to describe *The Devil and Mrs. Davenport* as haunting, and yet this book has undeniably haunted me—with its eerie imagery, its taut mystery, and unrelenting danger that crescendos below an outwardly perfect midcentury American life. A must-read for Shirley Jackson fans!"

—Olivia Hawker, bestselling author of *October in the Earth*

The Witch of Tin Mountain

"Hauntingly atmospheric and crackling with life, *The Witch of Tin Mountain* is an unforgettable story of family, magic, love, hypocrisy, and the power—for good or evil—we all carry with us. The richly painted Ozark setting leaps from the page, and all three interlaced storylines are captivating, heartbreaking, and triumphant in equal measure. I inhaled this book in two days. Witchy readers won't want to miss it."

—Allison Epstein, author of *A Tip for the Hangman*

"Kennedy beautifully captures the earthy, rural, charismatic traditions in her native Ozarks . . . Gritty and atmospheric, her alluring sophomore novel weaves spiritualism, demons, feminism, and folklore with more than a few twists before the book's satisfying ending. I loved every page!"

—Constance Sayers, author of *The Ladies of the Secret Circus* and *A Witch in Time*

"Electrifying! This multigenerational tale that travels across time and space is woven together like a delicate tapestry, and it will stay with you long after the last page."

—Mansi Shah, author of *The Taste of Ginger* and *The Direction of the Wind*

Parting the Veil

"Complete with LGBTQIA+ inclusivity, the suspenseful story will delight fans of historical fiction, horror, and mystery with twist after twist after twist."

—*Booklist*

"If you love a gothic tale full of twists and turns and things that go bump in the night, Paulette Kennedy's *Parting the Veil* is a not-to-be-missed treat. This debut is the perfect book to curl up with on a stormy night, but don't expect to put it down easily. And don't forget the Earl Grey and biscuits."

—Barbara Davis, bestselling author of *The Last of the Moon Girls*

"A darkly romantic old-school gothic novel with a gasp-inducing twist that's decidedly new school. In this lushly detailed page-turner, Paulette Kennedy piles on all the haunted house tropes you could hope for, and then some. Read this one with the lights on."

—Kris Waldherr, author of *The Lost History of Dreams*

The

ARTIST *of* BLACKBERRY GRANGE

OTHER TITLES
BY PAULETTE KENNEDY

The Devil and Mrs. Davenport

The Witch of Tin Mountain

Parting the Veil

The ARTIST *of* BLACKBERRY GRANGE

A NOVEL

PAULETTE KENNEDY

LAKE UNION PUBLISHING

Published by Lake Union Publishing, Seattle

www.apub.com

Amazon, the Amazon logo, and Lake Union Publishing are trademarks of Amazon.com, Inc., or its affiliates.

ISBN-13: 9781662524158 (paperback)
ISBN-13: 9781662524141 (digital)

Cover design by Kimberly Glyder
Cover image: © lambada / Getty; © Kittibowornphatnon, © Sergei Mishchenko, © Bojan Zivkovic, © Vlad Antonov / Shutterstock

Printed in the United States of America

For the cycle breakers

There is something fatal about a portrait. It has a life of its own.

CONTENT WARNING

This novel contains references to murder, traumatic death, suicide, racism, ageism, ableism, homophobia, alcohol dependency, adoption, traumatic birth, labor, miscarriage, dubious sexual consent, narcissistic abuse, and gaslighting.

Chapter 1

July 15, 1925

It's strangely soothing when everything goes wrong all at once. A bit like being in the eye of a cyclone. There you are in the middle, watching the chaos spin around you, knowing you can't do a damned thing but wait out the wind.

Today, the winds have been particularly harsh.

"I'm tired, Sadie," Ted told me, only minutes ago. I'd barely finished my vichyssoise when he took my hand from across our usual table at the Montpellier Tea Room and said he was tired. Tired of my moods. My moping.

But I was tired, too—of his lies and waiting for him to make up his mind. I never intended to fall in love with a married man twenty years my senior. What a mistake. I can almost hear Mama's voice in my head now: *Sadie Frances, what did you* think *would happen, getting wrapped up in a thing like that?*

I pick up my teacup and take a shaky sip. My rouged lips leave their imprint on the rim. A scarlet scream. I'm proud I didn't cry when Ted shattered my already fragile world into pieces. I only stared at him in disbelief as he broke my heart with cool indifference, then left me here, alone, with a tab I can't afford.

I didn't cry at Mama's funeral three weeks ago, either, come to think of it. Although the ache of missing her has grown deeper by the day.

"Miss Halloran?" Miles, the headwaiter, appears at my side, an expectant look on his face.

I open my handbag, eyeing the five-dollar bill inside. I hope it's enough for the tab. I've lingered too long, alone at this table. I don't belong here, not among Kansas City's upper crust. I haven't belonged for years. "I suppose you need me to leave."

"No, not at all. There's a lady over by the fountain. She says she knows you. She'd like to join you if that's all right."

I turn to look. A woman dressed in immaculate white lawn lifts her head, and I recognize her at once. My eldest cousin. Louise. She of the spotless manners and the glorious wedding at Our Lady of Sorrows and the three perfect blond children who came after. Louise is the last person I want to speak to right now. I wonder how long she's been sitting there. How much of my humiliation she's seen.

"Yes, Miles. You can have her come over." I sit up a bit straighter and dab my lips with my napkin. Louise's cloying gardenia perfume arrives before she does.

"Sadie!" she gushes. I rise to greet her. She kisses me on each cheek, then folds into Ted's vacant chair. She's just had her hair done. It lies in freshly set waves along her jawline, two shades lighter than my own dirty-dishwater blond, though our eyes are the same bright, crisp green. Thorne eyes. "How *are* you?" she trills. "It's been far too long."

It hasn't been long at all. I saw her at Mama's funeral. "I didn't realize you were a member here," I say, drinking down the last dregs of my tea.

"Oh, it's more of Toby's thing. He comes here with his doctor friends. We joined late last year." Louise fans herself with the menu card. "This heat. Can you believe it?"

I shrug. "It's July."

"I saw Ted on the way in," she says, placing her gloved hand over mine. "How are your wedding plans coming along? If you still need someone for the invitations, you can use my engraver."

I recognize the catlike smile on Louise's face—the smile that tells me she already knows what's happened. For a moment, I consider lying. Pretending I'm still engaged, even though we never set a date. How could we, when Ted never signed his divorce papers? I look down at the diamond he gave me at Christmastime. Fifty-eight stair-step facets, cold and bright as a winter day. At least I'll be able to pawn the ring. Generous of him to let me keep it. I can only imagine the jewels he'll give his wife as an apology.

"There isn't going to be a wedding, Louise."

Louise's mouth drops open in an exaggerated O. "Surely that's not true!"

I barely refrain from rolling my eyes. "I'm afraid so." I pick up my empty cup and silently curse myself for drinking my tea too quickly.

"What happened?"

"The very thing all of you *told* me would happen. Don't pretend to be surprised. And please don't be smug about it, either."

"I'm sorry, darling." Louise squeezes my hand. "Truly. But it's for the best. The scandal . . ."

"Yes. The scandal."

"Well. There's hope. You're still young."

I choke back a laugh. "Am I?"

Louise raises her hand to signal the waiter. "Could we have two mint juleps, please," she whispers when he reaches the table. "Heavy on the mint with mine, if you know what I mean. And don't try to tell me you can't do it, dear."

"More tea for me, please," I say to the waiter, motioning to my empty cup. "*Only* tea, thank you."

A few moments later, Louise's cocktail arrives, cleverly disguised in a gilded teacup. The Montpellier Tea Room, as a private establishment, is one of the more discreet speakeasies in town, catering to Kansas City's elite with its art nouveau decor and French cuisine. Few patrons would dare a daytime tipple. Not Louise. I cattily wonder whether she's an alcoholic. It does run in the family.

"Have you heard the latest about Aunt Marguerite?" Louise asks between dainty sips.

"No."

"Mother spoke to her nurse last week. She took a spill on the stairs. She wasn't hurt badly, just a few bruises, but it's worrying."

"I'm glad she's all right. How terrible," I say, although I'm selfishly relieved that my great-aunt's ill health has turned the subject from Ted and me. "Is she still in that enormous house?"

"Yes. She refuses to leave it."

I last visited Blackberry Grange as a child. Despite the name, the home isn't attached to a farm or granary. It's simply an overblown mansion with a rabbit warren of rooms and an abundance of gables, perched precariously on an Arkansas bluff. It was a place of wonder to my childish eyes, but I can only imagine how perilous the winding staircases and uneven floors would be for a frail, elderly woman.

"That can't be safe."

"No. She wanders about at night. They've placed an ad in the local paper for a round-the-clock companion, but Mother is concerned." Louise eyes me over her teacup. "The wrong sort of person might take advantage."

"I agree. It should be someone trustworthy."

A thought suddenly occurs to me, sitting there in the sunlight streaming through the arched windows—an impulsive one, but intriguing all the same. I've met Aunt Marguerite only a handful of times, but she made quite an impression on me. Unlike her older sister, our prim society matron grandmother, Marguerite was spirited. A chimera. An artist who broke rules and paved her own path in life. I'd long admired her from afar and regretted not knowing her better. Perhaps now might be my chance. I've nothing keeping me in Kansas City, after all. Not anymore.

"Do you think if someone in the family cared for her, it might be better?" I ask. "What if I did it?"

"Did what?" Louise's eyes narrow.

"Became Aunt Marg's companion."

Louise laughs, a loud, bright pealing that turns heads throughout the room. "Really? *You?*"

I bristle. "Why not me?"

"You're hardly the sort, Sadie. You're too impatient. Too *busy*. I can't see it. I'm sorry."

"I'm more patient than you realize. And what does 'busy' mean?"

"You're just not suited for that sort of thing."

"I think I am." My resentment simmers beneath the surface, as I think of all the ways I've never been good enough in my family's eyes. I'd always been the flighty one. The flapper. The good-time girl. No one ever considered that my "busyness" might be a distraction from my broken heart. From my grief.

"Do you want to do it because of Aunt Marg's money?" Louise arches her brow. "If so, you can admit it. I understand your predicament, Sadie. I do."

"No. That isn't it at all," I say stiffly. Although I must admit it is. At least in part. I received only a smattering of my mother's jewelry and a meager monthly stipend as my inheritance. As executor of her estate, my older brother, Felix, took her house and what remained of Da's investments. If I don't find a job, and soon, I could very well become destitute. Ted was my insurance policy. I'd been foolish to depend on his empty promises.

"You know," Louise says, her tone softening, "once you've had a chance to lick your wounds, I could set you up with Toby's friend Alan. The dentist? He's ready to settle down and won't mind about your . . . situation. Why—"

I rise swiftly, knocking against the edge of the table. The teacups clatter in their saucers, splashing Louise's mint julep onto the white tablecloth. "I think I'd better go. Before I end up saying something I'll regret."

Louise frowns. "Sadie. Really. There's no need to be angry. I was only—"

"Goodbye, Lou. Enjoy your *tea*."

I sweep from the room, leaving her with the tab. Unlike me, she can afford it. Presumptuous brat.

Outside the tearoom, I hail a cab and climb inside. The summer heat curls around me in the back seat, steaming thick as soup. I crank down the window, trying to catch my breath. "Waddell and Westport, please."

As the cab merges into traffic, I take out my compact to reapply my lip rouge and powder. I'm still shaking with anger at my cousin's words. But she's hardly alone in her opinion. No one in our family believed I would amount to much. No one but Da. And after Da? There was no point in proving them wrong. I reveled in their low opinion of me. In being the rebel.

I laughed in the face of my pain and became fun Sadie—a skinny, scrappy girl with sharp elbows who favored the new fashions and sat somewhere on the pretty side of plain. I wasn't born a great beauty like Louise, but I learned how to make men laugh. I learned how to please them in bed, too. But despite all the men I've charmed, none of them deemed me worthy of marriage. Ted gave me a ring only to string me along. To keep me content. If I were a better person, or smarter, I'd have ended our affair long ago. It's well past time to grow up and prove to myself, and everyone else, that I can be something besides an aging cigarette girl or a rich man's mistress.

I pinch my eyes shut against my angry tears as clouds gather outside the car windows, shuttering the sun. A crackle of thunder splits the sky. By the time the cab reaches my boardinghouse, the clouds open, streaming rain, and I've made up my mind.

The following day, I pack a single suitcase and go downstairs to pay Mrs. Dunlop for my week of room and board. I don't telegram to tell

Marguerite's staff I'm coming, nor do I tell Louise or anyone else in my family I'm leaving. I don't want anyone to talk me out of this.

"Where you going?" Mrs. Dunlop asks, opening her door wide. Smoke trails from her fleshy lips. Her apartment smells of liver and onions.

"Arkansas."

"You're coming back, hmm? You know I have a waiting list." She cocks a hip out and her floral-print robe slides open slightly, showing half a flaccid, white breast. "You ain't back by next Thursday, I'll be letting your room."

On my fifteen-dollar-a-month allowance, I can no longer afford to live here without Ted's help, but I'm not quite ready to let the room go. Not completely. "I'll be back."

"Sure, sure. This ain't about that man, is it, sugar? You know we've had complaints. About the noise."

"No," I say with a crisp shake of my head. "You won't be seeing him. Not anymore."

"Good." She pockets my money and turns back to her skillet of fried onions.

An hour later, I'm at Union Station, with the tickets for my journey to Eureka Springs clutched in my hand. I find the correct waiting room, sit on one of the long benches, and use my straw cloche as an ineffective fan. The train roars into the shed just as the heat becomes interminable. My head goes a bit woozy when I stand, and I clasp the arm of a well-dressed man to steady myself. He shrugs me away with indifference. Not pretty enough or young enough to warrant even the most common of courtesies anymore, it would seem.

Yes, I decide, I am quite done with men.

On the train, after some polite bargaining with a kind-faced woman traveling with her granddaughter, I manage to claim a window seat in our compartment. It's not the view that interests me. The first leg of the journey, to Joplin, consists of nothing more than endless green pastures and small, nondescript towns, but I'll be able to lean against the window and sleep. I caught only a scant hour or so of rest last night, too charged with spite at Louise's words.

I think of Mama, and all the ways I'd failed her. Even though she tried to hide it, I know she was embarrassed over my affair with Ted. She raised me to be better and I disappointed her, time and again. I'd disappointed myself. Caring for Aunt Marguerite feels like a chance at redemption. A chance to start over. Mama would be proud of me for doing this—for honoring my family.

The conductor comes through to tear our tickets as the train begins its slow chug out of the shed. I close my eyes against the white-hot July sun, the carriage's wood paneling cool against my cheek. Soon, I'm rocked into slumber. When I wake, the woman and the girl are gone and the sky outside the window is painted a seamless black.

My hunger rises, and I realize I've not had anything to eat since morning. I make my way to the club car. There isn't much on offer this late, but I order a turkey sandwich and a Coca-Cola. There's only one other person in the car—the same middle-aged man who brushed me aside at the station. In his double-breasted suit, he reminds me of Ted. I switch to the other side of the table, turning my back on him.

"How long to Joplin?" I ask the porter when he brings my food.

"Less than an hour," he says. "That where you're headed?"

"I have a connecting ticket to Eureka Springs."

"It's hotter than Satan's swimming pool down there, miss. You ever been?"

I smile at the young man's jovial tone. "It's been a while since I visited. My great-aunt lives there. I remember the humidity, though."

"Like that all through the South. Especially where I'm from. You let me know if you need anything else." The porter hurries back to the kitchen, and I tuck into the dry sandwich, washing it down with the cola. Mama wouldn't have approved of my hasty meal. She said food needed to be savored, not rushed. Our Sunday dinners together were always special occasions. If I'd been with her on the day she died, as I usually was on Sundays, things might have turned out differently. She might still be here.

But I was with Ted that day. Ted, who lured me with his lust and put me up in Mrs. Dunlop's flea-bitten boardinghouse, so he might have me whenever he pleased. I'll never reclaim the time I gave to him.

I push my dire thoughts away, locking them into the tidy box to deal with later. When I've finished my meal, I leave some change on the table as a tip. The rude man glances up at me as I pass by. I don't return his smile.

Chapter 2

July 17, 1925

I sit alone, outside the train depot in Eureka Springs, waiting for a car. A Duesenberg, according to the ticketing clerk, who phoned Marguerite's housekeeper on my behalf.

Rain sheets down, dripping off the awning and cooling the stolid air. This early in the morning, it's enough to send a chill through my thin summer frock and make me wish I'd packed a wrap. An hour or so later, the car—a fine thing painted a rich, deep green, with spoked tires and bronze fittings—splashes down the street and pulls to the curb. A tall, lanky man unfolds from the driver's seat, his flatcap pulled low over his eyes. He's dressed simply, in trousers with suspenders, shirtsleeves rolled to the elbow. "You Miss Halloran?"

I rise, lifting my suitcase. "Yes, I am."

"Well, come along, then."

I scurry to the car, shielding my head with my free hand. My leather shoes soak through immediately when I step off the curb. The man takes my suitcase and places it in the back seat, next to a box of groceries. I notice the slight limp in his gait as he walks around the car, and wonder briefly whether he's a veteran. It's certainly possible. Many came home wounded from the war.

"You'll be riding up front. With me," he says curtly. He opens the side door for me, and I slide in, uncomfortably wet. "You're lucky I had to go to town for the groceries this morning. The roads are likely to wash out with the storm. Should have let us know you were coming. Miss Thorne doesn't take kindly to unannounced visitors."

"I'm sorry. I really don't mean to be a bother." I turn to him, smiling tightly. "I appreciate the courtesy you've shown me, Mr. . . . ."

"Beckett. Just Beckett."

"I assume you're Aunt Marguerite's chauffeur?"

"Her gardener. Among other things."

"I see. Well, I'm Sadie. Just Sadie. Very pleased to meet you."

He merely grunts and pulls onto the street, windshield wiper slapping steadily back and forth. So much for Southern hospitality.

As we pass the hotels, restaurants, and spas lining Main Street, I remember the last time Mama and I came here, when I was twelve. Marguerite seemed so young then, her auburn hair faintly streaked with gray and her skin freckled from a recent European holiday. Her daring Paul Poiret ensemble turned heads up and down the boulevard. She'd spoiled me with sweet pastries and cocoa as she and Mama sipped aperitifs on a sun-drenched balcony and talked about things I found boring at the time but wish I could remember now.

As the car sweeps up the steep hillside leading to Blackberry Grange, I wonder just how much she's changed. If she'll even recognize me.

"Has Aunt Marguerite found a companion yet?" I ask the question directly, as "Just Beckett" seems to be a man with little patience for social graces. "My cousin mentioned she's in need of one."

"No. And she won't, most likely. She's already been through three nurses and two maids this year."

"Why is that?"

"You haven't kept in touch with your aunt, have you, Miss Halloran?"

I flinch at his judgmental tone. I turn my head to look out at the trees whipping in the wind, their leaves an incandescent, bright green against the gray sky. "I regret I haven't."

"You'll soon see for yourself why we can't keep staff." He retreats into stony silence as he shifts gears and maneuvers the curving road, his long-fingered hands flexing on the steering wheel.

The rain slows to a soft patter, and then ceases altogether, the sun breaking through the clouds. When the turreted roof of Blackberry Grange appears, I sigh in relief, eager to be free of the car and its surly driver. As Beckett brings the Duesenberg around in a slow circle before the elevated veranda, I take in the house with eager eyes. It's smaller than I remember, but still larger than any other house in our family by far. While the yellow clapboards and intricate abacus-chain millwork bear signs of genteel decay, the house, at least from the outside, wears its years with grace. The neatly manicured front gardens, dotted with evergreen topiaries, a trimmed lawn, and an espaliered blackberry thicket, show evidence of Beckett's diligent hand. I glance at him and consider complimenting his work but have the feeling my words would be met with icy disregard.

A short, solidly built woman comes out onto the porch, dressed in a modest gray frock. She waves as I step from the car, opening my own door this time. "Hello!" I walk confidently up the front steps and extend my hand. "I'm Sadie Halloran. Miss Thorne's great-niece."

The woman takes my hand briefly, then drops it, patting at her wren-brown hair nervously. "I'm Melva Percy. Miss Thorne's maid. I'm so sorry. If I'd known you were coming, I'd have laid something out . . ."

"I understand. It was rude of me to just turn up. Please don't make a fuss on my account."

As Melva leads me into the house, I wonder how long it's been since the last maid left. Though the house is neat enough, there's a faint veil of dust over everything. Memories wrap themselves around me as I enter the front parlor. Mama trailing down the hall from the library, a stack of books in hand. My brothers and I chasing fireflies through the yard. Marguerite and Louise dancing a soft-shoe routine before the piano. Coming here feels like being embraced by time—a halcyon time, before my life became what it is now, colored by loss after loss.

I turn in a circle, admiring the plasterwork cornices, the flocked-velvet wallpaper—a sun-bleached shade of bronze shot through with green, like aged copper. Portraits of my great-grandparents hang from the picture rail. Bram Thorne glares down at me stoically, next to his young French bride, Adeline. I see something of myself in her long, straight nose and downturned mouth.

"Would you like tea? Or perhaps coffee, miss?" Melva stands in the arched doorway separating the parlor from the entry hall, wringing her hands.

"Coffee sounds lovely."

She nods and leaves me. I remove my lace gloves and walk slowly through the room, gazing upon the array of old photographs arranged on the mantelpiece and sideboards. There's a portrait of my aunt Grace as a baby dressed in a ruffled gown, and another next to it, picturing her children, my towheaded cousins—cheeky Louise and Pauline—perched on a Shetland pony with their brother, Beau, holding the reins. Beau had died, taken by the Spanish flu, just like my little brother, Henry, pictured as a baby on a gilt-edge cabinet card. This room is a paean to loss. A family tomb full of bittersweet memories.

In the largest photograph, given a place of honor atop the tall parlor grand, my grandmother Florence stands in a church doorway, dressed in her wedding gown, flanked by a young Marguerite and their middle sister, Claire. Claire had also died young—in her early twenties—of the measles. My great-grandmother Adeline spent a year in a sanitorium after her death, stricken by the loss.

She wasn't the only one who had fragile nerves. Madness ran in our family, right alongside our proclivity toward liquor and a tragically young demise.

"I blame Florence, you know. For all of it."

I startle at the sound of a familiar alto voice and turn to see Marguerite at the foot of the stairs, dressed in a sheer emerald-green peignoir with not a stitch of clothing beneath it. I throttle my gasp before it leaves my throat. She eyes me suspiciously. "Who are you? The new help?"

"No. I . . . I'm Sadie."

"Sadie." Confusion laces her brows together. "Sadie."

"Laura's girl? Laura and Duke."

"Oh yes. Duke. The Irish boy."

I smile, my breath coming out in a rush. "Yes. The Irish boy. I'm his daughter. Don't you remember me? I suppose it's been a while." I pick up a fringed shawl hanging from the piano bench and approach my aunt slowly. "Here, let me cover your shoulders with this."

"Laura and Duke's girl. Laura . . . she had such a beautiful voice. It's awfully drafty for June, isn't it?" Marguerite shakes her head, white hair falling about her shoulders in a tangled mess. Why has no one bothered to brush it? Or dress her properly?

"It's July, but it's been raining," I say gently, averting my eyes as I wrap the shawl around her. "Your maid is bringing coffee. Will you come sit with me? I've been looking forward to our visit."

I lead her to the sofa. She lowers herself gracefully, fanning out the flimsy peignoir as if it's an ermine cloak. She crosses her ankles primly, knees together. Despite Marguerite's scandalous attire, all the etiquette my great-grandmother instilled in her youngest daughter remains apparent.

"How have you been, Auntie?"

"I've been well. I've just returned from Venice."

There's not a chance in hell Marguerite has just returned from Italy. "Venice? You're sure?"

"Yes, my dear. I go every year. Pia has an apartment near Campo Santa Margherita." She winks. "That's the saint I'm named for."

I squeeze her hand. "Saint Margaret. The willful and rebellious one." Although I know my saints well, I have no earthly idea who Pia is.

"Springtime is the best time to go to Venice. Summer brings miasma. Cholera. All that water."

"I've never been."

14

"That's a shame. You should see it while you're young."

When Melva comes with the coffee service and sees Marguerite's state of undress, her eyes widen. "Miss Thorne! My goodness." Teacups rattle together as she nearly drops her tray.

"Here, let me help you." I rush to the maid's aid, taking the heavy-laden tray from her. "Why isn't she dressed?" I whisper.

"I dressed her just this morning, miss. I promise. She takes everything right off again. She greeted the iceman last week, naked as a babe."

"Shhh," I say. "You'll upset her." I place the tray on the coffee table in front of Marguerite.

"You know, there's not a thing at all wrong with my hearing." Marguerite reaches for the silver coffeepot and daintily pours two cups, then adds cream and a single sugar cube to hers. "I don't know why everyone is always in such a dither over me," she says, tossing back her head. "I can manage my wardrobe quite well. And everything else, for that matter."

I take my place next to her and flavor my coffee with cream and sugar. "We're only concerned for you. Louise told me about your fall."

"The cat got wrapped around my ankles and I tripped. You can see for yourself I'm fine."

I look around for a cat but see no evidence of one. Melva meets my eyes, gives a slight shake of her head. "I'd better put the groceries away," she says, edging for the doorway. "Will you need anything else, Miss Halloran?"

"No, thank you."

"That one isn't very bright. But she's capable," Marguerite says conspiratorially after Melva leaves. "The last maid didn't change my bedclothes for a month."

I can't help the grimace that passes over my face. "I might stay on with you, for a while, if that's all right. Help you manage your staff and your social calendar."

Marguerite's eyes light up. "You'd do that?"

"Of course."

"But a pretty girl like you should be at parties. Courting with callers."

"I'm through with all of that. I'm ready for a quieter life, Aunt Marg."

"That's too bad. I was in my prime at your age. Oh, the stories I could tell you!"

"I can't wait to hear all your stories," I say, squeezing her hand. "I feel like I've missed out on so much of your life." And I have. Despite the short summer weekends I spent here as a child, my mother hadn't visited in years, even though she and Marguerite got along miles better than she and my grandmother, who never had anything good to say about anyone. But now, in this moment, sitting in this room, with the clouds clearing and cheerful sparks of sunlight shimmering through the lace curtains, I'm struck with a powerful feeling of belonging. This is where I'm meant to be. It was right of me to come here.

After a few moments of quiet conversation, Marguerite suddenly stands, sending her coffee tumbling. It sloshes over my already-wet shoes and across the rug at my feet. Her eyes are fixed, staring straight ahead. "Do you see him?" she says, lifting her hand to point at the stairs leading to the second floor.

"What?" I glance at the staircase. There's nothing there.

"That beast."

"What beast?" A chill walks between my shoulder blades. Even though I can't see a thing beyond the finely crafted banister and newel posts, an eerie sense of foreboding permeates the room, raising the hair on the back of my neck.

Aunt Marguerite pinches her eyes shut. "Oh, why won't he leave me be?"

"There's no one there, Auntie," I say, trying my best to calm her.

"He *is* there. Watching us." Marguerite stomps her foot like a child. "Go away!"

I take her by the arm, try to draw her back to the sofa. "There now, let's sit back down. We were having such a nice chat."

"I can't take this anymore." She wrenches free of my grasp with shocking strength and darts into the hall, shedding the shawl-covered peignoir as she flees. Panic floods my limbs as I follow her at a trot, unsure what to do.

Melva rushes out of the kitchen to meet me, eyes darting to the discarded clothing. "Oh, lord help us. We have to catch her before she gets outside. Harriet! Come quickly!"

A clatter of footsteps sounds from above and another woman in a maid's uniform appears on the stairs, this one at least a decade younger than Melva and dark skinned, her hair tightly marcelled away from her face. "Where did she go?"

"I . . . I'm not sure." Now I'm the one wringing my hands helplessly.

"We'll find her." Harriet smiles tightly, and rushes down the hall. Melva and I trail her.

We find Marguerite in the rear gardens, huddled under a wisteria bower. Just a few yards away, the grounds fall off—a sheer drop of rocky bluff into the valley below. I shudder at what might have happened if we'd tarried longer. "Melva, go get a wrapper, please," Harriet directs, doing her best to shield my aunt's nakedness from view with her body.

I sink down to the ground next to them, feeling helpless. "Is she like this often?" I whisper to Harriet. "She said something about seeing a beast."

"Yes. That's one of her recurring hallucinations. These delusions come on quickly, without warning. They're very real to her, and they're dangerous."

"I can see that."

Harriet turns back to Marguerite, murmuring softly as she draws a stoppered syringe and a vial of liquid from her apron pocket. She pierces the top of the vial and fills the syringe with the contents, squirting a small drop of liquid from the tip. My eyes widen. A memory of the injections I received at Elm Ridge rolls through me—the awful sedatives that made my mouth feel like cotton and my muscles weak as jelly.

"Don't worry," Harriet says, reading my expression. "I know what I'm doing. This will only make her sleepy. Calm her." She carefully inserts the needle in Marguerite's shoulder, whispering soothing words as she depresses the plunger. Soon, Marguerite whimpers, then stills, her eyelids falling to half-mast.

"I'm not really a maid," Harriet says. "As you might have gathered."

Melva returns with a cotton wrapper, Beckett in tow. He turns his back as we dress Marguerite, who's gone as limp and docile as a newborn kitten. "I'll carry her inside," Beckett says gruffly, bending to pick up my aunt. "This can't keep happening, Harriet. She's going to fall off that bluff one day."

"I know," Harriet says. "I'm doing the best I can, but she really needs to be in a nursing home. One with round-the-clock care."

"You know as well as I that she won't leave this house unless it's feetfirst," Beckett says, his tone softening as he looks down at my great-aunt. "This is her home."

I hesitate before speaking. Seeing the severity of Marguerite's condition for myself has lessened my earlier confidence in being able to care for her. Her turnabout in moods is shocking. Still, as I consider the frail, childlike form of my once vibrant aunt, I'm moved to compassion. "I'm going to stay with her," I say, steeling my spine. "That's why I've come. To help take care of her. She needs a companion. It should be someone in the family."

Beckett shakes his head. "I don't think you—"

My temper flares. "I *can* do this. I can."

Harriet frowns thoughtfully, brown eyes creasing with concern. "That's very noble of you. But you *do* realize she won't get better. Only worse. This was one of her tamer episodes. She's been violent with me. She may be with you as well."

"Will you show me what to do to help her when she's like this?"

"Yes, miss," Harriet says, "and I've promised to stay on with her indefinitely." She coolly assesses me. "I'm a nurse. I had my training in Philadelphia, but I married an Arkansas man, and well . . . the only work a colored woman can get down here is domestic work. But I don't scrub toilets, and I don't take kindly to disrespect." She smiles tightly. "Just so you understand."

"I do."

"Good. I'll do all I can to help you, but you should know this isn't going to be easy. Caring for someone with dementia wears on a person's nerves. Miss Thorne's mind is failing, but her body is still quite young. She's spry. Wily. You need to be prepared for long, sleepless nights and very little time for yourself."

"And there's no one who can help at night?"

"No." Harriet sighs. "Your aunt has a reputation for being difficult. I'm the first who's lasted with her for more than a month. The white nurses can get work anywhere. They don't need or want a patient like Miss Thorne."

"Well, that settles it. I'm staying. I may not be a nurse, but I'm family. That counts for something, doesn't it?"

Beckett and Harriet exchange a look. "Miss Halloran, this isn't . . ." Beckett begins again.

I frown at him. "I said, I'm staying."

Chapter 3

In the summer of my eighteenth year, I went blind. At first, my vision narrowed to a pinprick, then fell to a darkness as fathomless as the sea. I didn't see again for a week. *Profound shock and grief,* the doctors said. *The mind shielding itself from trauma.* The days that followed were a blur of white walls, nurses, bland food, and pills. So many pills. Mama had called it a "rest cure" for my nerves. But Elm Ridge had been anything but restful. After Da, everything changed. I went from a bubbly young debutante, ready to fledge and fly, to an object of pity.

My coming-out party had been scheduled for the first of June. At some point during the day, Da must have stolen away to the attic. Busy as we all were with the preparations for my party, no one noticed he was missing until later that afternoon. I was already dressed in my new white gown when I found him. I'll never forget how he looked, hanging there from the rafters, his eyes emptied of life.

Mama said I blabbered nonsense for three days straight. I don't remember. I remember only the darkness. The scent of rotting flowers. Tumblers of iced whiskey pressed to my lips. A cold washcloth on my forehead.

I didn't go to Da's funeral. They wouldn't let me.

They took me to Elm Ridge instead.

Da had been my world, and his loss left me unmoored. Broken. He'd hidden his darkness deep inside, behind his jocular wit and charming smile. If I'd only known how sad he was, I might have saved him.

Now I think of Marguerite, sleeping downstairs.

I couldn't save my father. Or my mother. Not even my little brother, Henry. But I still might save Marguerite.

I blink as my eyes adjust to the dim light in another attic, this one much larger than the one where my father took his own life. The ceiling balloons above me like a cathedral. Four windows face each cardinal direction. A simple iron bed, much like the one in my room at the boardinghouse, sits under the eaves, a colorful quilt spread across the mattress. Although it will be impossible to spend time up here during the hottest part of the day, it's pleasant enough now that the rains have tamped down the heat.

"You'll have more room to yourself up here, miss," Melva says. "It's quiet, too. The view is lovely, out over the valley."

I step over to one of the open windows. The sun has just fallen beneath the distant mountain ridges, throwing the hillside into purple shadow. "It's perfect. Thank you." I eye the edge of the bluff, with its perilous drop-off. "Why isn't there a fence? Guarding the bluff?"

"Miss Thorne won't allow it. She says fences are vulgar and they block the view."

Surely Marguerite's safety matters more than her view at this point.

"I'll leave you to get settled," Melva says. "Harriet will give Miss Thorne another check-over and put her to bed before she leaves for the night."

"And what about Beckett?"

"He lives in the stone cottage, up the hill above the grotto."

"He's the only one, then? That always stays on the property?"

Melva shifts uncomfortably under my question, crossing her arms about her plump waist. "That's right. The rest of us leave at night. But the sheriff is quick enough to come if you ever need anything. Doc Gallagher, too."

A nervous shiver runs through me like a many-legged centipede as I remember Marguerite's delusional spell this morning. Even though Harriet spent the better part of the day showing me what to do—how to calmly and gently restrain Marguerite—the thought of handling her on my own concerns me. I can't help but wonder if I've made a mistake in coming here. But where else was I going to go? What else would I do?

After Melva leaves, I roll my shoulders back and sigh, stretching. The attic floor creaks underfoot as I explore the expansive space. Furniture and heavy steamer trunks sit mounded under dustcloths along the walls. Near one of the other windows, I uncover a sofa and a wingback chair, its worn velvet seat stacked with books: *Gulliver's Travels, Moby Dick, Wuthering Heights*. I've read all but the last. I place the book on the nightstand and switch on the lamp. Someone brought my suitcase up earlier and left it next to the bed. Beckett, likely. I imagine him grumbling at the inconvenience. The man already goads me, although his earlier tenderness with my aunt showed an unexpected side to his character. I wonder how long he's been in her employ. He can't be much older than I am.

I begin unpacking, hanging my day dresses and dinner clothes in the wardrobe near the washstand. As I'm lining up my shoes at the bottom, I hear a strange sound—a faint rustling that carries through the cavernous room.

I pause to listen, kneeling there on the floor.

The frantic scratching continues, as if something is trying to claw through the ceiling. I remember my older brother telling me when we were children that this house was haunted—that he'd seen a strange lady in this very attic once. She'd simply stood there, staring at him, then faded from view.

Suddenly, a loud cawing screams through the open window, sending my heart into a gallop. A pair of crows take flight from the roof with a rush of wings. The scratching ceases. I let out my breath, chiding myself for my wild imagination. Only birds. Not ghosts.

Once it's dark, I settle beneath the covers with the well-worn copy of *Wuthering Heights*. My grandmother's maiden name is written on the frontispiece in girlish script: *Florence Marie Thorne*. I smile, imagining her reading this book as a young woman. After a few pages, my eyes begin to close. As I turn into my pillow and switch off the light, I hear the scratching start up once more. While it's much too late for crows,

I comfort myself with thoughts of raccoons or opossums—common enough in the attics of old homes.

Still, as I fall into a wary slumber, I'm unable to shake the uncomfortable sense that I'm being watched, and that there's more to this house than meets the eye.

I wake to an ungodly screeching, coming from somewhere below. I fling off the covers, feet tangling in the sheets as I scramble out of bed. The screeching continues—as if someone is dragging a heavy piece of furniture across the floor. As I make my way down the narrow, tightly spiraled attic stairs, I catch a glimpse of Marguerite's white hair on the landing below and see the source of the noise. She's dragging a small marble-topped table across the floor, rucking up the carpet. I creep toward her as soundlessly as possible to avoid frightening her.

She raises her head when I reach her, green eyes glassy, and I realize she's sleepwalking. I carefully pry her hands from the edge of the table and place it in the corner of the landing to deal with in the morning. I marvel at how she managed to get it up a flight of stairs on her own without waking me, and vow to keep the attic door open from now on.

I carefully lead her back to her room. I tuck her in, and she turns to me, eyes popping wide. She screams, hands flailing.

"It's only me. It's Sadie." I grasp her wrists, as Harriet showed me, and press her gently to the mattress. "You're all right. You're safe."

"Where's my penny? I've lost my penny." She begins to cry, tears tracking down her temples.

Go where she is. Don't argue with her. It only makes things worse. Harriet's earlier words of advice ring through my head. "We'll find your penny in the morning. I'm sure it's here, somewhere."

She turns away from me, crying. I rub her back in slow circles until she falls into a deep slumber. Bone tired and weary, I curl up in the chair next to her bed, unwilling to leave her alone, and sink into sleep. I wake to the sound of birdsong and the most beautiful morning light I've ever seen streaming through the windows.

And that's when I see the painting.

Chapter 4

I step toward the easel, entranced by the interplay of color on the canvas. It depicts an alfresco party by a river, the revelers' faces blank and featureless, save one. Though her image is unfinished, the woman at the center of the painting is arresting all the same—more handsome than beautiful, her dark hair piled atop her head, stark against her pale skin, lips outlined in bold crimson. She stares out at me, her blue-green eyes piercing. The background seems to swirl, the colors blending and morphing, as if the scene is in motion. I can almost smell the scent of the white rose tucked in the woman's bodice, can almost hear the rush of the river in the background. This painting is different from the art my aunt is known for—sweeping, unpopulated landscapes celebrated for their skilled interplay of light and shadow.

"That's Iris," Marguerite says, rising from her bed. "Do you like it?"

"It's beautiful. Lifelike and dreamlike all at once."

"I had to paint her from memory. It's been so long."

"Who is she?"

Marguerite smiles sadly. "An old friend. Another artist."

"I never knew you painted portraits."

"I did. Early on. But I couldn't find commissions. The society ladies all wanted to be painted by men. Sargent and Boldini. Bah." She waves her hand dismissively. "I left portraits behind for landscapes because that's what sold the best. But now, I can paint whatever I like, so I've gone back to them."

"Tell me about this scene. What's happening?"

"Oh, I took this study from life, dear. The summer of 1880. Iris and I were on a retreat in New York—the Hudson Valley. The light there is unlike anywhere else. After our lessons, the artists would unwind by the river, drinking and talking late into the evening. It was all very bohemian, as you might imagine. Papa threw fits about my going there . . . but he didn't have much say over me at that point. I was determined to make my own way in life by then. And I did. I sold my very first painting after that retreat."

I turn back to the painting, admiring the texture and movement in Marguerite's brushstrokes. The temptation to touch the swirling waves of paint is palpable. A feeling of vertigo washes over me. I could almost swear the woman's unfinished lips twitched into the faintest of smiles. I blink twice and shake my head.

"Don't stare at it too long," Marguerite says, chuckling. "You might fall in."

A soft knock sounds at the door and Harriet comes in. "Good morning, Miss Halloran. I hope the two of you fared well last night."

"We did. We had a small mishap with sleepwalking, but other than that, we've done just fine." I gesture toward the portrait. "Aunt Marguerite was showing me her painting."

"She started working on that one a few weeks ago. Isn't that right, ma'am?"

Marguerite's forehead wrinkles. "I . . . I can't remember. I thought I started it last year. But the paint isn't quite dry, so I suppose you're right, Harriet. The days blend together anymore."

Harriet hums under her breath and motions for Marguerite to sit at her vanity. "Let me take your blood pressure. Melva's made biscuits and gravy for your breakfast. She'll bring it up shortly."

"I think I'd like to eat downstairs today. I need to get up and about more. Keep pace with you young people."

Harriet smiles and wraps the blood pressure cuff around Marguerite's arm, tightening the leather straps and placing a stethoscope lens on the inside of Marguerite's elbow. She pumps the bulb a few times and listens, head cocked to the side as the dial jumps and then settles. "One-twenty-five over seventy. Perfect as usual."

"We've always had strong hearts in this family," Marguerite says proudly. "Not a heart problem to be found."

Until Mama. Her heart problem had lain in wait, hidden for years—a tragic arrhythmia that none of us knew about until it was too late. I look out the window, where the leaves blow gently in the breeze. I can't be sure whether Marguerite even knows about Mama's passing. Perhaps she was told, and she's forgotten. Surely Aunt Grace phoned her or sent a telegram . . .

"Would you like to help me dress Miss Thorne for breakfast, Miss Halloran?" Harriet asks, clearing her throat delicately.

"Of course. And you can just call me Sadie," I say. "Truly. I don't mind."

Harriet gives me the faintest of nods and moves to open a window, letting in a rush of cool morning air. "Her underthings are in the top drawer of the bureau. Bloomers and a camisole."

"No corselet or brassiere?" I ask.

"No," Marguerite says. "I haven't worn one in years. Do you know, in France, I spent almost the entirety of one summer in the nude? It was divine."

I see Harriet stifle a laugh as she pulls back the sheer curtains.

"What? The French are much more relaxed about that sort of thing." Marguerite unties her nightgown, and it slips off her shoulders onto the floor. "I'm an artist. I've no issue with the human form."

"I can see that." I bring a pair of silken underpants and a camisole from the bureau, and help Marguerite into them, sliding the silk over her soft skin as I avert my eyes. For her day wear, she chooses a lace tea gown in prewar style. Harriet and I button up the back, and then Harriet excuses herself to go downstairs.

I guide Marguerite to the vanity and begin brushing out her tangled locks, first with my fingers, and then a boar-bristle brush I find in one of the drawers.

"Where did you get your training?" Marguerite asks, sighing with pleasure as I use the bristles to gently massage her scalp.

"My training?"

"As a ladies' maid."

"Oh. I'm not . . ."

Go where she is.

"In Kansas City," I say. It isn't really a lie. I have a knack for hairstyling and cosmetics, and often helped style the cabaret girls at the Pepper Tree before their dinner shows.

"That's where I grew up," Marguerite says. "In Brookside. Our house had seven bedrooms."

"I know it well." Aunt Grace still lives in the handsome three-story redbrick house, with its Greek Revival portico and ornate gardens, built by my great-grandfather, who made a fortune in overland shipping before the Civil War. I finish my brushing and begin braiding Marguerite's long hair in a loose, single plait. "What brought you here?"

"Papa sent me here when I was eighteen," she says, closing her eyes. "I was in poor health, and he wanted me to take the waters. Eureka was little more than a pioneer camp back then, but I fell in love with the light. The landscape. There were artists here, even back then, so I fit in. After my travels with Iris, I came back in 1882 and bought this house for a song. It wasn't finished, on the inside, but the murder was the real reason no one wanted to live here."

I pause plaiting her hair. "Pardon me?"

"Oh, you've never heard about Lucy Blaylock?"

"I don't suppose I have." Suddenly, the cheerful birdsong outside the open window seems to diminish. "There was a murder?"

"Well, they *say* it was a murder. They put her husband away for it, at any rate. Lucy fell from one of the attic windows. A neighbor boy passing by saw her struggling with someone shortly before she fell. Mr.

Blaylock was a wealthy businessman. Kept a mistress on the side. That sort of thing never goes well for either woman, I'm afraid." Marguerite laughs under her breath. "Sometimes I see her. Lucy. She's still here, but she's not the only one. This old house holds many ghosts, my dear. Some of them are mine."

I'm held speechless by Marguerite's words—partly because of the strange sounds I heard in the attic, and my brother's childish ghost story, but mostly because of my own affair with Ted. In Lucy's situation, it was the wife who ran afoul of her philandering husband. But how many times has the mistress been on the wrong side of a man's ire and met a similar fate?

I remember an argument Ted and I had, late in our relationship, when I'd grown impatient with his ambivalence. He'd pinned me beneath him, his weight heavy as a boulder, and grasped my chin so roughly I bore the outline of his thumbprint there the next day. His overexcitability when we made love often frightened me. With his strength and size, he could have easily snapped my neck. Or choked me. And no one would have known where I was or how to find me. My mother never even knew where the boardinghouse was because Ted forbade her to visit me. He was paying my rent, after all. He paid for everything, so he made the rules.

Now here I was, alone. Abandoned like so many mistresses—and wives—before me. But better to be alone than dead. Because despite Marguerite's chilling words, a house full of ghosts frightens me far less than a man's rage.

Chapter 5

Over breakfast, Marguerite tells me more about Blackberry Grange and its history. The land it sits on once housed a small monastery of Trappist monks, who came to Arkansas in the middle years of the last century to enjoy the natural beauty and solitude. The monastery burned down one winter, after Christmas mass. According to local legend, the fire was an arson—allegedly set by one of the monks, who had fallen in love with an Osage girl and been denied leave of his order by the abbot.

"The abbot locked him in his cell, with only the light of a single candle to read by. That's what he used to start the fire." Marguerite blows across her coffee cup with pursed lips.

"Did he escape?" I ask.

"No one knows for certain. But people claim to see their spirits in the woods—the monk and his Osage maiden. Lights drifting between the trees."

I raise an eyebrow. "I'm going to need a special diary to keep track of all your ghosts."

"It might seem far-fetched, but this is one of those places where the veil between worlds is thin. There are all kinds of stories if you ask the locals."

While I'm still skeptical about spirits, I marvel at Marguerite's ability to remember things from the distant past, while I've had to remind her of my name no fewer than six times since my arrival.

Melva refills my coffee, then excuses herself to eat with Harriet in the kitchen. A few moments later, the front door scrapes open, followed by the heavy, uneven sound of Beckett's tread on the floorboards. My shoulders stiffen as he enters the dining room, dressed as he was the day before: gray trousers with suspenders, a collarless cotton shirt with sleeves rolled to the elbow. He doffs his cap and pulls out a chair to sit at the table. I glance at him sideways as he greets Marguerite, then helps himself to the biscuits and gravy. I've never known servants to sit at the same table as their employer. Once more, I find myself wondering about his history with Marguerite. How he came to be here. The nature of their relationship.

"Good morning, Miss Halloran," he says, noticing my gaze. I quickly look away. "Did you sleep well?"

"Yes. I did, thank you. Aunt Marguerite was just telling me about the history of the area. About the house."

"About our ghosts, you mean?" His lips tilt into a smile. "Are you a believer, Miss Halloran?"

"I . . . I'm not sure," I answer, stumbling over my words. "I suppose I'd like to believe."

"You will soon enough." His eyes glint with mischief.

"Don't scare the girl, Beckett," Marguerite says archly. "We want this one to stay, don't we? *She* knows how to dress my hair. Look." She twists in her chair so he can admire my braiding. "Isn't it fetching?"

"You look stunning, Marguerite. As ever."

She smiles and simpers as they make small talk, and I suddenly realize why she allows him at her table, the little minx. I only hope he doesn't use his flattery for improper advantage. Despite his unwelcoming attitude with me, he's quite a looker, with those dark-lashed aquamarine eyes and sly smile. A surge of protectiveness washes through me. I'll be watching the man and his motives. Closely.

After he finishes his breakfast, he excuses himself to his work. I watch him through the window as he walks the perimeter of the front gardens, stopping to examine the blackberries growing there.

"How long has Mr. Beckett been in your employ?" I ask.

"Years now," Marguerite answers, patting her hair. "He grew up here. His father was my gardener before him, his mother the cook. And he's Mr. Hill, dear. Beckett Hill."

"The two of you seem very familiar."

"Yes. He's like a son to me. The only one who's never left my side. I don't know how I'd have managed without him. He has such a talent with growing things—with roses, especially. They're difficult with the weather here. The rocky ground. But Beckett can coax anything to life."

I soften a bit in my opinion of the man. Perhaps I've misread him. "What happened to him?" I ask. "I've noticed his limp. Was he in the war?"

"No, my dear, although he tried to enlist twice, and they denied him. He was born with a severe curvature of the spine. It pains him at times, especially when the weather turns, but he's managed well despite it. He had to wear a brace as a child. I paid for his treatments." Marguerite's eyes grew wistful. "Such a beautiful boy. Happy, too. Until Charlie died."

"Charlie?"

"His younger brother. The war. He lied and enlisted before he was of age. Beckett feels guilty about that, I think. That it was Charlie who served and died instead of him. His poor mother's heart was broken, God rest her."

Many mothers lost their sons during the war. My older brother, Felix, came home unscathed by some miracle, but we lost Henry the winter after the Armistice. The rest of us had recovered from the epidemic of influenza raging through the country, but despite my constant vigil at his bedside, sweet Henry died. He was only thirteen.

Beckett and I have more in common than I realized. We've both lost younger brothers, and I gather he's an orphan, too. My thoughts are already on the future. If I ingratiate myself with Marguerite, I might inherit this house after her passing. I'd need a gardener and caretaker. So long as Beckett defers to me, I'll allow him to remain. If he persists in goading me . . . well. That's another matter. It feels calculating and selfish, having these thoughts, but my other prospects are dim. Perhaps it's opportunistic, but a woman like me, hedging toward thirty and past the prime of her youth, must be realistic. Practical. Besides, it's obvious Marguerite needs me just as much as I need her.

My gaze drifts out the window once more.

"You should go out, dear, have Beckett show you around the property," Marguerite says. "The grotto is lovely this time of year. Some of the hostas are as big around as this table."

"I think I might." I nervously eye the kitchen door, where I can hear the faintest thread of laughter. Hopefully Harriet or Melva will resume their watch over Marguerite once they've finished breakfast. "You're sure you'll be all right if I go out for a while?"

"Of course."

"Promise you'll stay put, right here at this table, until Harriet or Melva come get you."

Marguerite's face hardens. "Child, I don't need a keeper in my own home. Now run along. I'll be fine."

With one final furtive glance to the kitchen, I take my leave, smoothing my skirt and patting my hair. I catch up to Beckett at the fountain, where he's shin-deep in the basin, trousers rolled to the knee, scrubbing a metal nozzle protruding from a leaping carp's mouth.

"Hello," I say.

He turns toward me, taking off his cap and wiping the sweat from his brow with his forearm.

"Aunt Marguerite suggested I have you show me around the property."

He gestures toward the fountain. "I'm a little busy at the moment."

"I can see that." I cross my arms over my waist, defensively. "It's a lovely fountain." It isn't, with that cluster of horrible, gawping fish leaping from the water. I've always hated it.

Beckett laughs. "It's hideous."

I break into a smile, and bite my lip to contain it. "It really is, isn't it?"

"Yes, but Marguerite is very fond of it." He resumes scrubbing the nozzle. "There's too much lime in the water. I have to do this at least once a month."

I look around, taking in the freshly mowed green lawn, the arbor of climbing roses sheltering the path to the house, the blackberry thicket. "I can see you take a great deal of pride in your work. The gardens are lovely."

He says nothing in reply, only moves on to another stone carp.

"Marguerite and I were just talking about you." The words tumble out of my mouth before I can stop them.

Beckett stills, his hand cupped around the steel wool in his palm. His eyes narrow. "Oh? What did she say?"

I stand there awkwardly, not knowing how to respond. Where should I begin? Our dead brothers? His handicap? We hardly know one another—and certainly not well enough for such intimate talk. "Only that she greatly appreciates all you do for her. I'll leave you to your work, Mr. Hill. I apologize for the interruption."

I head toward the house, the humidity gathering around me and further inflaming the sudden heat on my face and neck.

"Miss Halloran!"

His voice seizes me midway across the lawn, and I turn to see him staring at me, an inscrutable expression on his face. "Yes?"

"Come out after dinner, before Harriet leaves for the night. I'll show you around the gardens then, if you'd like."

"All right," I say, offering him a smile. "I'd like that."

The house is in chaos when I return. In just the few minutes since I left her, Marguerite has gone missing. Melva accosts me as soon as I walk in the door. "Where were you?"

My defensiveness rises, accusatory words of my own climbing my throat. I push them back. If I'm to be lady of this house someday, I'll need to keep my emotions in check when addressing the servants. "I only went out for a moment to speak to Mr. Hill. You and Harriet were just there, in the kitchen, weren't you? Didn't you hear her?"

"Well," she replies, flustered. "Well. It don't take long for her to get a notion." Melva turns in a circle. "Oh, where has she gone now?"

"Do you think she's gone outside again?" I think of the sheer bluff behind the house, its edge protected by nothing more than a few scattered fieldstone boulders.

"No." Melva shakes her head. "No, not this time. I'm sure of it. I'd have heard the door."

Even though Melva's reassurances bring some level of comfort, Marguerite could be anywhere in this labyrinthine house, with its hive of interconnected rooms. I think of the steeply pitched staircases, the many windows, the weak spots in the floors. Even within the house, she's still in danger. "You search downstairs," I say. "Harriet can look for her on the second floor, and I'll search the attic. She must be here. She must."

I meet Harriet on the stairs and convey our plan, her coolheaded reaction a welcome contrast to Melva's panic, even though I can feel my own nerves jangling just below the surface. I think of Louise's words back at the teahouse in Kansas City—her judgmental chiding when I mentioned becoming Marguerite's companion. Perhaps she's right. Perhaps I'm not suited. For the second time since my arrival, I consider that I might have made a mistake. But I'm here now, and I must make this work.

I fly up the attic steps, and into the lofty, open space above. The daytime heat has already begun to gather beneath the eaves. A shaft of sunlight burns a bright path across the floor from the east-facing window, throwing the corners of the attic into shadow. "Aunt Marg," I call. "Are you up here?"

I pause to listen, my breath rasping hollowly. There's no response, but on the opposite side of the room, I sense movement and hear a faint rustling and scratching—the same sounds I heard last night. "Hello?"

I take two tentative steps forward and stop, my heart stuttering with shock as my eyes adjust. A man is sitting there, at a rolltop desk tucked against the wall. At first, I think Beckett somehow got past me and into the attic, but he couldn't have without my knowing. This man is taller, broad shouldered. Older than Beckett. He's writing, his pen flying across the surface of the paper, his silhouette limned with light. I wonder whether he's one of the household servants I've yet to meet. If so, we'll need to have a conversation about my privacy. I glance over at my unmade bed, my silk slip hung carelessly over the iron frame. This attic is my room now. He shouldn't be up here.

"Hello. I'm looking for Marguerite," I say crisply. "Have you seen her?"

The man turns, a slow smile forming on his face. "You must be the new hire. I saw you arrive yesterday."

"I'm . . . I'm not the help. I'm Marguerite's grandniece. She's gone missing. Have you seen her?"

"Marguerite goes missing often. You'll have to get used to that." His eyes glimmer in the half-lit room, flashing a devious, dark gray. "You might check the west turret. She likes to go there to read. There are hidden stairs behind one of the shelves in the library. Look for the red edition of Joyce's *Ulysses*, facing out."

His manner is haughty, bordering on arrogant, yet I find myself riveted to the spot. There's something strangely familiar about him—as if we met at some point in the past. He holds my gaze for a moment, then turns back to his writing. "Run along. Find her quickly now, before they all go into a panic."

His dismissive tone rankles me, but I do just that, rushing back down the stairs and toward the long hallway to the back of the house, where the two-story library sits, its tall windows framing expansive views of the valley below. It's one of the few rooms I remember well from the games of hide-and-seek I played here as a child. There are so many places to hide in this room, with its shadowed alcoves and heavy furniture, but I never knew about any secret stairs. I scan the shelves for the book the man mentioned—*Ulysses*—and find it, the leather binding a brilliant carmine red. I take it off the shelf and see a brass lever in the shape of a beckoning hand behind it. When I push down on the lever, the entire shelf swings open with a tired groan, revealing a twisting staircase leading up. A single set of footprints marks the dust on the treads. Marguerite's, I hope. I pause before going up, the stale air heavy in my lungs.

When I reach the top, my eyes widen in awe. Fractured light rains down on the floor from above, where a ceiling of steeply pitched glass catches the sunlight. The heat is fierce in this small space. Stifling. Marguerite stands before an arched picture window, looking out at the landscape below. The room is lined with bookshelves, but sparsely furnished otherwise, with only a cushioned, low bench under the window and a wingback chair. A covered easel stands at the center of the room. I resist the urge to lift the cloth covering it, and quietly cross the room to stand behind Marguerite, clearing my throat.

Marguerite turns, blinking slowly. "Hello," she says. "Who are you?"

"I'm Sadie, remember? We had breakfast together, just this morning."

"Sadie," Marguerite says, testing out my name. "I thought it was Sybil."

"You've given us all a fright. We'd no idea where to find you."

Marguerite frowns. "Find me? Why? I'm not lost. This is my home."

I smile, start again. "Yes, but . . . we all still worry about you. The man in the attic told me about this room. He said I might find you here."

Marguerite's eyes flash. "What man?"

"I didn't catch his name. Dark hair. Handsome. He was at the desk upstairs, writing. Is he one of your staff?"

Marguerite suddenly grasps my wrists, her bony fingers digging into my skin. I try to pull away, but she holds me fast. "You've seen him. That *beast*. I knew you would. Listen here, girl, stay far, far away from that man. Do you hear me? He's worse than any devil."

Chapter 6

My nerves are still a mess when I go out to meet Beckett that evening. Between the search for Marguerite and her strange admonition about the man in the attic, I'm feeling fretful and out of sorts. When I went upstairs to dress for dinner, the unsettling sensation of being watched persisted, although the man was gone. The rolltop desk he'd been seated at was covered with cloth and there wasn't a thing out of place indicating anyone else had intruded. Still, I'd unfolded the screen in the corner and undressed behind it for my own peace of mind.

As Melva cleared the table after dinner, I asked her if she knew anything about the man I saw.

"Yes. That man. The other maids talked about him," Melva said, brushing breadcrumbs from the tablecloth. "They said he's so real you'd likely feel flesh if you touched him."

"He seemed real enough to me. We had a whole conversation. Is he a neighbor? Another servant?"

"No. He's neither." Melva looked away, her eyes hooded. "Miss Thorne says there are spirits here, though I've never seen anything myself. I suppose he must be one of them."

A shiver ran through me like cold spring water. "You're saying he's a ghost?"

"Yes, miss."

Now, as I cross the lawn, I willfully turn my mind from ghosts to temporal matters. Haunted or not, this is my home now, and I'm eager to meet with Beckett and survey the entirety of the property and get a sense of what any future inheritance might entail.

The fountain plays merrily, water streaming forth with a musical sound—proof that Beckett succeeded at his morning chore. Being near the fountain feels pleasant, a cooling respite from the heat. I perch on the edge of the basin and wait, watching the sun slide behind the house. My grandmother would have frowned at my meeting with a man—much less a servant—unchaperoned. But times are changing. Girls much younger than I go out alone with men now. Petting parties are all the rage, Victorian morals having swiftly fallen by the wayside after the war. Besides, I'm hardly a blushing maid, and there's no risk of anything romantic happening with Beckett.

I lift my wrist, eyeing my watch. Nearly seven thirty. I rise and pace around the fountain, trailing a finger idly in the water. I'm making my third circuit around the fountain when I glimpse Beckett in the distance. I note his change of clothing immediately. He's no longer in his workaday clothes but a freshly pressed pair of linen trousers and a striped oxford with a crisp collar, a tie knotted at his neck. As he closes the distance between us, I see he's even combed his hair and oiled it, the sheen of pomade catching the warm evening light. From the cut of his clothes, my aunt must pay him a healthy wage, indeed. Once more, my suspicions rise.

"Have I kept you waiting too long, Miss Halloran?"

"Not at all." I ignore the fetching tilt to his lips and fiddle with the strand of pearls around my neck, suddenly nervous. "Harriet said she wouldn't leave until I return."

"Then shall we?" He motions toward the gardens.

"Of course."

An awkward silence descends as we cross the lawn to the stand of trees bordering the house. Maples, elms, and cedars. I imagine what the seasonal play of color will look like in autumn—flaming reds and yellows in contrast with the verdant evergreens.

"Marguerite told me your father was her original gardener," I say as Beckett leads me down a narrow, pebbled path through the wooded glen. "Did he do most of the plantings?"

"Yes. He did. My father was a follower of Frederick Law Olmsted. He believed in coaxing the land gently into submission instead of forcing things, allowing nature to hold dominion. Most of the trees on the estate are native, but the monks planted the blackberries and fruit trees long ago." Beckett motions toward an apple tree alongside the path, its fruit just beginning to ripen. "They fermented their own wine and cider. The old cider press is still here, on the property. I use it every fall."

"How fascinating. Marguerite told me about the monastery."

"Yes, you can still see remnants of the old foundation at the back of the house."

"When was the house built?"

"1880."

"So, not long before Marguerite bought it," I say, fingering a persimmon tree's leaves as we pass through an arbor woven out of willow. "She said she got it for a song."

"The man who originally built the house—Erwin Blaylock—didn't live here long. My father did most of the finish work on the interior. Blaylock's wife died on the property. People around here are superstitious about such things."

"Marguerite told me about his wife. Lucy. You know, my older brother claims he saw a lady once, in the attic here. He tried to scare me with ghost stories when we'd visit."

"Felix?"

"You knew him?"

"Yes. When you all came in the summer, we would run these woods together. I remember you, too. I thought you were a boy at first, with your cropped hair."

I laugh. "Ah, yes. I took Mama's pinking shears to it. I was tired of enduring her tight braids. I suppose I remember you, too, come to think of it." My memories are vague, but I do remember a boy with long-lashed, melancholy eyes. He asked me my name one summer afternoon as I sat pouting on the veranda after Felix stole my new kaleidoscope, then scurried away as quickly as he'd appeared. "You were very shy."

"Yes. But Felix wasn't, and that's why we got along so well. We were the same age, I think." Beckett's brow wrinkles with concern. "You said I *knew* him. Marguerite told me he served in the war. He came home, I hope."

"Oh. Yes. I'm sorry. I didn't mean to sound so dire. We just don't see one another very often anymore. We've never had much in common. His wife doesn't care for me, and my sentiments are equal. But they've two lovely boys. Felix is an attorney. Like our da was."

"That's grand for him. And what about your younger brother? As I remember, he was only a baby when you were here last. You were always toting him around."

"Henry. He died in '18. The flu. Two years after our da."

"I'm very sorry to hear that."

"Thank you." I clear my throat. "And what about you? Any family here?"

"No. Not anymore," he says with an air of finality. He points to where the forest closes in, the treetops allowing for only the faintest shimmer of light to fall to the ground. "The grotto is just ahead. You might take my arm. It gets a bit steep. You wouldn't want to roll your ankle."

I do as he suggests, winding my hand through the crook of his elbow. This near to him, I can smell the faint scent of his aftershave and something richer, like sun-warmed earth. I ignore the way my pulse is climbing, the way his steady strength reminds me of my best days with Ted, in far-flung places well outside Kansas City, where he might parade me around without risk of someone familiar seeing us—someone who would know what I *really* was to him. In those roadside hotels and restaurants in towns like Dubuque and Amarillo, I could pretend to be Mrs. Theodore Fitzsimmons. Only I knew I wasn't. I never would be.

As the path levels out, I let go of Beckett's arm and walk ahead, my eyes widening in wonder. The grotto is as magical as I remember. Yellow-gold coins of sunlight dance over the hostas and ferns. A statue of the Virgin presides over it all in her stone alcove, haloed by carefully groomed ivy. The faint trickle of the spring soothes my senses, the fairy-like array of moss roses and creeping Jenny soft underfoot. It's a tranquil place. Quiet and serene. A peaceful calm descends, and I close my eyes for a moment, letting out a long breath and lowering my shoulders.

"Restful, isn't it?" Beckett's voice is reverent, as if we've just entered a church, and we have, in a manner of speaking.

"Yes."

"I come here often, once my work is done for the day. The monks built this, too."

"You've maintained it beautifully. Truly. You should be proud."

"It calms me. My work. As it did my father. Being a steward of the land is a great privilege." Beckett brushes a fallen leaf from one of the stone benches facing the shrine and motions me to sit. I tuck my skirt smoothly and perch on the edge of the bench, crossing my ankles. He kneels to inspect a cluster of white lilies near the foot of the spring, then comes to sit next to me. "How long are you planning on staying with us, Miss Halloran?"

I'm taken aback by his question. "As I said yesterday, I hadn't planned on leaving."

He leans forward, elbows on his knees. "Marguerite is very special to me."

"She said the same of you."

"That's the reason I'm curious. About why you're here again, after all these years." His voice is soft. Level. But I see the suspicion behind his eyes. "I've never heard Marguerite mention receiving a single letter from you. Or even a telephone call. And here you turn up, ready and willing to be her devoted companion. Don't you think that's odd?"

I stiffen. "I'm not sure I like what you're implying, Mr. Hill."

He smiles that fox-like smile. "Just as I thought."

I rise, flummoxed, crossing my arms defensively. The sun has fallen well below the ridge, bringing a coolness to the shaded grotto. "I'm only here to care for my aunt, because it's obvious someone needs to."

Beckett stands, towering over me. All at once I'm back in my tiny apartment with Ted, liquor on his breath and his temper boiling beneath the surface. I take a step backward, and Beckett laughs softly. "Don't worry, Miss Halloran. I'm not in the business of hurting women. Or taking advantage of them, for that matter. I hope I can say the same for you."

"Oh? After your little flirtation with Marguerite at the breakfast table, I'm not certain you have the best intentions when it comes to my aunt, either."

"You read me wrong, Miss Halloran. Marguerite is like a mother to me. If I flatter her now and then to see her smile, it harms no one."

I glare at him steadily, refusing to cede any ground. "I'd like to go back to the house now, if you please."

He laughs. "Already ordering me around, I see."

"All right. I'll see myself back, then. Good night, Mr. Hill." Impertinent man! I turn and stalk ahead of him up the path, my face red with shame. His words settle in my belly, curdling like soured wine as I rush up the hill. Suddenly, my foot slides on a moss-covered rock, and I go down on one knee, a sharp cry leaving my throat before I can stop it.

Beckett catches up to me and offers his hand. "Let me help you."

I ignore him and lift myself from the ground, brushing my stockings. My palm comes away with a smudge of blood. "I'm fine," I lie through clenched teeth. Though my knee shouts at me, I stumble the rest of the way up the rise, refusing to give him the pleasure of seeing my pain.

"Miss Halloran!"

I don't turn at the sound of his voice. I walk on, through the trees and onto the front lawn, my back straight and my head held high as tears track down my cheeks. I angrily wipe them away, not wanting him to see that he's gotten to me—that he's right. For as much as I'd like to pretend my reasons for being here are selfless, I know they aren't. And so does he.

Chapter 7

Beckett and I do our best to avoid one another in the days that follow. It's not difficult, busy as he is with maintaining the grounds. I don't know how the man can endure this relentless, cloying heat. It pervades everything. In the front parlor, I lift one of the heavy window sashes, then open another across from it, bringing in the faintest cross breeze. I wipe the sweat from my brow with the side of my hand and sit on the sofa next to Marguerite, who I helped dress in the scantiest clothing propriety allows. I skim my thumb over the scab forming on my knee. Luckily, a skinned knee is the worst of my injuries, apart from my pride. Though Beckett's words vexed me, they have also spurred me to action. In the last few days, I've doted on Marguerite, determined to prove to him—and myself—that my motives for being here are pure.

"This heat reminds me of the canicule of '11," Marguerite says, fanning herself with a rattan fan.

"Pardon?"

"In France. The heat killed thousands that year. Christine and I fled Paris. Went to Antibes. Let a villa by the shore."

I settle in with my glass of iced tea, crossing my legs. "Who's Christine?"

Marguerite lifts an eyebrow. "If I tell you the truth, it will make you blush."

I laugh. "Try me."

"She was my lover. For many, many years."

I nearly drop my tea in my lap.

Marguerite smiles. "I told you I would shock you."

I've heard the rumors about Marguerite, of course. My grandmother shook her head at the company her youngest sister kept, judging her against their rigid Catholic upbringing. *Shameful and shameless,* I remember Grandmother saying after she read one of Marguerite's letters. She crumpled the letter into a ball and threw it in the wastebasket. I took it out later, smoothed the paper, and read it. I saw nothing more scandalous than a recounting of a day spent on Lake Michigan with a group of her friends. I didn't understand what my grandmother meant at the time. But now . . .

Marguerite watches me with steady eyes. "Would you like to see her?"

"Who?"

"Christine."

"She's here?"

Marguerite grunts softly. "In a manner of speaking." She lifts herself from the sofa. "Come along. I'll show you."

⤳⤶

Marguerite leads me upstairs, to a snug, closed-off room—no larger than a dressing room. I imagine its original purpose was to be a nanny's room or the housekeeper's quarters, situated as it is at the end of the second-floor hall, near the interior stairwell. Every surface is littered with artistic detritus. In the gloom, I can make out the shadowed forms of several easels, some standing, some stacked against the walls. Marguerite goes to the only window and draws open the heavy velvet curtains, letting in a blinding blade of sunlight. Dust flies, sending me into a brief coughing fit.

"I haven't been in here for over a year," she says. "This used to be my studio. Did you know Vermeer painted with light from a single high window just like this? It's how he got those marvelous deep shadows and catchlights in the eyes." She points to one of the easels. "That's her. Over there, I believe. Christine."

I wend my way across the cluttered floor to the painting and remove the dustcover. It's a portrait of a woman—one in her middling years and regal, with a saucy tilt to her chin as she reclines on the sand in an old-fashioned bathing costume. She has a large striped parasol anchored on her shoulder, shielding her from the sun. As I study the painting, a feeling of vertigo washes over me. The energy in the room shifts, and I can almost hear the sea in my ears, waves softly breaking over sand. Then suddenly, the woman *moves*. Her elbow lifts, ever so slightly, and the parasol spins. I step back from the painting with a gasp.

"She . . . she moved."

Marguerite comes to my side. "What did you say?"

"That lady. Christine. She moved."

Marguerite laughs. "Are you sure you didn't add some tipple to your tea, my dear?"

"No. I'm certain she moved." I step back to the painting, drawing Marguerite with me by the hand. "Look."

But nothing happens. There's only paint on canvas, artfully applied. Marguerite reaches out, tenderly stroking the line of Christine's jaw with her fingertip. "She was my last love. I didn't know that, at the time. I had other affairs after her, of course. But none like Chris."

"Just how many lovers have you had, Auntie?"

"I've had my share of flings, my dear, but I've only had three true loves."

I almost laugh. "That many?"

"What? Do you believe true love to be a once-in-a-lifetime thing? That's only the case in fairy tales." Her voice falls, growing solemn. "Something you realize, when you're older, is that you can and will fall in love more than once, and every lover you have teaches you something.

About the world. About yourself. The lessons aren't always pleasant. Or easy. And you won't always understand why things happened the way they did, until much, much later." She turns back to the painting and sighs. "It didn't end well for us. Christine wanted more than I was able to give. She begged me to give up my home here, move to France. But I still cared too much about what people would think. What my family would say. If I'd gone to live with her, it would prove the rumors about me true. Your grandmother Florence already suspected and judged me for it."

I remember the letter from Marguerite that my grandmother read scornfully and discarded, all those years ago. "I think you're probably right. About Grandmother."

"Bitter as the day is long, that one." Marguerite shakes her head. "She punished me for her unhappiness. With Florence gone, I can finally be who I am, but I wish things had been different between us. She was difficult. Domineering. But I secretly ached for her approval. I wish we could have found a way to make peace with one another."

"She loved you. She did," I say gently. "She told me such fond stories of your childhood together. About Claire, too." It's a bit of a lie—Grandmother had very few kind words in her repertoire about either one of her sisters, but rehashing their differences won't soothe Marguerite's regret.

"Claire . . ." Marguerite looks down. "Now there's a name I haven't heard in years. How did you know Claire?"

"She was my great-aunt, just like you are. I never met her, though."

"That's right. I remember now. You're Sybil, aren't you? Or is it Susan?" Marguerite shakes her head in confusion. "No, that's not right."

It's stunning how quickly Marguerite's recollection of who I am fades. I take her hand. "Sadie. I'm Sadie."

"Yes. Sadie. I like that name. It's a bit feisty."

I laugh. "It suits me, I think."

Marguerite covers the portrait of Christine, and motions to another easel. "I believe that's my portrait of Hugh, over there. I still need to finish it. I found it the most difficult to paint . . . my emotions got the better of me. Hugh was my first love. Things ended tragically for us. I don't like to think about him too often. It makes me sad." She moves to the painting and pulls away the cloth covering it. My eyes widen. It's the man I saw in the attic. The stranger. I recognize him immediately—his crisp jawline and that tumbling, dark hair falling over his brow. A face so handsome it's almost cruel.

"How?" Marguerite's voice drops so low I can barely hear the words. "I burned this one. I'm sure I did."

"Is that Hugh?"

"No," Aunt Marguerite says, her voice quaking. "Not Hugh. My Hugh was good."

"Who's this man in the painting, then?"

"My biggest regret." She crumples in on herself, hiding her eyes with her hand. "Cover it, please, Sybil. Cover it up."

I pick up the cloth and throw it back over the painting. As I do, I swear I see the faintest smile lift a corner of the man's mouth.

In the wee hours, after the house quiets and Marguerite falls soundly asleep, I decide to go back to the studio. I can't resist. The mysterious portrait calls to me. Who was the nameless man? Who was he to my aunt? If he was one of her lovers, their affair seems to have ended badly. And if he's a real person from the past, that means I've seen him—or his ghost—a troubling thought that chases me as I light an oil lamp and pad down the hall to the studio.

I slowly turn the knob and push open the door, its hinges creaking faintly. Between the undrawn curtains, trees sway in the indigo darkness. The air, even inside the house, is thick with the promise of rain. My lamp casts eerie shadows over the walls and shrouded easels as I set it on a small table near the man's portrait. I stand there for a moment, staring at the veiled painting, a tremor of anxiety at one with my curiosity as I remember the way his lips tilted in that insolent half smile. It might have been my imagination. But the same thing happened with Christine's portrait. Iris's as well. Each figure moved. There's something uncanny about my aunt's work. Otherworldly.

The hall clock chimes twice, startling me.

"Oh, Sadie, stop being ridiculous." I take a half step forward and gently pull on the dustcover. It falls away. The man stares out at me, his eyes dark with something dangerously close to desire. My head goes woozy as I study him. He sits in a wooden chair, one arm propped on the back, the light etching his face with shadow and carving away any softness. He's dressed simply, in a white shirt unbuttoned below the collarbone and black trousers with no jacket.

I step closer, my eyes roving over the surface of the painting as I examine Marguerite's brushwork. There's a difference compared to the other two portraits—her brushstrokes are more primitive, as if she made this painting when she was much younger, her talent nascent and still emerging. The swirls of paint are hypnotic, undulating across the canvas.

The wobbly sensation returns, my head spinning. I suddenly feel faint. I reach for something, anything, to steady myself as the edges of my vision begin to blacken. Before I can lower myself to my knees, the floor tilts at an odd angle, a strange, whining roar floods my ears, and I'm falling, the darkness reaching out to embrace me.

Interlude

Sadie sits up, her eyes wide as she stumbles to her feet and looks about. Confused thoughts knit together in a disarrayed tangle. Just a moment ago she was in Marguerite's studio . . . but she's somewhere quite different now. The room is lushly appointed, with high ceilings, wood-paneled walls, and velvet draperies. A billiards table sits at its center, brightly colored balls scattered over the red felt. It's a room familiar and unfamiliar to her all at once . . . some memory she can't quite pin down flits through her mind like an errant moth. She hears the distant tinkle of cutlery on china—a woman's high, spindle-sharp laughter. She presses her ear to the door, listens to the low hum of conversation in the next room.

A man's voice comes from behind her. "We can go in if you'd like. They won't be able to see you."

Sadie startles, whirls to face the corner. She hadn't noticed him sitting there, hidden in the shadows. A sinuous trail of smoke threads toward her. She looks down at her silk wrapper, the color rising in her cheeks as she tightens the belt, pulls at the short hem. "What happened? Where am I?"

"Kansas City, Missouri. 1875." The man takes a drag from his cigar and leans forward, into the frail light from the hissing oil sconce. It's the stranger she saw in the attic. The man from Marguerite's painting.

"But . . ." Sadie shakes her head, puts a hand to her forehead, as if checking for a fever. "I don't understand. Am I dreaming?"

"No, not exactly. I'll explain everything in time." The man unfolds from the chair, stubs out the cigar.

"You're him, aren't you? The man from the painting."

"Yes. I am." He closes the distance between them, covering Sadie with his gaze. "Weston Chase. We met the other day, but you were in a bit of a hurry. I regret we didn't have time for introductions."

"I was looking for Marguerite. You told me about the tower room. I saw you . . ." She shakes her head. "Are you real?"

"As real as I can be. I'm sorry, I don't believe I caught *your* name."

"Sadie. Sadie Halloran. I know where I am now," she says excitedly. "This is my aunt Grace's house in Brookside. There, that mantel. I had too much wine at a party here last year, and I hit my head. I needed stitches." Another peal of laughter rings from the dining room, this one familiar. Sadie turns at the sound, a soft gasp escaping her lips. "Is that my grandmother?"

"Yes. That's Florence. Would you like to go in now?"

"But won't we interrupt them?"

The man smiles with the slightest air of condescension. "As I said, they can't see you. You'll be like a ghost. They might feel a slight draft when you pass by. That's all."

Sadie reaches for the doorknob, all eagerness now, but her hand passes through it, her flesh as insubstantial as air.

The man chuckles softly. "Allow me." He swings open the door, and five heads swivel toward them at once. Weston lightly touches her back, urging her forward. Sadie slips through ahead of him, her eyes widening as she takes in the candlelit table, with its fine linens, crystal, and abundance of food. Her great-grandparents sit at either end—though she never met them, she recognizes them from their portraits. Bram and Adeline Thorne. Their three daughters, Florence, Claire, and Marguerite, are all there, too, dressed in dinner finery. The scene is a glittering palette of Gilded Age wealth. Sadie slinks to the wall, where she watches, taking everything in with awestruck attention.

"Weston, we were wondering where you'd gone off to," her great-grandfather says, motioning for a footman. "More wine, if you please."

"Pardon my poor manners, sir. I fancied a smoke and didn't want to offend the ladies." Weston takes his seat next to Florence, who turns to him with flushed cheeks and a winsome smile.

Bram waves away the apology. "How's the writing coming along?"

"Very well," Weston says. "I've the first five chapters complete."

"Good, good." Bram smiles beneath his impressive mustache. "Florence writes, you know. You should look at her work sometime, see if it has any merit."

"Papa," Florence says, shaking her head. "They're only silly stories. I'm sure Mr. Chase has more important things to do." Sadie watches Weston's eyes rove over Florence, taking in her youthful beauty. She looks so much like her granddaughter Louise, the candlelight suffusing her complexion with a lambent glow.

Marguerite's fork clangs loudly against her plate. Her green eyes are daggers, pointed at Florence. "Stop it."

"Marguerite!" Adeline scolds. "Qu'est-ce qui se passe?"

"Look at her," Marguerite says, her voice rising. "She's ridiculous. Surely *you* can see it, Claire."

Claire looks down at her plate, tracing a path through the cream sauce with her fork. "Marg, please . . ."

"You're all blind to it. Every last one of you." Marguerite stands, throwing her napkin down. "Well. I've had enough. I'm going to my room. I've lost my stomach."

Bram lifts a brow and sighs. "Very well, miss. As you're so fond of your room, you'll be spending the rest of the week there."

"Good." Marguerite stalks from the table, her bustled skirts swishing as she passes by Sadie, so close that Sadie can smell her lilac perfume. Her great-aunt pauses for the slightest moment, as if sensing her presence, then rustles on, the echo of her feet on the stairs fading into the distance. No one says anything in her wake, although Claire begins to cry, silent tears tracking down her angelic face.

"I apologize, Mr. Chase," Adeline finally says. "Marguerite is, how do you say . . . une rebelle."

Weston laughs. "I find all of your daughters to be quite charming, Mrs. Thorne."

"When are you going to take her in hand, Papa?" Florence says, fuming, her eyes now pinched and hateful, the expression ruining her delicate, pretty features. "She's jealous. That's what this is about. She's always been jealous of me."

"Florence, please." Bram passes a hand through his thinning hair. "Let's have our dessert in peace, shall we? I'm weary of all the bickering."

Weston glances over at Sadie as the footmen begin serving a decadent rum-and-cherry compote alongside fluted canelés de Bordeaux—a dessert her grandmother always favored. Florence lifts the spoon to her lips with a smile as Weston whispers something in her ear.

The scene shifts suddenly, as if a strip of film has been cut and spliced. Somehow, Sadie is now outside, the scent of summer jasmine heavy in the air. While the change in scenery is jarring to her senses, she recognizes this place, too—these gardens. She played in them as a child and once got lost in the boxwood labyrinth when she was small. The marble statues of gods and goddesses always frightened her. Now, up ahead, the cloistered walls of the labyrinth beckon, faintly edged in shadow. As Sadie nears the maze, she hears a soft giggle, then a muted male voice. She pauses, listening.

"There," he murmurs. "I'll help you up. But you must be quieter this time."

Sadie edges closer to the first open-air room of the labyrinth—a temple dedicated to Venus. A frisson of nervous dread wars with her curiosity. Somehow, she already knows what she'll see. The thought makes her stomach turn. Yet her feet move forward of their own volition.

"Weston . . ." Florence's voice, soft and pleading with want.

"Quiet now, or I'll stop."

Sadie rounds the corner of the hedge and gasps. Florence sits balanced on the altar at Venus's feet, her hair loose and her head tilted back as Weston pleasures her, the moon bathing her bare shoulders in silver light.

Chapter 8

July 21, 1925

"Miss Halloran." I open my eyes at the sound of my name. Blades of grass poke at my skin. I place a hand on the dewy lawn and sit up, my head spinning. The labyrinth is gone. The Brookside mansion is gone. Blackberry Grange looms in front of me instead, its dark windows cold and dismissive. The rising sun cuts a red gash in the sky.

"Miss Halloran." Beckett's voice comes to me again, hollow. I push myself up from the ground and stand, drawing my thin robe tight around me. The faint reddish light paints Beckett in monochrome as he rushes to my side. "Are you all right?"

"I . . . I don't know." I press the heel of my hand to my eye, where the beginning of a headache throbs. "I don't know how I got out here."

"You were sleepwalking."

But I've never sleepwalked. Not a day in my life. I shake my head. "I was in Marguerite's studio. Something happened . . . I was in the past."

Beckett frowns. "Let's get you inside." He takes me by the elbow, gently steering me up the porch steps. Pins and needles tingle my legs, making me weak. I stumble against him, and he catches me before I fall. "Easy, now."

We make it into the kitchen, and Beckett pulls out a chair at a simple, rough-hewn table, easing me into it. He flicks on a lamp on the sideboard, and soft light floods the room. "I'll make you some coffee."

As he stokes the embers in the stove, I comb through my memories from the strange, dreamlike encounter with Weston Chase. The thought of my young grandmother in the throes of passion brings a brief rise of nausea. She married my grandfather at twenty, and as far as I knew, he was her only beau. In the encounter I witnessed, she couldn't have been much younger, because Marguerite—five years her junior—wore a floor-length gown at dinner and the upswept hair of a young woman.

Was Weston Chase my grandmother's first, secret love?

"Would you like something to eat?" Beckett asks. He takes an iron skillet from the wire rack above the stove and places it on the cooktop. "Eggs?"

"No thank you. My stomach is a little wobbly right now."

He grunts and cracks two eggs into the skillet, then adds a pat of butter, scrambling everything together with a wooden spoon. I watch him, the crossed braces of his suspenders emphasizing the asymmetry of his shoulders. He sees me looking and shoots me a sly smile. "Never seen a man cook before, have you?"

"I can't say that I have."

"My mother taught me. Said I'd need to know how."

I'd never learned. We'd always had a hired cook and a maid, even after the Panic of 1907, when Da lost the bulk of our stocks and savings. In the boardinghouse, I got by with dry toast, boiled eggs, and canned beans warmed on my two-burner range, but it was hardly what I'd call *cooking*. "It's a good skill to have, certainly."

"Well. Men who look like me don't tend to marry."

He's a fine-looking man, but I've the feeling if I said as much, given his suspicions of me, he'd think the compliment ungenuine. The coffee gurgles in the pot, and Beckett pours me a cup, sliding it across the table. He heaps a plate with scrambled eggs and sits opposite me. "You're sure?" He gestures with his fork.

"Go on. It smells delicious, though."

He nods and tucks in, eating heartily as I sip my coffee. It's strong, just the way I like it first thing in the morning. I press my lips together before speaking, measuring my words. "I feel we've gotten off on the wrong foot, Beckett. Both of us want the same thing, I think."

"Oh?"

"Yes. I can see that you're very protective of Marguerite. I want the best for her as well. But I'll admit that you're not entirely wrong about me. About my reasons for coming here."

He cocks an eyebrow at me and continues eating.

"I was engaged to be married, but my fiancé . . . he changed his mind. Less than a month after my mother died."

"I'm sorry to hear that."

"Yes. It was a lot, all at once." I take another sip of my coffee. "There was nothing left for me in Kansas City. I used to work as a cigarette girl at a supper club, but I'm getting too old for that scene, and I'm running out of money."

He stops eating and leans back in his chair. "And so you came here."

"Yes. I've always felt a sort of kinship with Marguerite." I think of what I witnessed in my vision—the way Marguerite's mother and siblings dismissed her concerns and shamed her outspokenness. Felix, and even Mama, often did the same to me. "We're both outcasts."

"I can understand why you'd feel a pull to your aunt, but if you're thinking you'll garner Marguerite's affection and, someday, her fortune, she's savvier than you might think."

I bristle. "No . . . and that's rather harsh of you to say. I'm not a fortune hunter. Not at all. I merely thought I could be of use to her, while not becoming destitute myself in the meantime. If that makes me selfish in your eyes . . . well, I suppose you can't begin to understand my predicament." I clear my throat, soften my tone. "There are very few options available to unmarried women, Mr. Hill. Especially those of us past the first blush of youth."

"That may very well be, Miss Halloran, and you have my sympathies. But the fact is you shouldn't have come. It's not safe for you here." He pushes his chair back and stands. "This morning was proof of that."

"What do you mean?"

"Whether you choose to believe so or not, this place is haunted. That's why we can't keep staff. Harriet has her reasons for staying, with a husband away working and two little ones to feed. So does Melva. But the rest of them?" He shrugs again. "They start seeing things that shouldn't be there. Eventually those things become more real. Dangerous."

A shiver crawls up my back. "I saw something strange. Last night. In Marguerite's studio. There was a man. I saw him in the attic as well, the day after I arrived."

"Yes." His eyes lock with mine. "You're not the only one who's seen him. My cousin was Marguerite's last companion. She swore there was a man living here in the attic—a writer of some sort. I've never seen him, but she was adamant."

"Melva said the other maids saw him, too. Is he really a ghost?"

"In a manner of speaking. One who has a maddening influence on the living—especially young women."

"I'm not sure what you mean."

"It doesn't matter *what* he is, Miss Halloran, but I can assure you that his intentions are less than noble. For your own good, you should leave. The sooner, the better."

Try as I may, though the day shines bright and cloudless, I can't seem to shake my unease. My early-morning conversation with Beckett niggles like a stubborn hangnail during my walk around the rose garden with Marguerite and Harriet after breakfast. I've never believed in ghosts, but I can't explain what happened to me in the studio. I have questions for Marguerite—about my grandmother and Weston Chase. I've a feeling that although Marguerite's recent memory is a sieve, she guards the distant past like a precious coffer full of jewels.

We settle on the rear terrace after Marguerite has finished her daily inspection of the roses. Harriet covers Marguerite's shoulders with a crocheted shawl and excuses herself. I regard my aunt from across the heavy wrought iron table. It might be my imagination, but she seems younger today. More vivacious. There's a gleam in her green eyes, as if she's been up to something sly. She smiles at me and offers me the plate of delicate pastries Melva set out for us. I wave them away.

"Aunt Marg, now that I'm here, I'm curious about our family history. Grandmother especially. Did she have a beau before Papa James?"

Marguerite shakes her head. "No. Your grandfather was her one and only."

"You're certain?"

"Yes. She was nineteen when he proposed. They carried on the engagement for a year, as was proper in those days. All she could talk about was their wedding. Such a bore."

"Do you happen to remember a houseguest you had in Kansas City around the time of Grandmother's engagement? A man?"

Marguerite's brow furrows. "Oh, we had several visitors. Father's business associates would often stay with us when they came from out of state."

"Was there ever a writer?"

"A writer?" Her perplexed look deepens. "I don't recall."

I pause, taking a sip of my tea. If she's lying to me, she's hiding it well. I decide to try another tack. "The portrait. In the attic . . . the one that upset you so. Who was he?"

A sudden spark of recollection alights behind Marguerite's eyes. "Weston."

"How did you come to paint his portrait? Was he one of your beaux?"

Marguerite shifts in her chair, uncomfortable. "No. And I don't want to talk about him."

"Why not?"

"He and Florence. They . . ."

Ah. Now I'm getting somewhere. "What did they do?"

Marguerite clenches her teeth and slams her open palm on the table. "No. I won't talk about it. I want to go back inside now," she says, petulantly. "Take me inside, Sybil."

"Sadie."

Marguerite's eyes blaze. "What does the name matter? You're all the same. You all leave me. Every one of you. Whether Sadie, Sybil, or Amanda."

"I'm not leaving you. I promise," I say firmly. I help her to her feet, and wind my arm through hers. "You happen to be stuck with me, Aunt Marg."

She wilts against me. "You'll really stay?" she asks. "You promise you won't leave me?"

"Of course not." I pat her hand and guide her toward the door, steadying her gait. "Now, why don't we go inside. I'll play some music for you if you'd like. Or I could read you a story."

"Do you play? The piano?"

"Yes. I do. Not well, I'm afraid."

"I never could, either." Marguerite smiles up at me, her demeanor softening. "My wrong notes drove Maman batty."

No. It was my grandmother who had been the accomplished pianist of the family. The great beauty. The star debutante at the top of the Kansas City social register and a paragon of feminine virtue. But what secrets had she kept hidden? Perhaps she wasn't as virtuous as we all thought. I have a feeling, with enough time spent cleverly coaxing out Marguerite's memories, I'll discover more about my grandmother and her sisters than I ever imagined.

Chapter 9

That evening, in the brief interlude between dinner and Harriet's and Melva's departure, I return to my aunt's studio. The painting of Weston remains there, uncovered, his eyes boring into mine from across the small space. I approach cautiously, wary of any sound or movement, yet intrigued by the image all the same. I reach out, gingerly touching the surface with my fingertips. There's no movement, and no feeling of vertigo overwhelms me. It's only an arresting image, rendered in two dimensions.

"What are you doing?"

I snatch my hand back, turning at the sound of Marguerite's voice. She stands in the doorway, her arms crossed, her mouth set in a hard line. "You shouldn't be in here alone."

"I'm sorry. The door was unlocked. I was just enjoying your work."

Marguerite stalks past me and snatches the painting off its easel with surprising strength. "You aren't to look at this one anymore. I'll have Beckett get rid of it. He can burn it with the lawn cuttings."

"No!" I shout. The sound bounces off the walls. Marguerite flinches. My adamance surprises even me. I lower my voice. "Please . . . please don't do that. It would be a shame. It's such a unique piece."

"You mean amateur and childish. It was my first portrait."

"Then it's ever more special for that reason." I ease toward Marguerite, my eyes on the painting. She can't destroy it. I won't let her. It compels me—intrigues me—not only because of its handsome subject, but because of the uncanny sensations I experienced while looking at it. Was the scene from the past in Kansas City a dream? Or did this painting transport me there? Either way, I mean to find out. I won't be able to if she destroys it. I gently pry the canvas from Marguerite's grasp, my heart beating wildly. I set it back on the easel and cover it with the discarded dustcloth. "There. I've covered it. I won't look at it again," I lie. "Now, let's go back downstairs. Would you like some chamomile tea before bed?"

Marguerite sighs, shakes her head. "You talk to me like I'm a child. I'm only trying to protect you, Sadie. There's so much you don't understand." The sudden clarity in her words takes me aback. In the past few days, there have been times when Marguerite's mind is just as solid and lucid as my own. Times when I see a *knowing* behind her eyes that doesn't square with her delusions and confusion.

"Well, I'm not a child, either, am I?" I tug on her arm, coaxing her into the hall. "Now, shall we go downstairs and have some tea? I've been thinking. We should get a radio." One of the only things I miss about Mrs. Dunlop's boardinghouse is the radio in the lounge. I loved gathering with the other tenants on Sunday evenings to listen to news and music on WDAF.

"A radio?"

"Yes. That way we can keep abreast of the news. And listen to music and stories, too. Good ones."

I lead Marguerite down the stairs, pausing so she can catch her breath on the landing. "Georgia Merritt has a radio," she says. "A big one, in a cabinet in her parlor. She's a bit snooty, that one. She reminds me a little of Florence."

"Is Georgia your neighbor?"

"Yes. Two houses over. The blue steamboat gothic." Marguerite tosses me a sly smile. "She comes over sometimes, to play mah-jongg and bridge. You'll meet her. She doesn't like me, but she pretends to."

I sigh, thinking of Rosalie, my sister-in-law. "Yes. There are lots of women like that, I'm afraid."

We make our way to the parlor. As Marguerite arranges herself on the sofa, I wind the Victrola and choose a recording of French standards. I go to the kitchen and ask Melva to put on the kettle before she leaves, then rejoin my aunt, who has her head tilted back, eyes closed, as the music winds through the room.

"This music reminds me of Christine," she says wistfully. "There was a club we'd go to, in the early aughts, where it was safe for us to be ourselves. France was more accepting of our sort, all the way around, but it was a comfort to be around others like us at the club. Made our world seem a little smaller in the best sort of way. We'd drink absinthe and dance all night."

"It sounds wonderful."

"It was. We had some good times together. I came home in 1912— you and your mother visited me here that summer."

"I remember. You let me have all the warm cocoa I wanted."

"Yes." Marguerite smiles sadly. "Christine died the next year. Cancer. It started with a tiny mole on her shoulder. I used to kiss that mole, not knowing it would one day bring her death."

I'm not sure what to say, and I'm grateful when Melva brings our tea. She hurries out the door a few minutes later, pocketbook latched over her arm, mumbling something about airing out the linens tomorrow. After she leaves, Marguerite pushes the tea to the side. "I'm not in the mood for tea, after all, dear. I need cheering. How about something stronger? There's a bottle of Calvados in the cupboard under the stairs."

"Auntie! I'm shocked."

"You shouldn't be surprised by anything I do at this point. Now, go get that brandy."

I find the bottle shoved behind a row of dusty preserves, their contents somewhat suspect, and bring it out, wiping it clean with my handkerchief. It's old—from 1908—but when I remove the stopper, the unmistakable scent of good, aged brandy floods my nostrils. I find two snifters in the dining room hutch and bring everything back to the parlor.

Marguerite lights up at the sight. "I haven't had a proper drink in years."

"Things might get a little wild, then."

She arches her brow. "They might indeed."

I pour the brandy, and Marguerite wastes no time in taking her first sip, her eyes shuttering in pleasure. "There's no better brandy than Calvados. I've tried every sort. Hennessy makes the best cognac, though."

"My da would've agreed," I say, clinking my glass to Marguerite's. "He loved his Hennessy."

"I always liked your father."

"You seem to remember him so well."

"Well, he was unforgettable. That mop of black hair. Those blue eyes. He took up all the air in the room. Florence didn't like him. She wanted Laura to marry up. But I saw how he treated her. He was quite the charmer, but he was genuine. Determined to make something of himself."

"And he did."

"Yes, only to throw all of it away. What a shame." She sighs, shakes her head. "I don't know how Laura survived all that."

I finish my brandy to soothe the sudden pinch at the back of my throat, and quickly pour another two fingers into my glass. "She was strong because she had to be. For me and my brothers. But it took its toll." Since Mama's passing, I've often wondered whether Da's and Henry's deaths left an indelible mark on her heart, her grief weakening its rhythm.

"Why do you think he did it?"

"I've asked myself the same question, many times. He didn't leave a note. None of us knew why. We had a small loss of fortune after the crash, but Da recovered. There were rumors he'd had some dealings with the Irish mob in Kansas City, but we never saw any evidence of that."

"Sometimes, it's better not knowing the reasons why terrible things happen. It hardly changes the outcome."

If Da had known what the outcome would be—how his death would shatter me—he wouldn't have done it. I'm sure of it. The summer I spent at Elm Ridge, with its ice-cold baths and bitter tonics, was meant to shock my depressive nerves back into order, but it did little to allay my grief. Da's death was still an open wound. One that would never heal over completely. "Why don't we ride with Beckett into town sometime," I say brightly, hoping to turn the subject. Our conversation is hardly helping Marguerite's maudlin mood, or mine. "Melva mentioned she was going to send him for groceries later this week. I'd love to take a stroll downtown. Reacquaint myself. Maybe we could have a look at the general store. See if there's a radio you'd like."

"All right. I haven't been to town in months."

The record runs out, and I go to the Victrola cabinet and select a cheerful ragtime album to lighten the air. The brandy is just beginning to take effect, my limbs loosening as a slight buzz runs through my head. I want to keep the good feeling going, so I fill my glass again.

It isn't long before Marguerite's spirits lift, and we're soon laughing and tapping our toes to the beat of the music. She stands and dances around the room, twirling with surprising grace. "Do you dance, Sadie?"

"Oh, a little," I say. "Not well."

"Come on, then. Let's foxtrot."

I stand and shake out my skirts. "Shall I be the gent, or shall you?"

"Oh, my darling, I *always* take the lead."

Marguerite guides me into the dance, and we giggle as my clumsy feet tangle with hers. I'm at least a head taller than she is, so we make an off pair. "Didn't Laura send you to cotillion?" she asks.

"Yes, but I'm a hopeless case, as you can see."

"You really are, dear." Marguerite sends me into a turn, then draws me back in, her eyes bright and merry. "You're as boneless as a willow switch. Stiffen up, just a bit, and you'll be a better partner. The gents like it when you push back on their lead, just a little."

"I've a feeling my dancing days are over with anyone but you."

"Nonsense. Surely you have suitors."

"I did. But things didn't work out well for me."

"What happened?"

"I was with someone who never really belonged to me. It was good when it was good and it was very bad, all at the same time."

"Oh. I see." Marguerite nods sagely. "I've had my share of heart-ache, too, my dear. Regrets. Hugh and I were star-crossed from the start."

This is the second time she's mentioned Hugh. "Who was he?"

"My very first love."

I go to the sofa and sit, propping my hands beneath my chin. "Tell me about him."

Marguerite sits next to me, picking up her brandy. "Hugh was our groom's son. My best friend and, as we got older, more. It was no surprise we fell in love. My parents didn't know about us. Only Florence knew." Her eyes narrow. "I trusted her with all my secrets in those days. That was a mistake. But you should be able to trust your own sister."

The agitation in Marguerite's voice rises with every word. She downs the rest of her brandy and pours more into her glass, filling it almost to the rim, her wrist shaking. The bottle is nearing empty now. When she offers it to me, I set it on the floor by my feet and put the stopper in. The night has taken an abrupt turn—tension crackles in the room, replacing our merriment. We're on the edge of something dangerous. One of us needs to sober up.

Marguerite rises and begins pacing, muttering to herself, her lace tea gown trailing the floor. She pauses in front of the portrait of my grandmother on her wedding day. "She looks the perfect angel here, doesn't she?" Her words are scornful. Bitter. "Florence was always Papa's favorite. She could do no wrong in his eyes. But I knew better. I knew *her*. I saw everything she did."

I perch on the edge of my seat, ears pricking. "Do you mean you saw her with Weston?"

Marguerite whirls, her eyes sparking with anger. "How did you know about that?"

"I . . . I don't know. Not for certain. Just a lucky guess, I suppose."

"She asked me to keep her secrets. And I did. Then she turned on me. Turned on Claire." Marguerite sets the brandy snifter on the mantel, and liquor sloshes over the side, onto the crocheted runner. "Bitch."

I flinch at the word. "Aunt Marg . . . perhaps we should go to bed." I approach her carefully, keenly aware of the strength in her arms when she led me through our dance. How easily she lifted Weston's painting from the easel, even in its heavy frame. I've learned how quickly her moods can change. Her good cheer has gone, in an instant, and her sanity now perches on a needle-thin ledge.

She reaches for her snifter, and I gently pry it from her hand, pouring the liquor into the empty grate. "I think you've had enough, don't you?"

"What a waste of good brandy," she says with a haughty sniff. "I should fire you for that."

"You can't fire me, remember? I'm family."

"*Family.* What has my family ever done for me?"

"Let's go to bed. All of this will seem better in the morning." I wrap my arm around her waist, trying to lead her to the stairs. She pushes me away, making for the dining room. I rush after her, my mind wheeling with dire scenarios. We're alone. Anything could happen. I briefly consider leaving her to fetch Beckett, who seems to have a calming effect on her nerves, but I need to learn to handle her on my own. My legs are weak, my head fuzzy. I shouldn't have been drinking.

Marguerite begins riffling through one of the drawers in the hutch, where the silver is stored. Before I can reach her, she brandishes a carving knife at me, its tip curved and cruelly forked. I flinch, taking a step backward. "Get away from me," she growls, her eyes lit with a feral madness. "What are you doing in my house?"

My palms begin to sweat as she advances on me, my mouth dry. I think about screaming for help, but who would hear me? Beckett is at least a quarter mile up the hill, in his cottage above the grotto. The next house is even farther. I pull in a shaky breath to steady my voice. "I'm Sadie. Just Sadie. Your great-niece."

I take another few steps backward, crossing the threshold into the parlor. I'm tempted to turn and run up the stairs, where I might hide until she sobers up and this mood passes. But I'm frightened about what could happen if I do—of Marguerite harming herself. I can't take that chance.

"Aunt Marg, put down the knife. No one is going to hurt you. Please."

Tears spill over onto her cheeks, but her eyes are all fire as she glares at me. "Whoever you are, you shouldn't have come here."

It's the second time someone in this household has told me that, and right now I feel very foolish for coming here, indeed. Harriet warned me of Marguerite's violent outbursts, but the suddenness has me unmoored. If I survive the night, I'll be packing up every knife and bottle of liquor I find in this house and secreting them well out of her reach. I was foolish to let my guard down.

Marguerite stands her ground, hand clenched around the knife handle. "Leave," she says menacingly, taking a step closer. I mirror her in reverse, feeling my way toward the stairs. "You need to leave."

"If you give me the knife, I'll leave. I promise."

She stalks closer, sniffling, her eyes meeting mine. Suddenly, I feel a shift. Marguerite gasps, looking at me, then at her hand. She drops the knife, and it goes clattering to the floor. I step forward quickly, snatching it up and hiding it behind my back. She just stands there, stunned, as if she's woken from a dream. As if she's been sleepwalking.

"I'm so sorry," Marguerite sobs, hugging herself. "I'm so sorry."

I cautiously approach, my knees trembling. "It's all right. You weren't yourself, just then."

"No. No." She shakes her head. "But I'm getting like this, more and more."

I edge closer, drawing her in. She clings to me, and I hold the knife well away, arm extended behind me.

"I'm so frightened," she sobs, wetting my shoulder with her tears.

"Shhh, it's all right. Everything will be just fine, come morning. Now, let's go up to bed."

I lead her upstairs and tuck her in, turning down the lights as I leave her room. Once I reach the attic, I hide the knife beneath my mattress and sit on the edge of the bed, hands trembling as I shuck my shoes off. The day's heat still festers under the eaves, gathering like a boil beneath my skin. I shed my clothing, stripping down to my chemise and tap pants. One of the many bedrooms below would provide respite from the heat, but the memory of Marguerite brandishing that knife—the wild look in her eyes—keeps me in place.

For a moment, she wanted to kill me.

I've bitten off more than I can chew, coming here. That's obvious now. I should take Beckett's advice and have him drive me to the station tomorrow. Catch the first train to Kansas City, beg Hank for my old job back at the Pepper Tree. Life won't be easy, but I *could* survive on tips and my allowance from Felix. I'll scrape by, even without Ted. But knowing Mrs. Dunlop's greed, it's likely she's already let out my room, even though I paid for the week.

I settle in bed, turn on my lamp, and try to read. After the first few pages, I give up. None of the words make sense to me. My mind is far too muddled. Just as I lay my head on the pillow to go to sleep, I hear a commotion from downstairs. Something breaks. An enraged cry follows. Marguerite is up again. Panic floods my senses as I war with myself. I should go to her. Try to calm her.

I don't.

Instead, I creep to the attic door and lock it, ashamed.

Chapter 10

I feel him before I see him. It begins as a prickling along my arms as I wake, then a cold rush of air next to my bed. The faint, grassy scent of vetiver cologne. I lie there, silently, my eyes afraid to open. His presence is as palpable as if he were a living person. My heart thuds inside the cage of my ribs. I blink. Clamp my eyes shut. Then open them again.

Weston's form is silhouetted against the window, somewhere between ephemeral and corporeal. Watching. Waiting for me to wake. I sit up, startled. The covers slip down my shoulders, exposing my goose-pimpled flesh.

"You needn't be afraid of me," he says, his voice gentle. "I've no desire to harm you."

He moves to sit at the foot of my bed, although the mattress doesn't sink under his weight. "I've come because you need to understand who I am. They're trying to turn you against me. To frighten you into leaving." He sighs. "I saw everything, earlier. That bit with the knife."

I pull the covers back around me, shivering. "You saw? I didn't know what to do. To help her. I was scared."

"Of course you were." Weston shrugs. "The nurse and that idiot doctor from town dismiss Marguerite's episodes as demented ravings. But there's a reason for her anger. Her pain. She just has trouble remembering what caused all of it."

I could almost laugh. I never imagined I'd be face-to-face with a ghost, much less holding an entire conversation with one. This all seems like a dream, yet I can feel my bedclothes draped around me, the draft from the open window. Have I gone insane? It wouldn't be the first time my mind has played cruel tricks on me. I've had hallucinations in the past. But Melva and Beckett mentioned that others have seen Weston, too. I'm not the only one. He must be a ghost—the spirit of a real person who lived and knew Marguerite and her sisters. "Who were you to Marguerite?"

"An old friend. Something happened between Marguerite and I, a long time ago. We are tied together because of it, she and I."

He seems to be implying they were intimate, although Marguerite was visibly repulsed by his portrait and denied that he had been her beau. He seemed far more besotted with my young grandmother in the vision I had.

My fear fades, replaced by curiosity. "I saw you, with my grand-mother. In the garden. Did that really happen? Or was it a delusion? A hallucination?"

"No, not at all. It was a memory from the past, stored in time. You'll find that time moves differently here—the walls between past and present are less brick and stone, and more like sheer fabric." He smiles. "Iris is here, too. You'll see her eventually. We're both tied to Marguerite's paintings. Her past. What did you think when you saw me with Florence, that night in the gardens?" he asks, elegantly crossing one leg over the other.

"It was shocking. It . . . confused me. Upset me."

He nods, his eyes catching the sliver of moonlight knifing through the curtains. "Because you saw something you didn't expect. Florence had a side to her that few people saw. A passionate, adventurous side. I adored her. Even though she was already promised to another when we met, I took as much as she was willing to give me."

"Marguerite said Florence betrayed her. Did she know about your affair? Did Claire know?"

"Yes, Marguerite knew, and it made her angry, because she saw Florence as selfish. And even though I loved her, Florence *was* greedy.

Claire knew about us, but she was like the calm between two storms. Ever mediating. She just wanted everyone to be happy. There wasn't much room for what Claire wanted, between Florence and Marguerite."

I laugh, knowing all too well the plight of a middle child. "I understand, completely."

"Claire was the best of them. Her father hoped we might marry. I was willing, but Florence . . . she was jealous." Weston sighs. "She wanted me all to herself. Claire knew I couldn't resist Florence's charms. She would have made our marriage miserable. If I had it to do all over again, I'd never have gotten involved with Florence."

I'd seen hints of my grandmother's jealousy and selfishness, certainly— her insistence on always hosting Christmas dinner, despite Da's closeness to his own family. She'd pouted when Mama refused to leave us with a nanny to travel with her on her yearly holiday to France. Grandmother *was* petty and vain. Self-centered. But I never saw her as vindictive.

I study Weston, my guard still up, but eager to hear what he has to say. There's so much I never knew about my aunts and Grandmother. So much I want to learn. "Aunt Claire died. In 1881. Did you know?"

"Yes." He frowns, looks away from me. "Complications of measles. Florence wrote to me. I was heartsick over it."

So, my grandmother had stayed in contact with him, even after she'd married. "Did you move on, after Grandmother married Papa?"

"No. Florence and I still found ways to be together, through the years. Fleeting moments of happiness. James never knew about the affair. We continued meeting right up until I died." Sadness clouds his features. "It was difficult, not having her entirely to myself. But I accepted her sense of duty. She had a family. Children. I tried to be happy with our arrangement, but I was often very lonely."

I shoot him a wry smile. "That's something you and I have in common, then."

"What do you mean?"

"I fell in love with a married man. When my family found out about our affair, they nearly disowned me." I lean back against the headboard, letting the quilt drop to my bosom. "He said he wanted to marry me someday. Even gave me a ring. He lied."

"You deserve better. I suppose I did, too. We're quite a pair, aren't we?" He smiles sadly. "Some would call us pathetic. I prefer to see myself as a romantic. I suspect you are as well."

I should be angry with this man who despoiled my grandmother and made my darling, beloved Papa a cuckold. But as he looks at me, I sense a kinship between us. I didn't intend to fall for Ted, either, but I was swept along with what felt like true love at the time. Our affair seemed bigger than us—so big it consumed every ounce of my common sense and sent my better angels into flight. But even with my regrets, there's an inevitability to it all that seems fated. "I suppose we want to believe ourselves helpless in the face of love. That it can transcend everything. But it can't, can it? Not really."

"Indeed it can't. Not even death." He clears his throat. "Well, then. I'll leave you to your rest." He unfolds from my bed, eyes soft as he gazes down at me. "Thank you for a pleasant evening. It's been a long time since I've had someone to talk to, Sadie."

I feel color rise to my cheeks as he looks at me. Even though his arrival at my bedside was unsettling, I don't want him to leave. There's something mesmerizing in his manner—a cavalier brashness married with sensitivity. Understanding. "Come again . . . if you'd like."

"I'd prefer it if you came to me," he says. "I think you might know how." His lip curls into a mischievous grin that conjures an unexpected flutter—something I haven't felt in quite some time. "You have her eyes, you know."

And then he's gone, his form fading into the shadows.

When morning breaks, I dress for the day, my head pounding with the brandy's aftermath. I go down to check on Marguerite. She's sound asleep on her belly, a soft snore parting her lips. While she seems unharmed by last night's episode, her porcelain ewer is shattered on the floor—the source of the crash I heard—so I carefully pick up the broken shards and place them in the wastebasket near her vanity.

Downstairs, the house is quiet, the sun a burnished copper glow through the curtains. It's only six. Melva and Harriet aren't due to arrive for another hour. I open the hutch's drawers, searching for more sharp cutlery, and find only a butter knife. Still, I take it into the kitchen and stow it in the high cupboard above the sink with the other knives, then scour the parlor and hall for anything else Marguerite might use as a weapon in the future. I remove the poker from the hearth, a pearl-handled letter opener hidden behind a picture frame, and a set of keys on a worn brass chatelaine that I find in a drawer. I take the keys to the attic and put them on the top shelf of my wardrobe, under one of my hats. I'm curious to see whether they'll fit any of the locked trunks stowed there.

Weston's visitation last night still lingers as I go about my morning routine, enlivening me. Our conversation about shifting time and family secrets has me intrigued. I'm consumed by the urge to go to the studio, to inspect Marguerite's other paintings, to see whether they have a similar effect to Weston's. The pull follows me until I can deny it no longer. With the house still quiet, I creep down the hall to the narrow, closed door and twist the knob. It's locked. I try again, my frustration growing as the door holds, keeping me out. "Dammit."

Marguerite must have locked it, sometime during her restless night, which means she has a key. I could search her room, after Harriet arrives. Or perhaps one of the old keys on the chatelaine I found will fit the lock. As I turn to fetch them from the attic, I nearly run face-first into Beckett. He steadies me, hands on my arms. "Miss Halloran. What were you doing just now?"

"I left something in Marguerite's studio the other day. It's locked. Would you happen to have the key?"

"No, I don't. But even if I did, you shouldn't be in there alone."

"Why not?"

"There are weak places in the floor, for one thing. And there are reasons I hinted about before, though I doubt you'd believe the whole of things."

"I'm in the mood to believe all sorts of things this morning," I say. "Try me."

Beckett eyes me warily, taken aback by my frankness. Part of me wonders whether he's still the shy boy I remember, and his thorniness is merely testimony to his lack of social graces. He's been cloistered here with my aunt since childhood, after all.

"Well, for one thing," he says, "I've heard Marguerite calling you Sybil. Do you know why she calls you that?"

"I assumed it's just her memory lapses. That she's confused. I gather she's had several maids. Perhaps she's confusing me with one of them."

"She is, but . . ." He looks away from me. "Sybil wasn't a maid. She was the cousin I mentioned. Marguerite's last companion. She didn't leave like the others. She fell from the bluff behind the house and died. She was sleepwalking. Just like you were yesterday."

I'm taken aback by this revelation. "Goodness. I'm so sorry."

"I wouldn't have told you about Sybil, but I'm concerned by your similarities. Sybil was a lot like you—young, pretty, naive."

"I appreciate your concern, but I'm hardly young, sir, and the furthest thing from naive, although I'll accept your barbed compliment on my looks, thank you." I cross my arms, glaring at him. "I've never sleepwalked, Mr. Hill. It was only a fluke."

"That may be, but all the same, Sybil was obsessed with Marguerite's studio, too. Her work. One painting in particular."

I pause, considering him. "Was it the portrait of Weston Chase? Our ghost?"

He sighs, resigned. "Yes. She'd look for any excuse to visit the studio. I'd often find her, sitting and staring at his portrait, her eyes glazed over. And at night, she'd wander. I took to watching for her on the grounds. I saw some very disturbing things, Miss Halloran. Things I can't explain. I did my best to protect her, to keep her safe. But one night, I couldn't get to her fast enough."

"How dreadful." My pulse beats faster, thinking of the sheer drop of limestone behind the house—the deep gully below it paved with unforgiving shale. It would be nearly impossible to survive a fall from that height.

"Sybil was convinced Weston was real. She told me all about him one evening. How they'd fallen in love. I thought it all a young girl's harmless fantasy, at first."

I shudder, remembering how real Weston seemed to me as well. While there was a slight transparency to his features last night as he sat by my bed, when we visited the past, in Kansas City, he was just as real as Beckett is now. I'd felt the press of his hand on my back as he guided me through the door into the room where Marguerite and her family dined.

"And you believe he was responsible for her death?"

"I do. Whether he pushed her or she jumped, she wasn't in her right mind because of him." He looks away from me, then back. "Marguerite asked me to burn the painting after Sybil died. I did, but the next day, it reappeared, right where it had been. I've seen a lot of things I can't explain in my life, but that painting trumps them all. It's cursed. Evil. That's the reason it's locked away."

"That's quite a story," I say, lifting my chin, despite the tingle of fear dancing on my skin. But the jump in logic is a bit too much for me. Burned paintings don't reappear on their own. I'm still unsure of Beckett, of his intentions. It's possible he's only trying to frighten me away. It's obvious he wants me gone, and despite his protestations otherwise, I have a feeling it's not over any concern for my safety, nor any supernatural reason, but because we're at odds over Marguerite.

Last night, after Marguerite's violent spell, my first inclination was to leave. But now, my stubborn streak rises—the strong Irish will I inherited from my father. If Beckett thinks telling me scary stories will drive me away, he has another thing coming. Marguerite is my family, not his. I have a right to be here.

"Have you given any more thought to leaving?" he asks, confirming my suspicions. "I can take you to the station anytime you'd like. I'm going into town tomorrow. The depot is on the way."

I take a step back, regarding him coolly. "Thank you for the offer, Mr. Hill, but I've decided I'm not leaving. Marguerite had a bad spell last night. She threatened me with a knife."

"That hardly sounds like an argument for your staying."

"It *was* frightening. But I can't just desert her. What might have happened if I hadn't been there?"

He sighs, removing his cap and swiping his chestnut hair back. "You're determined, I'll give you that. Do you need anything, when I go to town?"

"Actually, I wondered if Marguerite and I might ride in with you. The outing would do her good, I think." I lower my defenses a bit and smile, doing my best to convey we're on the same side. That we both care deeply for the woman under our charge. "I've talked her into getting a radio."

He laughs, returning my smile. "Really? I told her we should get one years ago. It seems you're much more convincing than I am."

I resist playing smug, although his concession on this small, insignificant thing feels like a victory all the same. "You should come to the house in the evenings, after you've finished your chores. Have a listen with us."

"I might, at that." His eyes soften, the chipped edges of his demeanor falling away, just a bit. "I'm off to mow before the rain comes."

"How can you tell it's going to rain?" I ask, casting an eye toward the sun-drenched window above the stairs. "There's not a cloud in the sky."

"I can feel it in my bones, Miss Halloran," he says with a wink.

His wink leaves me flabbergasted and a bit off my feet as he walks away. I can't get a read on him, which is unusual. Normally I can read the intentions of men rather quickly. His story about Sybil and the painting has me rattled, but not enough to diminish my curiosity. I fetch the chatelaine from the attic, and I'm in the process of trying the keys on the studio door when I hear Harriet come in and call for me. I pocket the chatelaine and go down to greet her. She seems out of sorts this morning; her uniform wrinkled, as if she rushed out the door to get here quickly.

"I won't be able to stay all day, Miss Halloran," she says. "My mother-in-law is sick and can't watch my boys."

"I'm sorry. I hope it's nothing serious."

"I'm sure it's not, but I'll need to leave around noon. How was Miss Thorne last night? She seemed a bit agitated before I left."

I hesitate a moment before telling her the truth. I don't want her to think I'm incapable, but she should know what happened, all the same. "We had an . . . incident. I managed to calm her, but she came at me with a knife."

Harriet's eyes widen. "Are you all right?"

"Yes, yes, I'm fine."

"Where did she find a knife?"

"The hutch in the dining room."

"Oh, I must have missed it. I thought I took away everything she could use to harm herself or anyone else with, the first week I came here."

Harriet's tone isn't defensive, only matter-of-fact, but I touch her arm lightly to convey I'm not blaming her. "I didn't know it was there, either. She might have hidden it."

"They do that sometimes. We'll need to be watchful. It's the dementia. It makes her unpredictable. Especially at night."

"The brandy may have also been to blame."

Harriet hooks an eyebrow upward. "Brandy?"

"We were listening to records, and she asked for a drink. She had too much. We both did."

Harriet sighs. "Where is it?"

"What?"

"The brandy."

"I left it in the parlor."

Harriet marches into the parlor and snatches the mostly empty bottle off the floor. She upends it into one of the potted palms by the window, then hands me the bottle. "Put this in the rubbish bin. And for heaven's sake, no more alcohol of any kind. That goes for the both of you. You can't be off your wits with her, Miss Halloran. Not for a minute."

A part of me rankles at Harriet's authoritative tone. My grandmother would have never allowed hired help to talk to her in such a way, but I'm not my grandmother, and Harriet is right. And so I take the bottle to the kitchen, shamefaced, and bury it in the waste bin.

I shouldn't be drinking, anyway. Not with our family history. Grandmother was a closeted lush, with a proclivity for hiding gin in pretty crystal perfume bottles—something I discovered as a young girl. The habit caught up with her, and she succumbed to liver failure. I think of all the other secrets she might have been hiding. Did her guilt and regret over her affair with Weston drive her to drink? It's possible.

Weston's words from the night before sit heavily on my mind. If there are more secrets, more lies to uncover about my family's past, it all seems to begin and end with him. I reach into my pocket for the chatelaine and its keys. There are two keys I haven't yet tried. With a furtive glance behind me, I ascend the servants' stairs to the second floor, where Weston, and the past, await.

Interlude

WESTON

Sadie stands slowly, reeling from the uncomfortable vertigo created by her free fall into the past yet pleased by her successful escapade all the same. She lifts her hand, sees the faint outline of trees through it. While she is a ghost here, her senses are all still present. She breathes in the scent of soft rain, feels the breeze blowing across her skin, hears laughter close by—that of a woman, or a girl.

A few yards away, Sadie encounters a wooden gazebo set in a clearing—one she remembers from childhood. Grandmother gave her and the cousins birthday parties there. In her time, the gazebo had fallen into disrepair, its floorboards crumbling with rot and its delicate gingerbread ruined by the weather. Money had grown scarce for Aunt Grace in recent years, and nature was slowly reclaiming the Brookside gardens as a result.

But now, in this era, the gazebo is a luminous, whitewashed confection set against the verdant spring landscape. Inside, a man and a woman sit close together, their heads nearly touching. Sadie creeps forward, parting the rain-speckled shrubbery. It's Weston and Claire. Her long-deceased aunt lifts a sheet of paper from the open folio spanning her lap and reads from it.

"And Cecilia was the purest of heart," she recites, "though her eyes held an uncommon curiosity her elder sister lacked. Her charms were often disregarded when Felicity was about, but William saw in Cecilia the unrealized potential of the dreamer."

"Do you like it?" Weston asks.

Claire's chin dips. "I do. But Flor won't. She won't like it at all."

"It doesn't matter. It's my story, and in it you'll shine the brightest." Weston lifts Claire's chin to gaze into her eyes. "I've told Florence we can't go on, after she's wed."

"She won't listen." Claire laughs. "It will only make the game more interesting for her. A challenge."

"Do you think me weak, Claire?" Weston's thumb brushes her cheek. "Unable to resist her?"

"No." Claire takes his hand. Her eyes dance over the gardens, landing on the hedge of roses near Sadie. "It's only . . . Florence has never let me or Marguerite have anything *she* wants."

"Oh, darling. But it's you I want. *Only* you. Trust in that." Weston bends to her, kissing her deeply. Claire sighs, throwing her arms around his neck in surrender.

A clatter of hooves echoes through the trees. Weston and Claire spring apart as a horse and rider crash through the gardens, clearing the rose hedge in a spectacular jump. Marguerite sits atop a handsome dapple gelding, her long hair matted with wet leaves, her cheeks flushed. She brings the horse around in a circle before the gazebo and dismounts. Her hem is soaked, and a long tear in the fabric reveals the scarlet petticoat she wears beneath the dark woolen skirt. Claire stands, handing the leather folio to Weston. "Papa will have a fit if he finds out you brought Pepper into the gardens, Marg."

"I had to get out of that house," Marguerite says, exasperated. "Flor's throwing a tantrum over the seating for the wedding breakfast. She wants James's parents seated next to John Wornall and his wife instead of Maman and Papa." Her brows knit together as she regards Weston and Claire. "What are the two of you doing out here alone?"

"Weston was just showing me the new pages he's written." Claire smiles at him shyly. "They're quite good."

"Hello, Marguerite," Weston greets her. "Did you enjoy your ride?"

"I did," Marguerite says, lifting her chin. "Maman was looking for you, Claire. She needs your help choosing table settings. Why don't you take Pepper and go back to the house?"

"But . . ." Claire looks from Weston to Marguerite.

"Claire, it's all right," Weston says. "I should be leaving. I need to go back to the boardinghouse and pack."

"Oh? You're not staying for Flor's wedding?" Marguerite crosses her arms, pinning him with a cold gaze.

"I don't believe I will." Weston's eyes cut to Sadie. He gives her a slight nod, acknowledging her presence. "I'm due back in Bristol on Monday to give a lecture on Keats."

"Keats, is it? I'd imagined you preferring Byron." Marguerite and Weston regard one another in stony silence for an uncomfortable breadth of time.

"I'll go see what I can do to help Maman," Claire says. "Help me up onto Pepper, won't you, Wes? I'm not at all dressed for riding."

Weston lifts Claire, light as a feather, onto Pepper's back. As she rearranges her skirts over the sidesaddle's pommel, Sadie sees his hand slide up her leg. Claire's eyes widen and the faintest gasp escapes her lips. "I'll see you in August, won't I, my dear?" Weston asks.

"In August," she responds, her cheeks flushed.

She rides away at a trot, her hair bright as a bobbing flame through the roses.

Marguerite wastes no time in accosting Weston. Her face is a storm cloud of rage. She snaps her riding crop against the gazebo. "I saw the two of you. You were kissing her."

"And what of it? It's what Claire wants."

"To be your consolation prize?" Marguerite laughs.

"She isn't. I love her."

"Do you?"

"Yes." Weston runs a hand through his damp curls. "You think me a rake. A cad. But I care for both of your sisters a great deal."

"Oh yes, you've made that very clear. It sickens me how they fawn over you."

"But not you. You've never liked me, Marguerite. Why is that?"

"Because I've always known what you are. *Who* you are. What you're offering Claire isn't real. It's merely the illusion of love." Marguerite taps the riding crop against the gazebo in a staccato rhythm. "Florence is drinking now. Just like Papa. She tries to hide it, but I know. She was perfectly happy with James until you came around. You've ruined her. But I won't let you ruin Claire."

"I have no intention of ruining Claire. I can't help it that I fell in love with Florence first. It was a great misfortune that she was already promised to James when we met. But I *do* mean to marry Claire. And no one will stand in the way of that." Weston reaches out, grabs Marguerite's riding crop, stilling its perpetual motion. "Florence knows about you and your stable boy. She told me. But don't worry. I'll keep your secret. All of us deserve to be happy, after all. Don't we?"

The scene flickers, dying out like a spent candle, leaving Sadie with more questions than answers.

Chapter 11

When I come to, I find myself on the studio floor. I sit up, dust off my clothes, and pinch my eyes shut against the sun glaring through the split in the curtains. My hangover from the night before is slightly better, but confused thoughts run through my head. I'm not quite certain what Weston meant for me to glean from my latest foray into the past, but apparently he was honest about his intentions toward Aunt Claire, who seemed just as besotted with him as my grandmother. Something must have happened to derail their betrothal, because Claire was unmarried when she died. Did my grandmother interfere, just as Weston implied?

I cover Weston's portrait with its dustcloth and lock the studio door behind me. The upstairs hall is silent, apart from the ticking grandfather clock. Downstairs, Marguerite and Melva are sorting mah-jongg tiles on a card table in the parlor. A woman I don't recognize sits across from Marguerite, who looks up as I descend the stairs. "Ah! Here's our North Wind. I wondered where you'd gotten off to."

"Just reacquainting myself with the house. Your nooks and crannies."

"All morning? It's half past noon." Marguerite raises a brow and motions to the gray-haired lady across from her. "This is Georgia Merritt. My neighbor."

Georgia Merritt of the blue steamboat gothic and the fancy radio set. "Pleased to meet you, Mrs. Merritt," I say, offering my hand. "Sadie Halloran."

"Oh, it's *just* Georgia." She pats my fingers. Everything about her is tidy, from her attire to her trim, petite figure. "Marguerite, you didn't *tell* me how perfectly *lovely* she is." Her thick drawl rises in pitch with every word. I know that tone. All too well. It's the tone of a would-be matchmaker with some weak-chinned, clammy slob of a son, grandson, or nephew she'd like to set me up with.

"Are you a Sarah?" Georgia continues. "Sometimes *they're* called Sadie."

"No. Only Sadie." I smile tightly and fold into the chair across from Melva. I'd hoped to speak to Marguerite alone—to ask her more about Claire and Weston—but our long-hidden family secrets will have to wait.

Melva shuffles the tiles and deals out thirteen apiece. It isn't a fortuitous hand for me, and my losing streak continues through two glasses of iced tea, three cucumber sandwiches, and a rousingly shrill rendition of Verdi's "Sempre Libera" by Georgia, who claims she sang the role of Violetta in 1906, which I believe to be a confabulation of the highest order.

I applaud her all the same. We're having a nice time, and Marguerite seems to be in a high mood—a marked improvement from last night. She seems to have forgotten about the incident with the knife, and I won't say a word to remind her. After our game, Melva clears the table and returns to the kitchen, while Marguerite, Georgia, and I retire to the conversation nook in front of the parlor's bay window.

"I saw Beckett when I drove in," Georgia says, before daintily taking a sip of her tea. "What does *he* think of your Sadie?"

Marguerite presses her lips together and glances at me before answering. "We're all very glad that Sadie is here. It's nice to have family close."

"Hmmm . . ." Georgia smacks her lips. "Do you think he'll *ever* marry? Beckett?"

I turn my head, uncomfortable with the conversation and the pointed way in which Georgia studies me.

"He's never shown an interest in courting anyone," Marguerite says archly. "Why do you ask?"

"*Well* . . . it's just all so *sad*, isn't it? He's such a *handsome* young man. That *face*."

"There isn't a thing that's sad about Beckett," I interject, bristling at the implication behind her words. "He's quite capable."

"Oh, I didn't mean to *imply* . . ."

That his handicap makes him pitiable and less desirable in your eyes? The words are there, on my tongue, which I hold only for Marguerite's sake. I wonder at my own defensive reaction—at my sudden urge to champion him when he seems to hold me in low regard. But how many times have *I* been talked about in rooms where I wasn't present? I think of my time at Elm Ridge and how, after I came back home, my debut season fell by the wayside, and the women in Mama's circle no longer offered up their sons and nephews as my escort. Was anyone ever my champion when they called me "Mad Sadie"? No. They merely laughed behind my back. No one deserves that.

Marguerite smiles at me, as if she can read my thoughts. "Sadie's right. Beckett will be quite a catch, for the right sort of girl. He'll marry. Someday."

"Indeed." I clear my throat. "I think so, too."

Georgia looks at me for a long moment. "I have a nephew, just out of university. He's seeing a girl *now*. But she's a bit of a flapper. Wears her skirts *much* too short."

There it is.

"I used to be a flapper," I say, with a haughty lift of my chin. "I've aged out of the enterprise, but it was a great deal of fun while it lasted."

Marguerite snorts, covering her mouth with her hand.

"Really?" Georgia asks, flabbergasted. "But you're so *genteel*."

I hide my smirk behind my glass of tea. "Well. I'm twenty-eight, after all. I already have my burial plot paid for and *everything*."

"Oh. *Oh*. Are you ill, my dear?" Georgia's eyes widen.

"Only in the head, I'm afraid." I laugh, much too heartily. Being diagnosed with a nervous condition is beneficial in certain situations.

"I think I'd better *go*," Georgia croons. "Must tend to the . . . the *table* linens." She pats her upswept hair and twitters goodbye to Marguerite, who rises to see her out.

I'm still laughing to myself when I bring our dishes to the kitchen. Beckett is there, scrubbing carrots and potatoes at the sink. He glances over his shoulder at me and smiles. "I see you've met Georgia."

"She's a hoot," I say.

"And a gossip. By this time tomorrow, all of Eureka Springs will be talking about you."

"It's probably good, then, that we're going to town in the morning. The villagers can see for themselves that I don't have two heads and sixteen legs. I'm certain Georgia thinks I'm a lunatic. I won't be able to disprove *that* very easily. At least I won't have to worry about her pawning me off on her nephew."

He chuckles. "Just as well, for your sake."

"Yes . . ." I look at him, there at the sink, his strong, angled chin tilted down. Thunder crackles in the distance. I clear my throat. "Sounds like you were right, about the rain. Did you get your mowing done?"

He nods. "And more firewood cut for the stove."

"I wish I'd been as industrious. So far, the only thing I've accomplished is losing at mah-jongg. I had fun, though. Marguerite is having a good day, I think."

"I'm glad to hear it."

An awkward silence descends as the first patters of rain hit the kitchen's metal roof. Melva comes in from outside, a basket of laundry in her arms. Beckett takes it from her, setting it on the trestle table. "Fixing to come a gully washer," she says. "I should have sent you to the market this morning, Beck. Hopefully the road won't wash out overnight."

"This is the sort that blows over quick," he says, drying his hands on a towel. "It'll be done by morning."

"Lord, let's hope," Melva says. "We're out of everything. When you go, I need two heads of cabbage, white beans, and rye bread, the darkest you can find. Oh, and if you get the chance, swing by the butcher and ask Frank for some soupbones. I mean to make broth. Don't forget the coffee. This is the last of it." Melva fills the coffeepot with water, then slams it down on the stove.

"Yes, ma'am." Beckett glances over at me, a smile creasing the skin around his eyes.

"I hope ham and eggs are to your liking for breakfast tomorrow, miss," Melva calls to me. "About all I've got left. Nothing to be done for it now."

"Ham and eggs happen to be my favorite, Melva," I say, raising my voice above the storm. The soft, pattering rain has become a torrent.

She mutters something beneath her breath and goes to work folding the laundry.

"And you were worried about *me* ordering you around," I murmur to Beckett, teasingly. "Seems as if Melva has you well under hand."

He leans close to me. "I learned from my mother to never get on a cook's bad side."

"I should go check on Marguerite. See if she needs anything," I say, turning away from the surprising warmth in his eyes. One moment, he's charming, the next he seems determined to drive me away. Despite my attempts to convince him otherwise, I have the feeling he still only considers me a gold digger . . . and the fact that I care so much about what he thinks of me tells me more than I'm comfortable admitting, even to myself.

That night, as the storm rages overhead, blowing the tree limbs sideways to scratch against the house, I imagine I see Weston again, writing at his desk under the eaves, the lightning illuminating him briefly before he disappears. A frisson of fear and excitement runs through me, as I blink and refocus my eyes, willing him to return, to no avail. I can't help but wonder whether my encounters with him are only flights of strange fancy. I'm tempted to go down to the studio, to open myself to his world once more, but Marguerite's mood turned fitful and dark again after dinner, and I don't want to risk waking her.

She was convinced there was a crying baby in the house, and it took Beckett, Melva, and me more than an hour to calm her and ease her anxieties. According to Melva, the crying baby is another of her recurring delusions—one real enough to bring me to tears.

Beckett insisted on spending the night in one of the guest bedrooms, despite my assurance that I can manage Marguerite on my own. He still doesn't trust me. It's obvious. His mistrust rankles, but why do I care so much what he thinks of me?

I toss and turn, thoughts of Beckett, of Weston, of Marguerite and her sisters running through my head until morning glows pale gray through the attic windows. The rain slows to a gentle shower, then ceases before dawn. I rise, pull my wrapper on over my nightgown, then go downstairs to fill my ewer with warm water.

Light bleeds from the kitchen. Either Melva arrived incredibly early to work, or Beckett is up for the day. I'd bet on the latter. I'm suddenly conscious of my state of undress—a state he's already seen me in once before, after my episode with sleepwalking. I turn and start to pad silently back through the dining room, hoping to avoid another embarrassing encounter, when a shadow falls long across my path.

"Good morning, Miss Halloran." Beckett clears his throat. "Up early?"

"I didn't sleep well, with the storm." I turn to see him standing there in his undershirt and trousers, a steaming cup of coffee in his hands. "I . . . I just came to fetch some water, for washing up." My eyes flit from the dark stubble on his jaw to his narrow waist and broad shoulders, where freckles scatter the surface of his suntanned skin.

"Here," he says, setting his coffee cup down. "I'll get it for you. I'm warming a kettle of water to shave. You can have it."

"Oh, you don't . . ." He takes the ewer from me before I can finish, his fingers brushing mine. My belly tumbles. I cross my arms awkwardly as I wait. He returns a moment later and hands me a cup of coffee.

"Thank you," I say, inhaling the warm aroma.

"Come into the kitchen and sit with me. It'll be a while for the water."

I follow him and sit at the trestle table, feeling suddenly shy. I pat at my braided hair, rub the sleep from my eyes. Beckett sits across from me, propping his elbows on the table. I do my best to avoid staring at him. His work has made him lean and hard. Strong. I remember the note of pity in Georgia Merritt's words. If she could see him right now, she'd eat crow. He looks better than butter on sliced toast. The very picture of ideal masculinity. My skin warms and I quickly take a drink of coffee. "Marguerite sleep through the night?" I ask.

"She did. I didn't hear a peep."

"I hope Harriet's mother-in-law is feeling better, so she can come today. She's so good with Aunt Marg, even if she acts like Carry Nation with her hatchet around me."

"She doesn't care much for drinking, that's for sure." Beckett laughs. "I wouldn't expect her today. When one in the family gets sick, the others usually follow."

"True. I suppose it won't matter, since we're going to town today. The roads didn't wash out, did they?"

"I don't think so." Beckett raises his cup to his lips.

After a moment of awkward silence, I move beyond our stilted small talk. "Has Aunt Marguerite ever talked about her sisters with you, by any chance?" I ask. "Claire or Florence?"

"Not really. I know that your aunt Claire died when she was fairly young, and that your grandmother and Marguerite didn't always see eye to eye. I met your grandmother a time or two, when I was little." He chuckles. "She frightened me."

"How so?"

"She was imposing. Tall. Grand."

"We called her the Snow Queen, my cousins and I. Louise always claimed she was a witch."

"A very pretty one," he says, a smile playing on his lips. "I can see where you get your looks."

"Oh . . . I don't really look like her," I hedge, avoiding his gaze. "That's Louise. I favor Aunt Claire, most of all. I've seen her pictures. We have the same heart-shaped face. Same nose."

"It's funny, isn't it? How family traits skip generations."

"Yes," I say. "Do you favor your father, or your mother?"

"My father, although the curly hair comes from the Clemson side. My mother's. Charlie looked just like her."

"Marguerite told me about your brother. I'm so sorry."

"It's all right." Beckett's fingers flex around his cup. "Lots of people lost brothers over there. Sons. Husbands."

I reach out, lightly skimming the skin on his wrist with my fingertips. "Yes, but it doesn't make *your* loss hurt any less."

He looks at me through his long lashes. "I suppose you're right. Tell me about your little brother. What was his name again?"

"Henry." I smile, sitting back in my chair. "He was such a proud little stoic—from the time he was a baby. Once he could read, he had his head in a book from morning to night. Studying the lives of the saints. The works of Augustine. He was an altar boy at our church. Wanted to be a priest. He would have made a good one, I think."

Beckett nods. "I'm sorry. It's a shame."

"Yes." I take a long sip of coffee to soothe the ache in my throat. "It is."

The teakettle begins to steam but doesn't yet whistle. "Marguerite told me more about you last night, after dinner," Beckett says. "About your father's death. And that you'd had a tragic love affair."

I bristle. "She did?" I haven't talked about Ted at length with Marguerite, and she doesn't know much at all about us, other than things didn't end well. I've kept the details of our relationship sparse, but knowing Louise, she probably phoned Marguerite and told her everything, and in one of her moments of clarity, Marguerite remembered. I'm upset that she shared such intimate details of my life with Beckett. "What else did she tell you?" I hesitantly ask.

"Not much. She just said your engagement had ended badly and your man was a fool for letting you slip away."

"I'm sure *he* doesn't see it that way."

"What happened?" he asks.

I waver, unable to meet his eyes. It's none of his business what happened between Ted and me. If I tell him the truth—that Ted was married to someone else when I fell in love with him—it will only give Beckett another reason to judge me. To respect me even less than he does now. I think of the conversation I had with Weston, and how sympathetic he was. Only a person who's been in the same shoes can understand the complexity of that kind of love and how it tears a person apart and makes them feel alive, all at the same time.

The teakettle's shrill whistle interrupts my tumbling thoughts. "There's my water. I'd better get washed up and go dress for the day." I stand, tightening my robe.

Beckett rises. "I didn't mean to be intrusive . . . I—"

"It's all right." I grab the knitted square Melva uses as a pot holder and lift the kettle by the wire handle. Made of cast iron, it's much heavier than I expect it to be, and I fumble, nearly dropping it.

"Here, you'll burn yourself," Beckett says, his hand at my waist to steady me. "Let me help."

Let me help. How hard that is for me. To accept help from a man. "I can do it."

I tighten my grip on the handle and bring the kettle above the ewer. Beckett's hand is still on my waist, warm and strong, as he grabs a towel and uses his other hand to help me lift and tilt the kettle above the mouth of the pitcher. Together, we pour the steaming water inside.

I lower the empty kettle back onto the range and stand there, out of breath. Beckett is looking at me the same way he did yesterday, with warmth behind his eyes. His hand slips from my waist. "Would you like me to carry it upstairs for you?" he asks. "I'd be glad to."

"Thank you, but I . . . I can manage. I do it every day."

"All right," he says. "I'll be outside. Come get me when you're ready to go to town."

"Okay." The moment is broken, and I turn away, my pulse thrumming beneath my skin. I return to the attic with my ewer of water. As I'm washing up, I feel like I'm being watched. I glance over my shoulder, my senses heightened, but there's no one there, although for the briefest moment, I smell the warm scent of a fine cigar.

Chapter 12

July 23, 1925

I walk arm in arm with Marguerite down Spring Street, our steps small and measured. Eureka Springs was built to suit the lay of the land, without subjugation. The streets bend at odd angles and loop around one another, with uneven walkways and precariously narrow steps that threaten to turn ankles and send a person tumbling into the gullies below. Though quaint and picturesque, this is a true mountain town, made for hardy folk. Once more, I wonder at Marguerite's willingness to leave behind her plush, cosseted life in Kansas City for a place like this. When she first came here, it was little more than a wilderness camp, accessible only by stagecoach, where well-to-do ladies came to take the waters in the town's landmark springs, then journey back to their richly appointed lives elsewhere.

Not Marguerite. She had stayed—had carved out a place for herself among these pioneers.

"Right there, up ahead. That was where the sanitorium used to be. The one Papa sent me to in 1879." Marguerite points to a three-story building up the street, now a store, its stone shoulders hunched against the hill at an angle. "The original building burned in the Spring Street fire. It was one of the first buildings here. They housed us on the top floor, to make sure the consumption wouldn't spread, and so we'd get the full benefit of the sun."

"I never knew you had tuberculosis."

Marguerite nods, pausing to catch her breath. "Yes. I was one of the lucky ones. I survived. Many didn't. I credit the waters for my recovery. This was where I met Iris. Where I grew into my art." She points again to the building. "There was a window there, on the third floor. The morning light was perfect for sketching. I started out drawing the mountains. Those sketches turned into the first landscape I ever sold."

"How long were you here?"

"Almost a year. Then Iris and I traveled together, studying art."

"Did you ever go back to Kansas City?"

"Only once. For Claire's funeral." Marguerite's tone stiffens. "I felt like a stranger among my family at that point. Papa died two years later. I had to make it on my own after that."

We walk on for a bit, Marguerite pointing out landmarks and the special places tethered to her memories. I'm eager to set my roots down here, just as Marguerite did all those years ago. We're both outcasts—willful in our ways. I'd wavered a bit in my fortitude, out of fear, but now I'm resolute. It's been less than a week since my arrival, after all. Barely enough time for Marguerite to learn to trust me. Perhaps, with patience, her moods will stabilize as she grows more accustomed to my presence.

As we near the corner where the mercantile sits, its north wall bearing an ominous advertisement for Blocksom's mortuary services, Beckett pulls alongside us in the Duesenberg, its cloth top rolled down. On the sidewalk, heads turn at the sight of the car. Melva's groceries sit in the back, taking up more room than I anticipated. "If you find a radio you like, Mr. Blocksom can send one of his delivery boys to bring it up to the house after the store closes," Beckett says, as if he's read my thoughts. "He does that sort of thing all the time."

"You mean when he's not embalming bodies, he also runs this store?"

Marguerite titters. "Folks do a little bit of everything in a town this small, my dear."

"I'll wait out here for you," Beckett says, turning off the engine. "Take your time."

We go in, the bell on the door ringing a merry greeting. Counters and shelves lined with every sort of dry good one could imagine are on offer—from wire whisks and snow shovels to feathered hats and shoes. It's a neat, well-stocked store. I can see myself coming here often to peruse the shelves full of books and fashion magazines. On the way to the furniture and appliance department at the back of the store, I see a stunning garnet-and-pearl lavalier on a mannequin near the jewelry counter. A doe-eyed shopgirl looks up as we approach, noting my gaze. "Would you like to try it on?"

"How much?"

"Twenty-five," she answers. "They're real South Sea pearls, miss."

"I'd better not." I quickly turn away, murmuring an apology. Ted would have bought that necklace for me without a thought. But those days are over now. Spending twenty-five dollars of my meager savings on something so frivolous would be foolish. I think of the diamond ring hidden in the toe of my oxfords at the bottom of the wardrobe. I need to pawn it. I should. But a part of me still hopes that Ted will come to his senses. That he'll sweep through town one day, in search of me, and make everything right. It's a silly fantasy I must let go.

"You look sad, Sybil," Marguerite says, tugging on my arm. "What's the matter?"

"Nothing for you to worry about, Auntie. And I'm Sadie, remember?" I shudder at her use of Sybil's name, knowing about the unfortunate girl's demise.

We find the radios along the back wall, from tabletop sets to large cabinet models with built-in gramophones that Marguerite deems ostentatious—an ironic statement from a woman who owns the most ostentatious automobile in town. We settle on a modest RCA Radiola, which a young man named Floyd carefully wraps for us in brown paper and twine and brings to the car while Marguerite pays. I sit with the radio perched on my lap the entire way up the mountain, holding on extra tight as Beckett navigates the hairpin turns.

When we unwrap the radio in the parlor, Melva lets loose a squeal of delight, clapping her hands. "Land sakes! We'll be living the high life now, won't we?"

Marguerite chooses a place of honor on the sideboard next to the piano, moving family portraits and carefully arranging a velvet runner on the cherrywood surface. Beckett sets the radio down as she directs, then plugs it in. A loud screech emits from the speakers, making Melva shriek again. I can only imagine what Harriet will think when she returns to work.

Beckett sifts through dead air for a signal, the static dissolving as a smooth-voiced radio announcer comes on, delivering the news of the week: there was a solar eclipse in the southern hemisphere, Italy and Yugoslavia signed a treaty allowing immigration to Dalmatia, and the Scopes Monkey Trial had ended in Dayton, Tennessee, with school-teacher John Scopes found guilty of violating the Butler Act due to his teaching of the Theory of Evolution.

At this bit of news, Marguerite scoffs. "Why should it matter? I say let the children learn about Darwin's theories and come to their own conclusions."

"I'd agree, Auntie," I say.

The announcer breaks for an advertisement espousing the youthful glow imparted by Tanlac Tonic.

"I should get some of that tonic from the druggist," Melva muses. "Sounds miraculous."

I stifle a giggle and notice Beckett looking at me from across the room, an inscrutable expression on his face. I meet his gaze and then look away, suddenly shy, remembering the undeniable crackle of tension between us this morning.

Outside, the skies have grown darker, and thunder rumbles in the distance. More rain. Beckett rises from kneeling on the floor. "I'd better garage the car," he says. "I'll bring your groceries in, Melva."

But Melva isn't listening. She sits transfixed by the radio, her hand propped beneath her chin. Beckett shakes his head as he passes by me. "You'll be lucky to get any work out of her now."

"I think you're right." We share a conspiratorial smile.

"Come out with me," he says. "I have something to ask you."

"But Marguerite . . ." I glance at my aunt, who seems docile and occupied at the moment, yet I'm all too aware of how quickly things can change.

"Just to the porch."

I follow him, my curiosity piqued. Outside, the air is thick with the scent of rain. A chill wind picks up, flipping the sugar maple's leaves from green to silver. Beckett leans against the porch rail, crossing one leg over the other at the ankle. "I've been thinking about Marguerite's delusions. The violent spell you told me about."

"Yes?"

"I spoke to Harriet when she called this morning. We both think it would be best if I started sleeping in the house every night. In case you need my help. It's something I should have done a long time ago. Marguerite was always worried about what people might say, but we're beyond that now. She's getting more frail."

While I'm sure his intentions are noble, the proudest part of me, the part of me that still has something to prove, rises in protest. "I hardly think that's necessary."

"Don't you think it'll be better if I'm near at hand? For your sake as well as hers?"

"Because you're worried about Marguerite, or about me embarking on a love affair with a ghost and tumbling from a cliff?" I choke back a laugh. "Can't you see how ridiculous that sounds?"

"It wasn't ridiculous when my cousin died. Or when Marguerite accosted you with that knife." He grows somber. Serious. "I have reasons for being worried, Sadie. About both of you."

I rankle at his use of my Christian name. At his presumptuousness. At his insinuation that I can't protect myself.

I pull myself tall, squaring my shoulders. "Thank you for your concern, Mr. Hill, but I can manage Marguerite on my own just fine. And I can assure you I have my wits about me when it comes to men— ghostly or otherwise."

Rain begins to beat the veranda roof in a sharp staccato as we regard one another in stiff silence, the prior warmth in his eyes gone. "I'd better see to the car." Beckett pushes off the porch rail and stalks down the steps, a hand pressed to the small of his back. The change in the weather must pain him, as Marguerite mentioned. I watch as he cranks the roof over the Duesenberg's carriage and drives away, tires spitting gravel as I stand there, feeling foolish as a schoolgirl.

Chapter 13

Inside, Marguerite is gazing out the window, a faraway look in her eyes as she watches the rain. The radio plays muted jazz. "I like this sort of weather, don't you?" she asks absently.

"Yes," I answer, "although too many days in a row make me sad."

Marguerite turns to look at me. "You should let him in, Sadie."

"Pardon?"

"Beckett. I see him, watching you." She smiles. "And I see you tripping all over your words whenever he's near."

I laugh. "Don't be silly."

"Why is it silly? Because you consider him the help?" She frowns. "If that's the case, you're no better than Georgia Merritt. Too high and mighty for your own good."

I don't know what to say, because she's right. I've been rude. Snobbish. I've been so intent on asserting myself, on proving my independence and self-worth, that I haven't stopped to consider how callous I've been to the man my aunt regards as a son, not a servant.

Marguerite takes a small, tissue-wrapped package from her dress pocket and places it in my hand. "I saw you looking at this."

I unwrap the package to find the pearl-and-garnet lavalier from the mercantile. I gasp, lifting it. "Golly. I don't know what to say."

"Say you'll invite Beckett to dinner again, sometime. It would make me happy to see the two of you learn to get along. Even happier to see the two of you give things a go." She grins. "We were talking about you last night. The two of you have a lot in common. You can't see it now, but you'd be a good match."

So, that explains why she told Beckett more about me. About Ted. She has designs. While I'm none too keen on Marguerite's attempts at matchmaking, I'm honored that she thinks well enough of me to consider me worthy of her precious Beckett. And I can't deny that he's attractive, in a thorny sort of way. We both have our walls. Still, I can't imagine us ever becoming more than what we are now. He doesn't trust me, and I feel much the same about him. But it's vital for me to stay in my aunt's good graces, and if that involves inviting Beckett to dinner occasionally to appease her, I'll happily concede.

I wrap the lavalier around my neck and go to the mirror above the mantel, admiring myself. "Thank you, Aunt Marg. I love it."

"You should wear it with that pink silk frock you wore the other night. The one that shows off your legs."

Just then, the telephone rings, startling me. I realize it's the first call Marguerite has received since I arrived. Melva scurries to the dining room to answer it. "Thorne residence." There's a pause as she listens to the response. "Certainly, Mrs. Shepherd. She's here. I'll fetch her for you."

My good mood sours. I know only one Mrs. Shepherd. Louise. She must have found out about my coming here. When Melva fetches me, I reluctantly follow her to the telephone, bracing myself for the scolding Louise is sure to give me. I pull in a steadying breath and lift the receiver to my ear. "Hello, Louise."

"Sadie! Goodness. We've all been worried *sick* about you. Mama has been in a state. She nearly called the police."

I roll my eyes. Aunt Grace has always been a fabulist and instigator. Louise comes by her histrionics honestly. "Well, I'm alive and well, as you can hear."

"You're really *there*. I never thought . . . How is she?"

"She's grand. We've been having a time. I'm going to stay here with her, Louise."

The line goes quiet for a moment. "Well. Isn't that something?"

"How are things in Kansas City?"

"Dreadfully hot. And Sadie, I didn't want to tell you this, but I fear I must . . . it's about Ted."

I brace myself, knowing my cousin, and how she gloats over the least bit of schadenfreude. "What is it?"

"Toby saw him at the Montpellier Tea Room." She pauses for dramatic effect. "With another woman."

My stomach sinks. "It was probably his wife."

"No. It wasn't. She was young. *Very* young."

"Oh." I bite my lip to hold back the rising flood of tears. But what else did I expect? Men like Ted are strangers to fidelity. He'd never be satisfied with one woman.

"You're better off without him, Sadie. I know you don't think so, but you are." Louise's voice grows soft, almost tender. Almost. "Look, Pauline and I were thinking about taking the train down to see Aunt Marg for Labor Day. Now that you're there, it's even better. We'll bring the children. It'll be like old times."

"Yes . . . sure. I'd like that. I'll let Aunt Marg know." I rock back on my heels, clutching my new lavalier until the garnets bite into my palm, my eyes filling. But I won't give my cousin the pleasure of hearing me cry. "I need to go, Louise. I can't leave Marguerite alone for very long. Goodbye."

I replace the receiver, cutting off my cousin's response, and stand there in stunned silence, tears tracking down my cheeks.

The rain is relentless that night, washing the house in streams of water as thunder crackles overhead. I do my best to sleep after I've tucked Marguerite in, but even as exhausted as I am, all I can think of is Ted with his young ingenue. I imagine them doing all the things he used to do with me, and my stomach turns with envy and anger. I finally throw the covers off in frustration and pace the attic floor, fists clenched.

In the wee hours of the morning, after my anger simmers to a low buzz of resentment and I'm able to think straight again, I decide to go to the studio. I need a distraction from my thoughts, and the temptation of wandering into the past with Weston is as irresistible as it is frightening. Part of me still wonders whether what I experienced inside my aunt's studio was nothing more than an illusion. The only way I'll know whether it *was* is by trying to make it happen again. I want to know more. How Weston became enmeshed with my grandmother and her sisters. What happened between him and Claire? They never married—something I know for certain. I grab the chatelaine from my wardrobe, quietly make my way down the hall, past Marguerite's door, and push the studio key into the lock. The door opens with a satisfying snick. I go inside, my heart beating wildly.

But Weston's portrait is gone. The easel stands empty. Raw panic rushes through me as I remember my conversation with Beckett about Sybil. He'd burned the painting once. He might have done so again. I imagine the portrait going up in flames, the paint bubbling and melting, destroying Weston's likeness. Tomorrow morning, I'll confront Beckett. If he's done something to the painting, every ounce of my goodwill toward him will disintegrate.

And then . . . I have a thought.

Marguerite was concerned about my affinity for Weston's portrait as well. She was adamant about wanting the painting destroyed the first time I saw it. Might she be responsible for its disappearance?

I leave the studio, locking the door behind me, and rush to the heavy double doors leading to the library. I open them as silently as I can and ease inside. Moonlight spills through the high windows, illuminating the stacks and slipcovered furniture. I make my way down the rickety spiral staircase from the upper gallery to the first floor, then to the shelves hiding the secret passageway. The bookcase swings open with a tired groan, and I climb the narrow, steep steps, squinting to better see in the darkness. I emerge into the glass-ceilinged tower, the heavy patter of rain loud overhead. My heart beats with wild excitement. There are two easels there now.

I uncover the first and find an incomplete painting of a young girl.

But the second is Weston's portrait, just as I suspected. I reach out to touch the surface. It ripples and shimmers like water, and suddenly I am falling, falling, falling . . . like Alice tumbling down the rabbit hole.

Interlude

WESTON

It is nighttime. The gardens are illuminated, a soft summer breeze filtering through the air. A thread of orchestral music streams toward Sadie from the gazebo where she saw Weston and Claire, now lit with waxed paper lanterns and candelabra. There are others there—guests of this party—attired in evening wear, the men in cutaway coats and white cravats knotted at the neck, their high-waisted trousers accentuating the length of their legs, the women in full, bustled skirts. Weston appears at Sadie's side, dashing in his formal dress, his wild, dark hair framing his face in waves.

"What year is it?" Sadie asks, enraptured.

"1874. The year I first met the Thorne family."

"What's happening? What is this party?"

"Florence's coming-out ball. The night it all began."

Sadie sees Florence now—the golden penumbra of curls gathered atop her head, her white gown ethereal, her waist impossibly tiny. She flits among her guests, graceful as a butterfly, kissing them on both cheeks in greeting. Claire and Marguerite stand nearby. Marguerite wears a demure pink ballgown, her long, auburn hair spilling down her back.

Claire turns as they approach, her blue eyes widening. She nudges Marguerite, whose face pales, her mouth dropping open.

"Can they see me?" Sadie asks.

"No, darling." A flicker of irritation crosses Weston's face. "Only me, remember? You're merely an errant breeze. A trick of the light."

Sadie watches, motionless, as Weston leaves her side and approaches Florence. He touches her lightly on the elbow, turning her. Even from across the lawn, Sadie can see the scarlet flush climb her young grandmother's bosom, her easy confidence gone in an instant. Weston bends over her hand and kisses it. Florence closes her eyes as his lips graze her skin, her mouth parting softly in surprise.

The strings strike up a waltz. Weston leads Florence inside the gazebo, and they begin to dance, Florence limp in his arms as he clutches her possessively. They twirl in circles as everyone watches, as the women whisper behind their fans and the young men glare in envy. Sadie feels her own jealousy climbing as Weston consumes Florence with his gaze, wolfish and hungry and ever so dangerous. What she would give for him to look at her like that . . . to be ravished by those stormy eyes.

"Who is he?" someone asks, nearby.

"I haven't the faintest idea."

"Never seen him before."

Sadie spies Marguerite and Claire huddled together, furtively whispering, yet Marguerite's demeanor is far from quiet. "It's him. I'm sure of it," Sadie hears Marguerite rasp as she draws nearer to them on soundless feet.

"Don't be silly. It can't be."

Marguerite bats the air with a lace fan, her face aflame with anger. "It *is*, Claire. I should know."

"Well, whoever he is, he's holding her much too closely." Claire's eyes flit nervously from the dancers to Marguerite, to the star-scattered sky. "Papa should do something, or people will talk."

Sadie inches closer to her youthful great-aunts, her shoulder brushing the hedge of roses lining the allée. A scarlet petal drops to the ground. Marguerite's head turns, her eyes landing on Sadie for the briefest second—then falling away. Despite Weston's assurances of her invisibility, Sadie has the distinct feeling that Marguerite can feel her, that she can sense her presence somehow, although Claire seems none the wiser.

"What if James sees them?" Claire says. "What if he decides not to propose tonight? He's already asked for Papa's blessing. Tonight was supposed to be the night."

"I know." Marguerite frowns. "James isn't here yet, thank goodness. But people will gossip, and he'll hear it. If Papa won't do anything about this, I must." She marches past Sadie, her curls bouncing in time with her steps. Inside the gazebo, she taps Weston on the shoulder, and he slows the dance, Florence still in his arms, a look of rapturous adoration on her face. Reluctantly, Florence glides to the edge of the gazebo, ceding her partner to her youngest sister.

Marguerite's green eyes harden as Weston takes her in his arms and guides her along the dance floor, their movements more a battle than a waltz.

I always take the lead. Sadie can't help but recall Marguerite's words the night they drank brandy and danced in the parlor.

Suddenly the music changes tempo, becoming sluggish and muted. The crowd goes silent, the other dancers stilling as Marguerite pulls Weston away, everything frozen but the two of them. They disappear into the shadowed gardens, beyond the party's bright lights. Sadie sets off at a run after them.

She finds them sitting on a bench near the labyrinth, side by side. Marguerite's hand passes lightly over Weston's face, tangles in his hair. There isn't anything romantic about her caress; instead, curiosity is etched across her young face. Weston looks up as Sadie approaches. Their eyes meet for a moment, and then he turns back to Marguerite, whispers something to her that Sadie can't hear.

They rise, Weston helping her to her feet. He bows to Marguerite, and she nods with an enigmatic smile, as if they've come to a tacit truce. He watches as Marguerite flounces away. The string quartet starts up again, the laughter of the crowd carrying over the gardens.

"What just happened?" Sadie asks.

"I've brought you here tonight to show you where it all began, and to start over again. To do my part to make things right, as much as I can. It was a mistake for Florence and me to get involved. For me to ever think our love could justify all the pain it caused. So Marguerite and I came to an understanding."

"An understanding? About what?"

"Florence. My being here. Your grandfather will arrive at any moment. He'll propose, they'll marry, and she'll forget she ever met me."

"And what about Claire? I thought you loved her, too. I saw the two of you, in the gazebo last time. You told Marguerite you wanted to marry Claire. You're giving her up, too, that easily?"

"I'll always love Florence. Claire. They're a part of my past. But I don't want to live in the past anymore, Sadie."

Weston lifts Sadie's chin, his eyes drinking her in. "The simple truth is, I've found someone far more special. Someone who understands what it's like to risk everything for love."

Sadie's pulse flutters, falters as Weston clasps her around the waist, drawing her close, his lips a hairbreadth away from her own. "Who?"

"*You*, Sadie. Dance with me."

Chapter 14

I wake in a sweat, body feverish with want. With desire. The memory of Weston's kiss—his hands on me, sliding over my skin, tangling in my hair, the scent of crushed jasmine beneath my body. I sit up in bed, wondering how I got back to the attic, but not caring as I relish in the memory of what we did together beneath the stars . . . the way he made me feel.

My body is a drum, beating with longing.

I rise, the sun a hushed veil of silken pink outside the window. I shed my chemise, pour cool water from the ewer into the basin, sponge my heated skin with a cloth.

I gaze at myself in the mirror, skin flushed, pupils large and dark. Lips bruised and bitten. Did everything I experienced really happen? Somewhere in the past, did Weston and I truly enjoy a night of passion together? It seems mad. A hedonistic dream. One I want to have over and over, but I'd be lying if I didn't admit I'm a little afraid. I've taken a ghost as my lover, after all, not a man of flesh and blood. I briefly think of Sybil, and her unfortunate fate. But even Beckett isn't certain whether she jumped, fell, or was pushed. It might have been a tragic accident. It must have been.

I dress, humming softly to myself as I pull on my stockings, choose my outfit, and brush my hair. It's strange for the mundane world to keep running as usual, after what I experienced last night. When I go downstairs, I find Marguerite waiting for me at the dining room table, fully dressed. She smiles up at me, eyes bright. "Ah, there you are, dear."

"You're already up! Did Melva help you get dressed?"

"Of course not. I'm capable of dressing myself."

I sit at the table, unfolding the morning paper, although I'm distracted by amorous thoughts, imagining myself tangled up in Weston's arms, his lips tracing a line down my . . .

"Miss Halloran."

Beckett's voice startles me. I look up to see him holding a telegram, his face freshly shaved, the lingering scent of his aftershave crisp and pleasant, though a tinge of green faintly stains the skin around his fingernails. He's already been working. I wonder whether the man ever sleeps. "This came for you."

I take the envelope from him and open it. Inside, there are only three lines.

Rosalie and I are coming on August 8th. Disappointed. F.

Felix. Louise must have told him I came here. I shove the telegram to the side. "I suppose my brother and his wife are paying us a visit soon. Weekend after next." To scold me, more than likely, although hopefully with my allowance in hand.

"Oh, how lovely!" Marguerite exclaims. "Are they bringing the boys?"

"I'd expect," I said. "Louise and Pauline may come for a visit, too, for Labor Day weekend. I forgot to tell you." The thought of my family descending on us, at any time, is less than pleasant. "Louise mentioned they'd like to visit when we spoke last night."

"Louise reminds me so much of Florence," Marguerite says. "And it's not just her looks. She's always in everyone's business. Meddling."

"You're certainly right about that," I say, smirking.

Melva brings out breakfast, setting a steaming bowl of cornmeal porridge before me.

"This looks delicious," I say, stirring butter and maple syrup into the warm cereal.

"You're in high spirits this morning, Miss Halloran," Beckett says, taking the chair next to mine. "Did you sleep well?"

"Not at all," I say archly. "But I'm feeling delightful all the same."

He raises an eyebrow.

I hurry through breakfast, relieved when Harriet arrives to take Marguerite off my hands. After they've gone outside for their morning constitutional, I rush to the tower room, where my lover awaits me in another time. Weston crushes me against him, and soon we are flesh to flesh in a room draped in scarlet, aching and soaring and consuming one another like fire set to tinder, like the sweetest addiction I've ever known. This is all I need. *He* is all I need.

Time seems to accelerate in the real world when I'm in the past with Weston—something I've become aware of since our affair began, nearly two weeks ago. I carefully plan our liaisons between midnight and dawn, so that I won't chance waking Marguerite when I leave the attic. I'm barely getting any sleep as a result. I've learned to steal sleep during the day instead, when the rest of the staff is here and Marguerite takes her post-lunch nap. It isn't enough, though, and it's taking a toll. I'm becoming more forgetful. Moody and churlish.

But how can I resist what Weston offers? It isn't just our lovemaking, although it fulfills my need for passion and tenderness. It's the excitement of journeying to places I've never been before. I'd never be able to afford a grand suite in Paris or a holiday in the Tuscan countryside, where my only responsibility is to loll about in a villa with a glass of Chianti. Fifteen dollars a month won't get a girl very far. But with Weston, the whole world is open to me.

It all seems like madness in the light of day. But it's a madness I welcome. Tonight, we're in Rome, in an apartment overlooking the Spanish Steps. The bells of Trinità dei Monti ring vespers as Weston slides my gown down over my shoulders, pressing kisses between my shoulder blades and along my spine. He knows, instinctively, how I want to be touched, how I enjoy relinquishing myself completely. He dominates me, devours me, and I'm all too willing to be the tinder for his fire.

I can see why he had such a hold over my grandmother. Over Claire. It's intoxicating to be so desired. To be the object of his ardent admiration.

I turn in his arms, and he sets me on the wide windowsill. I wrap my legs around him as he takes me, not caring that anyone on the plaza below might see us. In this world, where no one knows me, and will never see me again, I am free. Without reservations.

Suddenly, I'm very cold, as if I've been standing in a drenching rain. I cling to Weston, seeking his warmth, but he pushes me away abruptly. "You must go," he says. I try to kiss him, but he rebuffs me, his eyes narrowing. "Leave, Sadie."

"Miss Halloran. Sadie!"

Rome fades away, the Spanish Steps crumbling, the stars falling from the evening sky. I blink—once, twice. I'm no longer with Weston. Instead, Beckett is holding me, his chest bare, his mouth set in a hard line. Thunder crackles overhead as rain sheets down, soaking my hair, a shirt flung over my naked shoulders. Beckett's shirt. I'm outside, without a stitch on apart from his shirt. Oh God. Shame and embarrassment flood through me.

"Come on. Let's get you inside," Beckett says gently. "You were sleepwalking again."

He guides me across the lawn and up the steps. The house is watchful. Wary. Once inside, I grasp the same velvet shawl I wrapped Marguerite in the day I arrived and cover my bare breasts. I let Beckett's wet shirt drop to the floor. He averts his eyes as I wrap the shawl around myself as best I can, my face on fire, even as my body shivers from the cold, drenching rain. "I'm sorry," I say. "I hope I didn't . . . I hope I didn't do anything improper."

"It wasn't for lack of trying." Beckett frowns. "You thought I was him. You called me by his name. Tried to kiss me."

"I . . . I must have been dreaming."

"Yes. You were." He picks his wet shirt up from the floor and turns away, his shoulders falling. "I'll stoke the water heater. Run you a bath."

"You don't have to do that." I stand there, awkwardly bouncing on my heels.

"Do you want a hot toddy?"

"No. It'll only make me tired."

"Yes, but you *need* to sleep. You're exhausted, Sadie. I'll stay in the house with Marguerite until Harriet and Melva get here. I can't do any work in this rain, anyhow."

I don't have the wherewithal to argue, so I accept the hot toddy when he brings it to me and let him lead me to the steaming bath. I'm shaky, out of sorts. After he leaves, I cast off the shawl and sink into the enamel tub. The water surrounds me, warming my skin. I'm horrified that Beckett saw me naked—that I was acting out my liaison with Weston in the real world. Did I really throw myself at Beckett, as he implied?

After my bath, I dry off and dress in the modest cotton nightgown Beckett placed on the hook by the door. I pad shyly into the hall. Beckett is there, sitting in a chair with yesterday's paper. He looks up at me, his eyes touched with sadness.

"You didn't have to wait for me," I say.

"I was afraid you might fall asleep in the tub."

"You're too kind." I bite my lip, study my bare feet. "Beckett . . . please don't tell anyone about this. I'll get hold of myself. I will. I just need some sleep."

He closes the paper and stands. "Sadie . . . you should consider what we talked about."

"You mean my leaving, don't you?"

"It's the only way you'll be safe. That man—that entity. Marguerite says he's attached to the painting." He sighs. "Sybil . . . wandered the property. Just like you. She wouldn't listen to my concerns. She became angry. Hostile."

I stiffen. "And you think the same thing will happen to me?"

"Yes. I do." His tone gentles. "Can't you see why I'm worried?"

I consider his words. His concern for me. Beckett isn't prone to hysterics or exaggeration.

I think about what I'm doing with Weston, and how my actions are carrying over into the real world. But while Beckett thinks I'm being reckless and that Weston is dangerous, what he and I have together *seems* so real. So good. I've not seen an iota of malice, or violence, or anything to fear from Weston. Nothing at all about him frightens me, apart from the fact that he's a ghost. We've had eight encounters since that first night of passion in the Brookside gardens, and after each one, I've only felt more alive. Happier than I've ever been.

I lay my hand on Beckett's arm. "Thank you. For taking care of me tonight. For your concerns. But I'm just fine, I promise you."

He sighs. "Go get some rest. Don't worry about Marguerite. Sleep as long as you can. I'll have Melva wake you before dinner."

I feel Beckett's eyes on me as I walk down the long hallway to the attic stairs. I must be more careful. More diligent about hiding my nocturnal affairs from him. I fall into bed, my body heavy with exhaustion, and allow sleep to overtake me.

Chapter 15

"Sadie. Are you listening to a word I'm saying?"

I lift my head, focusing on my brother. He looks so much like Da. Same dark hair. Heavy-lashed blue eyes. "I'm sorry. Could you say again?"

"Rosalie and I are moving to Florida. We've sold Mother's house on Charlotte Street and we're going to put the town house on the market this month."

"I'm tired of the cold winters," Rosalie says. "It never snows in Florida."

I ignore her. I think of Mama's little yellow house, her trim lawn, her cozy furniture. "You sold Mama's house without telling me?"

"We needed the money to help finance the builders." Felix shrugs. "Besides, I'm the one who bought it for her."

Yes, with the money Da had meant for both of us to share. That house could have been mine, were it not for my brother's greed. "Where in Florida?"

"Coral Gables. We're very excited," Rosalie says, smiling too brightly. Everything is too bright about her, from her hair to the outlandish orange frock she's wearing. She grips Felix's hand, squeezing until his knuckles turn white. When I don't return her smile, her painted lips purse. "Are you all right, Sadie? You seem a bit *off*."

I lift my teacup, squinting against the afternoon sun. "I'm feeling fine, Rosalie. Only a little tired."

"We were both surprised when we found out you'd come here," she continues.

"I've surprised everyone, it seems." I direct my attention back to my brother. "Did you bring my allowance, Felix?"

"Oh yes. Of course. And I'll continue to send the monthly stipend to you from Florida, so don't worry yourself over that." He leans close to me, his sharp bergamot cologne making my eyes water. "Have you spoken to Marguerite about the estate?"

"She's not out here. No need to whisper."

"I'd like to see the deed to the house, if you have it."

"I don't. But why?" My hands tighten on the chair arms.

"Marguerite doesn't have any children. Her estate needs to be in order before the inevitable happens."

Rosalie smiles. "Felix is always planning ahead."

"I can see that." Even through my sleepless haze, I know they're circling, like hungry lions, eager for blood. "Doesn't probate require the proceeds of an estate to be equally divided among all living heirs?"

"It does if a person dies without a will. That's why we need to make sure Marguerite *has* a will, so her wishes can be carried out. As I'm the oldest male relative, I should be the executor of her estate."

"Yes. Just like you were with Da and Mama. You made sure *that* was all in place. Felix the Fixer. That's what your clients call you, isn't it?" I narrow my eyes, noticing Mama's best pearls wrapped around Rosalie's long, turkey-thin neck. "Will I get anything from the sale of Mama's house? And the Troost Avenue town house? I remember what Da's will said, Felix."

Felix suddenly looks uncomfortable, as if my words have caused a bout of indigestion. "I've invested your share of Charlotte Street on a parcel of land in Florida. I plan on selling it later, at a higher price, and sending you the proceeds."

"I see," I say coolly. "How thoughtful of you." I already know I won't see a dime of that money. It'll all go to finance Rosalie's gaudy wardrobe.

"It's called buying a binder," Rosalie says excitedly. "You purchase a parcel of land and resell the binder later, at a much higher price. We've bought three parcels so far. We've already sold the first at two hundred percent."

Felix nudges Rosalie. Shakes his head.

"Sounds a bit like highway robbery," I say flatly. I couldn't care less about their real estate ventures. I want them to leave so I can make time with Weston in our Parisian hideaway before Harriet goes home.

"Truly, Sadie. You don't look well. Have you eaten anything today?" Felix's forehead creases with mock concern.

I lift a tea biscuit to my lips with a trembling hand. "There. I'm eating," I say, crumbs tumbling from my mouth. "Where are the boys? I thought we'd get to see them."

"They're at home with our nurse," Rosalie simpers. "We like to get away, from time to time. Just the two of us."

"How nice," I say. *Now leave. Please.* "Will you be spending the night?"

"We're staying at the Crescent. No need to go to any trouble." Felix rises, buttoning his sport coat. "If you happen to run across the deed, phone me, won't you? I don't trust the fellow who drove us here from the station. He seems a bit opportunistic. We need to get a proper will drawn up as soon as possible."

I rankle at my brother's insinuation. "He'd never take advantage. Beckett cares deeply about Aunt Marg."

"I'm sure he does," Felix says, smirking. "That's quite a car he gets to tool around town in."

"Well, Aunt Marg doesn't drive, and neither do I, so someone must. He told me the two of you were friends when we were children. He remembered you with fondness."

"How funny. I don't remember him at all."

Of course not, because in Felix's eyes, someone like Beckett was unimportant. A mere servant. But wasn't I just as judgmental and suspicious of Beckett at first? I stand, my knees wobbling. I feel rumpled, out of sorts, every movement like treading water. "You should come say goodbye to Aunt Marg before you leave."

They follow me into the library, where Marguerite and Harriet are sitting. Harriet's knitting needles click steadily as Aunt Marg dozes, her head tilted back against the leather chesterfield. My eyes drift toward the scarlet-bound book that hides the lever to the door to the room where my lover waits for me.

If only Felix and Rosalie would *leave*.

I clear my throat. Marguerite startles awake, eyes flashing. "What—what's the matter?"

"Nothing at all. Felix and Rosalie were just leaving. They wanted to come say goodbye."

Felix goes to Marguerite's side, taking her hand. "It was nice to see you again, Auntie. So sorry to rush off. Now that Sadie's here, I'll be visiting more often. We should have a chat about a few things the next time I come."

"What sort of things, Duke?"

"Felix." He scratches his head, flummoxed by Marguerite's confusion. "Oh, it's nothing important. We can save it for another day."

I clear my throat again. "Yes, you most certainly *can* save it for later, Felix. I'll fetch Beckett, have him bring the car around. He won't mind driving you to the hotel." They need to go. The sooner the better—before Felix starts going through cupboards and drawers. My brother hasn't always been greedy. He went into law because he wanted to help people, like Da did. He grew up in Hell's Half Acre and often represented the underprivileged pro bono. Due to the charity of Father Bernard Donnelly, Da was able to get an education and raise himself out of poverty, but he never forgot where he came from. Felix wanted to be just like him. Now, though, Felix is nothing more than a grifter, bent on opportunity and profit, driven by his wife's gluttonous ambitions.

He took Mama's property out from under my nose, slick as an eel. And now he wants this house. I'll need to find that deed and a local attorney who can fix things in such a way that there's no question to whom this house belongs after Marguerite is gone.

Rosalie bends to kiss Marguerite on the cheek, and Marguerite draws back. "Who are you again, dear?"

"Rosalie, ma'am."

"That's right. Your father is a plumber, isn't he? I sat next to him at your wedding supper."

"Yes," Rosalie says, her features pinching as if she's sucked on a lemon. "He was. He's retired now."

"There's nothing wrong with making a living in the trades, dear. Plumbers are vital. You shouldn't be ashamed of him."

"Of course not," Rosalie says. She latches onto Felix's arm, her chin high. "We should be going, darling, shouldn't we?"

I trail them to the front door. Beckett already has the Duesenberg parked in the circle drive, polishing the fenders with a chamois cloth. He glances up at me. "Could you please take my brother and Rosalie to the Crescent?" I ask. My head swims as I grip the banister, easing myself slowly down the steps.

"Sadie, are you all right?" Beckett asks. "You're pale as a ghost."

Suddenly, everything feels too warm and cold all at once. "I'm fi—"

But I'm not fine. At all. Beckett rushes forward to catch me as the ground tilts to meet me.

The bespectacled doctor lifts my wrist, taking my pulse, Harriet hovering behind his shoulder. "Dehydration. Common enough with this heat. Steady pulse. Pressure 150 over 85. A little high, but that's due to the dehydration."

I sit up, my head swimming. "I'm all right. I just need something to drink."

"Shall I get her some orange juice, Dr. Gallagher?"

"Yes, Harriet. Good thinking. She's probably hypoglycemic."

Harriet brings the glass to me quickly, pressing it into my hand. A memory washes through me, of someone handing me a glass of whiskey after I found Da, long ago. I close my eyes, letting the sweetness of the cold juice linger on my tongue. It's the best thing I've ever tasted.

"Have you had anything to eat today, Sadie?" Beckett rumbles from behind me.

"Just a tea cookie. With Felix and Rosalie."

I look around for my brother and his wife, but they're gone. Outside the library windows, the sky has turned a murky, violet dark, our images reflected in the glass, like actors on a lit stage.

"Where's Marguerite?"

"In bed with a headache," Harriet says. "She's very worried about you, miss. We all are. I'm spending the night."

"But your children . . ."

"My husband is home this week. He can see to them."

I think of Weston, of how it will be impossible for me to go to him tonight with so many people in the house. "I'm fine, really. You don't need to stay."

"Sadie, lie down," Beckett says, his voice firm. "She's staying the night. And so am I." He eases me back onto the sofa, propping a pillow beneath my head. "I'll go make you something to eat."

Dr. Gallagher kneels at my side. "I'll check on you tomorrow on my way to Tin Mountain. Get some rest, young lady. And make sure to drink plenty of water in this heat. It can get ahead of you before you know it."

Harriet places a cool washcloth on my head and urges me to drink more juice. I comply, trying best not to think about Weston. He and Paris will have to wait. For now.

Later, I swim up from sleep, to the sound of low voices from across the room. I lie still, eyes closed. Listening.

"It's happening again, Harriet," Beckett says. "Just like it did with Sybil."

"It does seem strange, how quickly this came on."

"Have you come across that painting? It's not in the studio."

"No, I haven't."

"If you find it, tell me."

Beckett's words fade as sleep pulls me under once more. He's wrong. I'm nothing like Sybil. As soon as I'm able, I'll hide Weston's portrait in a place where Beckett can't find it. Where he can't take my love from me.

Early the next morning, I creep up to the tower to retrieve the painting and hurry back to my attic room.

Interlude

WESTON

"They're suspicious of us. We must be more careful, darling." Weston glances up at Sadie from his desk, his pen stilling on the sheet of paper. It is autumn of 1883 in Paris, and the chestnut trees have turned deep gold. "Perhaps some time apart is in order."

"Time apart? How long?"

"A week. Perhaps two. Besides, I'm on a deadline. I must finish this novel, and you must learn to be more discreet. Lock yourself in your room before you come to me so you aren't traipsing about the place in a state of undress."

"I . . . I don't think I can go that long without seeing you." Sadie's voice wavers. Her emotions are rawer these days. More mercurial. Weston's presence is the only thing that soothes her.

He stands, goes to where she sits on the sofa, cups her jaw tenderly in his hand. "Oh, pet. Don't worry. I'll be ever more attentive when I'm not distracted by work."

"Can I see what you're working on?"

"No. Not yet."

"Why not?" Sadie asks.

"Because it's not finished. I don't show anyone my work until it's finished."

"You showed Claire. I remember." Sadie's words lash the air.

"Don't be jealous."

"Did you show *Sybil* your work, too?"

"Sybil? No." Weston skims Sadie's bottom lip with his thumb. "You'll see it. Eventually. Don't be petty. It's unbecoming."

Sadie bites his thumb, scraping his skin with her teeth, teasing him with her eyes.

He smirks. "You're such a naughty thing. You modern girls . . . shameless."

Sadie rolls onto her belly, arching her back. "You like my shamelessness."

"Yes. I do. But for your sake, and mine, we must put aside our play for now." He slides his hand up Sadie's bare thigh. "Let's make our parting a sweet one, shall we?"

After they make love, Weston returns to his work with a stubborn single-mindedness, barely glancing up as Sadie fades from view, as she falls back into another life—one that feels less like reality with each passing day.

Chapter 16

August 12, 1925

"I'm sorry, miss. Truly. I meant to give you more notice."

I swipe at my tired eyes, looking at Melva, her form wavering. I've been sleeping even less since parting with Weston. I'm left bereft by his absence. By his denial of my company. "When are you leaving?"

"This'll have to be my last day. I'm leaving tomorrow. I'm sorry."

"Oh."

"My sister needs me. With four little ones . . . she can't work. She's already found a post for me." Melva reaches out, squeezes my hand where it sits limply on my knee. "Now, I've made a list of all the things you'll need. You'll manage just fine, miss. You'll see. You've got Beckett. And Harriet for Miss Thorne."

Even though Melva's hasty departure leaves me anxious, I had a feeling this was coming. An ominous telegram arrived two days ago: a mining accident had injured Melva's brother-in-law in rural Tennessee, and he'd succumbed to his injuries. Initially, Melva took the news with a matter-of-fact manner, but I caught her crying in the kitchen later that day, dabbing at her eyes with a tea towel. I've been bracing myself for her notice ever since.

Given Marguerite's history with help, the chances of replacing the maid are slim. But the morning after Melva's departure, I phone the *Fayetteville Daily Democrat* anyway, and place an ad, hopeful that someone outside the immediate area might fill her post. The thought of keeping this house clean and running on my own seems an impossible task. Thank goodness Beckett can do the cooking.

After I place the advertisement, I go upstairs to check on Marguerite, who's at work on the portrait of Iris again, adding flourishes of color and detail to the nearly finished canvas. Though a slight tremor often afflicts her hands, when she's working, her motions are steady and sure. She looks up as I enter her room, giving me a shallow smile. "Good morning, dear. You look very tired."

She doesn't mean the comment to be unkind, but it annoys me all the same. I go to her bed and begin making it, smoothing out the sheets and fluffing her coverlet. "I phoned the paper. Placed an ad for a maid."

"Hopefully something will turn up." Marguerite swivels in her chair to look at me. "You know, I should paint you sometime. You remind me so much of Claire. You look just like her. All but the eyes and hair. She and Laura had the most beautiful hair in the family."

My mother's hair was a brilliant copper that fell to her shoulders in soft waves. She hadn't a single streak of gray when she died. She looked so young people often mistook her for my older sister. "Yes, Mama's hair was special, wasn't it?"

"Like a fresh-minted penny."

"Yes." I fluff the duvet and let it settle like a cloud over the bed. "I'm going up to the attic for a while to rest." I lift the porcelain bell by her bedside. "Ring this if you need me."

"I will, my dear. Try to get some sleep. I'll be just fine."

But though tiredness weighs every limb, sleep is the last thing on my mind. My heart races in anticipation as I climb the attic steps, hoping today might be the day Weston lets me back into his world. I take his portrait from beneath my bed and prop it on the chair behind my dressing screen, then kneel on the floor, touching the surface lightly, craving the feeling of vertigo that accompanies my plunge into this other world, this other place. But Weston's eyes only mock me, like they have every day since our last tryst. Nothing happens when I touch the surface of the painting. Nothing at all. I try again, pressing my palm to the canvas. Still, there's nothing but my longing, my lust, clouding my senses with want.

"Why won't you let me in?" I say aloud, my voice shaking.

After a few minutes, I finally rise from the floor, dusting off my knees. I'll try again tonight, once Marguerite is asleep. I'll try until he finally relents. This can't go on for much longer. I know he needs me, hungers for me, just as much as I do him. As I slide the portrait beneath the bed, something flickers near the west-facing window. I glance up, startling.

A woman stands there, her back to me, her dark hair swept atop her head, dressed in a simple calico dress. She turns as she feels my eyes on her. I gasp as I take in a face I've only ever seen in a portrait. The very portrait my great-aunt is finishing right now. "Iris . . . ," I whisper. She smiles, as if we're sharing a secret, then turns away, fading from view. Only dust motes dance before the window, sparkling in the sun.

The days pass, bleeding one into another, and Weston's painting—his world—remains closed to me. I vacillate between confusion, resentment, and longing as I become more desperate, begging him aloud in the night to come to me. As August leaps toward its end, I begin to wonder whether our affair was a delusion, much like Marguerite's recurring delusions of lost children and crying babies. Perhaps Weston was only an invention of my mind that I concocted to cope with my daily responsibilities and my grief. An escape from reality. A way to reconcile my affair with Ted, even. He and Weston certainly are similar in some ways—they're both dominant, worldly, and charmingly brash. But I've never been prone to wild flights of fancy or delusions. I hallucinated a few times during my darkest times after Da died, but not like this. Back then, it was only vague shadows, strange sensations where the world around me felt unreal, but I can think of no other explanation for my travels into the past with Weston. My mind must have merely played a cruel, if convincing, trick on me.

As for Beckett, he and I have settled into a routine since Melva's departure, and our earlier friction has diminished enough that we get on with what needs to be done without argument. He really is a marvelous cook—with much more sophisticated tastes than I predicted. When I go downstairs after dusting the pictures in the second-story hall, I find him in the kitchen, stirring onions in a pot with melted butter.

"Whatever you're making smells delicious," I say, pouring myself a glass of lemonade.

"Nothing special. French onion soup. Peasant food."

"Well, I've never had it." I sigh, leaning against the sideboard, watching him. I've found that I enjoy watching him cook a great deal more than I should. "I placed another ad today. Hopefully someone will respond soon, although I don't know how anyone will ever outdo your cooking. You may have missed your true calling."

"They're related, cooking and gardening." He smiles over his shoulder. "I enjoy both. How are you sleeping?"

"Better," I say. And I have been sleeping a bit better this week, now that my days have fallen into routine out of necessity and my nocturnal trysts with Weston have come to an end.

"I'm relieved to hear that. I didn't want to tell you this . . ." He looks away from me, then back. "But I saw you again before Melva left, wandering the grounds at night. Talking to yourself. And I've seen you do other things, too."

I blush at the innuendo in his voice. "I didn't know . . . how embarrassing."

"Marguerite is worried, too." He turns back to the stove, adds a sizzling splash of water to the pot. Steam clouds the air. "Your brother even mentioned how oddly you were acting when I drove them to the station after their visit."

Irritation flares beneath my skin. "The only thing Felix is concerned with is who will get this house when Marguerite dies. And he's very concerned you'll be that person, if you must know. He doesn't trust you."

Beckett stills. "Do *you* trust me, Sadie?"

"Of course I do. I stuck up for you, with him."

He smiles. "I don't know if I believe you."

"I thought we were past all that."

"You mean you no longer think I'm a gigolo, seducing Marguerite with my devious charms?"

I laugh. "Heavens no."

"Your brother has nothing to worry about from me. And I know I questioned your motives for coming here, at first . . ."

"You did."

"But try to put yourself in my shoes, Sadie. You hadn't visited Marguerite in years, and all of a sudden, you turn up. Wouldn't you be suspicious?"

"I suppose so. I had plenty of suspicions about you. I thought you were trying to drive me away. Frighten me into leaving with your scary stories about Sybil and the Blaylock murder."

He slides the pot to the back of the stove, then takes a step toward me, his eyes softening. "Only because I was worried. I don't *want* you to leave. I've grown rather used to having you around. We're managing things quite well, the two of us."

"I think so, too."

As he stands there, looking at me, I'm softened by his earnestness. I feel any remaining suspicions I had about him dissolve . . . only to be replaced by another feeling, something that Marguerite had hinted at. Attraction. Nascent and unexpected, but undeniably there, all the same. Perhaps it's been there all along, under the surface, and our shared sense of duty toward Marguerite has brought it to the fore.

"What are you thinking about?" He smiles that fox-like smile.

I'm thinking about what it might be like to kiss him, to lose myself in those marvelous eyes, but instead, I turn away, my cheeks blazing. Only two weeks have passed since I last saw Weston. Whether our times together were an illusion or not, I hardly need to complicate my life with another affair. Instead, I need to focus on finding the deed to this house, or a will, if one exists. Romance isn't the priority. Caring for my aunt and her household *is*. "I should go check on Marguerite."

I rush from the room, my emotions a torrent. Perhaps I'm only imagining the crackling energy between us. If I *had* followed my reckless impulse and kissed Beckett, would he have returned my kiss, or rejected me? A foolhardy impulse at this stage could wreck my chances at a stable future. A stable life. There's so much at stake, with Marguerite declining more by the day, and my brother and his greedy wife snapping at my heels.

That evening, after a tense dinner spent avoiding Beckett's gaze, I tuck Marguerite in, then go up to the attic and light a single candle. I need to put one lingering question to bed, once and for all, for the sake of my sanity. Tonight will be the final time I try to enter Weston's world. If he doesn't let me in, I'll know it was all an illusion. I'll return his portrait to the studio, lock the door, and do my best to move on.

I take out Weston's portrait and sit before it, fixing my eyes on his. "If you're real, show me. Show me the truth." I reach out, touch the painting's surface. It ripples invitingly, and with a soft *whoosh* and that familiar sensation of falling, I'm back in his world.

Interlude

WESTON

Weston stands looking out over the Scottish crag where he and Sadie trysted once before, high above the tumbling sea, his back to her as she approaches. Fog curls around her feet, wreathing the gorse like lace. The wind lashes at her, stealing her voice as she calls out his name. He turns slowly, a fierce glint in his eyes.

"I saw you," he says, his voice low, menacing. "With *him*."

"What? I don't know what you're talking about."

"After all I've given up. All I've sacrificed for you!"

Sadie cowers under the weight of his rage. "But we . . . I . . . I didn't do anything."

"You didn't need to do anything. I saw the way you looked at him." He turns away from her, his gaze falling on the sea. "Your heart is turning. You're fickle. Disloyal."

"No, Weston. I'm not." She lays a hand on his back. "I've tried to come to you several times and you denied me. If you wanted me here, why didn't you let me in?"

"I was working," he says stiffly. "Writing."

"For weeks? You've been ignoring me. It hurts. You know what that's like, Weston. What it was like when Florence did it to you."

He turns to her, with a cutting, sardonic smile. "Do not say her name again. I've forgotten her, for your sake. And this is how you repay me? By flirting with the *gardener*?"

"Nothing will happen with Beckett. I promise you." Sadie gestures at the wild, wide Highland vista. "There's no comparison. How could he ever give me this? Take me to places and times I've never seen?"

"He couldn't. He can't give you what I can. Not by half."

"Then you've nothing to worry about," she says, resolute. "I'm here now, aren't I? I'm here because I needed to know that what we have is real. I've been doubting whether it was all an illusion. A figment of my imagination."

"No, darling. I'm real. *This* is real."

"Then show me, Weston."

He closes the distance between them, enveloping her in his arms, lifting her off her feet as he kisses her, his lips brutal and hard. It is only them in this world—in a year she cannot name. Any thought, any consideration of Beckett flees, the foolish temptation she felt fading as Weston pulls her down into the gorse. Overhead, the clouds darken, and cold drops of rain begin to fall as Weston pushes her skirt above her hips to touch her. He smiles wickedly as she arches her back, as she invites him with her body. Some part of her recognizes the danger in his sudden jealousy, in his flare of anger. He could kill her here, if he wanted, close as they are to the edge of this sea-tossed oblivion. But isn't that part of the thrill? His raw passion, his animus—these things are what make him so intoxicating. So irresistible. Sadie surrenders to her fear. Surrenders to his touch.

"You are mine," he says hoarsely as he covers her with his body, claiming her. "Only mine. Never forget that."

Chapter 17

In the days that follow, it's as if the brief frisson of attraction I felt for Beckett never happened. I keep our interactions to a minimum when he comes to the house to prepare breakfast and dinner. I help him with the dishes after, as always, but I otherwise avoid being near him as much as possible as we see to our respective chores. If he notices my coolness, he says nothing about it. There's hardly time for socializing, on any account. We've had no luck acquiring another maid, and so my days have become a blur of domestic activities. Dusting. Sweeping. Gathering laundry and sending it out. I fall into bed exhausted most nights.

But not tired enough to deny myself the enticements Weston offers. He's forgiven me for my momentary flirtation with Beckett. I've come to my senses. After all, Weston affords me the kind of luxury and hedonistic pleasure Beckett never could. He dotes on me, lavishing me with delicious food, wine, and leisurely hours of lovemaking. In his world, I have no cares. No worries.

Last night, we were in Venice as the century turned, fireworks exploding over the Grand Canal. Marguerite was there as well, with the woman called Pia, walking arm in arm, their laughter ringing over the water as we followed them from a distance, then witnessed their kiss on a balcony overlooking the Campo Santa Margherita. In her younger years, my aunt lived a rich life, unconstrained by convention.

How could I want any less for myself? But seeing Marguerite in her prime has underscored just how much she's faded. Each day, her confusion grows deeper. She barely speaks to me now, and falls asleep earlier each night, sometimes in her armchair next to the radio. Her passion, the verve I admire in these vignettes from her past, has forsaken her. The only time I see her light up at all is when she paints. She sometimes works all day, eating only at my and Harriet's urging. She's resumed painting Hugh, her first love. I wonder whether his painting will have the same fantastical qualities as the others, whether he'll come to haunt this house once she's finished, just as Weston and Iris have.

I saw her again today. Iris. In the library, where I sat reading the worn copy of *Wuthering Heights* that once belonged to my grandmother. Harriet and Marguerite were there with me, happily playing a game of rummy. Neither of them reacted as Iris walked past us and through the wall, dissolving from view, leaving a preternatural chill in her wake.

I cannot shake the feeling that Iris is showing herself to me for a reason. That she has something important to tell me.

After Marguerite drifts off to sleep that night, I linger in her room to examine the finished portrait of Iris, propped on its easel, lit by moonlight. I look deeply into this long-dead woman's eyes, until my own eyes begin to cross. The familiar spinning sensation takes hold. I let out a shaky breath, touching the surface of the painting as softly as a feather. It ripples in the same way as Weston's, and reality tilts on its axis once more.

Interlude

Iris

Sadie stands on coltish legs, exploring this new landscape she finds herself in. It is sunset, golden-hour light slanting horizontally through the leaves. She can hear the rush of a river playing over rocks, laughter in the near distance.

She walks along a deer path, out of the woods, and into a clearing, where a group of young people sit in a loose circle. Some of them are idly sketching. Others are drinking wine. A young man strums a guitar, his eyes closed. They don't notice her as she takes her place among them. She looks about for Weston. He isn't here, but Marguerite is. She reclines against a fallen log, a lap desk propped across her thighs. Her hair is loose, as is her blouse, the high neck unbuttoned to her clavicle. A half-finished glass of wine tilts precariously at her side. She is older here than she was at the dinner party with Weston, the first time Sadie traveled into the past, but not by much. Perhaps nineteen or twenty.

Another young woman comes to sit next to Marguerite and whispers something in her ear. Iris. Sadie recognizes her angular, handsome face, her full, dark lips. She exclaims over the drawing Marguerite is working on. Sadie soundlessly approaches from behind, watching over their shoulders as they study Marguerite's sketch—a sensual-looking woman, chin tilted and eyes at half-mast, the long train of her black dress cascading down marble steps, her hand resting lightly on the banister.

"Is this your *Lady Moss?*" Iris asks.

"Yes. I'm almost finished with the preliminary sketches, thank goodness. She's been an impatient sitter. I'll begin painting soon."

"You're better than Boldini, you know. You are."

"I don't know about that," Marguerite demurs. "Let's just hope I'm good enough to gain commissions." She glances over her shoulder, as if she can sense Sadie's presence. "Do you feel that?" she asks.

"What?" Iris asks.

"That chill. It's as if someone just walked over my grave."

"No, I don't feel anything." Iris rises, shaking out her long skirt. "Let's go up to the conservatory so I can finish my sketches. The light is good right now and it won't last very long."

Sadie follows, from a distance, as Marguerite and Iris make their way to a small greenhouse perched on a shallow rise. The walls and ceiling are made of glass, the heady redolence of Asiatic lilies perfuming the air inside. Sadie watches as Marguerite places her lap desk on the tiled floor, then sits on a shabby, cushioned chaise, bending to unlace her boots. Iris stands behind her easel, charcoal in hand.

Marguerite unbuttons her shirtwaist, then stands to remove her skirt and undergarments. She and Iris share a long smile as Marguerite reclines on the chaise, tossing her hair over her bare shoulder. She places one foot on the cushion, the other on the floor, her elbow propped on her knee. The pose is insouciant. Bold. Unapologetically sexual.

"Beautiful," Iris says. "You look like a lioness at the hunt. Stay just like that."

Iris sketches quickly, her hand flying over the surface of the paper, her eyes locked on Marguerite. She looks down only once, to exchange the worn nub of charcoal for a fresh stick. The entire process takes less than ten minutes. When Iris is finished, she motions to Marguerite, who studies her own image, rendered in black and white and shaded with gray, fingers hovering over the surface of the drawing. The likeness is fierce. Erotic. Powerful.

"This is how you see me?"

"Yes," Iris says, a small smile playing on her lips. "It is."

The scene changes, suddenly. Now Iris and Marguerite stand looking at Weston's portrait on a gallery wall, his stormy eyes gazing out at the well-dressed patrons strolling by. Marguerite holds an inscrutable expression as the museum guests pause to admire her creation, whispering to one another. "They'd rather look at that dreadful thing than *Lady Moss*," she says, scoffing.

"It *is* an arresting portrait, Marg." Iris shrugs. "You've grown, it's true. *Lady Moss* is spectacular. But your use of light and shadow in this one . . . it's as if you knew chiaroscuro without having yet studied it. It's proof of your eye. Your talent." Sadie sees Iris's hand slide into Marguerite's, hidden in the heavy folds of their skirts. "You should be proud of it."

"I wish I'd never painted it. Truly. I'm sending it to Florence after the show. She's always wanted it, so she can have the cursed thing."

"What if someone wants to buy it?"

"I . . . I don't know. I don't think it should be sold. The cost might be too dear. There's something sinister about it."

Iris laughs. "Don't be silly, my love. You're being superstitious. And all of us have a price."

A pair of men pause before one of Marguerite's other paintings—a landscape rendered in vibrant, autumnal hues, Arkansan hillsides rimmed with deep, golden light. Iris gasps, tugging on Marguerite's arm. "Do you know who that is, dear? The one on the left, with the sideburns."

"I haven't the foggiest."

"It's John Taylor Johnston. I'd heard rumors he'd be here. He's a voracious collector. He seems taken with your *Last Light*."

Johnston murmurs something to the younger man at his side, who hastily scribbles across the pad of paper in his hands.

Iris squeals. "He's writing down the identification number."

"But I don't want to sell that one."

"Marg! Are you mad? If Johnston wants that painting, for God's sake, let him buy it! It could make your entire career. You need to sell *something*."

Inexplicably, a tear tracks down Marguerite's cheek. She swipes it away, angrily. "That one . . . you know why I painted it. *Who* I painted it for."

Iris guides Marguerite away from the wide-open space of the gallery, into a narrow corridor. They sit together on an upholstered bench, where Iris offers Marguerite her handkerchief.

"You need to let go of the past, my darling. Think of the life ahead of you."

"How can I let go? How? Not when my own sister . . ." Marguerite's fists clench on her lap. "I should have run away when I had the chance. I should have."

Iris embraces Marguerite as she succumbs to her tears, comforting her with words Sadie can't hear. The scene begins to flicker around the edges, like an out-of-focus stereoscope, until the two women fade from view, until all falls to the dark.

Chapter 18

September 2, 1925

I sit on the end of Marguerite's bed and watch her work, her brush swirling over the canvas. Hugh's features emerge more with each day. He's tawny haired with warm brown eyes, a dimple in his left cheek. She's painted him astride the same dapple horse she rode through the Brookside gardens, his posture confident, his smile easy.

"We used to ride this horse together. Pepper." Marguerite pauses to mix a brilliant shade of crimson with white. "Hugh loved horses, and so did I. That's how it all started when we were children. With the horses." She chuckles. "When we got older, he would lift me up on Pepper's back and sit behind me. We had a place we'd go to, by the creek. He wove an arbor for us to hide in, made of willow. It was only natural that we fell in love. He was my dearest friend." She dips her brush into the paint, adding a slight blush of pink to the boy's high cheekbones. "I often wonder how different my life would have been, had I married Hugh."

"Why didn't you? What happened?"

"Florence happened."

Marguerite had hinted at a betrayal by my grandmother, on the ill-fated night we'd shared the brandy, but she hadn't specified what it was. The more I discover about my grandmother, Aunt Claire, and Marguerite, the more intrigued I become. "What did she do?"

Marguerite pauses, turns to look at me, her eyes sharp. "Two years after she married James, I saw her with Weston, at a hotel in Kansas City. They were still carrying on. He was courting Claire at the time, and she knew all about the affair as well. Florence thought I told her about Weston, that I betrayed her confidence, but I didn't—Claire just knew. She was very intuitive. I threatened to tell James, but I never did. He might have divorced Florence and it would have ruined her. In society. Financially. She married James for his money, and Papa had encouraged her, because he was in debt up to his eyebrows, with his gambling and whoring and Maman's reckless spending. I just wanted Florence to stop using James. Using everyone. I worried about the girls. Grace, and later . . . Laura. They deserved a happy family." Marguerite's eyes fill. "So, in retaliation for my threats and my perceived betrayal, she went to our father and told him about me and Hugh. She implied he had raped me. Weston backed her story. Said he'd seen me in a state of ravishment, with a torn dress and leaves in my hair."

I sit there, in stunned silence, not knowing what to say. I remember the vision in the gardens, on the day Weston shared his manuscript with Claire and Marguerite interrupted them, her hair tangled with leaves and a rip in her skirt. *Florence knows about you and your stable boy. She told me. But don't worry. I'll keep your secret. All of us deserve to be happy, after all. Don't we?*

A chill runs through me. Weston's words had been a threat. A warning.

"Papa fired Hugh's father and told him if his *filthy mick son* ever came near me again, he'd have him locked up for life. They left, and I never saw Hugh again."

"Never?"

Marguerite shakes her head. "No."

"Did you try to find him?"

"Yes. I even went to Ireland, when I was older, to see if he'd gone back there. I found his uncle—he owned a saddlery in Tipperary.

He was friendly enough until he found out who I was. After that, he wouldn't tell me a thing."

"Goodness. Aunt Marg . . . I'm so sorry." The scene in the gallery I witnessed between Iris and my aunt now makes perfect sense. The scene in the gardens, too—the vision I'd seen of Weston, Claire, and Marguerite. Florence had destroyed any hope Marguerite had of being with Hugh. All the long years of estrangement between my grandmother and Marguerite make sense now—much more than when my mother excused their schism as a mere difference in temperament.

Marguerite lays her brush down, wiping her hands on a scrap of muslin. "If I'd been braver, I would have stood up to my father. Told him the truth. It's unlikely he would've listened, or believed me, but I might have spared Hugh and his family their humiliation." She glances at the painting. "There are lots of things I've forgotten. Forgiven. But I'll never forget how Florence wronged me." Marguerite rises, stretching, hands braced on her lower back. "I feel like going to town today. I need more turpentine. Let's have Beckett bring the car."

The ride into town is a tense one. I can't stop thinking about my conversation with Marguerite. About Florence's betrayal and Weston's manipulations. It has me seeing him in a different light—one I'm not entirely fond of. But can I trust Marguerite's recollection of events? Her memory is hardly reliable; her moments of lucidity wax and wane unpredictably.

At Marguerite's urging, I sit up front, next to Beckett. I feign indifference at his nearness and turn my head to gaze out at the late-summer landscape as my thoughts spiral, the trees rushing by in a green blur, the wind ruffling my hair.

Soon, summer will give way to autumn, and then winter will come to Blackberry Grange. I dread the short days and long nights. I inspect my hands, once soft and unblemished. Callouses and blisters now mar my skin. I hardly look like the lady I was raised to be. But I left all pretense of being a lady behind me long ago, even before I gave myself to Ted.

I compare my lovers, Ted and Weston—one alive in the real world, and the other in existence somewhere beyond the temporal plane. I find myself wondering what Weston does, in his other world, when I'm not with him. Is he writing, as he claims, or is he with someone else, in the past? His manipulations with Claire and Florence, if true, give more credence to Beckett's concerns about Sybil. About me. Weston claims to have loved Claire, but Claire remained unmarried until her death. Did he string her along for years, baiting her with false promises while he kept company with my married grandmother all the while? Can I trust Weston with my *own* heart?

Ted and Weston share many similarities. Passionate. Possessive. Dominant. And perhaps . . . duplicitous. I remember how vehemently I swore off men when Ted broke my heart. Part of me wonders whether my affair with Weston is my way of getting back at Ted for moving on . . . or for avoiding my grief over my mother, and how closely her loss and the end of my affair with Ted are tethered to my broken heart. What Weston offers me is familiar. But familiarity isn't always good. The familiar can be dangerous.

I shrug off my conflicted thoughts as Beckett parks the car along Spring Street in front of a coffee shop. He opens my door, then Marguerite's.

"I'll go up to the hardware store for the turpentine, then come right back," he says, avoiding my gaze. The tension between us is palpable. He's been acting strangely around me lately, and things have devolved between us once more. While my coolness toward him is calculated, his is guileless. It makes me wonder whether my actions in the other world are spilling over into this one again, despite my precautions.

"Take your time at the store, dear," Marguerite says to Beckett, patting his arm. She turns to me. "I want to talk to you about something, Sadie. Let's have coffee. They have wonderful lemon cake here, too."

"Sounds lovely," I say.

We enter the cozy café, the scent of freshly ground coffee beans warm and welcoming. Marguerite chooses a table by the window. A waiter comes, takes our order, and a few moments later, we're sipping the most delicious coffee I've had the pleasure of tasting.

Marguerite blows across her coffee to cool it. "They roast their own beans here. Good, isn't it?"

"It is."

Marguerite takes a tiny sip from her cup, then pushes it to the side, studying me hawkishly. "Now, I won't mince words with you, dear. What's happened between you and Beckett?"

"Nothing."

"Nonsense. The two of you were getting along just fine. Now you're nervous as cats around one another."

"I'm not sure where I stand with him. That's all. Sometimes I think we've reached an accord, and . . ."

"And?"

"Sometimes I think we only tolerate one another's presence, for your sake."

"Oh, I can assure you that's not the case. I've known Beckett a long time. I realize he can come off as brusque, but he's fond of you. He just doesn't know how to put it forward." Marguerite assesses me with cool eyes. "You care for him, too, Sadie. I can feel it."

I press my lips together, flummoxed by her directness. "I . . . I'm not sure that I see him in the way you hope, Aunt Marg. Beckett has his charms, certainly. But there's someone else."

"Nonsense. You've had no suitors coming to the house that I've seen."

"We're corresponding by . . . mail." Heat climbs my neck, reddening my ears.

"Oh? By mail, is it?" Marguerite's eyes narrow. "I saw you the other night, out my window. You were wandering around the gardens without a stitch on, my girl. Beckett found you near the bluff. Brought you inside, covered you up, put you to bed. Do you remember that?"

"What?" The heat beneath my skin flares, burning me from the inside. That would explain his mood—the awkwardness between us. I've tried to avoid this happening again, by locking the attic door, by going to Weston during only the latest hours of night, but it seems I can do little to control my actions in this world when I'm in his—a sobering thought.

"The other girl . . . oh, what was her name . . . she used to do the same thing."

"Sybil?"

"Yes. That's it."

How many nights has he witnessed me walking about in a trance? Did I act out the things Weston and I did together, while I was sleep-walking? The thought is so disturbing it makes my stomach turn. No wonder Beckett can't look me in the eye.

"Florence was just the same." Marguerite sighs, takes a sip of her coffee. "She was like a wanton thrall, sneaking out to the labyrinth every night to meet Weston. Did you know she spent a year in a madhouse because of him?"

"I . . . I'm . . ." Shock thrums through me. A madhouse? My grandmother was in a madhouse? I'd heard Great-Grandmother Adeline had gone to a sanitorium after Claire's death, but my own grandmother had never had any issues with her nerves that I knew of. But neither had I, until Da died. I'm not sure I believe Marguerite, but the conviction in her eyes is needle sharp. She's fully lucid today, and convincing.

"I can see you don't believe me." Marguerite arches a brow. "But I know what you're doing. Oh, there's no doubt he has you charmed, just like he charmed my sisters. Sybil, too. He was made that way—his very nature colored with seductive intent, down to his name." Marguerite chuckles. "*Weston Chase.* Like something out of a tawdry romance. He's a hunter, my dear. He *chases.* You fell right into his snare. But there's a price to his pleasures. A price you'll never be able to pay. I don't know where you're hiding his portrait. But when I find it, I'm going to destroy it once and for all."

I can't sleep. As the hours tick on toward morning, I pace the attic floor, wrapping my robe tightly around me. I feel Weston's eyes on me, even though I can't see him. I'm afraid. I wasn't before. But I am now. I remember his jealousy over Beckett. How close we came to the edge of that Scottish cliff, the wind lashing my body as he stood over me. From the west-facing window, I look down at the bluff Sybil fell from. Was she on that same Scottish cliff, somewhere in time, with Weston, when she fell from the very real bluff below? When he *pushed* her from it? Beckett found me there, too. Brought me inside. Kept me safe. But what if it happens again?

They say if you die in your dreams, you die in real life.

I'm no longer willing to cede control of my body, to consciously give myself over to a dangerous situation. I've realized I'm not really in love with Weston. I'm addicted to him.

When morning breaks, I take the portrait from beneath the bed and uncover it. Weston's eyes bore into mine, seething with the promise of passion. I waver, the temptation to fall back into his world—into his arms—strong. But at what cost? I've already lost my dignity. My self-respect. What will be next? My frail sanity, already tested and found to be lacking? My life? No. It's time to face reality. To give all my attention to the living. Those who care about me: Marguerite. Beckett.

I take the portrait from the attic and make my way to the edge of the bluff. I waver again, briefly, and then pitch the painting over. I watch it tumble through the air, hear the distant shatter as it hits the rocky ground far below. Tears prickle behind my eyes. It feels wrong to destroy the portrait. Cruel, even. As I turn to go, an icy-cold wind buffets me, chilling me to the bone despite the day's warmth. I almost swear I can hear Weston's laughter on the wind.

Chapter 19

September 5, 1925

If I thought disposing of Weston's portrait would bring me peace, I was wrong. My body still craves him like a drug—like an opium-eater craves their next dose. I need and want him as much as I fear the consequences of my desire. My ambivalence is maddening.

But I hardly have time to worry over carnal matters. Caring for Marguerite and the house now takes all I can give. Blackberry Grange seems to be crumbling in concert with Marguerite's decline. Mold grows in the corners of ceilings, where it wasn't before. The dust and cobwebs seem to multiply before my eyes.

I'm mopping the kitchen floor when I hear the doorbell ring. I glance at the clock. Perhaps it's the milkman, or the iceman, come with their deliveries. I comb over the days, which have all blended together in a blur, alike as they are for me. It's Saturday. Not Monday or Tuesday, when our deliveries usually arrive. Perhaps it's Georgia Merritt, or one of the other neighbors, come to call.

I place the mop in the pail, pat my mussed hair, and smooth my stained apron over my dress before going to the door and opening it. Louise stands there, blinking at me, dressed in airy summer lawn, her younger sister, Pauline, at her side, dour as usual. "Sadie, my goodness! *Look* at you."

"Louise. This is a surprise."

"I told you we were coming for a visit weeks ago, over the telephone. Don't you remember?"

Oh yes. The call where she gloated over telling me about Ted and his new mistress. She *did* mention visiting around Labor Day, but I'd forgotten entirely.

"Didn't you get my telegram?" she asks, whisking into the house and removing her gloves, plain Pauline at her heels like a loyal mutt. "I sent it on Tuesday. To remind you of our arrival. I asked you to send Aunt Marg's driver to the station to fetch us. We had to hire a cab instead."

I think of the unopened mail sitting on the tray in the parlor—a task I'd meant to get to but had also forgotten. "I must have overlooked it."

"Oh well. We're here now, aren't we? Children!" Louise calls over her shoulder. A tumult of footsteps clatters across the porch, then three bright-blond heads emerge, pushing past Pauline as they run into the house. Dottie, Philip, and Katie, if I've remembered correctly. They spread out, shrieking, everywhere all at once. A crash comes from the parlor, and I wince, thinking of Marguerite's priceless Ming vase.

"Louise . . ." I begin, but she's already off, sweeping through the rooms, peeking behind doors, running her hands over everything.

"I'd forgotten how simply *gorgeous* this house is!" she coos.

"I'll see if I can find something to eat for you all. You must be famished." Another loud bang echoes from down the hall, followed by a childish giggle. "Shouldn't you watch over them?"

Louise laughs. "Oh, they won't hurt anything."

I blink at her, incredulous, pasting a smile on my face. "Well. I'll go see what I can rustle up."

"Don't you have a maid to do that? Or a cook?" Pauline asks.

"Our maid quit us last month. She had a death in the family. We haven't found a replacement yet."

Pauline sniffs and sits in Marguerite's armchair, crossing her arms.

"I'll just . . . go make us some tea. Be back in a jiffy."

I fill the kettle and place it on the stove, stoking the embers, my irritation rising along with the heat. My cousins and I have always had a contentious relationship, and I very much suspect Louise's motives in coming here are similar to my brother's. Everyone wants a piece of my aunt. They're eager to get their hooks in now, before Marguerite passes away. Until she fell ill, she'd only ever been a name on a guest list for family weddings or a scandalous topic of conversation. While I'll admit my own motives for coming here were in line with theirs, to some degree, at least at first, a fierce protectiveness has replaced my earlier designs. My great-aunt is still very much alive. She is a person with memories, feelings, and intrinsic worth, deserving of respect and dignity. This house, and whatever else Marguerite's estate entails, should go to whomever Marguerite wishes. I need to find that deed—and a will, if it exists—and soon.

From the kitchen, I can hear Harriet and Marguerite outside in the gardens. I look through the window, watching as Marguerite bends to sniff a rose and says something to Harriet, who laughs. I'm bringing the tea service to the parlor when they come in. "Aunt Marg, we have company," I call. "Louise and Pauline came with the children."

"Who?" she responds, squinting at Pauline as they meet us in the parlor.

"Grace's girls," I say, motioning to my younger cousin, "Pauline and Louise, who must have gone . . . somewhere."

"Hello, Aunt Marg." Pauline rises and kisses Marguerite on both cheeks, then assesses Harriet coolly. "So you *do* have help."

Harriet's eyes dart to mine.

"She's not a maid, Pauline," I say. "She's Aunt Marg's nurse. Harriet Boyd."

"I see." Pauline smiles smugly, returning to the chair.

"That's Aunt Marg's chair, Pauline. Could you choose another seat, please?"

I place the tea service on the coffee table as Pauline vacates the chair with a dramatic sigh. Harriet helps Marguerite get settled, then hastily departs as Louise bustles in, clutching two children. The smallest, Katie, follows with a bedraggled palm frond in her hand, dirt smeared over her dress.

"I'm so sorry. She knocked over one of your palms," Louise says. "There's a mess in the hall."

That would explain the crash I heard.

"How *are* you, Auntie?" Louise trills, letting go of the children and bending to kiss Marguerite on the cheek before perching on the edge of the sofa next to Pauline. The children paw at the tea biscuits, sending crumbs scattering all over the Turkish rug. I hide my clenched teeth behind a smile.

A look of confusion darts over Marguerite's face. "Who are all of you again?"

"Oh." Louise pats at the lace collar adorning her dress. "I'm Louise. Your great-niece? Grace's daughter. This is my sister, Pauline. And these are my children." She plunks Katie, naughty thing, on her knee. "Katie is my youngest. Dottie and Philip are the twins."

Philip suddenly screeches and makes a beeline for the stairs. I run after him, anticipating the havoc he'll wreak unattended. I grasp him around the waist as he reaches the second-floor landing, and haul him, kicking and screaming, back to his mother. "Goodness, Louise. How on earth do you manage the three of them?"

"Oh, I don't, darling." She takes a dainty sip of her tea. "That's what Greta is for. Our nanny. She couldn't come with us and I'm worn through because of it."

More's the pity. "How long do you intend to stay?"

"Until Monday. Labor Day. We're taking the afternoon train back."

I nearly fall to the floor. Three whole days of this chaos.

"Did you get a hotel?"

"Of course not. Aunt Marg has plenty of room here, don't you, Auntie?"

"Yes, dear. I'll have Melva make up the spare bedrooms."

"We don't have Melva anymore, Aunt Marg," I say, doing my best to hold my smile. "Remember?"

"Oh, that's right." Marguerite tut-tuts. "My head isn't on straight these days."

I sigh. "I'll air out the spare bedrooms, after dinner."

"You seem out of sorts, Sadie," Pauline says, peering at me with her beady eyes. "What's the matter?"

If one more person asks me what's *wrong* or why I'm out of sorts, I'll burst. Instead, I school my face into what I hope is a pleasant expression. "Oh, nothing's the matter. It's so lovely you're all here. Truly. How's your tea, Pauline?"

"I usually drink orange pekoe, but this will do," she says, lifting her cup of Lipton and eyeing it with suspicion. "And Louise prefers Earl Grey, don't you, sister?"

"Yes, but I'm not picky. You're being rude, Pauline," she scolds in a stage whisper.

Katie soon falls asleep on her mother's lap while the twins sit at her feet and gamely shred the palm frond. The clock ticks on as our conversation devolves into chatter about the weather until the tea has gone cold and my patience is worn as thin as my pocketbook. Louise tries to liven things up with society gossip from Kansas City about people I barely know and Marguerite can't remember. It's at times like this that I realize just how little I have in common with my cousins. At a loss for anything else to talk about, I switch on the radio, and we all listen to a program about the benefits of daily calisthenics. Harriet comes to take Marguerite's blood pressure, then leaves for the evening, giving me a sympathetic look on her way out. As the minutes march toward dusk, Marguerite dozes off, head tilted backward, mouth agape. The children run about, then settle, then run around again. All I can think about is the work ahead of me.

When Beckett comes in after his chores and sees us all gathered in the parlor, he hastily doffs his cap. "I'm sorry, I didn't know we had visitors."

Louise's head whips toward him, a vixenish smile tracing her lips. "Who's this, Sadie?"

"Oh. This is Beckett—Mr. Hill. Aunt Marg's gardener and chauffeur." My eyes catch Beckett's and hold for the briefest moment. "And currently, our cook. He's very good."

"What a relief! I've been wondering who would make dinner. You *must* be a better cook than our Sadie," Louise says. "She could burn water."

"Very funny, Louise," I say, rolling my eyes.

Little Katie wakes, her blond curls falling in her face.

"And who might you be?" Beckett asks.

"Katie," she says, grinning, until she looks down and sees the shredded palm frond on the floor and immediately starts crying. "My flower!"

"I have a set of wooden blocks, in my cottage. I can bring them if you'd like," Beckett offers.

"Would you?" Louise says, relief flooding her features. "I'm at my wit's end with these children."

Beckett returns a few minutes later with the blocks. The children gather around him, clambering over his lap as he laughs and shows them how to build a house, and then a bridge. Marguerite wakes with a startled snore and looks around in confusion at the people who have become strangers once more. I go to her, take her hand, and explain who they all are again. Together, we watch the children play with Beckett, and suddenly, this unexpected family gathering doesn't seem so bad, after all.

"I'd better start dinner," Beckett says, gently setting Katie on the floor. She pushes out her lower lip in a pout. "We'll play later. I promise."

I follow Beckett into the kitchen, where he washes his hands and then begins peeling potatoes.

"Can I help you? With dinner?" I smile at him. "I mean to prove Louise wrong."

"If you like." He pushes a handful of potatoes toward me, and I fetch a paring knife from the cupboard and begin peeling them.

"I'm sorry to spring all of this on you," I say. "I didn't know they were coming."

"Your family has a habit of showing up unannounced, don't they?" He tosses me that wry grin of his, and a frisson of delight runs through me. It's good to talk to him again. I've missed our banter.

"Louise claims she telegrammed to tell us she was coming. But I didn't see it."

He places the potatoes into a pot, running water over them, his forearms flexing as he works. I remember what it felt like to have those arms wrapped around me that morning in the rain, wearing nothing but his shirt. I'd been soaked to the bone, but his scent and warmth had enveloped me. Sheltered me from shame.

"Beckett . . . shouldn't we talk? About what's happened between us?"

"I don't know what you mean."

"We can't keep ignoring one another. Even Marguerite's noticed the tension between us."

He sighs, leaning against the countertop. "I'm sorry. I'm not sure what to say. You started sleepwalking again. Slipping away, like before. You've thrown yourself at me, several times. You might not remember it, but you did, thinking I was him." He clears his throat and studies his boots, his ears growing red. "Marguerite doesn't want me to, but I'm going to have to build a fence. You almost fell from the bluff the other night."

My words rush out, filling the awkward silence. "Marguerite told me. I'm sorry for anything I might have done, in that state. You've been keeping me safe. Protecting my dignity. Thank you for watching out for me."

"Any decent man would do the same."

"Well, I haven't known very many decent men in my life, I'm afraid." I wipe my hands on my apron, suddenly shy. "I've not had the best history, Beckett. I tend to attract men who are less than . . . honorable. I don't know why. But you should know I'm in my right mind again, and I've gotten rid of that painting."

"What?" He lifts his head.

"Weston's portrait. I tossed it over the bluff. You were right. I was beguiled, just like Sybil. Aunt Marg warned me, too. Told me what I had with him wasn't real. That it was dangerous, and I believe her. I believe both of you." I shake my head. "I was foolish. Reckless."

"Sadie . . . you don't have to . . . you don't *owe* me any explanation."

"But I do. Because I've come to realize I care a great deal about what you think of me, Beckett. You're a good man. I've watched you, with Marguerite and just now, with my little cousins. I'm so sorry I ever doubted you."

I rush from the kitchen before he can respond, before he sees the unexpected tears brimming in my eyes. I don't stop until I've reached my attic room, where the horrific sight of Weston's portrait greets me, propped proudly atop my dresser, unblemished, his sardonic smile mocking me.

Chapter 20

I'm shaking when I come back downstairs. All through dinner, I think of Weston's portrait, dread filling my gut. His image looks slightly different since I last saw it—there's a crueler turn to his lips, a malicious gleam in his eyes that wasn't there before. I'm glad, suddenly, that it won't just be Marguerite and me alone in this house tonight, that we'll be surrounded by the bustle of my family. I'm afraid. Terrified. What was I thinking, all those nights, when I gave myself to him, when I took an *entity* for my lover?

The thought of it sickens me now.

I raise my wineglass to my lips—from a bottle of 1918 merlot I found in the kitchen pantry and eagerly uncorked—my food barely touched. Beckett looks at me from across the table, his forehead creased with worry. I've never had a poker face. I should tell him about the portrait after dinner. Have him help me destroy it.

Later, while Beckett resumes entertaining my little cousins, I air out two adjoining bedrooms on the second floor, the largest for Louise and the children and the smaller for Pauline. I open the windows and shake out quilts as Pauline watches from the doorframe.

"I saw that man looking at you, at dinner," she says. "Beckett. Do the two of you have something going on?"

"No. We don't. Not that it's any of your business."

Pauline frowns. "I just worry."

"Why?" I fluff the pillows, ignoring the implication in her words.

"Because I know how you *are*, Sadie."

I whirl on her. "What's that supposed to mean?"

She shrugs. "You should be more careful, is all. With your reputation. It reflects poorly on your family."

I laugh. "I'll never go back to Kansas City. You needn't worry about my reputation soiling yours."

"But people still *talk*, Sadie. I haven't had a single suitor since things came out about you and Ted."

I smooth the coverlet over and over with my palm, considering my words carefully. I could choose to be as petty as her. I could cut her in any number of ways—from insulting her looks (which she can't help) to criticizing her abhorrent personality (which she can) as reasons for her lack of suitors, but I choose not to. Instead, I smile at her. "It's just a matter of time, Pauline. The right one will come along. You're still quite young."

"I'm twenty-five. They're already calling me a spinster." She crosses her arms in front of her, her frown deepening. "Do you know what Aunt Laura told Mama, the week before she died? She said she was . . ." Pauline pauses, eyes searching the corners of the room. "Oh, it doesn't matter. I shouldn't tell you."

"What, Pauline? My mother was what?"

Pauline sucks in her lip. "She was ashamed, Sadie. Ashamed of you. She told Mama she couldn't believe how far you'd fallen, to take up with a married man. She said that worrying over you would be the death of her."

The words cut into me like thorns. Part of me pushes back—disbelieving that my sweet, caring mother would ever say such a thing about one of her children—but then I remember her words to me, when the truth came out. Words I'll never forget. *He's covered you in shame, Sadie. I raised you for better than this.* And she had, just as my grandmother had raised *her*, despite the dark secrets Grandmother had kept hidden from all of us.

A secret that now sits on my dresser, with hungry, heartless eyes.

"I don't believe you," I say to Pauline. "I think you're making things up to be mean. To hurt me."

"Why would I do that?"

"Because you've always hated me. Louise does, too, but at least she has the grace to hide it behind a smile."

"I don't hate you, Sadie. I pity you. You're just . . ." Pauline sighs dramatically. "You're just so *loose*."

I flinch, hearing such a crass word fall from my prim cousin's lips, but then I laugh, my lingering kindness taking flight. "And *you're* a prude. Perhaps that's why you can't find a beau, dear cousin. They take one look at you and know your bed would be a cold, barren desert." Her mouth drops open. "Tomorrow morning, I want you gone. All of you. You can tell Louise. I'll have Beckett drive you to the station."

Pauline's sallow face flares with pinpricks of red. "Louise says you're only here because you want Aunt Marg's money. This house," she sputters. "She and Felix have been talking. He thinks the same thing."

"Oh? Is that so? Well, I don't see anyone else in this family willing to give up their precious lives for Aunt Marg's sake. Not even one of you. Think of me what you will, Pauline. I care very little about your opinions. I never have."

I storm out of the room, my anger souring the wine in my stomach. *You're just so* loose. The word is vulgar. Offensive in what it implies. I was a flapper, yes. I'd flirted, gone to petting parties, had a handful of lovers before Ted, worked at a supper club with a topless cabaret. But I'm hardly the harlot they imagine me to be.

Not that it matters. Even if I'd been as chaste and prudish as Pauline, in my family's eyes, I'd always be a nothing. A nobody.

I'm halfway down the stairs when I smell smoke. I pause on the landing, sniffing. It's coming from above me. The attic. *Marguerite.* With Beckett occupied with the children and the hubbub over bedroom arrangements, no one was watching her. I take the steps two at a time, flinging open the attic door. The unmistakable flicker of flames reflects on the ceiling.

"Beckett!" I scream, covering my nose with my apron as smoke rolls toward me. "Help! Fire!"

I stumble upward, heat accosting me. Through the smoke, I glimpse Marguerite standing in front of my dresser, a bottle of turpentine in her hand, watching as Weston's portrait burns, flames darting toward the dry lath above us. Time seems to slow to a crawl as I push her out of the way and grab the covers from my bed, throwing them over the burning painting. It falls to the floor, still smoldering beneath the quilts. I stomp the flames out and then turn to the wall, where tendrils of fire are beginning to catch. I remember my basin full of wash water from this morning, and haul it out of the washstand, water splashing over the rim and cascading over my arms as I rush back across the room to douse the flames. They die with a wet sizzle, and I collapse onto the edge of my bed, my legs shaking. Marguerite sits next to me, calm as a windless sea.

"Are you hurt?" I ask, looking her over. No burns, at least none that I can see in the dim light.

"I'm just fine," she says. She gestures at the sodden mess on the floor. "That should have been done a long time ago."

"Maybe," I concede, "but not inside the house. You could have killed us all, Aunt Marg."

"I had things well under control, my girl. Well under hand."

I coax the bottle of turpentine away from her—the same bottle Beckett procured in town earlier this week. Another thing I'll have to hide, as well as the matches she must have found somewhere to start the fire.

Footsteps clatter up the attic steps. My cousins and Beckett burst into the smoky murk, eyes bouncing from me to Marguerite to the smoldering mess on the floor. The space reeks of turpentine.

"What happened?" Louise asks while Pauline merely scowls at me over her shoulder.

"Aunt Marg decided one of her paintings wasn't to her liking," I say lightly. "So she burned it."

"Oh. Oh *my*." Louise's eyes widen. For a moment, I think she might faint, but Pauline goes to her, fanning her hand in front of her face. Louise slaps her away in annoyance.

Beckett crosses to my side, helps me to my feet. At his touch, reality comes crashing down. I might have died. Marguerite might have. My knees tremble, my heart racing as delayed panic overtakes me, stealing my breath. "I need air," I pant. "I can't breathe. Louise, Pauline, can you take Aunt Marg downstairs? Stay with her. Please."

Beckett leads me outside, onto the front veranda, my head pounding from the acrid smoke. The air is cool, soothing. He guides me to the porch swing and sits next to me, rocking us slowly back and forth until my breathing steadies and my heart resumes its normal cadence.

"I'm moving into the house, Sadie," Beckett says. "I won't hear anything else about it. If you hadn't . . ."

"I know." If I hadn't noticed the smoke when I did . . . if I'd lingered even just a moment longer, the outcome might have been tragic.

"I'll take one of the bedrooms across the hall from Marguerite," he says. "I'm a light sleeper. I'll hear her if she gets up."

"Thank you. I'd . . . feel better having you here."

"I'd have done so weeks ago if you'd allowed it."

"I shouldn't have been so stubborn," I say. "I'm sorry. I thought I had something to prove."

"It's all right. We're both a little proud. A little stubborn. I think it's time to be done with all that, don't you?" He takes my hand, the warmth of his touch grounding me. "You were very brave tonight."

"I don't know about that."

"You thought so quickly."

"It was so strange," I say. "Time seemed to slow down."

"I've had that sort of thing happen to me before, as well. My little brother fell from the stone wall by our cottage when he was five, busted his head on a rock. There was so much blood. It was just a surface wound, but I thought he was dying. Still, I stayed calm and did what needed to be done, just like you did. Everything slowed to a crawl—as if time was giving me momentary grace to think. To act."

"It's such an odd thing, isn't it? Time. I often wonder if we're only imagining its passing—whether we're all still bumbling around in the past somewhere, replaying our scenes like a cinema film." I think of all the places I've been with Weston, where the others we encountered seemed just as full of life and vitality as the people in our time. "It would be a form of immortality, wouldn't it?"

He hums in agreement. We sway back and forth for a few moments in silence, listening to the cicadas sing. I see the parlor curtain twitch, and spy Pauline's baleful eyes glaring out at us. The curtain quickly drops back into place.

"Beckett?"

"Hmm?"

"They already think we're an item. My cousins. We might as well be, don't you think?"

He laughs, a low rumble. "You've had too much wine, Sadie. We'll see how you feel after you've sobered up."

I allow my head to drop against his shoulder, the tension between us melting, at long last. My eyelids begin to grow heavy. At some point, I feel myself being lifted and carried, then hear the squeak of a screen door and the slam that follows. I'm nestled somewhere comfortable and warm, covers pulled around me. The click of a light, and then the darkness wraps me in silence.

The dream feels real . . . so real that I smell the scent of sage, wafting toward me on a fitful breeze. I hear waves crashing against a shore but can't see their source. I look around, trying to get a sense of time and place. Perhaps I'm in France, or Italy, somewhere in the Mediterranean—places I've only been to with Weston in our nocturnal ramblings through the past. I walk along a sandy, narrow path, my feet floating above the ground. A woman stands in the distance, silhouetted against the dusky sky, her long skirt buffeted by the wind. As I near her, she turns. It's young Marguerite, but something is terribly wrong. Tears run freely from her eyes, a look of anger and immense pain lashed across her face. Her dress is stained crimson and a bloody knife lies at her feet. She points past the edge of the precipice she stands on, beckoning me to look. I come closer. The sea crests in satiny waves to the shore, its sound a soft whisper in my ears.

Where the smooth sandy sides of the dunes give way to the rocky escarpment below, a woman's body lies broken, her long copper-colored hair streaming in the breaking tide. It's Aunt Claire. Marguerite's mouth opens in a bloodcurdling scream.

Chapter 21

September 6, 1925

I wake with a gasp. My head pounds like a drum, and my cheeks are wet with tears, the horror of what I just witnessed imprinted on my retinas. The dream was too real. The sound of Marguerite's scream. The blood on her dress. The unnatural twist of Claire's neck, her open eyes—those brilliant blue eyes. An angelic face I've only ever seen in photographs and in my visits to the past.

But Claire died of the measles.

Didn't she?

I wake fully and realize I'm in the library. Beckett must have carried me here last night, after the fire made a mess of my room. Morning sunlight streams through the tall windows. I stretch, stiffly, the sound of conversation filtering to me from down the hall. My cousins. Memories of last night descend—my argument with Pauline. Marguerite standing before Weston's flaming portrait. Me and Beckett, on the veranda, swaying back and forth in the porch swing. I'd wanted to kiss him.

Outside, there's a hollow *thunk* as if something heavy has been dropped on the floor. "I have everything, Pauline. Carry Katie for me, would you?" They're leaving. Pauline must have told Louise we argued. I could stay here, pretend to be asleep until they're gone. Or I could go tell them goodbye, as I should.

With a resigned sigh, I go out to the hall, still in my stained apron and housedress. The terra-cotta pot and its uprooted palm lie on the floor, dirt scattered across the floorboards. Louise hadn't even bothered to clean it up. Pauline greets me stiffly, Katie squirming in her arms, suitcases at her feet. "Beckett is bringing the car. We'll be out of your hair soon."

"I'm sorry we had harsh words last night, Pauline."

She looks down at the top of Katie's curly head. "I'm sorry, too. I shouldn't have been so crass."

"You all can stay the rest of the weekend, if you'd like."

"That's all right. Louise wants to get home to her nanny, and I didn't sleep well at all last night."

"Was your bed not comfortable?"

"It wasn't the bed. Someone came into my room in the middle of the night. He woke me. Do you have another servant here? A man?"

I freeze in place, goose bumps trailing up my arms. "Yes," I lie. "He sometimes works nights. A friend of Beckett's."

"Well. You should tell him not to come into rooms unannounced. He just stood there, staring at me. I screamed. I'm surprised you didn't hear me. It gave me quite a fright."

"Oh," I say, composing my face. It must have been Pauline I heard screaming in my dream. "That won't do at all. I'll speak to him about it."

I have no doubt that Weston was Pauline's nocturnal visitor. He's letting me know he's still here. Watching.

Louise comes toward us, sunlight filtering through her breezy dress. The twins trail her. Philip shoves crumbling bits of pastry into his mouth, his hands grubby with jam. "Good morning, dear," Louise says cheerfully. "Before you ask, Aunt Marg is just fine. She's in the dining room. Beckett laid out breakfast for us." She leans close to me, her cheek resting on mine. "He and Harriet spoke to me at length this morning," she whispers. "It's good that you're here, Sadie. I mean that. And don't worry about Pauline. She was completely out of line last night."

She squeezes my hand and bends to lift her suitcase from the floor. I stand there, speechless, shocked by her goodwill.

"We'll be off, then," Louise croons. "Tell cousin Sadie goodbye, children."

I pat the twins' heads, and kiss Katie's chubby cheek, and then they're gone, leaving blessed silence in their wake. I collapse against the wall, letting out a long breath of relief, then go to the parlor, where Marguerite is sitting at the window, enjoying her coffee in a shaft of sunlight.

Harriet is making notes in her journal at the dining room table. She looks up with a faint smile as I enter. "Morning, Miss Halloran. That bunch was a lot to handle."

"They really were."

"I'll help you clean up that mess in the hall, later."

"You don't have to. It's not your job."

Harriet smiles. "I know. I'm *offering*. But I need my coffee first. My youngest kept me up half the night."

After Harriet excuses herself to the kitchen. Marguerite comes to the table, her eyes lighting on me. "Oh, there you are, Sybil. I was wondering where you'd gone."

"Sadie, Aunt Marg. I slept in. I have a bit of a headache this morning. Too much wine."

"Merlot does that to me, too. Papa favored it with dinner."

She sits next to me, and I take her hands. "I've been wondering something. Do you remember how Claire died?"

"Yes," she says, her brow furrowing. "She caught the measles. She got better, and then she got worse, all of a sudden."

"You're sure?"

"Yes."

"Are you sure there wasn't an accident? She didn't fall from a cliff? Near the ocean?"

Marguerite's eyes widen for the briefest second. I catch the look and mark it. "No. Claire was terrified of water. She never even went near the river, much less the ocean."

"You're certain?"

"Of course. I'd remember."

Harriet returns and places a steaming cup of coffee and a packet of soda crackers in front of me. "I *heard* you say you had too much wine." She raises a brow, and I know she's silently judging my overindulgence. "The crackers will calm your stomach."

After she leaves us again, I clear my throat gently. "You're absolutely certain something else didn't happen to Claire?"

"Why are you asking me about this?" Marguerite's expression hardens.

I grasp at anything to get her to open up, anything to trigger her memories. "I remember something Grandmother told me once. That after Claire died, your mother was so affected she went to an asylum."

"No. Maman grieved Claire, of course. Any mother would. But Florence was the one who went to the madhouse. I told you about that when we had coffee the other day."

"You told me she ended up there because of Weston."

"Yes. It *was* because of him. Lots of things happened because of Weston." Her eyes cut sharply into mine. "But there are some things I'll never tell you, child. I may be losing my mind. But I'll take some of my secrets to the grave."

My breath freezes in my chest. Perhaps it's the way my aunt's eyes grip mine. Her tone of voice. The way she opens her palms toward me, as if she's pushing me away. For the past few weeks, so much of what I thought I knew about my family has changed, as if I've been looking at them through distorted glass for all these years. Now I see them more clearly. How their well-bred ways were a facade for a well-hidden darkness. Though I don't want to believe it, there's a chance my aunt may have murdered her own sister. I think of my dream. The knife at her feet. Her bloodstained dress. My dream may have been just that—a dream. But it had felt far too real, the details much too clear. And after all, she'd come at *me* with a knife, after an otherwise pleasant night spent drinking and dancing.

If Marguerite had murdered Claire, her estrangement from her family would make more sense. They wouldn't have wanted her near them, but they also wouldn't want her to be prosecuted. It would have ruined their good name. Perhaps they'd lied, covering up Claire's true cause of death with a common illness—something that would be completely plausible. Grandmother told me that only Claire caught the measles, even though Claire still lived at home with the rest of her family in 1881. Even though measles was—and is—highly contagious. Suddenly, it all makes sense. Her cause of death was a lie. Just like my grandmother's fidelity to my grandfather.

And at the root of it all?

Weston Chase. Somehow.

That evening, I'm not surprised at all when I return to the attic and see Weston's portrait, completely restored and in pristine condition, the varnish on its surface gleaming in the setting sun as if Marguerite never set it on fire. The cruel twist of Weston's lips has grown sharper. His steely eyes bore into mine, accusing me. Fear gathers over me, like the dark shadow of some great beast, but I push against it as I touch the canvas and will his world to open to me one last time.

Interlude

WESTON

Weston's anger is a wall as he stands over Sadie, his eyes lit with rage. He backs her toward the bed in the Paris apartment until she feels the footboard against her hips. Even now, even as her fear crawls bitterly up her throat, desire is still there, that tender ache that tempts her into forgetting the real reason why she's come here. Almost.

"I knew you'd come to your senses, my love." His hands rove over her as he bends to kiss her neck.

Sadie pushes against his chest, locking her elbows. "No, Weston. No more."

"We'll see, won't we?" He grins and turns from her abruptly, crossing to the enameled liquor cabinet and withdrawing a decanter. "Wine? Whiskey?"

"No thank you."

He pours himself a whiskey, then leans against the wall, crossing one foot insouciantly over the other. "If you won't let me have you, why are you here?"

"I want answers. About the past. Marguerite. Claire. Florence. What happened between the three of them? And what did you have to do with it?"

He loosens his cravat, takes a long swallow. "Tell me what *you* think happened, and I'll tell you how wrong you are."

"I'd prefer it if you took me into the past and showed me. I don't trust a thing you say."

"I've never given you a reason not to trust me."

She laughs. "Oh, really? I heard about what happened to Sybil. How you encouraged Florence to betray Marguerite's confidence over Hugh. How you strung poor Claire along for years with promises you had no intention of keeping. Marguerite warned me about you. About how dangerous you are."

He laughs. "Oh, she told you *I'm* dangerous, did she? I had nothing to do with that girl's death. Sybil. She had a melancholy temperament. It got the better of her. Your *gardener* is only trying to scare you away from me, so you'll run to him." He gives a haughty sniff. "He's the least worthy rival I've ever had. And as far as Claire and me, Florence was to blame. She wouldn't let us marry. Every time I tried to end things with her, she'd threaten to kill herself. She was mad." He smirks. "Florence was delightful when she was happy. A tyrant when she wasn't."

"Why should I believe you, Weston?"

He shrugs. "Because I've only ever shown you the truth. Told you the truth, unlike your family. You're wasting your time, asking Marguerite about the past . . . she's full of false memories. Her disease has infected her mind. Made her believe things that aren't true."

"Did she kill Claire?" Sadie pins him with her eyes. "I saw her. In a dream. Standing on a cliff. Claire's body was on the rocks below. She looked dead."

"Iris," he hisses, slamming his whiskey glass down on the cabinet. "Oh, Iris, you cunning little bitch."

"What does Iris have to do with any of this?"

"She controlled Marguerite. Lorded over her. She's still trying to control her. Now you. I was worried when I saw Marguerite painting her portrait that she would meddle with things, influence you away from me."

"They were lovers, weren't they?"

He ignores my questions, paces around the bedroom like a caged lion. "At first, Iris liked me. Admired me, even. She loved it when I posed for her silly little sketches." He laughs. "I thought she was my ally. She wasn't. She was party to their deception. She did nothing to stop it."

"What happened? Whose deception?"

"It doesn't matter." He stalks toward Sadie, his eyes lit with desire. "I'll show you the truth, in good time. But for now, let's forget about all that." His hand curls behind her neck, drawing her to him. "Time is a slippery thing. All we might ever have is right now, Sadie, and you're such a delightful distraction."

Sadie turns her face away as he tries to kiss her, ignoring the way her body wants to curve into his, eager to cede the shaky ground she stands on. She thinks of Beckett instead. Kind. Honest. Hardworking. *Real.* "No, Weston. You don't get to have me anymore. This isn't real. It must stop."

Weston's hands tighten, holding her against him. "If it isn't real, could you feel this?" His tongue traces the sensitive skin below her ear, and she nearly swoons. "You can say what you like, Sadie. But you know I'm real, that we're both here, in Paris, in 1883, in an apartment overlooking the Avenue Millaud."

If this *is* all an illusion—some voluptuous figment of her imagination—could she smell the scent of spring lilacs filtering in through the open window? Hear the strike of horses' hooves on the cobblestones below or the shout of a street vendor hawking his wares?

Weston slides his hand down her thigh. "Your body betrays you, my love," he whispers. "Your blood runs as hot as mine. Give over to it. No one can make you feel the way I do."

"I hate you," she says, her last bit of resistance fading, failing. She surrenders, as she knew she would. He captures her lips with a vicious kiss and carries her to bed.

Chapter 22

September 7, 1925

I can no longer trust myself. The weight of what I've done follows me as I wrap Weston's portrait in a length of velvet curtain and carry it downstairs to Beckett, who sits at the dining room table, studying Marguerite's ledger. He looks at the rectangular bundle in my arms, his right eyebrow lifting.

"Do something with this, please. I don't care what."

He crosses to me and lifts the bottom of the drape, frowning at the image.

"He pulled me in again last night," I lie, biting my lip, ashamed, studying the toes of my shoes. I can't admit my own will in the matter. Not to Beckett. No matter my initial intentions—to find answers about my family in the past—I sought out Weston. Then fell under his spell once more. "Just take it. Hide it. It's obvious it can't be destroyed."

"I'll put it somewhere safe," Beckett says, gently. He takes the painting from me. "Somewhere you won't think to look."

"Tonight, after Marguerite's gone to bed, might we have a cocktail in the library?" I ask. "I'd like to spend some time together. Just the two of us."

His ears redden, and he stands very still, the painting clutched in his arms. "Sadie . . . I'm not sure that's a good idea."

"Not sure?" I stammer, taken aback. "It's only a drink. A nightcap after dinner, like the old folks do. I'll be on my best behavior. Just don't tell Harriet. She's chastised me enough about my drinking."

"All right," he says. "One drink."

"Just one."

After he goes, I find Marguerite sitting in the parlor, dozing in her favorite chair. I straighten the lace doilies on the mantel, dust the silent radio, and sit to go through the mail stacked on the sideboard. A letter from Rosalie lies on the top of the pile, postmarked Coral Gables. So, their move to Florida must be complete. I put it to the side to read later, when I have more of a stomach for my sister-in-law's boasting.

I've nearly reached the bottom of the pile when a letter falls to the floor. I pick up the envelope, addressed to me in a sweeping, feminine hand. The return address is Springfield, Missouri. I don't know anyone from there.

I slide the letter open with my finger, no longer bothered about the sorry state of my work-worn hands, and draw out the enclosed letter.

> Dear Miss Halloran,
>
> I realize this letter may come as a shock. I deliberated over writing you, but I'm desperate and need your assistance. My husband, as you know, has for many years carried on adulterous affairs. I'd always turned a blind eye to these situations, including his arrangement with you, simply because he provided me with a good life and maintained civil relations with myself and our children. I bear you no ill will. However, most recently, Ted has involved himself in illicit activities that frighten me, and I no longer wish to remain married to him. I have taken the children, and I am currently staying with my sister in Springfield, where it is safe for you to correspond with me by mail without Ted's knowledge. I would like to meet with you in

person. If you're willing, please write, so that we might arrange a time to discuss my dilemma in more detail.

Most Sincerely,

Blanche Selby Fitzsimmons

I fold the letter and place it back in the envelope, my hands shaking. Ever since Ted confessed to being married, I've fretted about the day when his wife would find out about me. I've imagined all sorts of horrific scenarios, but I never imagined this. How on earth did she know where to find me? Louise had mentioned that Ted and Toby were acquainted, due to their membership at the Montpellier Tea Room, but surely Toby doesn't know Blanche. Louise's husband would have hardly gone out of his way to put us in touch.

I open the letter from Rosalie next. Just as I thought, it's full of flourishes and grand proclamations about their new home—six bedrooms, five bathrooms, a full staff, tennis courts, and a swimming pool. And at the bottom, before her sign-off, a single question: *Have you found Aunt Marguerite's will?*

Marguerite wakes. She looks around in confusion, and then resettles, falling back into her slumber. She's been sleeping more and more, and she hardly eats, despite our best efforts. Harriet tells me this is all part of the disease—the natural, slow progression unto the death that will eventually claim my great-aunt's life. With Marguerite's condition growing graver by the day, her moments of lucidity will become fewer and farther between. I need to find the deed to the house and her will— if there is one—to make sure that her wishes are carried out when the end inevitably comes.

That evening, I take my time dressing for dinner. I choose a breezy, layered frock made of bronze chiffon and drape the garnet-and-pearl lavalier Marguerite gave me around my neck. I massage my hands with lanolin ointment, trying my best to reclaim some of my former vanity. Even though I'm not the celebrated beauty of the family—that's Louise—I've always managed to turn heads with my easy smile, posture, and my confident way of walking into a room. I lost all that, after Ted.

I think of Blanche's letter, tucked in my bureau, and wonder about the woman who wrote it. Ted didn't share much about her, even when I asked, but I know a few things. She is younger than him, but not by much. They have three children—two boys and a girl. Her refined handwriting and polite manner demonstrate evidence of an education.

While the prospect of meeting Blanche terrifies me, I imagine how much worse it must be for her—how desperate she must be if she's reached out to the woman who would have stolen everything that was rightfully hers. It was easy enough to dismiss Blanche when she existed only in my imagination, when I could paint her as the villain, as the uncaring, cold wife who had pushed Ted into my waiting arms. I thought myself special. A heroine of love. How foolish I was. How proud and vain and cruel.

I take out the ring Ted gave me and study its gleaming facets in the setting sun. Light reflects off it and bounces around the attic ceiling. The ring is at least three carats and worth more than all the other jewelry I own, combined. I need to pawn it. But something keeps holding me back. I place the ring in its pouch and hide it in the toe of my oxfords. I think of the young floozy Ted is now gallivanting around town with. I wonder what kind of false promises he's made to her, and how long she'll last. She probably thinks herself special, too.

Tomorrow, I decide, I'll write to Blanche.

When I go downstairs, Beckett is bringing a roasted chicken garnished with rosemary and thyme to the dining room table. I inhale the delicious aroma and take my place between Marguerite and Harriet, who's been joining us on occasion at the main table for dinner. Even though it's not the done thing, I'm glad for her company. Harriet is steady and thoughtful and a soothing presence for Marguerite.

After dinner, Harriet helps me dress Marguerite for bed and then prepares to leave for the evening. I walk her to the door. "My husband will be home for winter soon," she says. "I'll be able to stay some nights, now and then, to relieve you."

Relief floods through me. "Would you?"

"I can't stay every night, of course, but perhaps twice a week. I could use the extra money. And . . ." Harriet smiles at me, a knowing glint in her eye. "Perhaps if I'm here, you and Beckett might be able to steal some time away. Go out dancing, or to dinner. I see the way y'all look at each other."

I dip my chin. "Is it that obvious to everyone?"

Harriet laughs. "Yes. Very. He's just a little shy, but so was my Bill. Sometimes, you have to be bold with that kind of man. Otherwise, you'll be waiting around forever. Now, I don't mean to give advice when it's not asked for, but it would be good to have someone special in your life. It's going to get harder with Marguerite, not easier. A little sweetness could lighten the burden. Just think about it."

She tells me good night, donning her capelet to protect her uniform from the dusty roads. I watch her leave from the porch, amid the drone of cicadas. She secures her bag in her bicycle basket, then waves to me as she rides off down the drive.

I can hear Beckett finishing up the dishes in the kitchen. Instead of helping him like I usually do, I go to the library and slide the doors into their pockets. A rush of air comes through, greeting me with the scent of old books—slightly stale, but welcoming and warm all the same. I switch on the Tiffany lamps on either side of the chesterfield, then take the key from the snuffbox on the mantel and unlock the liquor cabinet. Inside, I find a half bottle of Booth's gin, Angostura bitters, and a decanter filled with amber liquid. I lift the stopper and sniff. Whiskey, of some sort. Ted would have been able to name the distillery, the year, even the kind of barrel it was aged in with the very first sip. He often teased me about my lack of knowledge when it came to spirits. Looking back now, there were so many things he *teased* and even shamed me about, all in the name of good humor. But tonight isn't about Ted. It's about being bold and giving something new the chance it needs to grow.

We'd moved the Victrola to the library after acquiring the radio, so Marguerite could listen to music here, too. I choose a King Oliver album and put it on the turntable. Beckett strolls in, wiping his hands on a dishtowel. His eyebrows lift. "Setting a mood, are you?"

I feel myself blush. I tinker with the Victrola's settings to avoid his gaze. "It's been a long day for both of us. I could do with a drink and some good music, couldn't you?"

He walks over to the liquor cabinet and lifts a bottle from its mirrored top.

"Not much of a selection, is there?" I say.

"No, but we can make do," he says. "Better than bathtub gin. I'll fetch some limes from the kitchen. That'll improve things."

I cross to the chesterfield and wait for him to return, arranging myself on the sofa in what I hope is a casually unassuming way. When he comes back, I watch as he mixes the bitters into the gin, stirring the mixture with a long spoon before cutting a lime in half and squeezing a bit of the juice into the glass. He carves a thin slice of lime and perches it on the rim, then hands me the glass.

I take a sip. Tart and crisp, with the warmth of the bitters rounding out the bouquet. It's a bit like summer and autumn, all at once. "It's good. Thank you."

He grins at me over his shoulder as he mixes his own. "I had a short stint as a bartender in town, before my father died. I learned how to blend spirits. Sometimes simple is better."

"It seems you know how to do everything. Truly."

"Hardly." He joins me on the sofa, leaving a respectable amount of space between us.

He's so different from the other men I've known. Uncomplicated. Hardworking and loyal. A salt-of-the-earth man with scars that echo my own. Now, without Weston's seductions complicating my mind,

I'm ready to declare my intentions in a way Beckett can't ignore. I take a deep breath, wetting my tongue with more of my cocktail before I speak. "Beckett, I was being honest with you, the other night, on the porch. I do . . . have feelings for you."

He doesn't say anything, just looks straight ahead, where our ghostly reflections mirror us in the glass.

"I wasn't expecting to feel like this. But I do, all the same."

"Sadie, I . . ."

I place a hand on his knee, the faint buzz from the liquor building in my blood. Before I can overthink things, before I can talk myself out of it, I lean toward him and press my lips to his. He stiffens at first, then surrenders as I deepen our kiss, my arms tangling around his neck. As his warmth and realness surround me, I think of how right it feels, being in his arms. How it feels like coming home. When we finally break apart, breathless, he shakes his head, wiping his face with his hands. "Sadie, I don't know if I can do this. I want to—God knows I want to. But I don't know if I can."

"What do you mean?"

"Give you what you want." He closes his eyes for a moment. "I've never . . ."

"Never?" I ask in awe.

"No." His ears redden. "You've just blown my world apart. When you were sleepwalking, and you threw yourself at me, I just thought . . . well, I *knew* it wasn't me you wanted, so I did my best to be a gentleman. I never imagined you would want me . . . like this. I never imagined anyone would."

"Golly." I look at him, flabbergasted. "Well, I've no idea why you'd think that. You're quite the catch. You can even cook, for heaven's sake!"

"Sadie. It's not because of anything I can or can't do—it's because of how I look." His lips press together in a thin line. "And if you're merely offering your . . . attention out of pity, you can stop the charade."

"Pity?" I sit up, my eyes widening. "I . . . Beckett, no."

"Women like you don't want men like me. No woman wants half a man. A cripple."

"That's not true." A fierce burning makes its way up my neck, and I realize I'm angry. I take a sharp swallow of my drink to quell it. "You're not half a man. At all. And if you think I pity you, you don't know me. I wish you could see yourself through my eyes. You're beautiful, Beckett. You are."

He leans forward, elbows pinned to his knees, the uneven arch of his back on full display. "My condition hurts me. Often. It will only worsen with age. I wear binders and braces, beneath my clothes. Lifts for my shoes. The ointments and balms Doc Gallagher gives me help, but they don't take all the pain away. On the very worst days, I take morphine, but mostly I've learned to live with it, because I don't want to fall into oblivion." He takes a deep breath, letting it out in a rush. "I don't know if I'm even capable of making love to a woman, Sadie. Or fathering children. The doctors . . . when I was young, the doctors said sterility was a possibility with my condition."

"But if that's the case, we would cope." I take his hand, press it between mine. "How can you know, if you never give things a chance? I'm willing to try. I want to, because I want *you*."

He looks up at me, his eyes glazed and vulnerable. I lean forward and kiss the tremble from his lips, pressing my mouth to his again, and then my body, boldly straddling his lap. I guide his hand up my thigh, pushing my dress over my hips, showing him where my want lives. My desire. My hands tangle in his hair as his lips softly press against my neck, my pulse thudding. I feel his body respond, his hips rising to meet mine, and I smile. "See, we won't have any problems at all," I purr, my hand going to his waistband to unbutton his fly.

His head falls back as he relinquishes himself to my coaxing touch. I've never felt more powerful, more alive. For all these years, I've been claimed and taken by men who asserted their dominance over me, who pursued me, who took ownership of my body. This—this is new. And it is decadent. Heady. Delicious.

Suddenly, a loud crash echoes from the hall. Beckett's eyes fly open. He pushes me off his lap, hastily buttoning his trousers. "Marguerite," he rasps, and rushes to the door. I follow him, panic replacing my desire.

But when we get to the hall, there's no one there. Only the same potted palm little Katie upended the other day, lying on its side once again, dirt spilling across the floor, the pot now irretrievably broken.

"How did that happen?" I wonder aloud. I check the single window in the hall. It's locked, not the faintest hint of a draft around the sill.

"I don't know. I'll go get a broom."

I remain in the hall, an eerie sense of watchfulness pervading the air. Outside, a soft misting rain begins, gently pattering on the windowpanes. The perfect weather for making love. I feel a gentle touch on my shoulder, brushing aside my hair. I turn, expecting Beckett, hoping to fall into his arms and regain the ground we've lost to this strange distraction. But there's no one there, only an empty hallway, lit with clouded moonlight.

Chapter 23

In the days that follow, Beckett and I have very little time alone. Marguerite has grown more restless, her moods scaling up and down. She wakes one morning in hysterics, swearing there are strangers in the house, hiding in the walls. Harriet and I take her from room to room, opening cupboards and closets. Still, she clings to the notion well into the afternoon, insisting they've come to abduct her. Sometimes my aunt's delusions and hallucinations are harmless—even beautiful—like the musical flowers she sees blooming on the ceiling. Other times her hallucinations are so frightening they make the hair on the back of my neck stand on end. Given my encounters with Weston, my own sense of reality has warped a great deal since coming here. Who's to say what is truly real, and what is not? The mind is a powerful engine.

Despite Marguerite's decline and my increasing responsibilities, I still manage to write to Ted's wife, and she sends me a telegram a few days later. We make plans to meet in town the following week, at the same coffee shop Marguerite and I visited. Thankfully, Marguerite's moods settle, and on the morning I'm due to meet Blanche, Harriet assures me she has things well in hand. I dress demurely, pinning my hair into a tidy bun, and go out to meet Beckett in the drive. I haven't told him or Harriet the true purpose of our trip—only that I want to have coffee with a friend in town on holiday.

But as I take my place next to him in the car, a twinge of guilt convicts me. I need to tell Beckett the truth about Ted. I want to build our relationship on a foundation of honesty, because that's what he deserves. What I deserve. After learning more about the faulty scaffolding in my family—lies stacked upon lies—I don't want to make the same mistakes as my forebears.

I look over at Beckett and smile as we turn onto the road leading to town. It's a beautiful day, with a bright azure sky arching overhead, but the gorgeous weather does little to soothe my apprehensions. He shifts gears, then places his hand over mine on the leather seat, glancing at me shyly through his lashes. When he pulls alongside the curb in front of the coffee shop, I turn to him, my nerves raw. "Beck, there's something I need to tell you. About why I'm here."

"Here? You mean the coffee shop?"

"Yes." I hedge, twisting my hands together in my lap. "Do you remember when you asked me what happened with my fiancé?"

He nods. "You said things didn't end well."

"No. They didn't. They didn't end well because he was still married to someone else."

Beckett is quiet for a moment, and my apprehension grows. "Did you know?" he finally asks.

"Not at first. But later? Yes. I did." I reach out, place my hand on his arm. "It wasn't my intention to fall in love with a married man. Ted pursued me. He was relentless. But I'm—I won't deny my own guilt in the matter. We carried on for over two years, well past my knowing about his wife."

"Is it him you're meeting here, then?" I see the fear in Beckett's eyes. The vulnerability. He's afraid of losing me, just as much as I'm afraid of losing him.

"No. No! His wife. She sent me a letter and asked to meet me. She's suing for divorce and needs my help."

Beckett's shoulders fall. He lets out a long breath.

"Beck, I'm only telling you because I want you to know everything about me. If this changes how you feel . . ."

"It doesn't, Sadie. Do you know how crazy I am about you? I was just afraid . . ."

"I know. And I understand why. But you don't have to worry about anyone else. I promise. I'm awake now. To everything." I lean forward and press a chaste kiss to his lips. While I want to linger longer, want to drive far, far away from here and spend the day in his arms, it's time to put this last remnant of my past to rest, so the future will be fully ours.

Blanche isn't at all what I expect. She's small, diminutive. Shy. Pretty in a way that doesn't threaten, just like me. She lifts her coffee cup to her lips, and I see her wrist shake with nervousness. She's the only other customer here, and I'm relieved for the both of us. Still, she glances around the café furtively as I approach, as if she's worried someone has followed her. "Thank you for coming to meet me, Miss Halloran," she says by way of greeting. "I didn't know what to expect."

"Nor I," I say. "I've been a ball of nerves. This is all a bit strange, isn't it?"

She smiles. "Yes."

"I've been wondering how you found me."

"I hope this won't be too upsetting, but I hired a private investigator. He followed you for weeks in Kansas City, then followed you here, on the train. That's how I found out where your aunt lived."

I vaguely remember the stranger on the train, the one I bumped into at the station and then saw again in the dining car. It must have been him. "But why go to such great lengths if you already knew Ted was having an affair with me?"

"I needed proof. About the affair . . . and Ted's illegal dealings, although my investigator reassured me that you were innocent in all that."

"Illegal dealings?"

Blanche's small hands grip the edge of the table. "Didn't you ever wonder where all his money came from, Miss Halloran?"

"I assumed it was from his businesses."

"Yes. His businesses." Blanche's lips tighten. She lowers her voice to a whisper. "Do you know what cocaine is?"

"Yes . . . I'm aware of what it is."

"Well," she says, "that's where Ted's money comes from. He runs it all over the country, along with liquor and hashish. He's in thick with the mob, which is why I'm so nervous. I'm working with a federal marshal. But it's taking more time than I'd hoped to get Ted arrested. I'm very afraid of him and I'm growing more desperate."

I sit back in my chair, stunned. I had my suspicions about the bootlegging, given Ted's encyclopedic knowledge of spirits, but drugs? "I had no idea."

"Well. He fooled the both of us, didn't he?" She laughs and shakes her head. "Ted and I were both schoolteachers when we first met. Did you know that?"

"No. But he was always cagey about his life. Now I see why. And this new girl? Who is she?"

"Oh, there are several girls, dear. There always have been. You were never the only one." Blanche smiles sadly. "I'm sorry if you thought you were."

I sigh, not the least surprised. "How can I help?"

She reaches into her pocketbook and draws out a piece of pink paper. "If you'll read this affidavit and go with me to a notary to sign it, I need it to file for divorce. As concrete proof of Ted's adultery. After the divorce is granted, I plan on taking the children and getting as far away from Missouri as possible."

I read over the document quickly, then together, we walk to the post office, where I sign the affidavit and the clerk notarizes it with his seal. I'm not worried one iota about what having such a confession on record will do to my reputation. It feels good to come clean. To be honest about my past. I'm starting over, and so is Blanche. We're more alike than I ever could have imagined.

"Thank you so much, Miss Halloran," Blanche says, hastily stowing the affidavit in her pocketbook, her eyes brimming with tears. "I only want my life back. To live with my children and be free. I never asked for any of this."

"I understand," I say, reaching out. She gives me her hand, and I squeeze it gently. "I have something for you. Something that may help you and the children."

I pull Ted's ring from my pocket and offer it to her. Her eyes widen at the sight. "Oh my."

"I'm so sorry for all the grief I've caused you," I say. "I should have never . . . I should have known better. I wasn't raised that way, Mrs. Fitzsimmons."

"We all make mistakes, Miss Halloran," she says, her tone gentle as she takes the ring. "What matters most is what we learn from them."

I watch her walk away, brisk little thing, and think about how strong we women truly are. How strong we have to be, in this man's world.

Chapter 24

September 18, 1925

The morning after my meeting with Blanche, I find Marguerite's bed empty, covers knotted and twisted, as if she wrestled someone—or something—in her sleep. Thunder crashes, shaking the house. The light patter of rain that began late last night has become a deluge, water sheeting sideways against the clapboards, the sky an ominous shade of green. I frantically search the rooms upstairs and down for Marguerite as the lights flicker, threatening to plunge the house into darkness.

I quickly amass as many oil lamps as I can find, and place them on the dining room table, just in case we need them. If we lose power on this hillside, it might be weeks before it's restored. The roads have already washed out—Harriet phoned to say she couldn't get to us shortly before I discovered Marguerite missing.

Beckett meets me in the hall, dressed in his rain slicker and hat, his face solemn. "I'll search the grounds. She might have gotten outside."

"Did you hear anything last night?"

"No, not a thing. But this noise could drown out anything." Thunder rumbles through the house again, shaking the floor. He gives me a tight smile. "We'll find her, Sadie. Try not to worry."

"Be careful."

He squeezes my shoulder and goes out the front door, letting in the roar of the rain.

After I've finished my fruitless search of the second floor, I go to the library and then up to the tower room, hoping to find Marguerite in her favored hideaway. It's empty, but the canvas with the likeness of the young girl is uncovered, and a palette with fresh paint lies on the floor, next to a low-burning kerosene lamp and a tumbler of brushes soaking in turpentine. She's been here. Recently. And somehow, she'd found turpentine, even though I'd taken on the task of cleaning her brushes to keep all of us safe. Lightning flickers all around me, the sound of rain deafening on the ceiling. At any moment, I imagine it shattering in the howling wind, glass raining down and cutting me to shreds where I stand.

"Marguerite!" I shout, desperate. I turn in a circle, looking for anything that she might hide behind or inside.

I hear a low moan. I whirl around, my ears straining. "Aunt Marg?"

I rush to the window seat, remove the cushion, and raise the lid to reveal a storage area beneath. I find old books and papers stacked inside, spotted with mildew, but no Marguerite. A dull thumping comes from the staircase. There must be another hidden room. One I don't know about.

Sure enough, when I make my way back down the treacherously steep steps, I notice a small door in the stairwell wall, its exterior hasp latched. Lightning flashes, illuminating the space just enough that I can see to pry it open. I spy Marguerite inside, slumped on the floor of the windowless, small room. I go back for the lamp and crawl inside.

Once inside, I can stand, just barely, my head brushing the top of the sloped ceiling. It's a storage closet. Half-finished canvases lean against the walls, landscapes and portraits of unknown people. I rush to Marguerite's side. To my relief, she blinks at me drowsily and pushes herself up from the floor. The lamplight reveals a thread of dried blood trailing from her left temple to her chin.

"What happened? How did you get trapped in here?"

"I . . . I don't know. I was working and needed something from this room. I can't remember what it was. I heard a noise on the stairs.

Scratching. I was worried it was those people again—the ones living in the walls. I went to see what it was, and the door slammed shut behind me and wouldn't open. I hit my head trying to get out."

Scratching. The same noise I heard on my first night in this house. I shudder.

"Let's get you out of here. Beckett and I have been worried sick. He's outside in this weather, looking for you. You shouldn't be up here without one of us." I don't mean to scold, but my fatigue and fear have stolen the better part of my patience. There are so many ways Marguerite's actions might have resulted in tragedy. Even though her injuries don't appear serious, she could have a concussion. I think of the tumbler of turpentine next to the kerosene lamp. She could have easily knocked over the lamp and set the house ablaze again. She seems unaware of her limitations and how dangerous her delusions can be. It frustrates and frightens me.

"Here," I say, moving to a crouch, "put your arm around my neck. I'll help you up. Watch your head."

I lift her to her feet as she clings to me, guiding her slowly and carefully toward the door, and down onto the narrow landing, the lamp lighting our way. She stands still for a moment once we're out of the cubby, placing a hand on her head. "I'm so dizzy," she says.

"I'm not surprised. I'll telephone Dr. Gallagher, but he may not be able to make it up the hill in this storm. Harriet called earlier. She said the roads were all washed out."

"Oh my."

"Yes. It's very important for you to stay close to me just in case we lose power. No more wandering off."

"I'm sorry, Sadie." She begins to cry, tears spilling down her face.

"It's all right." I soften my tone, urging her on with gentle words as we navigate the last few steps into the library. Beckett is there, to my great relief, building a fire in the hearth, his hair and clothing soaked. At the sight of us, he hurries to help, taking on Marguerite's weight as we ease her onto the sofa. I kneel and remove her shoes, massaging her feet to warm them, then cover her lap with a quilt.

"She may have a concussion," I say. "She hit her head pretty hard."

"Where was she?" Beckett asks, his forehead creasing with concern.

"In a closet, off the tower stairs. She had another delusion about the strangers in the house."

A hard clap of thunder crashes overhead. The lights flicker, once, twice, then blink out.

"I'll fetch more lamps," I say. "You need to go dry off, Beck. You're half-drowned."

"Don't worry about me. I'll stay with Marguerite until you're back."

I walk quickly to the dining room. The rain drums like fists on the roof, and then the sound becomes sharper still, like rocks fired from a slingshot. Hail. Fear floods through me. The last time I experienced a storm like this was in 1920, when a rash of them broke out across the Midwest on Palm Sunday. We were spared a tornado, but the hail and wind were harrowing. Now, perched as we are on the top of this bluff, I worry that we won't be so fortunate.

I hurry back to the library, two lamps clutched in my arms. Beckett takes them from me and places them on the side tables near the sofa, removing their glass chimneys and lighting the wicks with a match. Marguerite watches him, her eyes heavy. I nudge her with my knee. "You can't go to sleep, Aunt Marg. It's not safe."

"I'll go change clothes and make some coffee. Should I call Doc Gallagher?" Beckett asks.

"You might. I'm worried. Even if he can't come, he might tell us what we should do." He squeezes my shoulder, and I place my hand on his, grateful for his calming presence.

Marguerite stares vacantly at the fire. "I remember now, why I went in there. I was looking for my penny."

"Your penny?" It's the second time I've heard Marguerite mention a lost penny. I wonder what could be so special about a single coin, worth very little, that could have her so fixated on finding it.

184

"Yes. Her portrait. Penny was beautiful. Did you know her?"

Realization dawns on me. Penny was a person. "No, I'm afraid I didn't."

"That's too bad," Marguerite says.

"Tell me about her."

"She was tall. Willowy. She had the most beautiful voice. I used to go to Our Lady of Sorrows in secret to watch her sing in the choir. She was in the novitiate. I talked her out of taking her final vows." Marguerite chuckles. "She was so lovely. So sweet."

Penny must have been another of Marguerite's lovers. This one young and a novice nun. Had Marguerite seduced her away from her order? The thought makes me slightly uneasy.

"I started painting Penny months ago, but I put her portrait in that room, and I can't remember why. Something happened . . ." Marguerite shakes her head, the heels of her hands digging into her forehead. "Oh, why can't I remember anything?"

I coax Marguerite's hands into mine to keep her from hurting herself. "Try to keep still, Aunt Marg. I'm sure you'll remember where her portrait is. I can help you look for it once you're feeling better."

Her agitation eases and I shift our conversation to more pleasant things—Louise's children, Beckett's plans to build a greenhouse, and her painting of Hugh, which is nearly finished.

"Tell me more about Hugh," I ask. "I remember you saying he was your first love. How old were you when the two of you met?" I've started asking Marguerite more questions lately—especially about the past. Not only to satisfy my curiosity, but to exercise her mind, to keep her thoughts agile. I've learned that boredom brings about agitation in Marguerite. Frustration.

"I was eleven when we first met. That's when the Nolans came to work for us. We were fast friends almost immediately. I didn't have any friends until Hugh, you see, only my sisters. We had a governess, so we didn't go to school. When Hugh came, my world opened a little more. We both loved horses . . ."

"Yes, you told me. You'd ride Pepper together."

"Yes, Pepper." Marguerite smiles. "I was quite the equestrienne. I won several ribbons riding Pepper. Show jumping. That's what we did best."

"What else drew you to Hugh?"

"He was fun. Ever smiling and happy. My homelife was lonely and depressing, before Hugh came. Papa was often at Annie Chambers's brothel, and Maman was miserable because of it. Her misery carried over onto us, and Florence's demands didn't help matters. She was always ordering Claire and me around." Marguerite frowns, her good mood souring.

Thankfully, Beckett returns, carrying a tray with coffee and scones. He's dressed in clean clothes, his hair attractively mussed. He sets the tray in front of us, and I pour a cup for Marguerite and myself, flavoring hers with cream.

"I phoned Doc Gallagher," he says, sitting in the chair closest to me. "He can't come until tomorrow morning, but said he'd ride his mule here if he had to. He said we should keep Marguerite as calm as possible and watch her closely. If she starts having seizures, he wants us to call him immediately."

I look over at Marguerite, whose eyes have grown heavy. She seems likely to fall asleep at any moment, even with the strong coffee. I wonder how long she's been up, or if she even really slept at all last night. "*Should* she sleep?"

"He said she could." Beckett leans forward and lowers his voice. "But we'll need to wake her every few hours to make sure she doesn't slip into a coma."

"All right. We'll take shifts." I rise, stretching. "I'm going to get a washcloth to clean her face."

I see Beckett's eyes trace my body, then flick away. I tip his chin up, forcing him to look at me. "I don't know what I would do without you, truly," I say, letting my thumb brush his lower lip. "And I promise, when we *do* have time to be alone together again, I'll make it worth the wait."

He closes his eyes, a faint smile lifting the corner of his mouth. "I'll hold you to it."

I take a lingering look at him, over my shoulder, then make my way to the downstairs powder room. The rains have slackened a bit, but the light outside the windows still holds a sickly, green tinge. I warm a cloth under running water, then wring it out. I study myself in the mirror. I look tired. Haggard. My overlong hair has escaped the coronet braid I've been wearing of late, unruly waves sticking out here and there. There's an unidentifiable stain on my Peter Pan collar. I look a sight worse than I did a year ago, when my face was plump with steak dinners and I dressed to the nines on Ted's money. He'd kept me in the latest fashions while I otherwise lived in squalor. I think of all those beautiful, beaded dresses I abandoned at the boardinghouse, and how, by this time, Mrs. Dunlop and the other women living there surely have picked through my belongings like vultures. And why shouldn't they? I have no use for fine dresses anymore.

I'm on my way back to the library when I hear the radio kick on in the parlor. It screeches, then settles on a channel. "Beckett! The current's back on!" I call. But then I notice that none of the lights are on. I switched them all on when I was searching for Marguerite before we lost power.

Something isn't right about this.

My skin prickles as I turn and head for the parlor. The music from the radio grows in intensity, then fades, as if the electricity is ebbing and flowing. As soon as I near the front staircase, the radio abruptly clicks off, its lighted dials going dark.

I stand there, stock-still, listening to the wind howl like an ungodly beast. That same uncanny feeling crawls over me. The sense that I'm being watched. The radio suddenly clicks on again, music surging and filling the room, horns and strings screeching. I drop the washcloth and clap my hands over my ears.

The next moment, the room abruptly falls silent again. Whether this is a trick of electricity or something else, the utter randomness of the radio along with the somber moan of the wind have me unsettled. I bend to retrieve the washcloth and hurry down the hall, my heartbeat surging. I'm almost to the library when someone—or something—shoves me hard from behind, sending me toppling to the floor. I catch myself with my hands. Blows strike my back, as if someone is kicking me. I gasp, try to cry out for help, but my voice comes out as only a panicked whimper. And that's when I know. It's him. Weston. I can feel his anger all around me, just as if he were here in the flesh. I try to claw myself forward, to where daylight leaks through the bottom of the library doors, my fingers scrabbling to find purchase on the wooden floor as my ankles are lifted and I'm pulled backward on my belly, my skirt riding up. I panic, flailing against the air, against his unseen hands, until finally a ragged scream leaves my throat.

Beckett comes rushing down the hall, his eyes wide as he sees me lying there, my clothing in disarray. He kneels, helps me up. I collapse against his chest, sobbing. "It was him," I say, clutching his shirt. "Weston. He . . . he . . . the radio, and then he . . ."

"Shh, you're all right. I've got you." Beckett holds me tightly. "You're safe."

But am I? Are any of us? I think of Marguerite trapped in that tiny closet. It might have been an accident, her getting locked inside, but it might not have been. I shudder to think what might have happened if I hadn't found her. I got a taste of Weston's jealous, vengeful nature in that other world—his world—when I mistakenly allowed myself to fall for his charms. Now that he knows I've rejected him again, he could be capable of anything.

Beckett leads me back to the library, where he covers my shoulders with a blanket and presses a cup of coffee into my hand. I look over at my aunt. She's sound asleep on the sofa, oblivious to what just happened, her lips softly parted. I begin to shake, all over, as fear settles into my bones. Despite Beckett's calming words and promises of safety, I have a feeling nothing can protect me from Weston's wrathful jealousy, and that our troubles are only beginning.

Chapter 25

September 19, 1925

The sun creeps slowly through the library, filling the room with light. A rooster crows, somewhere in the distance. I sit up from my makeshift pallet on the floor. After Weston's attack, I was much too afraid to sleep alone in the attic, despite Beckett's reassurances he would keep vigil. Marguerite and Beckett are awake and gone, but I can smell bacon frying and hear the low hum of his voice down the hall. I rise and look around me, the events of yesterday casting a disturbing pall over the morning. Outside, puddles stand on the flagstone terrace, and several downed tree limbs lie on the back lawn. An aftermath of the storm. Beckett will have his work cut out for him today.

I think of how tender he was with me last night, soothing my fears. He stayed awake and watchful until I'd fallen asleep. For all his initial gruffness—which I now know to be shyness—he's someone quite different from the man I first judged him to be. A man who puts the care and welfare of others before himself. I wanted this house to be mine someday. Now I can't picture myself living here without Beckett. But regardless of where our relationship leads, I'm determined to honor Marguerite's wishes when she dies. And that begins with finding her will. Because if I don't, my brother and my cousins will find a way to rip everything away from us. I can't let that happen.

Remembering the papers I saw in the tower room, I decide to go upstairs to sort through things, to see if I can find something of merit. I wedge a chair against the hidden door, holding it open just in case Weston's spirit attempts to shut me in. I have my suspicions he was responsible for locking Marguerite in the closet. I climb the steep stairs, the fractured light from the tower's glass ceiling illuminating my way. I emerge into the hexagonal room, where the portrait of the young girl stares at me with blank, pupilless eyes. I wonder who she is and why Marguerite has resumed work on her portrait. All her other paintings have been images of her former lovers, but this one is obviously of a child, no older than twelve or thirteen.

I lift the lid to the window seat and riffle through the contents. I don't find anything of great importance. Only ledgers noting household expenses, old Montgomery Ward and Sears, Roebuck and Co. catalogs, and receipts from purchases Marguerite made decades ago. Most disturbingly, I find a box filled with knives and scissors, and wonder whether Harriet hid them for safekeeping or Marguerite put them there as a secret cache of weapons.

"Sadie!" I hear Beckett call. "Breakfast."

"I'll be right there!"

I turn to go back down the stairs, the box of sharp objects in hand. A small slip of pink paper on the floor catches my eye. I bend to retrieve it. It's a receipt from a Kansas City seamstress. At the bottom, scrawled in Marguerite's handwriting: *L's wedding gown—5 Jan. 1895.*

1895. The year my parents married. Did Marguerite pay for Mama's wedding dress? It's likely, since my grandmother hadn't approved of my father. She'd looked down her nose at his common Irish roots and only came around once Felix was born. But Marguerite had always liked Da—perhaps because he reminded her of Hugh. All these seemingly disparate things are weaving together, like threads in a tapestry, telling me more about my family than I've ever known.

I hide the terrifying box of knives in the liquor cabinet, locking it with the key. After breakfast, Beckett brings Marguerite's easel and paints from the tower to the library, so I can better watch her while he goes about his outside chores. Dr. Gallagher arrives just as he promised, astride a sturdy gray mule. He checks Marguerite over efficiently and declares her safe from any immediate peril. Before he leaves, he draws me aside, addressing me with a solemn look. "Miss Halloran, your aunt is deteriorating quickly. She's lost a significant amount of weight. You must begin preparing yourself for the inevitable."

"How long?"

"In my experience with this disease, once anorexia sets in, it's a matter of months, if not weeks."

I think of all the years I've missed with my great-aunt, of how becoming her companion has opened my world in ways I never imagined. I'm not ready to lose her. Not when I've just found her. Not when I've already lost so many people I loved in this life. "Isn't there anything that can be done?"

"Give her whatever she would like to eat. Anything easy to swallow that will stir her appetite. Keep to a routine with meals, and in general. People in her condition find a great deal of comfort in their routines. There's also a nursing home, in Fayetteville, that has a ward dedicated to dementia. It offers groundbreaking care. However, an abrupt change in her surroundings at this late stage in her condition could prove to be catastrophic."

"I think you're probably right. She doesn't want to leave this house." I sigh, my weariness and exhaustion apparent. "Harriet mentioned she'll be able to spend the night from time to time this winter. I'm hopeful that together the three of us can manage things until the end."

He nods, placing his hat on his neat blond head. "I'll begin calling on her once a week, during my usual rounds. Take care, Miss Halloran. Marguerite is very fortunate to have you."

I rejoin Marguerite in the library, where she's deliberately working, adding the final details to the background of Hugh's portrait. Her tremors have become more apparent, visible now even as she works. I rest my hands on her shoulders and kiss the top of her head, fighting back tears. She frowns up at me. "I don't know why that man brought everything down here. I much prefer working in the tower."

"I know, Aunt Marg, but I need to be able to see you while I do my chores. The stairs are dangerous and we don't want what happened yesterday to happen again."

"What happened yesterday?" She blinks at me, her eyes clouded with forgetfulness.

"You hit your head. In the closet off the tower steps."

She brushes her hand over her temple, wincing. "Oh yes. I remember now."

"Would you like to listen to some music while you work?"

"Yes, that would be lovely, dear."

I put a record on the Victrola and settle on the sofa, taking up my half-hearted attempt at cross-stitch. Without Harriet here today, I'll have no respite from my watch. Even going to the powder room and leaving Marguerite unattended carries risk I'm not willing to take, given yesterday's events and her increasing frailty. I try my best to push my concerns to the side and concentrate on my needlework, but I can't help thinking of all the things I should be doing instead—namely, searching for Marguerite's will or anything else that might clue us in to her wishes. Dr. Gallagher's words were sobering. We're running out of time. Perhaps tonight, after Marguerite retires to her room, I can finally search through the trunks in the attic.

But part of me is afraid to be up there, alone, in the place where I first encountered Weston's spirit. My back still aches from him throwing me to the floor.

"He's not going to leave you be, dear," Marguerite says, startling me.

"What?"

"Weston. He's not going to leave you be." She wipes her brush on her smock, leaving a smudge of yellow. "Florence wanted to be free of him, too, but he kept drawing her back in, over and over. She was afraid of him. She couldn't go to sleep without the lights on."

"I remember that. She'd fly into a panic if the electricity went out during a storm."

"Yes. I offered to take the painting. Asked her to send it to me. Yet she never would. I tried to help her. Tried to reason with her. But he had her captivated until the day she died." Marguerite turns to me, the clarity in her eyes as sharp as the needle in my hand. "My sister . . . didn't understand what she did. What she called forth. What she made me a party to."

"What she called forth?" The hair on my arms rises as chills dance over my flesh. "What do you mean by that, Aunt Marg?"

Marguerite chuckles softly under her breath. She shrugs and turns back to her painting. "There are so many things you don't understand about my sister, Sadie. About Weston. But you'll see. In time."

That night, after the house has settled deep in its bones, I go to the library. I flick on a single light and stand before the portrait of Hugh. Marguerite's love for him is apparent in his likeness—she's captured him in the peak of his youth, with his sparkling brown eyes and wide smile. I wonder where he is now. Whether he's still alive. Marguerite is only in her midsixties, so the chances are high Hugh is still out there, somewhere. Did he move on? Marry someone else? Perhaps, if I knew more about him, I might be able to find him again and help bring a sense of closure to Marguerite before she passes. I step closer to the canvas, curious to see whether Hugh's portrait has the same uncanny quality as the others. It does. As soon as I reach out, my fingertips tingle, and the tawny leaves in the background begin to flutter. I take a deep breath, prepare myself for the free fall into the past, and close my eyes.

Interlude

HUGH

It is late in the day—near sunset—the clouds tinted pink. Sadie sits up, getting her bearings. A brisk chill barbs the air. Autumnal gold and scarlet cloaks the trees. As she makes her way through the underbrush, Sadie slowly recognizes the area from her girlhood—when it was the golf course and country club Papa James belonged to. Now, in this time, the road that will one day become Ward Parkway is nothing more than a dirt lane winding alongside Brush Creek, cutting through a swath of picturesque but still wild land, where one of the bloodiest battles of the Civil War took place. Her family's Brookside mansion had served as a field hospital in the aftermath.

The clatter of hoofbeats rings on the packed earthen road. Sadie steps back into the trees as two horses bolt past her. She recognizes Pepper's Appaloosa coat immediately. Marguerite sits astride him, trailed by Hugh on a bay mare. Marguerite reins in her horse and glances over her shoulder, smiling playfully at Hugh, then steers Pepper onto a path through the woods.

Sadie races to follow as they ride side by side, talking in low voices. She can hear the creek's muffled rill, Marguerite's girlish laughter in harmony with the water. Sadie catches up and inches forward, peering through a maple tree's branches. Marguerite and Hugh sit at the edge of the creek, his arm draped around her waist, her head resting on his shoulder as the horses drink from the creek's crystal clear waters.

"I don't want to go. I'll plead sick," Marguerite says.

"But you must, Maggie," Hugh says. "They'll be suspicious if you beg off."

"Florence said the same thing." Marguerite sighs. "Papa won't let it rest. I'm a burden on his finances. So is Claire. He's bound to see me betrothed by year's end."

"Try not to think about that." Hugh raises Marguerite's hand to his lips, presses a kiss to her skin. "Play their game while I figure things out. I've been saving everything I can. I almost have enough for a wagon and a team. There's a group of Irish going to Colorado this spring. We can head out West with them once winter breaks."

"That long?"

"We can't make the journey this late in the year. It's too dangerous."

"Does your da know your plans?" Marguerite asks.

Hugh shakes his head. "No. Only Mam, and she swears she won't tell him." He turns to Marguerite, cupping her face in his hands. "It's all going to work out, Maggie. You'll see."

Sadie turns her head as their affections become more needful and passionate. Hugh stands and leads Marguerite deeper into the forest. The scene flickers, the trees fading, replaced by the Brookside mansion's gravel drive. It is twilight now, and the front gardens are drenched in a deep, gloaming blue as Marguerite trots past on Pepper, alongside Hugh on his horse. Florence stands in front of the mansion's raised porch, her arms crossed. She's dressed in a modest lavender shot silk gown—half-mourning, probably for Papa James's father, who died in 1878. Her pale hair is gathered becomingly atop her head. Diamonds sparkle at her neck. In her ears. "Where have you been?" she scolds, eyes narrowing as her gaze travels up and down Marguerite's form. "James will be here with our carriage any minute."

Marguerite dismounts, and Hugh leads Pepper away, still astride the bay mare. He sends a lingering look over his shoulder at Marguerite.

An inexplicable shudder travels through Sadie's stomach. Something terrible is going to happen tonight.

Florence grasps Marguerite by the arm and marches her inside. "Papa is upset with you. I heard him arguing with Maman earlier. We need to get you into your gown and do something with your hair before he wakes from his nap."

Marguerite pulls free from Florence's grasp. "I haven't been feeling well, Flor. I don't want to go."

"You must, you little fool. It won't be long before *everyone* knows what you've been doing. I'm trying my best to protect you!"

Marguerite flounces past Florence and rushes up the stairs. Sadie trails them as they go to a bedroom she slept in many times when she was little, when Mama and Da went out for the evening and Grandmother tucked her into the plush bed with its pleated, satin tester.

Florence hastily begins helping Marguerite undress, unbuttoning the bodice of her riding habit. "Frank Wornall will be there. One of Colonel Swope's nephews, too. Either of them would be a good match for you."

Marguerite steps out of her skirt and petticoats as Florence rushes to the wardrobe, flinging open the mirrored doors. "You must wear your lowest-cut gown, tonight, Marg. The green one. I'll corset you as tightly as I can."

"Flor, stop. Please. We have a plan. Hugh and I are going to Colorado, in the spring. We're joining a wagon train."

Florence stands very still. "You can't. Do you know how dangerous that is? You could die, Marg. Indians. Cholera . . . any number of things. I won't let you do that."

Marguerite's jaw clenches. "You won't *let* me?"

"Someone has to look out for you. You've been very lucky. But everyone's luck runs out eventually." Florence pulls a green gown trimmed with gold ribbons from the wardrobe. "Here. This one."

Marguerite crosses her arms, standing there in her corset and drawers, her face aflame. "I told you, I'm not going to the ball."

Florence tosses the gown onto the bed, squaring up to Marguerite. "Your stubbornness will be your undoing. This thing between you and Hugh must end. I understand how you feel. God *knows* I do. But you must put your duty to your family first. Before your own happiness."

"I suppose you know all about that." Marguerite laughs, shakes her head. She sits on the edge of the bed. "Shall I marry Frank Wornall then, to appease Papa, and keep Hugh as my lover? Will you teach me how to deceive my husband, Flor?"

Florence wilts. "Yes. If that's what it takes, I will. Right now, you're blinded by romantic notions. But marriage isn't about romance. Not at all."

"It should be. You should marry for love."

"In a perfect world, yes. Everyone would marry for love. I'd have run away with Weston, if I could have. But I couldn't. And neither can you, darling. I won't stand by and let you ruin your life." Florence gentles her voice. "Now come. Get dressed. You're going to look ravishing tonight."

Marguerite rises, reluctantly, and crosses to Florence, who turns her and begins loosening the laces in her corset. "You're lucky. You can't see it now, but you are. You're going to make your husband very happy."

The sisters fade from view, the darkness closing in around them, the uncomfortable feeling of dread lodging deep in Sadie's spine.

Chapter 26

September 20, 1925

Harriet returns to work the next day. She hands me a basket of freshly baked bread and strawberry jam when she comes in. I'm so relieved to see her I set the basket on the kitchen table and hug her, catching her off guard. Tears brim in my eyes. All my emotions are too close to the surface these days. Loneliness. Worry. Frustration. Helplessness and fear of the unknown in a constant, unending loop. The dread I felt after witnessing the scene from Marguerite's past has followed me into the present. Everything feels dire, as if I'm teetering on the edge of disaster.

Harriet pats me on the back awkwardly and pulls away, forehead wrinkling in concern. "What's this about? Has something happened?"

I nod, wiping my eyes. "Marguerite wandered off again during the storm. She got trapped inside a closet and hit her head. She's okay . . . Dr. Gallagher came to call on her yesterday, but things are getting worse. He says we should begin to prepare for the end."

"He's not wrong." Harriet sighs, pulls off her coat, and hangs it on a peg by the door. "I've seen the same progression with other patients. Is she eating?"

"Like a bird," I say. "I have to remind her constantly."

Her brown eyes are soft, sympathetic. "Are *you* eating? Sleeping?"

"Barely."

"Well. I'm here now." She squeezes my shoulder. "You need to get out of this house. Do something fun. There's a dance at the Crescent tonight. You should go with Beckett. I'll stay here with Marguerite and spend the night."

"Really? You'd do that?" The thought of a night out—a night of dancing and pleasure—almost makes me drunk with relief.

"Yes." She arches a brow, smiling knowingly. "You're going to have a life, after your aunt is gone, Miss Halloran. Right now, it might seem like this is all there is. I *know* the kind of fatigue you're feeling. I cared for my daddy before he passed. But there are thousands of tomorrows yet to come. For you."

Beckett comes in just then, his eyes flitting to me, to the sudden flood of tears running down my face. "What's wrong?"

"You just need to take this girl dancing tonight, Mr. Hill," Harriet says with a sly grin. "Give her a reason to dress up. Get pretty."

Beckett clears his throat, looking at me shyly. "I'd like that. Would you like that, Sadie?"

"Yes. I would," I say, laughing through my tears.

"Well. Now that that's settled, I'd better get to work." Harriet grins at us and pushes through to the dining room.

Beckett takes my hand. I turn to him, pressing my forehead to his. "Harriet's playing the matchmaker, too, isn't she?"

He smiles, brushing away my tears with his thumbs. "She is."

"I think we deserve a night out. What do you say?"

He answers me with a kiss, surprising me with his forwardness, and I melt into the sweet, earthy reality of him. A reality I never want to let go of again.

Beckett hands me out of the Duesenberg, my heart lighter than it has felt in weeks. The iridescent jet beads on my hem sway back and forth as we walk into the hotel ballroom, the bright, vibrant sounds of a five-piece jazz band flooding the lofty space decorated with bouquets of chrysanthemums, cornstalks, and sunflowers to convey the harvest theme. We're dressed to the nines, the both of us. It felt good to get ready for a night out again—to primp and paint my face. I've even rouged my knees for the first time in months and pressed the sides of my hair with Marguerite's marcel iron, pinning it back into a faux bob. Beckett looks dapper in his well-tailored suit, his chestnut waves parted in the middle and combed with pomade. He draws me forward, into the crowd, pressing me to him as we sway together to the music, our bodies aligned perfectly for dancing. We're a handsome couple, drawing admiring glances from the locals.

Before I know it, we're kissing, feverish and hungry, and the rest of the crowd seems to fade away. When we pull apart, breathless, Beckett closes his eyes, leaning into me again. "God, Sadie, you're something else."

"Say, you kids need to get a room!" someone says, followed by a shrill wolf whistle. "Who's this sweet thing, Beck?"

"Larry," Beckett says, his voice flat. "Haven't seen you around in a while." His arms lock around me possessively as the short young man with greasy blond hair looks me up and down.

"I ain't on your route no more. After that old dame you work for opened the door naked as a jaybird, I asked Hal to change me to a town route." Larry laughs, showing a set of crooked, yellow teeth. "Won't ever get that image out of my mind. Holy hell."

I feel Beckett tense. He doesn't like this man, and neither do I. He's crass. Loud. And he just insulted my aunt.

"Well, who's the doll, Beck?" Larry leers at me. "Ain't from around here. I can see that much."

"I'm Sadie Halloran," I say, my eyes sliding over his shabby suit. "Marguerite Thorne's great-niece. You must be her former iceman." I say the word with as much disdain for his station as I can muster.

Surprise lights his eyes. "Golly, Beck. You got high hopes, I see."

"That's enough, Larry."

"Sure, sure." He winks at me. "You ever want a man who can show you a *real* good time, sugar, you just let me know. Maybe I'll ask Hal to change my route again."

"I'm plenty happy right here," I say, smiling up at Beckett.

"Lucky dog." Larry laughs, shaking his head. "Guess if a cripple can bed a dame like you, there's hope for me, after all."

Anger courses through me. I slap the man, hard, before I can stop myself, my palm hot as fire. My handprint blooms in red relief against his cheek. He glowers, takes a step toward me. "You little . . ."

Beckett pushes me behind him, widening his stance. We're drawing stares from the other dancers now. "Back off, Larry. You've had too much to drink."

He shakes his finger at Beckett. "I'll remember this. Mark my words. I will. We'll settle up later."

"Sure," Beckett says, laughing. "Sure we will."

The man stalks off, muttering beneath his breath.

"You didn't have to do that, Sadie," Beckett says, pulling me back into his arms. "Larry's just a kid. He's too big for his britches and doesn't mean half of what he says."

"Well, I couldn't let him insult you like that."

Beckett nuzzles my hair. "It's not the first time someone has called me a cripple. It won't be the last."

A full-figured woman steps to the front of the band, her beaded silver dress gorgeous against her deep-brown skin. The music slows as she begins to croon with a soulful alto voice. Beckett and I rock together, my heartbeat settling into its usual rhythm. I kiss his neck, where his pulse beats softly. "What do you say we get out of here while the night's still young?" I say.

"I'd like that."

I lead him out of the hotel, and we drive away with the top down, letting the night air cool our skin. "There's a spring here, nearby, isn't there?" I let my hand stray to his knee. "Somewhere we can be alone?"

He glances over at me, that sly smile lifting his cheekbones. "Yes. There's a spring nearby. But I know a better place, not too far from here."

We drive up and over hillsides, along gravel and dirt roads so deeply furrowed I worry we might bust a tire, trees hanging low overhead. Beckett pulls off the road, the Duesenberg's headlamps lighting up a wall of rock covered with moss and lichen. Trickling rivulets of water flow down its face, like black tears. "There's a hot spring behind that bluff. We'll have to squeeze through a cleft in the rock, but no one will see us there."

He cuts off the engine and leads me through the underbrush, with only the full moon's light as our guide. We find the narrow cleft of rock, and Beckett eases through sideways, reaching out a hand to help me through. "Watch your step. The rocks are slippery."

Once through, my eyes widen in wonder. The night sky stretches above us, twinkling with stars, above a steaming pond edged all around with limestone. It's like being at the bottom of a marvelous natural bowl, carved by the gods.

"I've come here to bathe since I was a child. My brother and I discovered this spring when we were little. The warm water soothes my back." Beckett lets go of my hand and removes his sport coat, laying it on a low, flat rock. "You can sit here, if you'd like."

I remove my shoes and roll my stockings off, letting my feet dangle in the deliciously warm water as Beckett shucks his clothes until he's down to his drawers. My eyes trace his muscled chest, the line of tawny hair leading to his waistband. With a sly grin, he turns and strips all the way, giving me a full-on view of his chiseled backside.

"And here I thought you were shy, Mr. Hill," I tease, leaning back on my hands and watching him.

He walks forward, hands trailing through the water, sending star-light shimmering in waves across the surface. "You should join me."

"I should, shouldn't I?"

I stand and undress slowly as he watches, taking my time, letting moonlight bathe every inch of me. Even though he's likely seen all of me before, when I was sleepwalking, tonight I'm under no delusion. Tonight, my body is a gift meant only for him. A shiver of anticipation trembles through my body as I descend into the steaming water, clad only in the pearl-and-garnet lavalier. I walk carefully along the silty bottom until I reach him in the middle of the spring, where the water laps at my waist. Heat rolls through me, uncoiling my muscles, quickening my pulse. Beckett's eyes darken with desire as he takes me in.

I kiss him, wrapping a leg around his thigh, feeling the bloom of want at my core as I press myself against him. He's ready, his body well primed to claim mine, but I'm determined to take my time. I don't want either one of us to forget this. We have this night, this luxurious, beautiful span of time alone beneath the stars, without responsibility or care. I don't intend to take a moment of it for granted.

I take his hand, show him how to touch me, how to please me. After falling apart with eager abandon, I lead him to the shallows and show him all I'm capable of, what I've learned about a man's body. When I look up at him, drunk on my own power over his pleasure, he cups my face in his hands, his breath coming in sharp pants. "Sadie . . . I can't . . . much longer."

I claim his lips with my own, pushing him back onto the rocky shore and rising over him like a siren emerging from the water. He arches up to meet me, to fill me, and I cry out, triumphant as we move together, our rhythm as ancient as the land around us. Afterward, we lie still, breathing, holding one another in silence, until our skin dries in the soft breeze. When the air grows too brisk, we dress quickly, throwing bashful smiles at one another, and make our way back to the car.

On the way home, he twines his fingers with mine on the leather seat, raising my hand to his lips as he drives. "I never knew it could be like . . . that," he says. "I've been to peep shows, of course. Looked at pictures. But you're like something from a beautiful dream."

"And to think we're only getting started," I say, biting my lip. "To think you were worried about pleasing me."

"Did I? Please you?"

"Oh yes." I laugh. "More than once. Couldn't you tell?"

He squeezes my hand. "On the nights Harriet stays over, you should come to the cottage. There's a double bed."

"Already thinking about an encore, I see."

"How could I not?"

"Mmm. I'm happy. Aren't you?"

"Very."

I scoot closer to him, my head resting on his shoulder as the darkened countryside rolls by, the lights of town peeking through the trees. The closer we get to Blackberry Grange, the more dread fills me at the thought of returning to the house. Of what might happen.

"What's the matter?" Beckett asks, his voice rumbling below the wind.

"I'm worried. About what might happen when we get back."

"With Marguerite?"

"No. With him." I can't bear to speak his name aloud.

Beckett's hands tense on the steering wheel. "I'll protect you. I won't let anything hurt you."

"The other day when he pushed me to the floor, I was completely helpless, Beckett. I couldn't even scream. It was terrifying." I shudder. "I've been thinking about Sybil a lot. Imagining how horrific it must have been for her. And my grandmother as well." Looking back, my grandmother's insistence on leaving the lights on all through the night makes much more sense. While she'd hidden her fear well, she'd been kept in thrall by Weston for decades, a servant to his demented attentions.

He grows silent. "I don't think you should sleep in the attic anymore. It'll be too cold up there in the winter, anyway. Take the room next to mine. If anything happens, I'll hear."

"There's a door between those rooms, you know."

He chuckles. "Yes. I know. But if you come visit me, you'll have to be much quieter than you were tonight."

"Perhaps we'd better use the stone cottage, then," I tease. "Nice thick walls."

He pulls into the driveway, the windows of Blackberry Grange shining like half-shuttered eyes. I tidy my mussed hair as best I can as Beckett helps me out of the car, then drives away to garage the Duesenberg. Harriet opens the door, her lips curving into a smug smile. "Have fun?" she asks lightly, sauntering into the kitchen.

"We did."

"I'm glad."

"How's Marguerite?"

"She's been agitated most of the night. Kept wanting to go to the attic to find her penny. Do you happen to know what that's all about?"

"A little. I thought she was talking about a lost coin, but Penny was a person. Marguerite was looking for her portrait when she got locked in that closet. I think she and Marguerite were . . . friends."

Harriet pours a cup of coffee and pushes it toward me. "Something else happened while you were gone. I wasn't going to say anything. But after I put Marguerite to bed, I heard some noise up in the attic. At first, I thought it was my imagination."

I brace myself, a sense of foreboding falling over me.

"The maid before Melva was always hearing things. Amanda. Seeing things. I never have, so I didn't think much of it. But when I went up to the attic, there was a man there—just as real-looking as you or I. Dressed in old-time clothes and sitting at that rolltop desk, writing." She takes a drink of her coffee, pursing her lips. "I closed my eyes, for just a second. When I opened them, he was gone." She snaps her fingers. "Just like that. Now explain that to me."

I choose my words carefully, pondering them at length before I speak. "I've seen him, too. On my first day here. I thought he was a servant. I asked Melva about him, and she said the other girls had seen him as well. I . . . I think he's harmless." I feel bad about lying to

Harriet, now that I know Weston is anything but harmless. But I don't want to scare her away. We need her too much. Hopefully her seeing him will be a one-time occurrence.

"I'm not so sure that he is. Harmless." Harriet frowns. "Amanda told me a dark-haired man locked her in the linen closet. Slammed the door on her while she was sorting laundry. She couldn't open it for several minutes. She left after that. Melva told me he's the reason y'all can't keep any help. Word gets around about things like that. Folks are superstitious in these parts. People talk about Sybil Vaughn, too. They say her fall wasn't an accident."

"Did you know her?"

"All of that happened before my time with Marguerite. But I'd seen her around town. Young. Pretty. Beckett told me she was his cousin. She was English, so she stood out here, as you can imagine." Harriet shrugs. "There was lots of talk when she died. Some folks say it was suicide. Some say she was pushed. Beckett saw it all happen. The sheriff suspected him, for a while."

"Surely not."

"There was no one else around. They had to question him."

Even though Harriet's words give me pause, I have no reason not to believe Beckett's version of the story. And after Weston's violent assault in the parlor, his angry outbursts in the other world, I know too well what he's capable of. "Do you remember seeing a portrait of a man, with dark hair?"

"I recall seeing it a time or two."

"It's . . . haunted." I pull in a deep breath. "That man, in the painting, he's the same one you and I both saw. Marguerite painted him when she was young, and his spirit is tied to that painting somehow. He was my grandmother's secret lover for years. None of us ever knew about him."

"That's quite a story." Harriet shakes her head, looking skeptical. "I don't like to mess around with spirits and things like that. But whoever he is, he's not going to run me off. I can promise you that." She stands and stretches. "I'm off to bed. I'm going to sleep in Marguerite's dressing room tonight. Hope that's all right with you."

"Are you comfortable in there?"

"Have you *seen* that dressing room?" She laughs. "It's bigger than my house."

"I think I'm going to move downstairs for the winter. Across the hall from Marguerite."

"Next to Beckett?"

"Yes, Harriet," I say, smiling. "Next to Beckett."

"Good," she coos. "I'll see you lovebirds in the morning, then."

Beckett comes in the kitchen door a few moments later. I go to him, pull him in for a lingering kiss, the memory of our lovemaking still hot in my blood. He smiles against my lips. "Aren't you tired?"

"Not at all," I purr.

"Me neither."

"Marguerite's sleeping?"

"Like a lamb."

"Want to sneak out with me?"

"Mmm. Are you going to show me your stone cottage?"

"I plan on keeping that cottage, and you, very . . . occupied, Miss Halloran."

Chapter 27

September 21, 1925

Dawn is breaking pink through the trees when I stumble out of the cottage, satiated but bone tired. I reluctantly untangled myself from Beckett's arms and left him sound asleep in his cozy double bed. I need a hot cup of coffee, a long bath, and a few stolen hours of sleep before the day's responsibilities set in.

I pick my way through the woods above the grotto, admiring the view. The air is crisp without being cold, the leaves just beginning to change color along their margins. The whole world seems brighter to me, despite my tiredness. I think of Beckett, and our newfound love, of where it might lead. While I probably should have considered taking precautions, I didn't. Ted had always used Trojans when we made love. He was dreadfully afraid I'd fall pregnant.

And what if I do with Beckett? I've never imagined myself as a mother, but now . . . now I can almost see it. He was so patient with Louise's children. I imagine Marguerite's house filled with a family of our own. Wouldn't that surprise Felix and my cousins? I smile to myself. Yes. I can see it all so very well.

I emerge into the rose garden, where the rear exposure of the house sits silent. The sun crests over the hillside and I pause to take in the view from the bluff, where the distant ridges ebb and flow like deep purple waves. I close my eyes, tilting my head back and breathing in the morning air. I never imagined I'd fall in love again. Never imagined I could feel so settled. So happy.

Suddenly, I feel a sharp tug on my lavalier. My eyes fly open. I turn, thinking the necklace must have snagged on a branch. But there are no branches near me. The sharp yank comes again, the pearls tightening around my neck with unrelenting pressure. Panic funnels through me. I pull at the necklace, my breath coming in short gasps. When the pressure releases, I fall to my knees, perilously close to the bluff. I look up, my eyes watering. A dark, shadowy figure stands above me. Weston. I use the precious air flooding into my lungs to scream, the sound ricocheting off the rocks and echoing all around.

Through sheer force of will, I rise on shaky legs. I stumble forward and run. Dark laughter surrounds me. Bitter. Cold. Loveless. And then I realize this is a game. It's all just a game. Weston *wants* me to run.

I run anyway, because what other choice do I have? I cut through the trees, my feet pummeling the ground.

"Sadie! Where are you?"

It's Beckett. He heard me scream. Relief floods through me. I pause for a breath, and glimpse him through the trees, close enough I can see the pinstripes on his shirt. "Beck!" I take off running again, my side screaming with pain, my heavy, beaded dress hobbling my thighs.

I make for a break in the trees, anchored by tall pines. But I don't find the clearing I expected. Instead, I'm on a flat outcropping of rock, jutting like a narrow table over the gully. I skid to a stop, panting. I whip my head from side to side, looking for Beckett, but see nothing but sky and the dizzying treetops below.

I'm cornered here. Defenseless. Trapped, just as Weston wants me to be. Suddenly, I'm sent hurtling backward, pain radiating through my body as I tumble to the edge of the outcrop, the wind knocked from my lungs. I futilely try to keep my hold, loose rock crumbling beneath my fingers as my body tips over the edge. I hit the side of the bluff, tumbling toward the earth far below. And then suddenly, the lavalier pulls tight again. My eyes pop open, my throat screaming in pain, the lavalier stretched in a taut line above me, its knotted pearls caught on a point of stone. I eye the ground, still so far below, through the corner of my eye, clawing at the necklace, my feet scrambling against the wall of rock as my consciousness begins to flicker. The rough-edged garnets cut into my flesh. Something wet and warm runs down my clavicle. Finally, the pearls break, shattering over my head like rain, and I'm falling again, into a fathomless blackness, into darkness and death.

Chapter 28

In the darkness, I see Da. He looks as he did when I was little. Handsome and young, dressed in white linen to combat the heat, his blue eyes lit with the same cheerful glow they always held. I'm on the swing in the pin oak, behind our town house on Troost Avenue, the moon shining overhead as brightly as the sun.

"Sadie, mavourneen," Da says, and leans close, his hands above mine on the ropes. "How high do you want to fly?"

"High. As high as the stars and higher still."

"Then that's where you'll go." He pushes me, hard, and I swing through the air, the wind whistling in my ears. I laugh because it *feels* like flying. It feels like life and love and everything I've missed so very much. He laughs with me, pushing me again when I swing low to the ground. I pump my legs, pushing myself to go higher and higher, until the stars are so close I can almost touch them, until the moon is as big as a dinner plate.

If this is what dying feels like, it's not so bad.

When the swing reaches the apex of its highest arc, I close my eyes, and jump, knowing Da is there. Knowing he'll catch me. He'd always caught me.

But he doesn't this time.

I fall back into my body—that leaden weight, that anchor of pain, with all the gravity of loss pulling me to earth. It hurts to open my eyes.

There's a roar in my head like the ocean. "No," I murmur. "No . . . I want to go back. Da . . ."

"She's severely concussed," a man says, distantly. A bright light shines into my eyes. "She needs to go to the hospital. She may be hemorrhaging. Bring the car."

I hear someone crying. Keening. Da always said when someone was the next to die in our family, the banshee would wail. I'd heard her myself, two nights before Da took his own life. I'd thought it was the wind.

"Take Marguerite out of here, Harriet," the man says. I recognize his voice now. Dr. Gallagher. "Sedate her and put her to bed if you must."

I try to focus my eyes, to look around me, but everything is blurry and doubled. Someone is holding my hand. Beckett. I can smell his distinctive scent—sun-warmed earth and the spice of his aftershave. "I'm going to get the car. I'll be right back, darling. I promise."

He kisses my forehead, and there's a rush of air behind me as he leaves. I don't know how I got back to Blackberry Grange. I can't remember what happened. I only remember leaving the stone cottage, leaving the warmth of Beckett's arms, then walking through the woods. Nothing after.

Minutes pass in silence, and then I'm lifted, gently, like a magician's assistant levitating off a table. "Support her feet, Beckett. There. Just like that. I've got her head. Slowly, now. Is the top down on the car? Good. We'll lower her into the back seat from above. I'll ride with you."

I blink in and out of consciousness. I hear the wind whistling overhead. The steady hum of tires on the road. Bright blades of sunlight pierce the thin skin of my eyelids. Children shout as we pass them. The smell of something delicious filters through an open window. When I went blind, after Da, all my other senses became heightened, just as they are now. There's so much richness to the world, beyond sight. More than anyone could ever know. It's the reason I'm not afraid of the dark.

Cool fingers press the inside of my wrist, checking my pulse. "You're doing just fine, Miss Halloran. We'll be there soon."

The next few days go by in a blur, my consciousness coming in and out of focus, along with my vision. Even when I can't hear him or see him, I know Beckett is at my bedside.

Through the fog, I've gathered that I'm at a hospital in Fayetteville, that I have what is called a "traumatic brain injury." Despite the doctor's best efforts to conceal his whisperings from me, I learn that I nearly died, and even though I'll survive, I may never regain all my brain function. When my faculties do begin to return, after a week, and I'm able to sit up and stand without the room spinning, I'm allowed to go on short walks around the ward with the nurses. Being here reminds me of my time at Elm Ridge. I'm concerned that they'll find some way to keep me or, given my confusion and amnesia, transfer me to an asylum, but my worries are unfounded. My progress is deemed exceptional. The next week, Dr. Gallagher comes for a visit. He reassures me that Marguerite is safe and well, and that he's dispatched his own nurse to relieve Harriet, who has been staying round the clock since my incident.

The incident.

My memory is still fuzzy, but bits and pieces are coming back to me. I remember running through the woods, being chased. Someone choking me. My throat still bears faint marks and bruises. The rest is lost to me. A symptom of concussion, the doctor tells me.

On the day I'm due to be released, Beckett comes in, his hat in his hands. He sits next to my bed, his eyes full of sadness.

"What's the matter?" I ask. "Did something happen to Marguerite?"

"No, Sadie. Marguerite is fine."

"I can't wait to be home, Beck. To see her. Harriet, too."

"Sadie . . . I can't take you back there."

"What?" I sit up, ignoring the persistent ringing in my ears. "Why not?"

He presses his lips together. "He almost killed you. I saw it happen. I won't ever get that out of my head. The doctors here think I did it.

213

That I hurt you. Doc Gallagher doesn't think that, but the others . . . They wouldn't believe the truth, even if I told them."

"The truth?"

"Do you remember what happened that day? Any of it?"

"Not really. I remember a man chasing me through the woods. But I don't know who . . ."

Beckett's eyes grow cloudy. "Not a man. A spirit. Do you remember the painting? In Marguerite's studio? The one you asked me to hide."

"I . . . I think so." I scrape the corners of my mind, trying to recall what he's talking about. I come up with only vague shadows.

"He tried to kill you." He chokes on his words, squeezing my hand. "I can't let that happen again."

"But . . . what about us?"

He pinches his eyes shut. "Perhaps, after Marguerite has passed, I can come to you, in Kansas City. Until then we can call. Write. But it's not worth the risk. You can't go back to Blackberry Grange, Sadie. Your life is more important than us being together right now."

"Beckett, no! I won't give you up. Not for a week or a day. And I won't leave Marguerite. I won't." My voice grows frantic. "I'll be all right. Take me home. Please."

"I can't, Sadie." He stands, suddenly stern. Unyielding. "Now, get dressed, and I'll meet you in the hall. I've packed your things. Your suitcase is in the car. I called Louise. She said you could stay with her until you find your feet again."

Hot tears spill from my eyes. "So, you'll give up? Just like that."

"Sadie . . . I'm not giving up. But it's best for us to be apart. For now. Even if you weren't in danger, I've been thinking a lot about us, and *you* need to think about where this is going, too. You deserve someone who can give you everything you want. You're used to the sort of life I could never give you."

"That's not true, Beckett. No. You're exactly what I want. What I need!"

One of the nurses comes in, her brow wrinkled with concern. "You mustn't become distressed, Miss Halloran. Sir, if you could please leave the room." She glares at Beckett. His head drops as he leaves.

"Is that your husband, miss?" the nurse asks as she helps me dress. "No."

"He didn't do this to you, did he?"

"No," I snap. "He would never."

"I'm sorry to ask. We just see these types of injuries when homes are unhappy. You're certain you're safe with him?" She looks at me with soft, kind eyes. I regret snapping at her. My emotions are untethered by Beckett's tacit rejection. Raw.

"Yes. I'll be fine."

Beckett is stony and silent on the drive back to Eureka Springs. It's almost October—my favorite month of the year. The leaves are stunning, the air crisp with the scent of fall, but all I can think about is how I might be losing the purest, truest thing I've ever known. What if his promises to write and call are empty? I see his assurances for what they are—a way to let me down easy. When we get to the depot, Beckett turns away from my attempts to kiss him, and hands my suitcase to me. His coldness breaks me in half. Steals my grace. "You're being a coward, Beckett Hill," I say to his back as he turns to go. "If you really cared about me, you'd fight for me. For us. We'd find a way through this, together."

His shoulders stiffen. "I love you, Sadie. I do. But it's better to lose you for now than to lose you forever."

I wait until he drives away, and then I begin walking.

There's no way in hell I'm going back to Kansas City.

Chapter 29

October 5, 1925

I walk the uphill mile to the Basin Park Hotel and book a room. I need to organize my thoughts, buy some time, and make a plan. Though my head pounds from exertion, I remember everything now, clarity coming to me with every passing hour. Beckett was right: Weston did this to me. He nearly killed me.

I have dinner brought to my room, then lie down to take a nap. When I wake up, it's sunset. A cheerful banjo tune streams through my open window, along with the tantalizing scent of popcorn. I rise, relieved that my headache has abated. I pull my cardigan on over my dress and slip my oxfords on, drawn by the music. When I go out to the street, I see a plethora of electric lights twinkling in the dusk. There's a carnival in the park. Booths line the curved wall below the bandstand, offering all sorts of handmade wares. One booth in particular catches my eye—a simple, hand-stitched tent of patched calico fabric. A sign hangs from a tree made of blue bottles out front: GRANNY WOMAN CHARMS, HERBAL CURES, FORTUNES READ.

My curiosity piques as I approach the tent. Figures and shapes woven from grapevine and willow dangle from the makeshift awning, along with bundled, dried herbs. A woman with bobbed, fiery red hair sits outside the tent's opening in a rocking chair, holding an equally redheaded child. The woman smirks at me, her eyes skimming over my clothes, marking my measure. "Mama!" she yells over her shoulder. "You got a customer!"

"You don't have to yell so loud, Valerie, I'm right here."

A striking woman with long silver hair emerges from the tent, her deep-blue eyes creasing at the corners as she smiles at me. "Well, come on in, child. Don't be shy. I can see right now why you came."

I follow her into the tent, which is lit with a dim combination of kerosene lanterns and beeswax candles. Spicy herbal scents surround me. A round table with two chairs sits in the middle of the tent, with a deck of cards stacked on top, larger than a typical deck. Tarot cards. I've seen them before, but never had a reading.

"We don't need to bother with a reading," the woman says, noting my gaze. "Your aura is pitch black. How long have you been under this oppression?"

"What?"

"The demon spirit, sugar. How long has he been bothering you?"

"I don't know . . . if that's what he is."

"Whether he's a demon or a vengeful spirit who once lived, he's put a seduction on you. I can sense it." She rummages around in a tall apothecary chest, glancing over her shoulder at me. "Some people mince their words about these matters, but I'll tell you straight. Butter wouldn't melt in his honey mouth, would it?" She laughs. "His kind is mighty sweet, until you get on his bad side. Oh yes. I know just what you need." She motions to the table, tells me to sit. I drop into the chair, stunned.

She slides a burlap pouch toward me, tied with twine. I pick it up. Sniff it. It smells like sulfur.

"That's asafetida and cemetery dirt. Sprinkle it on all the thresholds, say a prayer, anoint the door lintels and posts with oil. Any oil will do, though some say olive oil is the best since that's what our Lord was most likely to use." Next, she slides a coin-shaped medal on a chain toward me. "You're Catholic?"

I nod, speechless.

"Here's Saint Michael. You wear that, and you don't ever take it off. Do you know the prayer?" I nod again. "Pray it every night before you go to bed."

"These charms will protect me from him?"

"Yes."

Protection is a start. But I want more than protection. "How do I get rid of him?"

"Give me your hand."

I reach out hesitantly and take her extended hand. Her touch is soft and warm. Comforting. She closes her eyes, breathing deeply. A few moments later, she lets go of my hand. "I wish I had better news for you."

Dread builds to a low hum, at one with the constant ringing in my right ear. I've never met this woman a day before in my life, but I have the feeling she knows everything about *me* with a single touch. "Go on. Tell me."

"The women in your family are under a curse. A spiritual attachment that goes back for generations." She closes her eyes, opens them again, a look of distant, personal pain on her face. "This entity lingers because of something that happened down your family line. A mistake someone made in the past. This spirit wants vengeance. The only way you'll ever be free of him is by discovering the root of the curse. You must confront the wrongs of the past and make atonement—or the one who wronged him must, if they're still alive." She presses her lips together. "Have you had an easy life, honey?"

I think of my long line of losses, all the heartaches and hardships stacking one atop another like masonry and brick. "No. I haven't."

"Just as I thought." Her eyes slide from my face to my hands, which she takes in her own, gently squeezing them. "Find a way to break the attachment and give this spirit the peace he seeks, and you'll be free, along with all the generations that come after you. You'll find your answers in the past." She stands. "Those things I gave you will help protect you in the meantime. If you need more of that powder, or anything else, you can find me up the road in Tin Mountain. Deirdre Werner."

"Thank you, Mrs. Werner. What do I owe you?"

She waves me off. "It's 'miss,' and you don't owe me a thing. I never charge for what I do. I'm called to help others. But if you want, you can leave whatever feels right to you with Val out front."

I emerge into the night, blinking, and offer the redheaded woman a silver dollar. Her eyes light up. She snatches it from me and deposits it in the bucket at her side. "Thank you kindly. Mama help you?"

"I think so."

"Good. You come back anytime, ma'am, you hear me?"

I walk back to the hotel, stunned by the granny woman's words. Her uncanny knowledge. I've heard of demonic possession—something the esoteric side of my church recognizes, but seldom speaks about openly. But she used a different word: "oppression." And that's what it feels like. A heavy burden, following me at every turn. With some surprise, I realize the heaviness has always been there—a constant presence in my life. The thought of Weston weighs on me with visceral fear and dread. I got "on his bad side" when I chose Beckett, and he'd nearly made me pay with my life. While he seems to be tied to his cursed portrait, with me gone, he'll surely turn his anger elsewhere—onto the people I care about. Harriet. Marguerite. Beckett. Or some other poor, unwitting girl in the future. Someone like Sybil.

After hastily repacking my suitcase, I check out of the hotel and ask the desk clerk to call for a cab. The granny woman said that the answers to the curse could be found in the past. And I know just where to find them.

Harriet opens the front door at my knock. She rolls her eyes heavenward. "Oh Lord. You're back."

I set my suitcase on the floor and take off my hat, hanging it on the coatrack by the door. "I am. And I'm staying. I can't desert Marguerite. It's not right." I take in Harriet's tiredness, which she wears beneath her eyes and in her slow, sluggish movements. "Besides, Harriet, you're worn to a frazzle. You can't do this alone. Your family needs you, too."

"Doc Gallagher's nurse has been helping some." She shakes her head. "Beckett won't be happy about you being here, though."

"I know. But he and I have been at odds before. Nothing I'm not prepared for. Where's Aunt Marg?"

"In the library. Working. It's all she wants to do these days. I can barely get her to stop long enough to eat. But she's been feeling better lately. More lucid. Folks often rally toward the end. Can I get you some tea?"

"Absolutely not. Go lie down. Get some rest. And then I want you to go home. Take a few days off, with pay. I can manage. I just want to carry on and do what needs to be done." Apart from my troubles with Weston, I still need to find Marguerite's will. In the hospital, I was afraid Felix would swoop in and do his best to gain control of the estate. There are matters both corporeal and spiritual that need my attention, and I don't intend to waste any more time.

I put my suitcase in the room across from Marguerite's, where Pauline slept, then try the adjoining door to Beckett's room. It's unlocked. The large, four-poster bed is made, corners tucked neatly, a pair of worn, slouching boots sitting on the floor in front of his night-stand. I rest my hand on his pillow, where the slight indentation of his head is still visible. An earthy sweetness permeates the room. Clover, dried leaves, and sunshine. His smell. I hope, with everything in me, that he'll understand why I've come back. That we can resume our affection and he'll accept my love. Because I know that's what this is, now. Love. Something worth fighting for.

Marguerite is painting when I enter the library. The portrait of Hugh is finished. It sits on an easel by the window, its vibrant autumn colors blending with the changing leaves outside. After witnessing their tryst by the creek, and the promise Hugh made to Marguerite, my grandmother's betrayal bears more weight. Why did she work so hard to drive Hugh and Marguerite apart, when she well knew the pain of hiding her own forbidden love?

Marguerite is working on the image of the young girl again, humming softly to herself. I approach her quietly, clearing my throat to get her attention.

She turns, her green eyes widening. She looks a decade younger, the wrinkles on her face diminished, a youthful glow blooming on her cheeks. "Sadie! You're back. I've been so worried about you."

"I'm just fine. Only had a little headache. That's all. You're looking well, Aunt Marg. Did you get some of that Tanlac Tonic from the ads?"

She chuckles. "No. But I've been sleeping better."

"Who's this?" I ask, motioning to her canvas. "She looks familiar."

"Oh, that's because she's me, darling."

I lean closer, admiring her work. "I can see that now. How old were you here?"

"Thirteen. I started this one a few years ago as a practice study. Now that all the others are done, I want to finish it before the autumn light fades away." She looks out the window. "The days are getting shorter. The sun already so low."

"Winter will be here before we know it."

"Yes." She smiles sadly. "And this one will be my last."

"Don't say that."

She shrugs, dabs her brush in a bright crimson. "A person just knows these things." She turns back to her work. "Beckett is working in the rose garden. You should go to him. I'll stay right here, I promise. I want to get this part finished before it gets dark."

"Harriet's lying down. You're sure you won't go wandering?"

"Yes, dear. I'm sure." She lifts a small porcelain bell from the folding table that holds her brushes. "I have this bell if I need anything. It rings loudly enough you can hear it from the rose garden."

I leave her to her work and go out the french doors to the rear terrace. Beckett is cutting back the roses, pruning the spent flowers one last time before the cold sets in. He looks up as I approach, an inscrutable expression on his face. I cross my arms over my waist, awkwardly.

"I saw the cab. Why did you come back, Sadie?"

I sit on the ground, my legs folded to the side. "What would *you* have done if you were me? Really, Beckett. Don't lie."

He turns back to the roses, pinching a thorny branch between the blades of his pruners. "I don't know."

"You'd come back. If not for me, for Marguerite. You know you would."

He looks at me, pain darting from his eyes. "I can't protect you, Sadie. Do you know what it was like for me, watching that happen to you?"

"Yes. But I'm the one who nearly died. I'm afraid, too. I'd be lying if I said I wasn't. But I talked to someone. And she gave me some answers. Charms—to help protect me from Weston."

"Charms?"

"Yes. I saw a granny woman," I say. "She told me Weston's spirit is restless because of something that happened in the past. A mistake. Someone in our family must have wronged him. That's why he's vengeful. Angry. She said that if I use these charms and wards, it will protect us."

"And you believe her?" He shakes his head. "Sadie, the only way you'll be safe is if you leave. I've told you that, a thousand times."

"You say that, but what if I go back to Kansas City and that accursed portrait turns up there? Who's to say he won't follow me? He didn't leave my grandmother alone. Not until she died. This entire situation confounds logic." I stand, my chin lifted. "But whether it takes charms or spells, or ten thousand prayers on my rosary, I refuse to live the rest of my life in fear. I'm going to find a way to break this curse. Because that's what it is." I stand there as he looks at me in silence, my breath coming in sharp pants.

"If you're determined to stay, I can't stop you. But we can't go back to how we were, Sadie. It's too dangerous for you. Every time he attacked you, it was after we were together."

"But can't you see that's why I want to fight? To try. Because I can't bear not being with you, Beckett. This is our home. *You* are my home." My fists clench at my sides, my frustration welling at his stubbornness. "While you decide whether or not I'm worth fighting for, I'm going to fight for myself. For us."

I turn and walk away, squeezing my eyes shut against my angry tears.

Late that night, I arrange Marguerite's finished paintings side by side in the library. Hugh, Iris, Christine. I try not to think about the other portrait, hidden somewhere on this property, in a place only Beckett knows. I hope to never lay eyes on it again. I spread the asafetida powder across the threshold, finger the amulet around my neck, and whisper my prayer to Saint Michael. If what I'm attempting works, chances are I'll encounter Weston, somewhere in Marguerite's past. I need all the protection I can get—there, and in the present, too, where my vulnerable body will remain while my consciousness travels beyond the temporal plane.

I stare at the images of Marguerite's lovers, in turn, perched on their easels. I could attempt to go back the furthest in time again—to Hugh's time, in the brightness of his and Marguerite's youth. But when I touch his painting, there's no spinning sensation of vertigo like I've had before. No invitation to enter. I move to Iris's portrait. Weston mentioned that she was once his ally, but something changed. He insinuated Iris was party to some sort of betrayal and had manipulated Marguerite, yet Marguerite still held Iris in fondest regard. There was something missing. Some obscure thread that bound everything and everyone together. And at this point, I trust Iris to show me the truth more than I trust Weston's words. I tentatively touch the surface of the painting, which ripples like water on a pond. I suck in a deep breath, close my eyes, and let oblivion take me.

Interlude

Iris

Sadie finds herself in a room with a view of the sea, draped with sheer lawn curtains. Outside the open window, she hears the muted susurration of waves and the shriek of gulls. Wind-twisted trees stand stalwart through the lifting fog, and the scent of sage drifts on the wind. This place is familiar and foreign all at once.

Sadie turns just as a perfume bottle sails through the air, shattering on the wall near the window. The smell of gin fills the room, woodsy and sharp.

"How could you!" Florence collapses on the floor beside a four-poster bed, in a heap of lace and satin.

"I'm sorry," Claire says, her voice steady. "But we've waited long enough for your sake, Flor. Too long."

Florence laughs madly, her blond curls shaking. "He was with me just last night!"

"I don't believe you." Claire kneels and begins carefully gathering the shattered pieces of glass in her hands. "You're very good at making up stories."

"So are you, Claire. You've concocted a happy ending in your mind, but he won't be loyal to you. Even if I deny him, he'll find someone else to seduce. It's who he is. What he does."

"I understand. You're hurting, so you want to hurt me. But you must learn to be happy with James. To be *grateful* for the life you have." Florence shakes her head. "You tell me to be happy with James, but you can't know what it's like for me. No one knows how truly alone I am."

Claire rises and places the pieces of glass on Florence's vanity. "I think it can be repaired. This bottle. I'll take it and try to glue it back together later." She crosses to Florence, pats her head with a pitying look. "Now, get dressed. Marg and the others are waiting for us. We'll have our ride this morning, then our picnic later. Everything will be all right."

"You think yourself so much better than the rest of us, don't you?" Florence turns away. "You madden me."

There's a gentle tap on the door and Iris strides in, dressed in riding clothes, her dark hair gathered in a long waterfall down her back. Iris's eyes land on Sadie briefly, and she gives her the slightest smile in acknowledgment of her presence. "We heard a commotion. Is everything all right?"

Marguerite pushes past Iris into the room, solemn-faced in an equally somber riding habit. She takes account of the broken bottle on the vanity, Florence's state of deshabille. "You're indulging in histrionics again, I see. Get up, Flor. Weston is waiting with the trail guide. He's being paid by the hour, you know."

Weston. Weston is here with all of them.

"I've decided I'm staying in." Florence stands, propped against the bedframe. "I ate something that didn't agree with me at dinner."

Marguerite snorts. "Very well. Stay here and pout while the rest of us go enjoy ourselves."

Claire hedges, eyeing Florence. "Perhaps I'd better stay with her . . ."

"No." Marguerite takes Claire by the hand, turning her. "We've a beautiful day ahead of us. Florence will be just fine. Won't you, Flor?"

"Yes. Go on, Clairey. I'll come out for our picnic this afternoon. I promise."

There's another knock at the door. "Claire? Are you in there?" It's Weston. Sadie stiffens as Iris opens the door a crack, whispers something to him, and departs. Weston stalks into the room, his mouth set in a hard line. His eyes skate past Sadie. He must be unable to see her in this version of events. Relief floods through her.

"What's the matter?" he asks, his demeanor softening as he goes to Claire's side.

"Flor isn't feeling well," Claire says. Sadie can hear the resignation in her voice. "I think I should stay with her. I don't care much for riding anyway."

"Nonsense," Weston says. "I've chosen a gentle old mare for your horse. We'll have a grand time. The guide told me he's taking us to a redwood glade, with ancient trees, tall as giants. You don't want to miss that, do you? Come along, darling."

Realization dawns on Sadie. Redwoods. They must be in California. One more piece of the puzzle slots into place.

"*Darling.* Darling *sweet* Claire." Florence cackles, rolling her eyes toward the ceiling. She brazenly sheds her ruffled dressing gown, and stands staring at Weston, clad in only her shift. Weston's eyes trail to the beamed ceiling. He runs a hand through his hair, his jaw clenching. "Why so shy, Mr. Chase?" Florence says. "You saw me in far less last night."

"Enough!" Marguerite shouts.

Weston hurriedly leads Claire from the room as Florence's eyes spill over with tears, her fragile hauteur fading as she falls onto the bed, muffling her sobs in a pillow. Compared to the last scene Sadie witnessed between Marguerite and Florence, just a few years in the past, where Florence was steady, calm, and determined, it's now Marguerite who dominates the room, and her sisters.

"Why must you be so self-centered?" Marguerite scolds. "You act as if you're some long-suffering martyr, and I'm sick to death of it. I *hate* the thought of them together. I do. But this is what she wants, and

Claire deserves a chance at happiness. Let him go, Flor. For everyone's sake."

"Oh, let her believe she's won, then! But Weston and I will never be parted. Not in life, and not in death. I swear it."

"Death? I hope you're not planning anything rash."

"What would it matter?" Florence says. "No one would miss me. I should throw myself into the sea and be done with it."

"Yet more selfishness." A hard shadow drifts across Marguerite's face. "Laura and Grace. *They* would miss you. Terribly."

"You hate me."

"No, I don't, Flor. But you're acting like a spoiled child who's lost her plaything. Now. Get hold of yourself. I've had quite enough of your moods, and so has everyone else."

Florence wails pitifully, burrowing beneath the eiderdown. Dread spills toward Sadie after Marguerite leaves the room, spreading like black ink across paper as the light fades and the sea whispers *hush-hush*.

Chapter 30

I come back to my senses, the last vestiges of my trance fading as the present overtakes the past once more. Yet the feeling of dread lingers, haunting my thoughts. I remember asking Marguerite whether Claire had ever been to the ocean, on the morning after my strange dream where I'd seen Marguerite with the bloody knife. She told me Claire had never been to the coast, that she was terrified of water. Yet in the scene I just witnessed, Weston, Claire, and her sisters had obviously been somewhere near the Pacific.

I think of the conflict and agitation I observed in that room by the sea. Claire's slightly sanctimonious worry over Florence, my grandmother's jealousy and distress, Marguerite's disdainful anger. There was a hard edge to her ire—a flinty look in her eyes that told of her resentment and bitterness. But despite this new insight into my aunt's past, I still don't have the answers I'm seeking. Either Marguerite purposely lied to me about Claire going to California, or she's forgotten it entirely. I'm left with the sinking suspicion that something terrible happened that day. I turn to Iris's portrait. I need to go back. To see more. I reach out, my fingertips just brushing the surface, when I hear someone come into the library.

Beckett clears his throat. "I couldn't sleep. I checked your room. Saw you were gone."

"I couldn't sleep, either," I say, turning.

He gestures at Iris's portrait. "She was my aunt. Iris. The likeness is astounding."

"Oh? Marguerite never told me she was your aunt."

"Yes. That's how my father came to work for Marguerite. Iris was his sister. She married an Englishman and moved away to London."

I cross to the chesterfield and sit, tucking my legs beneath me. "Come sit with me," I say, patting the leather seat. "I won't bite. I promise."

He sinks down next to me, sighing. "I'm sorry about earlier, Sadie. I am glad you're back. I didn't want you to think I wasn't."

"You were only worried. I understand." I look around the library, listening to the soft ticking of the clock on the mantel, the hushed whisper of wind outside. Things seem quiet. Peaceful. The quiet feels less comforting than it should, though. As if a tiger is crouching in the shadows, waiting for the right moment to pounce.

"You should phone Louise. Tell her you're not coming," he says.

"I will. She'll be relieved, I'd imagine." I laugh. "She and Pauline don't like me. They never have."

"They seemed nice enough when they were here."

"You don't know my family. They're like shrikes. Sweet and innocent looking, but ready to barb you with harsh words and hidden knives when you least expect. It's ridiculous."

He sighs, twisting from side to side, wincing in pain.

"Your back?"

"Yes. It's been hurting all day. The weather's getting ready to turn again."

"Let me help you. Take off your shirt and lie down on your belly."

"Sadie . . ."

"I happen to be very good at massage. Now, do as I say."

He unbuttons his shirt, grumbling, but I can see the hint of a smile on his lips as he shucks his undershirt and lies prone on the sofa. The curvature of his spine is more apparent from above, the sideways shift to the left in the middle of his bare back. I rub my hands together to warm them, hitch up my skirt, and straddle his hips, leaning forward and gently pressing the heels of my hands against his skin. He groans as I begin kneading, slowly building pressure as I feel his resistance to my touch lessen. I can't help the wave of arousal that warms me as I rock back and forth atop him. What we're doing is undeniably sensual. Even though it's not my intention to seduce him—I merely intend to lessen his pain—I feel a shift in the room's atmosphere all the same. The attraction between us is still there. It always has been.

"You're driving me crazy," he says, confirming my suspicions.

"Do you want me to stop?" I ask teasingly, pushing my hands from his tailbone to his neck. He practically purrs beneath me.

"My god, no."

"I told you I was good. Sit on the floor in front of me, and I'll do your shoulders."

He acquiesces, his shoulders pressed between my knees. I knead the firm, knotted flesh until it softens, savoring his groans of relief. After his muscles have relaxed beneath my touch, he stands and stretches. I look away as he pulls his undershirt over his muscled chest, remembering his eagerness when we made love. I push my want and disappointment to the side, go to the liquor cabinet, and pour each of us a finger of whiskey. "This will help your muscles stay loose," I say, handing him a tumbler. "Sláinte."

He tips his glass to mine and takes a long sip.

We sit in silence for a long time, watching the flames die in the hearth. "There's something I never told you about Sybil," Beckett finally says. "I'm the one who convinced her to come here. That's why I feel so guilty."

"How could you have known what would happen, Beckett?"

He ignores my question, as we listen to the embers pop and crackle. "She was just out of finishing school and wanted to earn some money over the summer to go to Hollywood. Become an actress. She idolized Marion Davies. Mary Pickford. The first few months were fine. Marguerite loved her. She brought new life to this place. When that painting arrived, we didn't realize what it was. How it would change her."

"When it arrived? I thought it had always been here."

"No. It came after your grandmother died. She left it to Marguerite in her will."

I scrape my memory, trying to recall whether I'd ever seen Weston's portrait in my grandmother's house in Kansas City. I hadn't. But once, I wandered into a room when I was very young, while I was playing hide-and-seek with my cousins—the old schoolroom on the third floor, where Grandmother and her sisters had studied under a governess as children. Apart from three dusty desks and a chalkboard, a shrouded picture leaned against the wall. I'd started to lift the velvet covering, exposing the gilt frame, when Grandmother stormed into the room, snatched me up, and put me in the hall, locking the door behind her. "You're never to go in that room again! Do you hear me?"

Had it been the portrait of Weston? Had she kept it locked away, all those years, so she might go to him whenever she liked? I think of the scene I witnessed in the gallery, the first time I entered Iris's world—the art show where Marguerite had debuted her work. Marguerite told Iris she was going to send the portrait to Florence. She obviously had. Her deep-seated anger toward her eldest sister was apparent. Florence's betrayal over Hugh, and her continued dalliance with Weston had left a wound that Marguerite couldn't forgive. Everything that's happening to me, everything that's happened to our family, points back to my grandmother and her sisters and all the secrets they kept for all these years. I think of the granny woman's parting admonition to me: *You must confront the wrongs of the past and make atonement—or the one who wronged him must, if they're still alive.*

My grandmother has been dead for almost three years. Aunt Claire for much longer. If either one of them was the source of the curse, it will never be finished. That leaves Marguerite.

"Did your aunt ever talk about anything tragic that happened to Marguerite, in the past?" I ask, pushing back my growing apprehension.

"Nothing of note, that I recall. They became companions for a few years, traveled, studied together, before Iris met my uncle in London."

"When did she die?"

"Nearly ten years ago. She had a stroke. It was sudden."

"I'm sorry."

He shrugs. "I barely remember her. She and my cousins would come for the holidays occasionally when I was young, with piles of steamer trunks loaded with presents. She brought me those blocks I gave your little cousin to play with. She came to see my father, of course, but she was mostly here for Marguerite."

"They were more than friends, I think."

"Yes. My father always suspected as much."

I glance over at the portrait of Iris, wondering whether her spirit is here, listening to our conversation. The ties between my family and Beckett's are deep, going back generations. If Iris was anything at all like her nephew, she's the most trustworthy source at my disposal. If I'm to get any answers, they'll come from her. From her memories of the past.

As the liquor seeps into my bones, and weariness begins to take me over, Beckett eases me down onto the sofa and covers my shoulders with a blanket, then dozes off next to me, my feet resting on his lap. I imagine I see Iris's spirit as I drift off to sleep, standing by the fireplace, her eyes gentle but determined. She lost a granddaughter to Weston's machinations. Now I wonder whether Weston targeted Sybil as revenge against Iris. He obviously holds contempt toward Iris over some perceived betrayal. But for what reason? Perhaps Iris wants vengeance, just as much as I do. Perhaps together, we'll get it.

Chapter 31

The next few days go by in a rush. With Harriet taking a much-deserved break, Marguerite's care has fallen squarely on my shoulders. While I've recovered well enough from Weston's attack to see to my many responsibilities, I'm always on edge. Jumpy. Even though I've never been afraid of the dark, I've begun leaving the lights on overnight, just like my grandmother did. The ringing in my ears and occasional headaches still plague me. Most concerningly, my memory remains full of holes. It's mostly harmless, small things—forgetting where I placed the dustpan, or put my watch. But then, one afternoon, as Marguerite feverishly works on her self-portrait while we chat about our family history, I find myself unable to recall the year my little brother, Henry, was born.

"I . . . I think it was 1905. Yes. That was the year. Mama went into labor during a snowstorm. The doctor came to the house to deliver him." We didn't have a telephone at the time, so she'd sent Felix to the doctor's house, rousing him from sleep.

Marguerite smiles placidly, feathering painted shadows between the pleats on her younger self's skirt. "It's curious how time can make our minds slip, isn't it? Some things that happened many, many years ago seem to have only happened yesterday. But others . . ." Her brush pauses on the canvas. "Others I'd give anything to remember. I have entire years missing, Sadie. Years."

"I'm sorry."

"Well. Dr. Gallagher says that I must do my best to hold on to the things I *can* remember."

"Do you remember going to California? Or perhaps Oregon? With Claire and Florence?" I ask. "Did you see the redwoods?"

Marguerite's brush stills again. "I've been to lots of places, my dear, but never out West. Hugh and I—we wanted to go to Colorado. Together. But Florence put an end to all of that." She sighs. "I went looking for him there, after Claire died." She shakes her head. "But that's as far west as I've been."

I don't believe her. Not for a minute.

The next morning, I hear Marguerite talking to someone inside her room. I cross to her closed door, listening. She laughs softly, her voice low. "You always were. I adored that one. You should have shown it in Chicago."

There's a pause in the conversation. "She doesn't." A dramatic sigh. "I can't tell her. You know that."

A moment later, Marguerite begins to sob. "Oh, leave me be!"

I rap on the door, realizing she's in the midst of a hallucination. I know how quickly these delusions can turn from pleasant to terrifying. "Aunt Marg, it's Sadie. Can I come in?"

"Yes," she says wearily.

I open the door to find her sitting on the edge of the bed, her head hanging low. She glances up as I come in, a haunted, distant look in her eyes.

"Who were you talking to just now?" I ask, sitting next to her.

"Iris." Marguerite's lips thin as she scowls. "She won't leave things alone."

"Won't leave what alone?"

"The past."

I take her hand. It's icy cold. I rub it between my own to warm her skin. "You can tell me what's bothering you if you want. I promise I won't tell another soul."

"I can't, dear. I made a promise to Florence. To my family. I've forgotten a lot, but I haven't forgotten that."

"Grandmother is dead now. Whatever secret she made you keep—you can't hurt her by telling me."

"I could care less about hurting Florence. She never cared about hurting me." Marguerite's lip trembles. "Oh, Sadie. I'd give anything to go back. I would. How different things might have been."

"What would you change, if you could?"

"So many things," she says enigmatically. "Help me get dressed. I need to get back to my work."

She paints for the rest of the day, pausing only long enough for tea in the afternoon, saying very little to me. I leave her in the library, with an admonishment to ring the bell if she needs me and go up to the attic to search for Marguerite's will, a deed to the house—and any other clues I might uncover about her past.

It's been weeks since I've been up here. The bed is made, a fresh quilt smoothed neatly over the mattress. The faintest odor of smoke still lingers from the fire. The curtains are closed, so I open them, allowing the light to reach into the darkened eaves, where layers of steamer trunks are stacked. I'm daunted by the prospect of sorting through Marguerite's things. I've no idea where to start. The chatelaine and its bronze keys still sit on the top shelf of the wardrobe, where I left them. I try the trunks near the west-facing window first. The smaller keys fit the locks, just as I suspected, and soon I'm burrowing through the detritus of my aunt's past. She's saved everything over the years, it seems. Mail. Old receipts. Notes scribbled in her fine, delicate penmanship. It's an interesting, yet arduous task. I make two stacks—one to burn in the rubbish heap, one to look through more carefully.

I roll my head back on my shoulders, stretching my aching neck before I open the next trunk. My heart jolts at the sight of my parents' wedding portrait sitting on top of a pile of family pictures. In the photograph, my young mother is full-cheeked and happy, wearing the high-necked, wasp-waisted gown Marguerite evidently paid for, her lace veil pooling on the church floor, my father next to her, handsome in his white tie. They were little more than children when they married—sixteen and eighteen—with Felix well on the way. Though tightly corseted, my mother's pregnancy shows in the fullness of her bust and her plump face.

The trunk is filled with family memorabilia. Photographs. Knickknacks, trophies, ribbons from Marguerite's equestrienne days. I sort through things slowly, taking the time to read old postcards and letters from my aunt Grace, my mother, my grandmother. Most of them simply recount their daily lives—births, illnesses, our growing-up years, what they did on holiday. In a letter from 1920, I learn that my grandmother disliked Felix's wife as much as I do, laughing to myself as she decries her *insipid smile and weak-chinned blathering.* Grandmother always treated Rosalie with abject kindness and respect, at least in front of us. I find it both humorous and intriguing knowing what lay beneath her refined politeness. Her histrionics in my journeys to the past were shocking as well. When I was young, she seemed less like a grandmother than a queen trapped inside a snow globe. Beautiful, regal, and untouchable. How many secrets had she kept? How many faces had she worn? Did *she* ever really know who she was?

I continue searching through the trunk until the light fades to a wash of rusty orange through the windows. Near the bottom, beneath a neat stack of letters tied with grosgrain ribbon, I find an envelope with a notary seal. I open the folded papers within, my heart beating wildly. It's Marguerite's will.

I peruse the handwritten document carefully, tracing each line with my finger. The will was drawn up decades ago, in 1887, and it bears the markings of its age, the faded ink nearly illegible in some places, although it's quite clear to whom Marguerite wanted to leave her fortune once she departed this life. My mother. Her maiden name, Laura Bethany Knight, is notated throughout the will. She would have inherited everything—the house, Marguerite's entire artistic estate, and even the silverware and china.

Marguerite's bell rings from the library, the sound piercingly loud. "Coming!" I call, placing the parcel of letters back inside the trunk. I'll return to them later. My hands tremble as I hastily refold the three-page will and secrete it in my apron pocket. If Felix ever lays eyes on it as it's written now, he'll fight me tooth and nail over the estate. We must get the will redrafted. Soon. Whether Marguerite decides to leave everything to me or to Beckett matters not. Felix took our childhood home and my mother's cottage. I won't let him take Blackberry Grange.

That night, Marguerite is restless. Petulant. She refuses to change into her nightclothes, her lucidity fading with the light. I finally manage to calm her with recordings of Enrico Caruso and a cup of chamomile tea. The music takes her back to another time, in Venice, with Pia, who she's never painted but loved all the same. I listen as she recounts their adventures, going with her into the past. I've learned it's best to meet her there, in the life she's constructed from happy, comforting memories. When drowsiness begins to take hold of her, she trails me to her room, where she shows me the collection of Venetian masks she collected on her travels, unwrapping them from their tissue one by one, their colorful feathers and beads still vibrant.

"We should start looking through some of these things—start planning for who will get them after I'm gone," she says. "Set aside whatever you'd like now, Sadie. Before the others come. Florence will take everything."

She's forgotten that Grandmother died nearly three years ago. "Aunt Marg, let's not think about all that tonight." I immediately chastise myself for my words—the folded papers in my apron pocket remind me that we do indeed need to talk about who will get her belongings after she's gone. "If you'd like, we can summon an attorney. Have him come to the house, catalog your belongings, and draft a will."

"Oh, I had a will done ages ago, my dear. I made my wishes very clear concerning the estate. Laura's to get everything."

I've avoided talking about my mother's death with Marguerite for months, slipping away from the subject like a skater avoids razor-thin ice. But who am I trying to protect by doing so? Marguerite? Or myself? Keeping Mama alive in Marguerite's imagination serves no one. And now, it's a matter of my own survival and security to tell her the truth.

I sit on the edge of Marguerite's bed and pat the mattress. "Come sit with me. We need to talk about Laura."

Marguerite shuffles over and sinks down next to me. I take her hand in mine, capturing her eyes with my own. "Laura died, Aunt Marg. This summer."

At first, she doesn't react, only blinks, the impact of the words delayed. Then a soft sigh escapes her lips. She begins to tremble all over, her eyes frantic. "But she was just here, last month. For a visit. She brought the children."

"That was Louise." I squeeze her hand. "We used to visit you in the summers when me and my brothers were little, though. That's probably what you're remembering."

"Laura's . . . dead? You're sure?"

"I'm afraid so." My mouth suddenly feels dry, the back of my throat burning like an ember. "Her heart. It was very sudden."

Marguerite's hands fly up, hover in front of her face for a moment, then tangle in her hair. She rocks back and forth, wailing. The sound ricochets from the ceiling and reverberates through me. It's the most pitiful, most painful sound I've ever heard. The rawness of her grief breaks me, cracks open my fragile shell, my own long-denied tears flowing as I wrap her in my arms, both of us weeping together over a beloved niece. A treasured mother.

"No, no, no," Marguerite says, over and over. "No, no, no."

"I know," I say, smoothing her hair out of her clawed hands. "I don't want to believe she's gone, either. But we're going to get through this. We must."

Beckett knocks, and asks to come in. "Everything all right?"

"No," I say, smiling sheepishly as I wipe the tears from my eyes. "I'm going to stay with Marguerite tonight. Sleep in her room."

His eyes bounce from me to Marguerite, his consternation at our mutual distress apparent. "Let me know if you need me."

"I will."

The door snicks shut. I turn down the bed, and ease Marguerite under the covers. I switch off the lights, then lie next to her, cradling her back as she sobs into her pillow. Sometime later, she drifts off to sleep, and I soon join her, the two of us bonded by our grief, by the terrible weight of love.

Chapter 32

Early the next morning, I rise without disturbing Marguerite, and cross the hall. I knock lightly on Beckett's door. There's a muted rustling from within, as if he's dressing. "Come in," he says gruffly.

I ease into the room. Birdsong ripples from the window, open a crack to let in the cool air. I linger there awkwardly, fingers laced together, still unsure of where we stand with one another and incredibly conscious of the fact that I need to figure out my place in his life before we help Marguerite settle her affairs.

"What happened last night?" he asks. "I've never seen Marguerite in such a state."

"That's what I came to talk to you about." I perch on the chair by the window. "I found her will yesterday, in the attic. She . . . wanted to leave everything to my mother. I had to tell her she died. She didn't take the news well." I cross my legs at the knee. "Didn't anyone phone or write to tell her?"

"If they did, I never heard about it."

"I'm not surprised. Aunt Grace was probably afraid to upset her." I clear my throat. "But it's important because my mother's death leaves the will open to contest unless Marguerite has it revised. My brother already has designs. So does Louise."

Beckett comes to the window and looks out, his hand resting lightly on my shoulder. I cover it with my own, relief coursing through me at this show of tenderness. "We'll call Peter Bruce on Monday," he says. "Her attorney. Have him come here. If she wanted this house to go to your mother, then it should rightfully go to you."

"Yes, but Marguerite needs to have the final say. Her feelings might have changed. She might want to leave it to you instead. You've been like a son to her."

"Maybe. But no matter what, Sadie, this is your home."

"And yours," I say, squeezing his hand.

He looks at me then, with a softness in his eyes I've not seen in some time. Hope blossoms in my chest. I reach up, touch his cheek. He leans into my hand, his lips brushing the inside of my wrist.

I stand to face him, my pulse a drumbeat in my ears. He hesitates for the sparest moment, then pulls me to him, kisses me, his lips testing mine. Our kiss deepens, becomes hungry and needful as his fingers work loose the buttons on my dress. When the cold breeze from the window touches my skin and his hands warm my breasts, I gasp, delight fracturing my reserve. He backs me toward the bed, and I kick free of the rest of my clothing as he kneels on the floor and slowly traces the inside of my thigh with his tongue, looping my leg over his shoulder.

Suddenly, a loud crash echoes through the room. My eyes fly open. The mirror above the dresser lies shattered on the floor. Beckett lifts his head. "What the—"

Something sends him toppling sideways, with a cry of surprise. I scramble to cover myself with my discarded dress and clutch the Saint Michael medal, speaking the prayer aloud into the room:

"Saint Michael the Archangel, defend us in battle.
Be our defense against the
wickedness and snares of the Devil.
May God rebuke him, we humbly pray,
and do thou, O Prince of the heavenly hosts,

by the power of God,
thrust into hell Satan, and all the evil spirits,
who prowl about the world seeking the ruin of
 souls.
Amen."

As I repeat the prayer again, sheer terror floods through me. Invisible hands yank Beckett to his feet, his shirt collar knotted. His head snaps back, as if he's been punched. He tries to fight, just as I did, wrestling against Weston's evil grasp as my voice rises in crescendo, the last words of the prayer a shout. And then, abruptly, it's over. The room falls silent again, the birdsong resumes, and Beckett limps to his feet, wiping a thread of blood from his lip.

I fly to him, checking him over frantically, running my hands up his chest.

"I'm fine, Sadie. I'm fine," he reassures. But I see the haunted look in his eyes, the fear. I think of the pouch of asafetida and cemetery dirt the granny woman gave me, sitting on my nightstand. It's nearly empty. I sprinkled my threshold, Marguerite's, the entry leading to the attic stairs, as well as the library threshold, but I didn't use it at the door to Beckett's room. I hadn't thought to. Now I see my mistake. I won't be so careless again.

Beckett and Marguerite wait in the car as I approach the granny woman's cabin, its low-slung roof loamy with moss. The same redheaded woman who was outside the tent at the festival sits on the porch swing, smoking a cigarette and rocking back and forth, heel to toe. She looks up as I draw near, grinning. "Back already, huh? Mama's inside. She'll fix you up."

The air inside the cabin is stolid and earthy, the rafters hung with drying herbs. The granny woman comes out of a curtained alcove, her silver hair glowing in the dim. "Oh, it's you," she greets me, squinting. "I figured I'd be seeing you again. He still botherin' you?"

"Yes. I'm afraid so. He didn't harm *me*, because of this." I pull the medal from beneath my shirt collar. "But he attacked my beau. I need more of that powder you gave me, please."

"Of course. Wait here, child. I've something else for you, too. You've been on my mind lately."

She turns back to the alcove, rummages around behind the curtain as I listen to the clink of glass bottles. She emerges with a knotted burlap sack. "Your warding powder is inside. I also put everything in there that you'll need to build an altar."

"An altar?"

"Yes. A wall of protection for your home. Set it up tonight. Keep those candles burning and he shouldn't bother you or anyone else in the house."

While the thought of lit candles around Marguerite terrifies me, I nod politely and thank her all the same.

"Now, take this work seriously, girl, because it's serious work," she admonishes as I leave. "You know where I am if you need me again."

"Thank you, Miss Deirdre," I say, smiling at her from the porch.

She leans forward to look out the door. "That man in the car? He's your beau?"

"Yes."

She chuckles warmly. "He'll be your husband, soon enough. Mark my words. He has the glow of love on him."

"I wouldn't be opposed to that," I say, blushing. "Not at all." I press three dollars into her hand, and wave at the redheaded woman, who merely stares at me as I depart.

Beckett looks at me quizzically when I slide into the front seat, tucking the satchel between us. "What is that? Smells like rotten eggs."

"It's asafetida powder. And it works. Just trust me."

He grins. "If you say so."

I glance back at Marguerite, dozing in the back seat, her head lolling to the side as Beckett backs down the steep drive and turns onto the narrow mountain road. It's a crisp fall day, still warm enough to leave the top down on the Duesenberg, but with the promise of winter in the wind.

That night, after I've tucked Marguerite safely in bed, I clear a space on the dresser in my new room and pour out the contents of the satchel. There are two white candles, a black one, a prayer card with the image of Saint Michael slaying a fanged serpent, coarse salt, and a large pouch of asafetida and cemetery dirt. A handwritten note is tied to the bag, with directions for setting up the altar.

I carve my name and Beckett's on the white pillar candle, as instructed, with Marguerite's and Harriet's names beneath, as Harriet is due to return to work tomorrow. I place it in the center of a mirrored tray atop the dresser. To the left of the candle, I prop the prayer card against the mirror on the wall. Saint Michael. Our protector. Outside the circle, facing me, I place the black candle, representing Weston. The enemy.

I carefully pour a ring of salt around the white candle, then light the black candle. I feel the hairs on the back of my neck prickle before the warding words leave my lips. "Weston. I know you're there. I sense you. From this day forward, you may harm me no more, nor anyone I love. Do as you will but leave me be."

Next, I move to the white candle and light it, the flame flaring in the darkness. "I am my own, as are those that I love. No harm may befall us. We are protected. No evil can enter this home."

I then repeat the prayer to Saint Michael, closing and binding the spell with his protection before making the sign of the cross. A weight seems to lift from the room as I finish, a brightening of the shadows as the candle flames flicker gently, magnified by the mirrors beneath and behind.

A few moments later, Beckett knocks on the door adjoining mine. I turn from the altar as he enters the room. A faint bruise stains the skin beneath his right eye—undeniable proof of Weston's attack. "You were serious," he says, smiling. "It looks like a church in here."

"It works. I can feel it. I can't explain how."

"I don't know if I believe in magic, but I suppose anything is possible." Beckett brushes a hand over his injured jaw and closes the distance between us. He wraps his arms around my waist, pressing his forehead to mine. "Sadie, I'm sorry I doubted you. I'm sorry for all of it."

"Hush. There's nothing to be sorry for. Now that it's safe," I whisper, leading him to my bed, "let's finish what we started this morning."

Afterward, we lie together, limbs entwined beneath the sheets. I nestle against Beckett's chest, breathing in his salty skin, pleasure drunk and happy. The candles dance and play hypnotic shadows on the wall. "I want to spend every night in your arms from now on," I say. "No more of this false propriety or keeping separate rooms."

He laughs softly. "Harriet will tease us about living in sin."

"Oh, I think Harriet already knows what we've been doing."

"I've been thinking about what we talked about this morning. About this house, and Marguerite's will." Beckett grows quiet, contemplative. His hand circles low on my back, tracing the divots in my hips. "I'd like to marry you, Sadie. Make this right. If you'll have me. That way, no matter what Marguerite decides, this'll always be your home. You won't have to worry about anyone taking it from you."

"Marry you?" My heart leaps. I duck my head beneath his chin. "You're sure?"

"Yes. I am."

"Oh, Beck. You've just made me the happiest girl on earth."

We make love again, slower this time, indulging in one another. As I watch him drift off to sleep, my mind whirs with wakefulness, with his promise, with the earnest simplicity of his proposal. I don't need a flashy diamond or a big church wedding to prove to the world that someone loves me. I need only Beckett and thousands of perfect, peaceful moments just like this.

Chapter 33

October 13, 1925

The attorney looks at Marguerite over his spectacles, one eyebrow lifting. "So, if I'm to understand, you wish for your estate to go to Mr. Hill *and* Miss Halloran?"

"Yes, Mr. Bruce," Marguerite says with a crisp nod. "That's what I'd like."

"We're . . . going to be married," I say, reaching for Beckett's hand. "Probably this spring, though we haven't yet set a date."

"I see." Peter Bruce clears his throat. "Might I have a word with both of you, privately?"

We trail him into the hall, where he fixes us with a gimlet stare. "You do know I cannot redraft this will as she's requested and guarantee it will be upheld by the probate court. If she has it written in this way, it's very likely to be contested by another member of your family, especially since Beckett isn't a blood relative. I often see property held up in probate when left to someone other than a client's next of kin." He opens the folder in his hands, studies the paperwork inside. "I believe Marguerite's next of kin is Grace Cameron, your deceased mother's sister. Is that correct?"

I worry the lace on the edge of my sleeve. "Yes. But Aunt Grace already has a house—in Kansas City. A big one. She's a widow of little means and can barely maintain one home, much less two." Which means Louise, with her covetous ways, will prevail upon her mother to make Blackberry Grange *hers*. I imagine those three terrible children running roughshod over the house, Marguerite's priceless porcelain and crystal heirlooms shattered on the floor.

"I can empathize with your concerns," Mr. Bruce says, "but according to the law . . ."

"What do you suggest we do, sir?" I ask. "To ensure Marguerite's wishes are carried out?"

"I suggest the two of you marry, as soon as possible. You don't have to tell anyone but myself and Miss Thorne, but in the eyes of the law, it will solidify your claim to the estate and give your great-aunt what she wants, as the two of you will become a legal entity. Have your ceremony in the spring, if you'd like, with all your trimmings, but don't waste any time making things legal, especially given Miss Thorne's condition. Once you're married, we can redraft the will."

Beckett and I look at one another, my nerves tight beneath the surface until he smiles. "I'm as ready as I'll ever be," he says. "What do you say, Sadie?"

"Now's as good a time as ever, I suppose."

"You'll just need to go to the county clerk's office to get a license. Then the judge could marry you as soon as next week." He turns to me. "I'm sorry to hear about your mother's passing, Miss Halloran, but it's good that you contacted me once you found the will. I see families torn apart by such matters all the time. Let's do our best to make sure your aunt's wishes are honored, and you receive the inheritance you deserve."

"Thank you, Mr. Bruce."

"Of course. Make sure you call me as soon as the ink is dry on that marriage certificate."

He goes back into the library, and Beckett and I face one another. I suddenly feel as giddy as a schoolgirl. "This time next week, I'm going to be your wife."

"Yes, and I think it's for the best, Sadie. For lots of reasons. When you said you wanted a spring wedding, I was worried."

"Why?"

"Because I don't think Marguerite will last that long."

"Don't say that, Beckett. She's been feeling better lately. She's even eating again."

"Yes, but . . . I want to be sure she's at the wedding. Even if it has to be a courthouse affair."

His eyes glaze, and he looks down. I lean into him, resting my head beneath his chin, listening to the steady beat of his heart. "It's going to make her very happy, our marriage."

"It's going to make me very happy, too."

We're married the following Wednesday, inside the judge's chambers at the Carroll County courthouse, with Marguerite and Harriet our only witnesses. I wear my best dress—a gorgeous ecru crepe de chine Lanvin accented with seed pearls. The drive home is filled with laughter, my heart light and heavy all at once. I'd felt my mother's absence keenly as I took my simple vows. With some absurdity, I think of how pleased she'd be that my initials will remain the same. Sadie Frances Hill. It has a ring to it, I must admit. That evening, we celebrate over dinner by opening a dusty bottle of Veuve Clicquot Harriet found in the root cellar. Even she raises a glass to toast us, relaxing her teetotalism to celebrate our wedding. Later that night, I lead Beckett to my room, where the protective altar burns with fresh candles from the five-and-dime. My gown has hardly hit the floor before we're consummating our union, his body melding with mine, our eagerness for one another undeniable.

"My brother will be furious when he finds out what we've done," I say later, as the moon shatters silver light over us. "Even more so once he sees that will."

"Let him be mad," Beckett says, pressing a kiss to the back of my neck. "You deserve to be happy, Sadie. You're the only one who stepped up to care for Marguerite. She wanted this place to go to your mother. There must be a reason for that."

I've pondered the reasons ever since I discovered the will. In recent years, my mother and Aunt Marguerite had barely kept in touch. Though they got along well when me and my brothers were children, we rarely saw her, apart from our summertime visits and the occasional family wedding. But perhaps, like me, Mama was one of the few relatives who tried to maintain a tie with Marguerite. Grandmother certainly never went out of her way to spend time with her, nor Aunt Grace and my cousins.

After Beckett drifts off to sleep, I leave his side and go to the library. I stare at the half-finished portrait of Marguerite as a girl. In the background are two faceless figures that weren't there yesterday. I peer closer. Marguerite's brushstrokes are more erratic now, given her increasing tremors, and the shakiness of her work sets my equilibrium off-balance. The feeling of vertigo starts in my belly and spins up through my head, although when I touch the painting, the dizziness ceases abruptly, like a door slamming shut.

The other portraits remain still as well.

It frustrates me. With every passing day, and Marguerite's health fading, the chances of uncovering the secrets in her past narrow more and more.

Unable to sleep, I light an oil lamp and make my way to the attic to finish going through the steamer trunk where I found Marguerite's will. A feeling of unease prickles along my spine as I enter the darkened room, the lamp casting a spare ring of light in front of me. I whisper the prayer to Saint Michael as I kneel on the floor and open the trunk, wary of any small sound. Wary of being watched. I pull out the bundle of envelopes and untie them. The first is postmarked with a London address. I slide it open with my finger, drawing out the folded letter. It's from Iris, her bold signature slashing across the bottom of the thin onionskin paper.

April 2nd, 1881

My darling,

I am sorry to hear of your illness. The London damp has
me in a state as well—it is still wretchedly cold here most
days, though I've enjoyed my studies. Rossetti is just as
much of a recluse as rumored. Yet he deigned to entertain
me all the same, thanks to the solicitude of Miss Wilding.
His command of oils is extraordinary . . . I have pages of
notes to share with you. I'm eager to return to your side.
This California holiday will do us good—and it will be
good for you to be reconciled with your sisters as well.
We'll have a merry time, the four of us. You mustn't hold
on to the past with any sort of bitterness. I'm looking
upon your portrait now and counting the days until I
can kiss you.

Ever yours,
Iris

So, there *was* a California holiday. Iris was there, too, in 1881—the
same year Claire died. I open another envelope, this one dated January
1882, and read Iris's slanting hand.

My darling,

There is no use trying to reason with her. She will
never see your side. The three of us are bound together
forever by this terrible thing, and for your own good,
and Laura's, it's best if you try to forget. Pretend it was
all an awful dream. Come to me this spring. Neil is
eager to meet you. He knows about our great fondness
for one another and won't mind if you steal me away
for a time. I miss you dreadfully.

Iris

Just as I suspected, something must have happened on the California trip. Something terrible. But what? I remember the interlude I witnessed when I journeyed to the past through Iris's painting. The disturbing dream I had, of Marguerite on the edge of the cliff, a bloodied knife at her feet, and Claire's broken body on the rocky beach below—a beach that must have been in California, despite Marguerite's denial. Did Iris witness what happened?

The three of us are bound together forever by this terrible thing.

I open the other four letters in the packet, reading them one after another. There's no more mention of the *terrible thing*—only the same sort of recounting of events I read in the letters from my grandmother. Iris's wedding. The birth of her son. Her 1883 show at the Tate Gallery, after which she received several commissions.

I re-tie the letters and replace them, then parse through the rest of the trunk. Near the bottom, I find a small canvas turned on its face, with a lock of red-gold hair tucked beneath the bracing. I turn over the painting, my breath catching as I do. It's an unfinished portrait of my young mother in profile, her hair swept beneath a novice's white veil, a crucifix dangling from the rosary in her prayer-folded hands. Above Marguerite's signature and the date, there's a name.

Penny.

I pace the halls until the wee hours of the morning, my mind and emotions scaling up and down. I'd never known my mother entered the novitiate, intending to become a nun. No one ever spoke of it, least of all her. And why had she gone by the name Penny? Of what significance was it?

I have so many questions for Marguerite. Questions I'll no longer delay. The temptation to wake her is strong. She's at her most lucid early in the day. But I restrain myself.

I'm on my way to the powder room when a flicker of movement catches my eye. A flash of white, almost like the tail of an old-fashioned nightgown. A soft susurration follows, a whispered word. A woman's voice.

I turn to go to my and Beckett's room, suddenly afraid. But as I reach for the doorknob, a pallid form passes in front of the mirror near the staircase and gracefully descends.

Iris.

I follow, my heartbeat ratcheting higher as she turns toward the library. The air is frigid in Iris's wake and scented faintly with verbena. Inside the library, she points to her portrait, her eyes filled with sadness. My anxiety climbs as I touch the surface and find it pliable as water. I pull in a deep breath. "Show me, Iris. Show me everything."

Interlude

Iris

The room is completely white. Sterile. Gauzy curtains blow softly in the open window. At first Sadie thinks she's back in the California house. But she's not. This is a dormitory. Or a hospital ward, much like her room at Elm Ridge. She turns to see Marguerite seated on a cot, reading from a book, her skin unnaturally pale. She lifts her head, looks directly at Sadie, and smiles. "You've finally come," she says, her voice musical.

"I have." At first, Sadie thinks Marguerite has seen her, but it's Florence who speaks. Sadie whirls to see her grandmother, dressed in striped summer poplin, a wide-brimmed hat perched on her blond curls. "Stand up, sister, so I can have a proper look at you." Marguerite stands, her nightgown fluttering to the floor. Her belly arches out from her slender body, convex. Unmistakably pregnant.

"It won't be very long now." Florence crosses to Marguerite, places a hand on her belly, her wedding ring glinting in the light. "James has the nursery ready."

"I'm afraid, Flor," Marguerite says. "Will it hurt?"

"Yes. But our bodies are made to do it. And the pain stops once the baby comes." Florence sits on the cot, drawing Marguerite down with her. The hem of Marguerite's nightgown lifts, exposing painfully swollen ankles. "Next year, this will all seem like a dream. I've already spoken to Papa. He's willing to send you to Europe for your grand holiday."

"Really?"

"Yes." Florence strokes the side of Marguerite's face. "You'll be able to see all the places you've dreamed of going. Work on your art."

Marguerite takes Florence's hand. "You'll let me see her, won't you?"

"Of course I will. As often as you'd like. But remember—you must promise to never tell her the truth, darling. She needs to believe she was always mine. Do you understand why that's important?"

"I . . . I think so."

"Good girl." Florence presses a kiss to Marguerite's cheek. "I'd better go, for now. But I'm staying here, in town, until your time comes. I'll visit you again tomorrow." She moves toward the door, bustled skirts swishing in her wake.

"Is James here? With you?" Marguerite asks. "If so, I'd like to see him."

"No, I came alone this time."

Marguerite's eyes narrow. "Is *he* here, then? Is that why you're rushing off?"

A shadow falls over Florence's face. "That isn't your concern."

"It *is*, Florence. If I'm to give you my child, I want to make sure she grows up in a happy home. Where is Gracie?"

"With our nurse."

"In Kansas City?"

"Yes."

"I see. And does James suspect anything?"

Florence sighs, her hand clutching her parasol handle. "If he does, he's never said as much. I know James. He won't."

"Tell me the truth, Flor. Is Gracie James's, or Weston's?"

Florence whirls to face Marguerite, her face suddenly livid. "How dare you ask me that?"

"You don't know, do you? You're lucky she resembles you," Marguerite says, smirking. "Lucky you can't have another child."

"*Lucky?* I should hit you for that, Marg."

"Do it." Marguerite stands, tears pricking at the corners of her eyes. "You've already destroyed my life. Taken Hugh from me. All out of spite."

"You can't see it now, but I've protected you. From dishonor. From a life lived in some shameful tenement or a shanty. Hugh couldn't have given you the sort of life you want." Florence is shaking now, her barely contained rage near the surface. "He only wanted to take what he could get. And you were so willing to give it."

"I think you're talking about Weston now, not Hugh. Isn't he taking what *he* can get? From you? It disgusts me to see him stringing Claire along. Making promises he has no intentions of keeping. You're selfish, Flor. Hateful. Someday you'll reap what you've sown."

Florence's arm snakes out, the resounding slap on Marguerite's skin like a thunderclap. Sadie covers her mouth, shock and anger and betrayal flowing through her as the truth settles into her marrow.

Marguerite slumps onto her cot, presses her palm to the handprint seared on her face.

"You are still such a child," Florence says, seething. "You don't have any idea how the world works. I should have let you run away with him. Let you see your folly, on some godforsaken trail out West. I've saved your *life*, Marguerite." She spares a final glance at her youngest sister, then flounces out of the room, letting the door slam behind her.

Marguerite bursts into tears, sobbing so hard her shoulders shake. Iris comes in a few moments later, dressed in a white gown, reed thin with hollow, young eyes. She goes to Marguerite and gathers her in her arms.

"I . . . don't want to give her up," Marguerite wails, her hand clutching her belly. "I can't."

"I know, darling. But we must think of what's best."

"I'm what's best for this baby! *I* am, Iris. I can do this!"

"How? Without a husband? Without your family's help? You know as well as I do that your papa will stop sending you money eventually." Iris knits her fingers with Marguerite's. "At least she'll be with family. Your sister. You'll be able to see her grow up."

"You don't know Florence. She's wretched. She lies about everything." Marguerite stands, goes to her dresser, removing folded clothes. "I'm leaving tonight. After Nurse makes her rounds."

"And you'll go where?" Iris stands, incredulous. "Marguerite, think! Do you plan on having this baby in a hotel room? By the side of the road? I've been through it, remember? It can be dangerous. The cord was tangled around Victor's neck when he was born. If the doctor hadn't been there . . . he might have died."

"I'll figure it out. I'll find Hugh. We'll go to a doctor. Or find a midwife."

"How?"

"I . . . I don't know. But I'll find Hugh. I will."

"And what if you do? Your father accused him of rape. Do you think his family will open their arms to you, after what they've gone through? I know the Irish. They're a proud, stubborn people."

"Then we'll run aw—" Marguerite suddenly stills. She clutches her head, wincing. "Something's wrong." She staggers to the bed, a grimace of pain shooting over her face. "Oh God, my head . . ."

"I'll get the nurse." Iris runs from the room.

The scene shifts. Marguerite lies on a gurney, nurses surrounding her. Florence is there, too, in the same poplin dress, clutching Marguerite's hand as she strains and cries out, her hair dark with sweat.

"We have to get this baby out," the bald doctor says to one of the nurses. "She's in eclamptic distress. Mrs. Knight, you'll need to leave the room."

"But I . . . ," Florence protests. "I can't."

"We'll call for you soon, ma'am." One of the nurses guides her from Marguerite's side. "It won't be long."

Once Florence is out of sight, a nurse climbs atop Marguerite, pressing both of her hands on Marguerite's stomach. "When you feel the pains come again, push with all you've got, love."

"I want my baby," Marguerite says, panting. "Please don't let them take her."

"Now, now. Enough of that."

The contraction comes. Marguerite pushes, and the nurse atop her pushes, too.

"There, that's it!" the doctor exclaims. "One more push should do it."

Marguerite collapses back against the pillows, weak, frightened. She turns her head and looks at Sadie. This time, Marguerite sees *her*. Truly sees her. "Who?" Marguerite whispers. "Who is that, in the room?"

"What, dear?" The nurse looks over her shoulder at Marguerite, giving a quizzical look.

"That woman. In the corner. Who is she?"

"There's no one there. She's hallucinating," the doctor says, his voice rising. "We need to get this baby out, nurse. Give it all you've got this time."

Marguerite squeezes her eyes shut as the next contraction sets in, a throttled scream escaping her throat as she bears down. The nurse presses hard on her belly, elbows locked.

"Aha!" the doctor exclaims. A thin, reedy cry floats over the din, the excitement in the room palpable as the doctor raises the baby up where Marguerite can see. "A girl. You've done well, Miss Thorne. You've done well."

Marguerite raises herself onto her elbows, her eyes lividly green against her pale face. "Let me have her. Please."

The nurse clambers off the cot, takes the baby from the doctor, and swaddles her as he clamps and cuts the cord. The baby is red-faced and angry, her bright copper hair contrasting with the linen sheath they've wrapped her in.

Sadie is crying, watching her own mother come into this world, watching her take her first, greedy gulps of air, all the puzzle pieces of the past slotting together in this singular, shocking moment.

"You're bright as a fresh-minted penny!" Marguerite exclaims, clucking her tongue at the little girl, who soon quiets in her mother's arms, puckering her lips. On instinct, Marguerite opens her gown, brings the babe to her breast. The nurses and the doctor are too distracted to notice, busy as they are with delivering the afterbirth.

And then suddenly, as if time has sped up, the room goes quiet. It is nighttime. Only a single nurse keeps vigil, the room lit dimly with oil lamps.

Florence and Weston enter. Sadie startles at the sight of him, her fear and her dread as one, but he doesn't seem to notice her, not in this timeline. She's as invisible to him as she is to Florence.

"Why is he here?" Marguerite growls. She holds the baby closer.

"It's nighttime. I needed an escort."

"Well, you shouldn't have come. You can't have her. I've changed my mind."

"Marg, please," Florence entreats, extending a hand to Marguerite. "It will only be harder, the longer you wait."

The nurse rises from her chair, clears her throat, her dark eyes creased with care as she goes to Marguerite's bed. "Miss, if you'll give her to me now, I'll take care of the rest."

"Get away from me." Marguerite's eyes go wild. The baby cries, softly, in her sleep.

"Now, don't make this more difficult than needs be." The nurse's voice grows stern. "We've given you long enough with her." She reaches for Laura—for Penny—and Marguerite strikes her. The nurse steps back in shock.

"I'll claw your eyes out if you come any closer," Marguerite threatens, baring her teeth.

"You signed the papers months ago, Marguerite," Florence says, her voice wavering. "You can't change your mind."

"Can't I?" Marguerite swings her legs over the side of the bed and stands. Weston and the nurse surge forward. Everything happens so quickly. The baby wakes, cries. Weston swears, and the nurse gives a frantic shout as Marguerite thrashes like a wildcat. An orderly rushes into the room, wrestles Marguerite to the gurney, holds her down as the nurse transfers the baby into Florence's arms.

Marguerite screams her baby's name, then a string of curses as the nurse hurriedly ushers Florence and Weston from the room. The scene fades, grays out around the edges, and Sadie finds herself standing in the library with the morning sun flaming white through the windows.

Chapter 34

I sit by myself for a long time that morning, thinking over everything I witnessed. I have no reason to doubt the truth of what Iris showed me—that Marguerite is my grandmother by birth. It's no wonder that she took the news of Mama's death so hard. After my tears are spent and I've considered the words I want to say, I wipe my eyes and go to Marguerite. Harriet looks up from her knitting as I enter the library, which has become our favorite room as fall's chill sets in. I ask Harriet to leave us, and she does so graciously, eyeing the items cradled in my hands. I pull a chair next to Marguerite at her easel and sit, but her concentration never wavers. Her brush makes smooth, delicate swirls through the paint. Even though her hand often trembles when lifting her fork or a teacup, the tremors seem to dissipate when she paints. The self-portrait is nearly done, Marguerite's young features fully formed. The figures in the background have taken on more presence as well— two girls dressed in summer muslin, one blond, the other redheaded. Though their features are still vague, I know it's Florence and Claire.

"Aunt Marg," I say softly, "I was hoping we could talk. How are you feeling today?"

"Oh, hello, dear. I'm well enough, I suppose."

"You're almost finished." I gesture to the painting. "Tell me what's happening here, in this moment."

Marguerite smiles. "The beginning of everything," she says cryptically.

"Everything?"

"Yes. I remember that day *so* well."

"I found something you were looking for." I lift the unfinished portrait of my mother from my lap and show it to her, along with the lock of red-gold hair.

Her hands fly to her face. "Penny."

"I never knew Mama wanted to be a nun," I say.

Realization slowly dawns on Marguerite's face. "You know."

"Yes. You never had tuberculosis, did you?"

She shakes her head, a single tear tracing a path down her cheek. I reach for Marguerite's hand, my own emotions still near the surface, ready to break free at any moment. "Why don't you tell me everything. I think it's time. Florence is gone now. So is Mama. I'm ready to listen—to help ease some of your burden."

Marguerite's lip trembles. "How much do you know?"

"Not everything, but enough. And I'm so very sorry that things happened the way they did."

Marguerite traces my mother's painted profile with a slender finger. "She had Hugh's nose and his chin, but my eyes—the Thorne eyes. You have them, too. And to answer your question, she didn't want to be a nun. She only became a postulant to get away from Florence. From home. That's why I talked her out of taking her final vows."

It's a revelation, hearing her speak the truth aloud, one that shakes me to my foundation. Even though I saw my mother's birth in the scene Iris showed me, a part of me had still wondered whether it was an invention of my mind. A strange dream. Now there can be no doubt. A tear escapes my eye. I wipe it away, determined not to succumb to my emotions.

"When your aunt Grace was born, Florence nearly died. She hemorrhaged and had to have a hysterectomy. She'd always wanted more children . . . always wanted to be a mother. When I became pregnant, she saw the opportunity. When I refused to marry the men she threw at me, early in my pregnancy, she told Papa about me and Hugh. Our plans to run away. She claims she did it to protect me—couched it as if taking Laura off my hands was a blessing. A favor. And in some ways, it was." Marguerite gestures toward her paintings. "After all, if I'd run away with him and kept the baby, I wouldn't have had the opportunities I had. To travel. To study." She pats her heart. "But there was always an emptiness here. I loved her so very, very much. More than I thought I ever could love someone."

"Did Grandmother let you see her?"

"No. Not really. Only on holidays and the like. I'd get the occasional picture, with Florence's letters. Laura started writing to me in her teenage years. I became her confidante. It was wrong of me, of course. She had a mother. But I longed for anything I might have of her. Once she went to the convent, I visited her as much as her Mother Superior would allow. Which wasn't often . . . but all the same, I was glad for any opportunity to see her." Marguerite smiles. "When she left the Sisters and took up with Duke shortly after, Florence was furious. Cut her off. I started sending Laura money. I helped them out a lot, over the years."

"Did Mama ever know the truth?"

Marguerite sighs. "I never told her. I promised Florence I wouldn't. Besides, what good would have come of her knowing? I had carried her in my body, and then I carried her in my heart. Even though it wasn't enough, I knew keeping the secret was for the best. And I *enjoyed* being the doting aunt. Florence had taken her from me, and yes, I was bitter. Angry. But I refused to make Laura—Penny—suffer for it."

I squeeze Marguerite's hand. "You loved her more than you loved yourself. And that's noble of you, Aunt Marg. Selfless."

"Perhaps." Marguerite shakes her head. "But if I had it all to do over again, I'd never have signed those papers. I'd have found a way to keep her. I regret it to this day."

We sit in silence for a while, contemplating what might have been, the portrait of Penny perched in front of Hugh's likeness. I can see the resemblance clearly now, with them side by side. Can see it in myself. I have my grandfather's bronze-blond hair. The dimple in his left cheek. Possibilities crowd my mind. If Marguerite and Hugh had run away together and gotten married, would my mother have grown up in some Colorado mining town? Or in Ireland? Would Mama and Da have ever met? Would my brothers and I have existed at all? It's a lot to ponder. To consider. Not that any of these conjectures, these theories of fate and chance, truly matter. Because here we are now, in this moment, bound by common blood and choices made. And while I have some of the answers to my questions about Marguerite's past, a knot of dread remains lodged in my gut. There are still missing pieces, concerning Marguerite and her sisters and something terrible that happened on a holiday by the sea two years after my mother was born.

The next day, Peter Bruce comes with two witnesses, a stenographer, and a notary. Marguerite's state of mind is keen and her hand steady as she signs her name to the documents. The will is duplicated, signed by both witnesses, notarized, and sealed. I place my and Beckett's copy safely inside my dresser, beneath my underthings.

The telephone rings not half an hour after Mr. Bruce and his entourage depart. "Hello?" I answer, out of breath from my jog down the stairs.

"Sadie! It's Felix."

My stomach drops. It's as if he has a sixth sense.

"How's Florida?" I ask, my mouth gone dry.

"Oh, it's grand! You should see Rosalie's suntan. She's always in our swimming pool."

"How nice. How are the boys?"

"Good, good. Say, have you had any luck finding Aunt Marg's will? Rosalie said you never answered her letter."

Dammit. I lean my forehead against the wall, squeezing my eyes shut. "There's a will, yes."

"Well, what does it say?"

"Listen, Felix, I can't talk right now. Dinner's on. I need to see to it."

"Sadie, come on. It's only two o'clock there and you don't cook. What are you hiding?" His voice grows stern. "What does the will say?"

My mind grasps, grapples for what I might tell him, but lying won't change anything, and better he find out now, from afar, than in person. I pull in a shaky breath. "First of all, before you get angry with me, as I know you surely will, you need to know we've thought everything through very carefully."

"What are you talking about? Who is *we?*"

"Marguerite, Beckett, and I."

"Beckett? The chauffeur?" He barks a laugh. "What does he have to do with anything?"

"He's my husband now," I say. "Beckett and I got married. This week."

The line goes deathly quiet.

"I know you're upset with me. But this is my life to live, Felix. This is my home now, here with Marguerite and Beck."

He sighs. "You've always been impulsive. But this . . . this astounds me, Sadie. Marrying the help. What would Mother think? Grandmother?"

"Mama would like him. I know she would. And I don't give a whit what Grandmother would think."

"Very well. If you're determined to make a wreck of your life, that's your choice. Seeing as you're a married woman now, you'll no longer need an allowance. This month's check will be the last."

"You can't do that. Da intended that money for me."

"Until you married. That's what his will said. That your monthly stipend will continue until the termination of your life or until you marry, whichever occurs first, at which point it reverts to me. Now.

What does Marguerite's will say? Specifically, please. And if you think to deceive me, know that I have ways of going above your head."

Felix's voice has grown cold. Clipped and mechanical.

"She wanted everything to go to Mama. The house. Her accounts. All of it. Down to the silverware."

"I see. How unusual. Seeing as Mother's dead, we'll need to get the will redrafted with a proxy to speak on Marguerite's behalf; otherwise Aunt Grace is next in the line of consanguinity and stands to inherit everything if Marguerite dies intestate."

I won't tell him the truth about our lineage unless I'm forced to, but I must tell him the rest. I press my lips together and say a silent prayer for strength. "Aunt Marg . . . already had the will redrafted. She made her wishes very clear. She wants me to have the house. Me and Beckett, together."

Felix laughs. He laughs so loudly and heartily that I nearly drop the phone. "She's in no state of mind to declare her wishes. She's incompetent. Did you coerce her? You must have. You do realize if a will is written under duress, it's not legally binding."

"There was no coercion. Her attorney reassured us it was all upstanding and legal, Felix."

"Well. We'll see about that, won't we? What absolute and utter bull, Sadie."

My anger flares then, boiling my guts. "When Mama died, you took *everything*. Both houses. Rosalie flaunts Mama's jewelry. I only got one strand of pearls and a check for fifteen dollars a month. You are despicable, Felix. You ought to be ashamed of yourself. I used to think you were a good person. What happened?"

The line goes silent, and I realize he's hung up on me. I replace the receiver, my hands shaking. I think of the time Felix wanted the handsome Gladiator bicycle our cousin Beau had received from Marguerite at Christmastime. Felix claimed she'd intended it for him, since Beau favored riding horses, not cycles. He'd argued that the Hermès saddle he'd received was meant for Beau, and Aunt Marg had accidentally tagged them wrong in the shipment. His argument was so firm, so solid, that the adults caved to his charming manipulations. He'd won the bicycle and taken it out for a ride after Christmas dinner, leaving Beau in tears, the saddle in his lap. Beau had half a dozen saddles already, a point I'd argued to no avail, because Felix always got what he wanted. He was the golden child. And just like Beau's bicycle, if he wanted Blackberry Grange badly enough, he'd find a way to take it from me.

In speaking my mind, in asserting myself, I've shaken our already fragile bond and made an enemy.

Chapter 35

October 27, 1925

I hear nothing further from my brother after our phone call, although I expect some sort of threatening legal letter to arrive any day now, demanding my cooperation in his attempt to seize Marguerite's estate. Instead, things remain deceptively peaceful as autumn fades slowly toward winter. I've made three attempts to reenter Iris's world since the night I discovered the truth of my mother's birth, to no avail. It's as if she's withholding the rest of the story. But why? Almost everyone who might be affected by what happened back then has passed away. It makes no sense.

I take a drink of coffee and stand looking at the morning fog through the library windows as Marguerite paints, the blaze of maples in the distance bright against the gray.

Beckett emerges from the dim, hauling a wheelbarrow to collect the fallen hedge apples from the lawn. He's had a surge of industriousness before winter. Since my return, he's built a handsome split-rail fence along the edge of the bluff, which has greatly improved everyone's peace of mind and done little to sully Marguerite's view of the valley below. Our marriage isn't at all what I expected when I was a girl, but I fall more in love with him every day. His quiet steadiness grounds me, keeps me tethered to reality.

"Mrs. Hill?" Harriet says after clearing her throat. "May I speak with you?"

"Certainly." I follow her down the hall, concerned by the expression on her face. She leads me to the sofa in the parlor, and we sit side by side. "Is something the matter?"

She shakes her head. "No, ma'am." Her hand flits lightly to her stomach. "It's just that . . . I need to let you know I'm in the family way."

I've noticed the booties she's been knitting, but I assumed they were for a friend's or a relative's baby. "Well, that's wonderful news, Harriet!"

When Harriet doesn't return my smile, I know. Dread rolls through me. "You're not leaving us, are you?"

"I . . . I can't. I can't afford to. But my midwife wants me off my feet. My last pregnancy was a difficult one. I went into labor too early, and the baby . . . she didn't survive."

"I'm so sorry."

"Thank you." Harriet drops her head. "This one was a surprise."

"Well, you must think of your health and the baby's. Let me talk to Beckett and Marguerite. See if we can afford to pay you to take a leave. You can come back after the baby is born. Whenever you're ready."

"You'd do that?"

"Of course we would."

She pulls in a dignified breath before continuing. "I'll just take a couple weeks off, after the baby comes, then return to work as soon as I can. I just worry Miss Thorne won't be with us by then."

We share a long look in the space between words because she's probably right.

"You already know how to do everything for her, but I'll still call to check in on you from time to time. My neighbor has a telephone she lets me use. I'll give you her name, in case you need to call me."

"That's very kind of you, Harriet."

"Well. Miss Thorne has been very kind to me. So have you. That's not often the case with white folk."

I squeeze her hand. "You'll always have a place here with us."

Even though Harriet's departure comes with more warning than Melva's, and Harriet has schooled me well in caring for Marguerite, my mind swirls with anxiety. I think about my long days, and how they'll soon be even longer. The overwhelm I already feel crests like a gigantic wave, threatening to crash over me and pull me under.

I wait until Harriet returns to her duties, then go to the powder room on the first floor and sob into a towel to muffle the sound. I think of how much I wanted this house to be mine. My inheritance. But now . . . the monstrous responsibility of it all threatens to consume me. We've had no luck finding help after Melva's departure, and I don't have high hopes for Harriet's return—despite her best intentions. With three children underfoot, she'll have her hands full at home.

I pull myself together and pat my face with a cool washcloth to soothe the blotchy redness from my cheeks. I run into Beckett on my way to the kitchen. He reads my face immediately. "What's wrong?"

"Harriet is expecting. She needs to take a leave of absence. I don't know how we'll manage without her, but I wonder if we might pay her while she's away, to help ease her burden."

"Of course." Beckett pulls me close. "It's nearly winter. I won't have to do as much work on the grounds. I'll be able to help more with Marguerite. We'll get through this, darling."

Beckett always brings me back down to earth, when my anxieties threaten to send me into a tailspin. He pulls away from me, a mischievous grin playing on his lips. "I need to burn some brush. I could build a fire, in the stone cottage. Why don't you find a reason to slip away? Make the most of the time we have left with Harriet here."

"I think I could manage that."

He kisses me, nuzzling my neck with his nose. "Don't keep me waiting too long."

I bring tea to the library and tell Harriet I'm helping Beckett with his work, ignoring her sly smile and arched brow, then make my way to the cozy stone cottage. Beckett is waiting for me next to the crackling fire, the bed turned down in anticipation. As the day rolls on toward afternoon, the patter of soft rain against the shingles makes for a pleasing accompaniment to our leisurely lovemaking.

After, I curl against Beckett's chest, contemplative. "Do you think *we* should have a baby, Beck?"

"Only if you want," he says, kissing the top of my head. "We can be more careful, if not."

I think of my grandmother, Marguerite, and Harriet—all of whom had difficult pregnancies and deliveries. But my own mother didn't. My brothers and I were born without complication. While a part of me is terrified of being pregnant and then bringing a child into this world, with all its horrors and troubles, I consider how wonderful it would feel to see my and Beckett's love reflected in our child's eyes. I imagine the unique blend of our features. Our personalities.

"I don't want to be careful," I say, lacing my fingers with his. "I think we should let fate take its course. I'll be happy, and settled, either way."

"Even if our baby is born like me?" he asks, a tinge of sadness in his tone. "It could happen."

"And it might not." I turn to him. "But if it does, we'll make sure he or she has all the help and care we can afford. We'll cope. Besides, do you think your mother regretted your birth for one second?"

"No," he answers. "She always reassured me of that."

"Then I'm willing to take the chance if you are." I run my fingers through his thick chestnut waves. "I know one thing . . . our baby had better get your glorious hair and eyes."

Later, we return to the house, hand in hand. Harriet greets us at the door, her eyes tired. "Marguerite is in some sort of state all of a sudden. I can't get her to respond to me."

"What happened?"

"She finished that painting, then seemed to slip into some sort of trance."

"The self-portrait?"

"Yes."

I rush to the library, Beckett behind me.

I find Marguerite sitting in the chair in front of her easel, her lips moving soundlessly, eyes glazed over.

"She's just asleep," I say, pulling a chair next to hers. I have a feeling I know what's happened. What she's done. The self-portrait is finished now. It's another portal into the past. One *she's* walked through this time. Her sisters stand in the background, their faces fully rendered. I see Claire blink, see Florence's hem ripple in the wind. The familiar vertigo washes over me. "She's dreaming and we don't want to wake her by force. Leave me with her. I'll watch over her until she wakes. Beck, close the doors when you leave."

"Sadie . . ." Beckett gives me a concerned look. "Are you sure you're all right? You've gone pale as a ghost."

"I'll be fine. Please. Just trust me."

He squeezes my shoulder, and he and Harriet depart. "Show me what you're seeing, Aunt Marg," I say, after the library doors close. I take Marguerite's limp hand in mine, reach toward the painting with the other, and pull in a steadying breath as the past opens to me once more.

Interlude

THREE SISTERS

Florence is reading, sitting in the swing beneath the maple tree, her dress blowing gently in the breeze as she thumbs through the pages of *Wuthering Heights*. She sighs dramatically, studying her younger sisters. Claire watches Marguerite sketch, her fingers clenched around a nub of pencil.

"What are you drawing?" Florence asks.

"You," Marguerite says. She turns over her tablet, shows Florence the sketch.

"You've made my nose too big."

"No, I haven't," Marguerite says. "That's how it looks."

"I have an idea," Florence says, standing. The swing knocks against the back of her thighs. "I want you to draw me a picture. One to go with the story I'm writing. I want you to draw the Baron de Havilland."

"Baron de Havilland. What a name." Marguerite sighs, rolling her eyes. "What does he look like?"

Florence smiles. "He's wickedly handsome, of course. Tall, with dark hair, the edges touched with auburn. Storm-colored eyes. An insouciant smile. He's a rake. Secretly."

"I've read her story," Claire says. "It's tawdry and shameless. You'd better hope Papa never sees it, Flor."

"And you'd better not tell him, either one of you, or I'll have your hides."

"I don't know how to draw someone who isn't real," Marguerite says. "Why don't *you* draw him?"

"Because I can't. You're the artist. I'm the writer." Florence glances at Claire. "And Claire is just *Claire*."

Claire pouts and turns her head, the hurt skating across her pretty-plain face, so much like Sadie's at the same age.

"You'd better let me read this story of yours, then, if I'm to draw him well," Marguerite says. "He might look any sort of way, otherwise."

"I can't show you."

Marguerite sighs. "Claire's seen it."

"She's not as judgmental as you are."

Marguerite laughs. "She is, she just doesn't say things out loud like I do."

"Use your imagination, Marg. I'll give you all my penny candy if you do this for me."

"Fine, but you'd better give me the candy first."

The scene shifts, morphs. Marguerite sits before an easel, painting, covering the original pencil lines of a sketch with careful brushstrokes. Sadie recognizes the subject instantly. It's Weston, his dark features unmistakable on the canvas. There's a knock at the door, and Florence enters.

"Oh, Marg," she exclaims, "he's just as I imagined. You have such a gift."

Marguerite smiles. "Do you really think so?"

"Yes. If you finish it for my birthday, it will make me so happy."

"That's just five days away . . ."

"You can do it. I know you can. It'll make the perfect gift." Florence comes nearer, her lips softly parted. "Goodness, he looks like a real person—like you've captured him from life."

Marguerite frowns. "I'm not sure I like him. He looks dangerous. Like a scoundrel."

"And dashing and remarkable. Just as I wrote him." Florence's eyes close, her hand trailing over her collarbone, the color flowering on her cheeks.

"James would be jealous, if he could see you right now, all moony over an imaginary man."

"Don't be silly."

"What happens, in your story, Florence?"

"Oh, it's a tragic romance. Just like *Wuthering Heights*."

"And he's your hero?"

"Yes," Florence says. "And the villain, all at once. I'll give you one of my Meissen figurines, as payment, once you're finished. Consider it your first commission."

"Oh!" Marguerite's eyes light up. "The pink dancer, with the fan?"

"Yes. If that's the one you want."

Marguerite cleans her brush on her smock, then dips it in lampblack. "All right, then. I'll do my best to finish it before your party. Now, leave me alone. Let me work."

Sadie watches young Marguerite paint as the scene slowly fades from view, and an uncomfortable understanding breaks over her. She remembers the scene she witnessed at Florence's coming-out party. The same night Florence and Weston met, in that other time and place. Had it all begun because of this painting?

Was Weston ever a real person? Or did Marguerite's painting and Florence's words bring a figment of imagination to life?

Chapter 36

October 31, 1925

I discover Weston's portrait by accident. Beckett and I are in the old barn, making cider with the ancient press, when I see a bit of purple velvet peeking out from behind a stack of baled hay. I do my best to ignore it, handing him apples as he works the press, forearms straining below his rolled sleeves. We've begun to ready ourselves for Harriet's departure, finishing the last of the outdoor tasks before winter's sharp lash descends.

When Beckett goes to fetch more cider pails, I ease the painting from its hiding place. Ever since the last scene I witnessed with Marguerite and her sisters, my questions have multiplied. Louise always claimed our grandmother was a witch—that she'd seen her doing strange things, late at night. After the events of the past few months, I'd almost believe it. Marguerite's words from a few weeks ago haunt me. *My sister . . . didn't understand what she did. What she called forth. What she made me a party to.* Is Weston the ghost of a man who once lived? Or some sort of demonic entity my grandmother summoned in the guise of a man?

I uncover the painting. Weston's deep-set eyes greet me, his expression mocking mine. The old, uncomfortable desire blooms low in my belly, and I quickly cover the portrait with the velvet drape, replacing it behind the hay bale just as my husband returns.

"What's wrong?" he asks. "You look upset."

"Oh, it's nothing. I only thought I saw a rat. It startled me." I'm not sure why I lie. I should tell him I've found the portrait, so that he might hide it somewhere else before my irrepressible curiosity gets the best of me. The temptation is still there—to abandon my senses and return to Weston's world and all its dangerous charms. Whether my grandmother invented or conjured him, his allure is potent. Seductive.

Beckett hums beneath his breath, interrupting my thoughts. "I'll get some traps the next time we go to town. We don't want them burrowing in the hay and making nests."

"What?"

"The rats. We don't want them nesting in the hay."

"Yes, you're right. A good idea."

I return to his side, my pulse thudding in my ears. We resume our work, but my mind is distracted, the pull toward Weston's portrait unmistakable. I touch my neck, where my Saint Michael's medal usually rests. It's gone. I search frantically, pawing at the hay-strewn floor with my feet.

"What's gotten into you, Sadie?" Beckett frowns.

"I lost my necklace. My Saint Michael medal."

"I'm sure it will turn up."

But it doesn't. I can't find it anywhere. And that night, when I go to our room, the ever-burning candles on my protective altar are out. I relight them, speak the protective prayer aloud, and turn in, exhausted from my day of chores.

I wake sometime later, to the feel of my husband's caress, his hand trailing up my thigh and across my belly, his fingers teasing me. I sigh as his tongue flicks against my neck, as he cups my breasts. I roll over, offering myself to him fully. But when I open my eyes, Beckett isn't there. No one is there. The room is pitch black, the altar's candles extinguished once more.

I scream and hurtle myself from the bed, fear bristling beneath my skin.

The door creaks open, letting in a cone of yellow light. Beckett squints at me. "Sadie?"

"Don't . . . come in," I say. "He's here."

"Who?"

"Weston."

Just then, the candles fly from the dresser as if thrown, one after the other. I chant the Saint Michael prayer. The lights flicker on and off, the bed shaking like a child's plaything. Then everything stills.

Beckett rushes to me, taking me in his arms. "It's all right. You're all right."

I sink down on the bed next to him, trembling. I think of what might have happened, had I not come to my senses. Weston might have ravished my all-too-willing body. Or killed me. Helplessness floods my limbs. I was foolish to think I was safe. That we were safe. It will take more than white candles and incantations to protect us.

Beckett and I go to the kitchen, where he makes a mug of warm chocolate for me. Marguerite shuffles in a few minutes later, no doubt roused by the noise. After I've calmed down, Beckett presses a kiss to the top of my head. "I'm going up to bed," he says. "I'll make sure the candles stay lit in our room."

After Beckett leaves, Marguerite leans toward me across the table. "He was here again, wasn't he?" she asks. "Weston."

"Yes. I found his portrait in the barn, where Beckett hid it. I think I stirred things up again by looking at it."

"I told you he wouldn't let you go. He's angry. Angry that he can't have what he wants anymore. He wants to keep you captivated, just as he did Florence."

"What is he, Aunt Marg?"

She smiles sadly. "My invention. Mine and Florence's. She wrote the story. I painted him. Made a graven image for her to worship, like a god. One that should never have existed."

"Your . . . invention."

"You saw us there, in the past—I know you did. I could feel you there, watching me paint." Marguerite shakes her head. "I had to paint my way back to the beginning, to remember everything. Now I know what I must do to make things right. To protect you."

"What do you mean?"

"I have to return to that day, a week before Florence's eighteenth birthday, and unmake the past. Unmake Weston."

"Is that possible? Even if you could somehow undo your part in his existence, if Florence wrote the story, created the original idea of him, how can you unmake him all on your own?"

Marguerite sighs. "I'm not sure. But if I don't try, you'll always be in danger. Just like Sybil. Just like Claire."

"Claire?" I ask.

"Yes, Claire. She fell into his orbit as well, child."

"She didn't die of measles, did she?"

"No." Marguerite squeezes her eyes shut. "That's the other secret I promised my family I would keep. But you need to know the truth. Claire killed herself because of Weston. Jumped from a cliff in California when we were on holiday. I tried to save her. I couldn't."

I remember Iris's letter, the lines about the "terrible thing" that had happened in California, and the vision of the woman's body broken on the rocky beach, the bloodied knife in Marguerite's hand. An uncomfortable sensation claws at my mind. Something is still missing. Claire didn't seem suicidal at all when I saw the three of them together in California. If anything, Florence was the one who seemed at risk of doing something rash and impulsive. "And you're certain Weston wasn't a real person? Only an invention?"

"He *seemed* real enough, at first. After Florence's coming-out party, he ingratiated himself with our family, my father. He was our houseguest for months. Lived in our garret. He claimed to be a writer from Connecticut. But something seemed off about him—about his mannerisms. He was amused by conflict. Enjoyed evoking quiet chaos between my sisters and I. Florence wrote him that way, you see. He was always plotting and scheming in that wretched story of hers. Kidnapping ladies. Coercing them into bed. She wrote a devil into life."

"And what about you, Aunt Marg? Did you ever fall under his spell?"

"No," she says, with an adamant shake of her head. "Never. I knew he was mine and Florence's creature, and I knew him for the evil he was. Claire never believed me about the painting. I tried to tell her what he was and what he was capable of. But Claire chose to see the best in people. That was her temperament." Marguerite's eyes drop. "As for Florence, she thought he was the love of her life, because he was just like her. A reflection of the worst aspects of her personality. Florence always loved herself more than anyone else, and Weston was an extension of that love. He encouraged her vanity and selfishness. If it hadn't been for Weston's influence, Florence wouldn't have done all the things she did to me. To Claire. To Hugh."

I drink my chocolate, contemplating Marguerite's words before saying, "When I've visited the past through your paintings, I'm unable to influence anything. I'm only a bystander—a watcher. How can you be sure you can change anything? Influence what's already happened in the past?"

"It makes sense, don't you see? You didn't create the paintings. Your actions didn't bring about what happened in the past. *Mine* did. So I can very much influence the outcome. I can repaint my memories from the past, make them reflect a new reality. The right one. The just one."

"How did the paintings come to be this way? How did they become portals into the past, your memories?"

"I'm not sure. But everything shifted after Weston came along. I can't explain it. I wish I could. Sometimes I think I sold my soul for a handful of penny candy—as if some unseen devil heard Florence's wish and granted it, using my talents as a vehicle for evil."

"Louise told me Grandmother was a witch. Was she?"

Marguerite shrugs. "Oh, she dabbled in things. Girlish magic. Love spells and séances in our rooms. With Weston, she might have stumbled on something beyond her scope of understanding. It's possible."

"None of it makes any sense. It seems to defy logic," I say. "But the granny woman I met told me that the only one who can break Weston's hold over us is the one who wronged him and created the curse. I don't know how you can do that alone, since Grandmother was just as culpable."

"You're right. I don't know if I can do it," Marguerite says, her jaw firm. "But I have to at least try. Righting these wrongs is the only thing that will bring me peace before I die. And it's the only way you'll be safe."

⤚✣⤙

Early in the morning, Beckett and I move Marguerite's portraits back to the glass tower, where she insists on working in private. A gentle, soft rain patters on the roof as we arrange the easels side by side. Christine. Iris. Hugh. Marguerite. And finally, Weston's portrait. If Marguerite is successful, his image will cease to exist in this world, taking his vindictive and vengeful spirit with it.

Despite my concerns for her safety and my pleas to accompany Marguerite on her journey into the past, she refuses me. "This is something I must do on my own, Sadie. Your presence might upset the balance—influence me to do something that could jeopardize the future. I must go alone. There are several threads that need to be cut and stitched back together."

We leave her comfortably seated before the bank of portraits. As we go out, I seal the threshold with prayer and a sprinkling of asafetida powder and salt, hoping it will be enough to protect us all from Weston in the corporeal realm.

She remains in the tower room for hours, as I fret and pace the library. Beckett tries his best to distract me with a game of chess, but my mind is far too addled to concentrate. A dull headache crowds my temples—a common occurrence after my concussion. I take a swallow of whiskey and lay my head on Beckett's lap, drifting into a fitful sleep.

When I wake, Beckett is gone, but Marguerite sits across from me in her favorite chair, gazing out the window at the muted afternoon sun. I sit up, rubbing my eyes. "Oh, you're here. Are you all right?" I ask.

Marguerite turns to me. "Yes, dear. Beckett led me down after I finished working. I've accomplished a lot today." Her voice is haunting. Wistful.

"What do you mean?"

"You'll see. All sorts of things are changing. Perhaps, if I'm successful, I can even prevent Claire's death."

"How wonderful that must be to consider."

"Wouldn't we all change our pasts, our regrets, if we could?"

"I think so." I hold my aching head in my hands. The buzzing in my right ear returns, with more intensity. A trickle of warmth runs from my nose.

"You're bleeding, dear," Marguerite says.

I wipe under my nose, startled by the sight of fresh blood on my hands.

"It's probably just the dry air," Marguerite soothes.

But it's not dry at all. We've just had rain. And I have the uncomfortable sensation that, despite Marguerite's best intentions, something isn't right.

In early November, the day after Harriet's tearful departure, the first killing frost of the season comes, lacing the world in white. In the front parlor, the radio announcer relays rising stock prices, sinking commodities, and news of the wider world as I go through the mail. There's a letter from Blanche Fitzsimmons. She's successfully sued for divorce from Ted, thanks to my affidavit, and used the money from the engagement ring to help finance a move for her and the children to Arizona. I fold the letter, pleased with the sense of closure it brings me.

Marguerite is at work again in the tower, obsessed with undoing the past. At dinner, when I ask if her efforts have borne any fruit, she gives me a cryptic smile. "I'm working it all out. Sorting through things. Trying to find the eye of the needle, my dear." I've come to believe her task futile, and somewhat delusional, but even if it is, the effort has given her purpose and her life fresh meaning. I decide to let well enough alone, given that the hauntings seem to have diminished, and Weston has not reappeared, much to my relief.

As the days grow short and the nights long, sleep eludes me. Despite my husband's presence, I find myself growing more and more restless. I'm distracted. Forgetful. I long for the relatively carefree days when Melva and Harriet were here to help. Marguerite's decline has become precipitous. Between her confusion and increasing physical frailty, I'm worn thin, making sure she remains safe while also completing my daily household chores. With his tasks—weatherproofing the house and gardens for winter, and preparing our meals, I know Beckett is just as exhausted. Our marriage begins to show the strain. We're more agitated. Short tempered. One morning, after gathering firewood for the kitchen stove, I forget to latch the screen door. A few moments later, while Beckett makes breakfast, the bitter north wind rushes across the hillside, ripping the door from its hinges with a sharp crack. I watch it tumble end over end across the lawn, before it comes to rest against a bare-limbed hedge apple tree.

"Dammit, Sadie!" Beckett scolds. "I've told you a thousand times to latch the door when you come in."

"Well, if you'd filled the hod last night, like you usually do, I wouldn't have had to go out to get more wood."

"Watch the bacon." He stalks outside, slamming the door behind him.

I watch the bacon sizzle for a few minutes, my eyes smarting with tears, then sit at the table, thumbing through the new Sears and Roebuck catalog. Then I remember my coffee cup, which I left in the parlor. When I return to the kitchen, the bacon is charred, acrid smoke filling the small room. I throw open the window over the sink and hurriedly wipe out the skillet before Beckett comes in and sees even more evidence of my carelessness.

I pull fresh rashers from the icebox and start again. I hear Beckett hammering new nails into the door hinges, cursing as he works. After breakfast, we spend the day in stony silence. He doesn't apologize, and neither do I. My grudge settles in, as I consider all the ways Beckett has fallen short of my expectations since our wedding. He's often aloof. Emotionally stilted. Driven by his work. Today wasn't the first time he's shown a lack of patience with my mistakes. With the weight of our responsibilities and Harriet's departure, our pleasure in one another's company has diminished. Our lovemaking has fallen to the wayside as a result.

As the days roll toward December, the lapses in my memory grow sharper. I find myself forgetting what day of the week it is. And when I insist that it's 1922 and Harding is still president, Beckett shows me a newspaper to prove otherwise.

"Sadie, what's gotten into you?" he asks. "You sound like Marguerite."

Worse yet, my urges to seek out Weston have returned. Late at night, while my husband sleeps beside me, I find myself longing for the scrape of teeth against my flesh, for the carnal, wicked pleasures I once enjoyed with Weston. It's shameful. Dangerous. Yet the temptation is ever near. If Marguerite succeeds in destroying his painting in the past, or never painting it at all, I may never see him again. And so one frigid night in early December, when the moon hangs low and yellow, I'm far too weak to resist my own curiosity. In the wee hours of the morning, I find myself walking, trancelike, to the library and Marguerite's tower, where Weston's portrait awaits.

I place a lantern on the table next to the easel and uncover the painting. It's changed. It's no longer in its gilded frame, and there's a dull sheen over Weston's features, as if a wash of translucent white paint has been applied. When I touch the surface, nothing happens. Nothing at all. I try again, frustration and longing flooding through me. "Why won't you open to me? I'm here, Weston. Don't you still want me?"

Sadie . . .

The whispered sound of my name startles me. I snatch my hand back from Weston's portrait, glancing up. There's no one there. But out of the corner of my eye, I see Iris move inside her portrait. I gasp. The background of the painting has changed—the scene by the river is gone. In its place, the same seaside bluff I saw in my dream, the soft sound of breaking waves audible even though we are hundreds of miles from any ocean. It no longer looks like a painting; it looks like what it truly is: a window into another world.

Come, Sadie. It's time you learn the truth.

Iris's lips don't move, but I can hear her voice inside my head. I hesitate, for the briefest moment, my emotions tangling. I have a feeling if I go through that painting and see what Iris wants to show me, it will change everything. Still, I step toward her portrait and reach out, unable to resist the pull of my curiosity. Vertigo washes over me, sending my senses into a spin.

Interlude

IRIS

Iris stands in front of an easel in a room overlooking a fog-wreathed mountain, its grassy slope angled sharply down to the shore. Sadie approaches and sees that she's sketching Weston. "He's such an engaging subject, isn't he?" Iris asks, glancing up. "It's not just his looks, but his presence. I can see why you were taken in by him."

"You called me here, didn't you?"

"Yes. I did," she says. "Because you need to know the truth, Sadie. All of it."

Sadie looks out the window at the dramatic coastline. "We're in California, aren't we?"

"Yes. Big Sur, south of San Francisco. In 1881. We're here because you need to see what happened that summer. So you can confront Marguerite with the truth and help her right the wrongs of the past before she dies."

"I'm not sure how I *can* help," Sadie says. "Aunt Marg said that I can't interfere—that only she can change what happened in this world. In the past."

"Yes, but what she's doing is a waste of precious time. Painting over Weston. Destroying Florence's manuscript. None of it will matter, because she still believes her own delusion." Iris motions to the sketch of Weston. "It's the way her mind has protected itself for all these years. How she's justified what really happened."

"'Delusion.' You're talking about Weston."

"Yes," she says, "he's merely the scapegoat."

"What do you mean?"

Iris rises, wipes the charcoal from her hands on a scrap of linen. "Do you trust me, Sadie? To tell you the truth? All of it?"

"If you're anything at all like your nephew, who I trust more than anyone else, then yes."

"Good. Because what you're about to see won't be easy. I wouldn't lie about this. That would be cruel."

A chill dances over Sadie's skin—a chill that has nothing at all to do with the wind ruffling through the window. "I'm ready. I want to see. I want to know the truth."

The scene shifts, warping and fading. Sadie finds herself alone, standing on the same desolate cliff she saw in her dream, the sea pounding against the rocks below. In the distance, silhouetted against the sun, she sees a man and a woman. From their agitated motions, Sadie can sense that they're arguing.

She approaches, weaving through the thorny chaparral and scrub sage. It's Weston, with Claire, her face streaked with tears. "She'll hate me if I do," Claire says. "I cannot go through with this, Weston. I'm sorry."

He reaches for her, but she turns from him and walks away, arms clutched around her waist. "Claire!" Weston calls, his voice ragged. "Please!"

The scene shifts once more. Marguerite and her sisters are having a picnic on the same cliff, the sun a beacon in the afternoon sky as gulls scream overhead. Nearby, Weston poses for Iris as she sketches him in profile, looking out to sea.

Sadie approaches the plein air tableau cautiously, but no one seems to sense her presence. Marguerite cuts a tea sandwich, serves one half to

Florence and the other to Claire. "I'm not hungry," Claire says, pushing away the plate Marguerite offers.

"Claire, please, you need to eat."

"Now *you're* the sour goose," Florence chides. Her hair is mussed, gathered in a tangled clump atop her head. Her eyes are swollen into slits, as if she's been crying all day. Sadie remembers the scene from the past she witnessed in Florence's bedroom—the tantrum Florence had thrown. This must be later, on the same day. The picnic she promised to attend.

"I'm going for a walk." Claire rises, shaking out her muslin skirts. She walks away in a meandering line, toward the edge of the cliff. Apprehension fills Sadie's gut, remembering Marguerite's words. *Claire killed herself because of Weston. Jumped from a cliff in California when we were on holiday.*

"Please don't," Sadie whispers, following Claire as she comes to a stop on the perilously loose shelf of rock and sand. Claire bends and picks up a handful of stones. She pitches one over the precipice, her mouth knotted in concentration as it bounces down to the sea.

Florence approaches, her blond curls whipped loose by the wind. "Come away from there, Clairey. You're getting too close to the edge."

Claire says nothing, a look of placid calm on her face as she pitches another stone.

"If you think pouting is the way to get his attention, you're wrong," Florence says. "Now, come away from there before you fall."

Claire whirls on her older sister, her freckles sprinkled like stardust across her nose. "Why can't you let the rest of us be happy, Flor?"

"Happy? Do you think *I'm* happy?" Florence asks, exasperated.

"You're far happier than you have a right to be. Do you know what Marguerite calls you? The Monster. And she's right. You take whatever you want, and you hurt people. You don't care what happens to anyone else."

"You're wrong. I care *too* much. Marguerite can't see that, and neither can you. My affair with Weston has been my solace. My joy. But the guilt has made me miserable, Claire. Do you think this is how I imagined my life? You can't fathom all the lies I've had to keep straight. The stories I've had to tell. It's exhausting."

Claire says nothing, her eyes narrowing.

Florence looks out to sea. "Do you know I've never been able to be my true self outside of his arms? Not once! My only choice as the eldest was to please Maman and Papa. To do their bidding. To placate. To be a good example for you and Marg. I don't love James. I didn't want to marry him. I wanted to break off our engagement and marry Weston instead. From the first moment I met him, I knew he was the love of my life. We were two halves of a whole. I tried to tell all of you that, but no one would listen. All Maman and Papa saw was James's money and how it would bring us back from the brink of ruin. Papa was too worried about our reputation to let me have the life I wanted. The *husband* I wanted."

"And so, because you can't have what you want, you'll destroy all of us." Claire's lip trembles. "You want to keep Weston, yes. But it's not because you love him—only because you can't bear to lose. Because you're *selfish*. Heartless. Weston wants *me*, Flor. Me. Not you. He's sick to death of you."

Florence begins to shake, her eyes brimming with tears. "That isn't true."

"Ask him, if you don't believe me." Claire laughs. "You find it impossible, that he could choose me over you. Plain little Claire. Quiet little Claire." She chucks another round stone over the ledge. "I told him I wouldn't marry him because you'd make our marriage a living hell. But I might change my mind, after all. Why should I sacrifice what *I* want to appease you, when you'd never do the same?"

It happens so quickly, so unexpectedly, that at first, Sadie doubts her own eyes. She sees Florence strike Claire, sees the slap land so hard that Claire's head jerks to the side, so hard she stumbles and loses her footing on the perilous bluff, her arms wheeling for balance. Claire's blue eyes pop wide, and then she falls, tipping over the cliff's edge, her hair a scarlet flag against the sky. Sadie and Florence scream in tandem, the sound echoing off the rocky shoreline.

"Claire!" Marguerite shouts and runs toward the bluff. Iris and Weston follow, their faces marked with horror. "Oh, Florence, what have you done!" Marguerite wails, peering over the edge to where Claire's body lies broken on the rocks, blood trailing from her head.

"She . . . she fell," Florence says, frantic. "I warned her she was too close to the edge. She wouldn't listen."

"You were arguing," Marguerite says. "I saw you!"

"No. You're wrong. She tripped over a rock and fell."

A low moan of grief leaves Weston's throat. He falls to his knees, hands knotted in his hair.

Florence paces back and forth, her face pale. "No. She—she jumped. That's what happened. She was upset over Weston, and she jumped."

"You liar! You hit her! I saw you!" Marguerite screeches.

"I did no such thing." Florence begins to cry, shakes her head violently. "No. No!"

"We have to fetch the constable, Marg," Iris says, the only calm voice in the midst of this frenzied anguish. "He'll know what to do."

"Did no one else see them?" Marguerite asks, frantic. "Did *none* of you see what just happened?"

"It *must* have been an accident. A terrible accident." Weston shakes his head, wipes his eyes. He goes to Florence's side, and she wilts against him, sobbing. "It was an accident, wasn't it, Florence? Please tell me it was."

"Yes, yes," Florence says. "Of course it was. You believe me, don't you?"

"I'll go down to the beach," Weston says gently, disengaging Florence from his arms. "She might have survived."

"Yes," Florence said, nodding rapidly. "She's still alive. She must be."

Something shifts in Marguerite's demeanor. A hardness enters her eyes. "You're mad. Both of you! She's dead!" She stalks forward, seething. "This is *your* fault, Florence. Every bit of it." Marguerite grasps a handful of Florence's hair, twisting it. Florence cries out, sinking to her knees. Marguerite wrestles her to the ground, teeth clenched, eyes wild as she stands over her sister.

And that's when Sadie sees the knife clutched in Marguerite's hand, half-concealed by her long skirts. A simple table knife, the same one she used to cut the tea sandwiches, its edge serrated.

Weston sees the knife at the same time, terror in his eyes as he hurtles forward. "Marguerite, no!"

Everything that happens after is a frenzied blur as Weston tries to pull the women apart, like two vicious, feral dogs. Suddenly, he cries out, eyes lit with shock. An arc of blood shoots forward, painting the ground crimson. Weston stumbles, clutching his neck, blood spouting like a fountain between his fingers. Marguerite screams, dropping the bloodied knife. "No! Weston!" She rushes to his side, futilely trying to catch him as he collapses, panic blanching her features as she wraps the tail of the skirt around his neck in an attempt to stanch the bleeding.

Iris rushes to Marguerite's side as Florence begins to wail.

"God, help!" Florence cries, clambering across the ground and shielding Weston with her body, desperately clawing at his chest. "Oh God! Please don't die, my love, please don't die."

❧

The scene fades from view, the whispering sound of the sea muted. Sadie realizes she's back in Iris's room. She sinks onto the edge of Iris's bed, her mind reeling from the horror she's just witnessed.

"We dragged Weston's body into the sea, at high tide," Iris intones, her voice hollow. She continues sketching, adding shading to Weston's jawline with a thin stick of charcoal. "No one questioned his disappearance. He had no living family. No one to miss him. As for Claire, Bram had enough social standing to ensure no one would ask the sorts of questions that would endanger his reputation, nor those of his daughters. They shipped Claire's body in a private railcar back to Kansas City, gave her a full requiem mass, and buried her in hallowed ground without incident. Only I, Florence, and Marguerite ever knew the full truth of what happened. I loved Marguerite enough to keep her secrets. I protected her. And Marguerite protected Florence, for Laura's sake. Florence went mad. Spent a year in an asylum. It was terrible. You can't begin to imagine. Marguerite was never the same after that day. None of us were."

Sadie stands and paces the room, her mind reeling. Marguerite, a murderer. Her grandmother, guilty of potential fratricide. She doesn't want to believe any of it. She can't. "But Marguerite said that Weston wasn't real, that he was an invention—the hero of Florence's romantic story that she painted into reality."

"No. He lived, Sadie. He was a real person. Marguerite can't face the truth of what happened that day, so she made up a story. A delusion. She's been in denial for decades. And it's cost all of us dearly." Iris shakes her head. "Weston's spirit wants vengeance. He's angry. And so he's punished us by destroying those we love. First Sybil, my only granddaughter. Now he's trying to destroy you."

"To what good end can any of this come? How can I change things?"

"The only way you can is by confronting Marguerite with what I've just shown you. Help her remember. So that she uses the time she has left to make things right. I'll help her if she comes to me. If she prevents Weston's murder, her actions will ripple down through time, to you. It's the only way you'll ever be safe from Weston's vengeance . . . and I have the frailest hope that if she's successful, it might bring my Sybil back, too." Iris looks up at me, her eyes brimming with tears. "You have to make her see the truth, Sadie. You must."

Chapter 37

December 7, 1925

I come to my senses gradually, wading out of the fog of time and memory, warm morning light spilling into the tower's windows. I'm so horrified by what I've witnessed—Claire's fall, Weston's death—that I don't know if I can bring myself to look Marguerite in the eye. I return to my and Beckett's room. He's already up, the covers pulled taut over the mattress. As I'm dressing, he raps on the door, then enters.

"Where were you?" he asks. "You were gone when I woke up."

"I . . . I couldn't sleep. I went to the library to read," I say, turning my back to him. I shrug a sweater over my slip and step into my skirt.

He crosses to me, wraps his arms around me from behind, resting his chin on my shoulder. "I was just worried about you. That's all."

I turn in his arms and kiss him, my guilt over seeking out Weston the night before keen. I'm grateful that my temptation didn't yield success. In the light of day, I can see how foolish I was. "How's Marguerite doing this morning?" I ask.

"She's in the dining room. I made breakfast," Beckett says. "I can't get her to eat anything, but perhaps you can. She was having a hallucination when she woke. About the lost baby again. I managed to get her calmed down."

I know who Marguerite's lost baby is now. My mother. A pang of sympathy runs through me. Although I witnessed Marguerite kill

Weston last night, my compassion for her remains. It was likely an accident—a terrible one. And according to Iris, there might still be a chance she can save him and, in the process, save Sybil. Maybe even Claire . . . if I can convince her to finally face the truth.

Marguerite is sitting in a puddle of sunshine when I enter the dining room, staring out the window, her hands folded in her lap like innocent doves. On the sideboard a tray of pastries and a steaming tea samovar await. I pour myself and Marguerite a cup, add three sugar cubes to mine, and cross to her with a plateful of pastries. "Beck made all sorts of good things for us this morning, Aunt Marg. Won't you have something?"

She waves the food away. "I haven't been able to change a thing," she says, her voice haunted and low. "I've tried. Five times now. Each time I go back, I refuse Florence's request to paint him. I even burned her manuscript. Yet Weston still appears at her debut. They still dance. Still fall in love, no matter what I do."

Because he wasn't a figment of your imagination. He was a real person, and you killed him. "Aunt Marg, we need to talk about Weston." I reach out for her hand. "I went through Iris's painting last night. She showed me what happened all those years ago, in California."

Marguerite's eyes widen. "I don't know what you're talking about."

"I believe you do. I think it's probably easier to cling to the falsehood you've created, and I can understand why you would. But Weston was a real person, Aunt Marg." I pull in a shaky breath. "I know he was, because I saw him die." *I saw you kill him.*

Marguerite snatches her hand from mine, her mouth a hard line. "Nonsense."

"Iris showed me everything. The argument between Claire and Florence. I saw Florence hit Claire. She lost her balance. Fell to her death."

"Stop it. Stop it right now." Marguerite shoves away from the table, her voice frantic. I stand, facing her. I'm tempted to call for Beckett, but part of me wants to protect Marguerite, and him, from knowing her most shameful secret. It might color how he thinks of her. I don't want that. I want him to remember her as the benevolent, generous woman he's known his entire life. I only want her to face the truth.

"Aunt Marg, think. Think back to the summer of 1881. You, Florence, and Claire went on holiday to Big Sur, in California. Iris and Weston were there with you. Florence and Claire were quarreling over Weston's affections. Florence threw a tantrum one morning, refused to go on a trail ride with all of you. You had a picnic on the bluff later that day. Do you remember?"

Marguerite stills, her shoulders falling. "How could you know about any of that? We've never talked about it."

"Iris showed me."

"I can't do this." Marguerite falls back into her chair, resting her face in her hands. "I can't . . . I can't talk about the rest."

I kneel at her side, my hand resting on her knee. "You don't have to tell me anything, Aunt Marg. I saw it all. I saw Claire fall. Saw you charge at Florence. Saw you accidentally stab Weston. It was a crime of passion. A sudden madness, wasn't it? It doesn't make it right. Of course it doesn't. But it happened."

"Yes." Tears flow unrestrained down Marguerite's face. "I loved Florence and yet I hated her so much at the same time. I just wanted her to stop meddling in Claire's life. In my life. I hated her for what she did to Hugh. How she drove us apart and kept me from the life I wanted. We were all puppets in Florence's play. When I saw Claire fall, something came over me. I wanted to hurt Florence. I didn't want to kill her. And I certainly didn't intend to kill him. But I just . . . oh, Sadie, what did I *do*?"

I'm at war with myself. I want to offer her words of comfort, to tell her it wasn't her fault. But it *was*. And no matter how good I know Marguerite to be, it doesn't erase the past. She killed Weston, got away with it, and then covered it up with Florence's and Iris's help—and a delusion so convincing she fooled herself and me into thinking he was her creation.

"Aunt Marg, I want you to listen to me." I lower my voice. "Iris told me you can make this better. You can fix things. You said yourself that what you've been doing isn't working. Iris said she would help you, if you go to her. But there isn't much time."

Marguerite looks down at me, wipes her eyes. "It isn't too late, then? To undo my biggest regret?"

"Iris seems to think there's a chance."

"I *have* been able to change some things. In the past. I'm not sure why these things and not the others. I managed to conceal mine and Hugh's love affair from Florence. And my pregnancy, at least for now. Or is it then? I'm not sure what difference it will make, in the present, in the future, but perhaps . . . in that other time, Hugh and I will find some way to run away together. To be happy. I've the feeling he's still alive out there. Somewhere. Perhaps we'll find one another again, before the end."

"Yes, but even if you do manage to run away with Hugh and raise Mama together, there's no guarantee you won't still kill Weston. It's the reason he's here, haunting us, Aunt Marg. The reason he haunted Florence for all those years, killed Sybil, and why he's threatening me. He's angry. Vengeful. All of you played a part in his death."

"Yes, I understand that now."

"And you realize that your actions in the past have impacted all of us, don't you?" I prod.

She raises her teacup to her lips, her wrist shaking. Her tremors are growing even more pronounced, another indicator we haven't much time. She takes the tiniest sip of tea. "Of course, my dear. I remember. The whole reason I went back in time was to try to save you from him."

"I understand that. But I don't think you should go back and try to alter how things happened with Hugh anymore. I think, perhaps, it might be best to accept that part of the past as it is. As it was. If you go back, I think you should just try to save Weston, since he's the problem at hand. Don't you agree?"

"And let go of Hugh? Penny?" Marguerite's face grows stony. Hard. "You've no idea of the pain I've endured, child. None. I didn't tell you everything. Your mother knew about the adoption. I didn't tell her, but she figured things out for herself. She asked me for the truth, the last time you were here, after I came home from France, and I couldn't lie. Not to her. She was so angry. At Florence for lying to her all those years. At me, for lying, and for giving her up. She thought I didn't want her." Marguerite's lip trembles. "That's the reason you never came back, Sadie. Why she never called or visited after that summer. And now that she's gone, where does that leave me?" Tears break free from her eyes, flowing down her cheeks.

So, Mama knew. She knew the truth of her birth. And she never told me or my brothers. It makes sense now, her sudden reserve whenever I'd bring up Marguerite. How she'd hedge when I asked her why we no longer spent summers at Blackberry Grange. A shallow echo of the hurt and betrayal Mama must have felt nudges at my heart. I don't know what to say. All this is too much at once.

"Ever since you told me about her death, I've tried to go to Penny," Marguerite says. "To prevent it from happening. I can't. All I can do is watch my own child die, again and again. Do you know what that does to a person?"

I choke back a sob, my fingernails biting into my palm. "Please, Aunt Marg . . . don't."

She shakes her head, the hardness returning to her face. "Now that I'm at the end of my life, I can see all of my regrets spread out before me, like some horrible, hellish landscape. You can't understand how I feel because you're still young. But someday, *your* regrets will come home to roost, Sadie—mistakes you're making now, and mistakes you have yet to make. You'll wish you had the chance to do things over again, too."

I know this look. This tone. My aunt is about to descend into obstinance. I attempt another tack. "Perhaps you should try to go to Iris. Listen to what she has to say. She loves you. She wants to help."

"I don't suppose it could hurt anything. She keeps coming to me in my dreams, anyway. She's been trying to get me to tell you the truth."

"I'm glad someone has. There are far too many secrets in this family. I'll help you up to the tower if you'll eat something first."

"Oh, all right. You're always after me to eat."

"Only because I care. I want to keep you around as long as I can. We've missed out on a lot over the years." I offer her a danish, and she takes it.

After she's finished eating, I guide her up the narrow steps to the sun-drenched tower, where the portrait of Hugh has taken center stage on the easel, her chair parked in front of it. I ease it off and replace it with Iris's portrait. "There. All settled?"

"Yes, dear."

"I know Iris will be happy to see you." I pick up the porcelain bell from the side table next to her chair. It rings faintly. "Ring this when you're ready to come down. I'll just be in the library, reading."

In the library I leave the door to the tower cracked, ever so slightly, and tuck into one of the club chairs by the fire. I open my grandmother's dog-eared copy of *Wuthering Heights*, still unfinished, and resume reading. It's little wonder where she got the inspiration for her fictional Baron de Havilland . . . or that she fell for Weston. Heathcliff, with his dark good looks and passionate, fiery temperament, reminds me of Weston.

Lulled by the crackling fire and the stillness of the room, I soon find myself growing drowsy. As my eyes shut to half-mast, I sense Iris's spirit nearby. *She's listening to me about Weston, but she won't listen when it comes to Hugh. The baby. Her selfishness could destroy you, Sadie. You must find a way to stop her. You must.*

I sit up, blinking, and she disappears, like smoke from an extinguished candle.

Chapter 38

December 10, 1925

The telephone rings, startling me. I rub at my sleep-starved eyes and go to answer it, my voice vacant.

"Hello, Sadie, it's Rosalie."

Rosalie . . . Rosalie . . . I don't recall knowing anyone named Rosalie. "Pardon me?"

"Ros-a-lie," the woman enunciates, her voice rising. "Your sister-in-law?"

"Oh! Oh yes." Felix's wife. "I'm so sorry. I haven't been sleeping very well lately."

"Well, I'm calling because we're planning on coming for a visit, at Christmastime. We'll bring the boys. They're very excited to see their aunt Sadie."

"Oh. Oh, no. You can't . . . I mean, I'll need to talk to Beck and Aunt Marg . . ."

"The boys will be heartbroken if we don't get to come. They miss you so."

I think of Felix's boys, both dark headed and blue eyed. Leslie and Grant. I think. Or is it George? "Won't they want to be in their own beds on Christmas morning?"

"They're still too young to care about such things." Rosalie pauses, her breath soft over the phone. "Is it because of the argument you had with Felix over the will? Is that why you don't want us to come?"

"It's not about the will, or anything other than Beckett and I are overworked. We won't be good hosts. We're stretched thin, Rosalie. Well and truly. We can't find hired help and Marguerite's nurse went on leave. Aunt Marg isn't doing well."

"I'm so sorry to hear that. Perhaps I could stay with you for a few weeks, with the boys. Help you get things sorted. I'm used to hard work, you know."

The last thing I need is Rosalie underfoot, prying into our business, peeking in cupboards, and cataloging everything she finds for her and Felix's benefit. "Aunt Marg doesn't do well with houseguests. It confuses her to have new people staying in the house."

Rosalie sighs. "Look, Sadie. I know you don't like me. I've known it from the start. But I *am* on your side with all of this. Truly. You've really stepped up. I saw how you were with Aunt Marguerite this summer, and I . . . I just want you to know, that when the time comes, I'll do everything I can to help with the estate. And not for selfish reasons. I promise."

I want to believe her, that I've misjudged her. But then I remember her hungry eyes, devouring Mama's jewelry at every family gathering. Her flattering words. Her shallow compliments. If her intentions are truly altruistic, all will be revealed after Marguerite's passing. We'll see then.

"I'll tell Felix we won't come, then," Rosalie says, her voice dripping with disappointment. "He won't be happy about it."

"He put you up to calling me, didn't he?"

The line goes quiet again. "Yes. He did."

"I knew it," I scoff.

"Between us, he doesn't trust your husband. He thinks he's manipulated you into marriage and coerced Marguerite into leaving everything to you. I told him he was being unfair. But you know how he is."

"I do. And thank you, at least, for being honest with me, Rosalie."

"Well . . . I've known your brother for many years now, dear. We're not always on the same side of things. And I, for one, am very happy about your marriage. He's quite a looker, your husband. Those divine eyes! He seems to be levelheaded. And he's very polite."

"He is. All of those things. And more."

"Are you happy, Sadie?"

I think of our recent bickering. But despite our petty arguments, Beckett is a good man. An honest one, without guile. And he hasn't changed at all from the person he was when I met him. The man I fell in love with is still very much there, weathering my fickle affections and my impetuousness with his characteristic pragmatism.

"I am happy. Very."

Rosalie sighs again. "Good. Because marriage is dreadful, if you're not. It can seem very much like a prison."

I'm not sure what she's implying. I've never considered that she might be unhappy with my brother, cosseted as she is in the lap of luxury. I don't know what to say, so I promise to write soon and tell her goodbye, then go to check on Marguerite in the tower. She sits ramrod straight in front of her self-portrait, her eyes glazed over in a trance. I glance at the easel next to it, which holds Weston's unframed portrait. She's completely covered his image with white paint. I'm saddened by this. Evil or not, it was a beautiful likeness of him. I can see a light pencil sketch on the whitewashed canvas, but I can't make out what she's drawn from here.

I pause by the door, watching her, but I don't want to interrupt her trance. I go to the powder room, let down my hair, and brush through it with my fingers. I hardly recognize myself in the mirror. I look older, dried up, my eyes creased with worry, shadowed in their sockets. A sudden wave of dizziness overtakes me as I'm washing my hands. I lean over the sink, breathless. A faint *plop plop* hits the porcelain. Blood tracks slowly down the drain. In the mirror, I see the thin line of blood streaming from my left nostril. I pinch the bridge of my nose to stanch the flow and try my best not to panic as the other side begins to bleed as well. Iris appears behind me in the mirror, her form flickering.

She's making a terrible mistake.

Suddenly, the floor pitches, the hexagonal tiles rise up to meet me, and everything fades to black.

Interlude

Iris

Sadie finds herself in the sunlit room at the sanatorium again. Marguerite is sitting on her narrow cot, heavily pregnant, rocking gently back and forth, her mouth an angry slash. There's a light tap on the door. Florence enters, dressed as she was the first time Sadie witnessed this scene, in striped summer poplin.

"Good morning!" Florence chimes. "You look—"

"I've changed my mind," Marguerite says, cutting her off. "I'm keeping the baby."

Florence wilts. "Marg, we've been over this. It's for the best if James and I raise her. It is. You can't see it now, but it is."

"Oh, I see it now. I've seen it all, because I've already lived it once, Flor. I've endured watching her grow up from a distance, on holidays, through pictures. You told me you'd let me see her as often as I liked. You lied. You've lied about so much."

"You're not making any sense, darling. Are you sick?" Florence crosses the room, sinks down next to Marguerite. She places the back of her hand on Marguerite's forehead, frowns, her dainty rosebud mouth pinching. "You don't feel feverish."

"I tried. I tried to make things right with you. Tried to accept our differences and forgive you for your selfishness. Because that's really why you want the baby. You're selfish. At least you've let *him* go," Marguerite mutters beneath her breath. "At least perhaps, now, Claire might live. We'll see in two years, I suppose."

"What on earth are you talking about?" Florence's brow furrows. "Are you quite well, sister?"

"I'm fine! It's all of *you* who are broken. You with your vanity, your hypocrisy. Your hidden darkness. Maman and her creditors, trying to heal her heartache over Papa's affairs with pretty dresses and jewelry. Papa, with his drinking. The drinking will kill him, you know. And you, too, eventually, because you're going down the same road."

Florence looks at Marguerite, aghast. "You're not making any sense."

"Oh, but I am. Claire was always lying down and letting you walk all over her. She hates you for it, secretly. We all did. But I see everything now, Flor. All of it. And I'm fed up. I'm fixing things. I am. For once and for all. For Sadie's sake."

"Sadie? Who is that?" Florence asks.

"Never mind. You'll think I'm mad if I tell you."

"Marguerite, what on earth are you talking about?"

The scene shifts, the light fading to a dull coppery orange outside the window. Sadie watches as Marguerite goes to the dresser, frantically removing clothing from the drawers.

Iris comes in, just as she did before. "Marg, what are you doing?"

"I'm leaving this place."

"You can't! You're due any day now."

Marguerite stills, turns to Iris, softness in her eyes. "Listen to me, Iris. Listen very carefully. I've seen the future. You're going to be successful. You're going to marry well—an English lord. You'll travel the world with him. He'll finance your art. You're even going to meet Rossetti. You'll have more children—children that you'll get to see grow up. It will always hurt, giving up Victor, and you'll always miss him, because a mother's heart never forgets, but as you once told me, we must move on and try to find our happiness in the present." Marguerite crosses to Iris, presses her forehead to hers. "My granddaughter and your nephew are going to meet someday, and they'll fall in love, just like us. They won't get along at first, but in time, they'll see how much they need one another." Marguerite bends to kiss Iris, long on the lips, making her gasp in surprise. "I'm so sorry for everything I put you through. The terrible secret you had to keep for me. What I made you do. You were one of the greatest loves of my life, Iris, the truest and best of friends."

"'Were'? What do you mean?"

Marguerite hoists the carpetbag over her shoulder, opens the window, and lingers on the sill for a moment, before turning one last time to look at Iris, her lips curving into a tender smile. "I love you, my darling. I'll carry our memories for always."

And then, with a flash of auburn hair lit by the setting sun, she's gone.

Chapter 39

December 11, 1925

"Sadie. Sadie, wake up." Beckett's voice floats to me, as if through a tunnel. "You need to wake up. Something's wrong with Marguerite."

"What?"

"She's had a seizure. A fit. I found her in the hall. Doc Gallagher just got here. It's not looking good."

"Why didn't you wake me earlier?"

"I've tried, several times."

I sit up, my head pounding. The room swims before my eyes. I close them as a wave of nausea rolls over me. My tongue feels like a lump of dry clay. "Water."

Beckett hands me a glass, his hand shaking. I see that he's been crying, his eyes red around the edges. "Should we phone your aunt? Your brother?"

"No. Not yet. Let's see what the doctor says first." I wince as a lance of pain shoots through my temple. "Good God, my head hurts."

The telephone rings, the shrill sound piercing my already painful head. Beckett rushes to answer it, then comes back a few minutes later. "That was Claire. She's coming down on the train from Kansas City. She'll be here tomorrow."

The walls seem to shrink, closing in around me. "What did you say?"

"Claire. Marguerite's sister."

"Claire . . . but Aunt Claire's dead. She died in 1881."

Beckett gives me a strange look. "She came to our wedding. Are you sure you didn't hit your head when you fainted, darling?"

"Maybe I did." I claw through my hair. The pain in my head is almost unbearable. "Could you bring me some aspirin? Please. I have a horrible headache."

He returns a few moments later with a tin of aspirin. I take two tablets and down them with the rest of the water. I have no recollection of coming to our room. The last thing I remember is having a nosebleed in the powder room. Beckett mentioned that I fainted. I *must* have hit my head.

But I remember enough to know Aunt Claire is dead. I saw her die, with my own eyes, in the past.

At least . . . she *was* dead.

Was Marguerite truly able to change the past? Did she save Claire? And what about Weston?

I fling off the covers and stumble across the hall to Marguerite's room. Dr. Gallagher sits at her bedside, taking her pulse. He glances up as I enter, eyes scraping over my disheveled appearance. "Mrs. Hill. Please sit down. I've got some news about your aunt, and it isn't good, I'm afraid."

I sit heavily at the foot of Marguerite's bed. "What's happened?"

"A cerebral hemorrhage. A stroke. A bad one." He glances at Marguerite. "She's in a coma now, which is for the best. She may linger for days. But she won't regain consciousness."

"She's . . . she's dying?"

"Yes. I'm very sorry."

I glance at Marguerite. Her face is placid, her skin soft and ruddy with life. Her chest rises and falls steadily, as if she's only asleep. "She looks fine. Are you sure there's nothing you can do for her?"

"No. She may look healthy, but her brain has sustained irreparable trauma. All of her reflexes are gone, apart from basic autonomic functions. The best we can do is keep her comfortable until her body gives way." He shakes his head. "It's so strange. These things are usually brought on by exceptionally high blood pressures. Marguerite's pressures have always been normal. The seizures I witnessed when I first arrived are more in line with what I've seen with eclamptic mothers."

"What does that mean, 'eclamptic'?"

"Before labor, it's called 'pre-eclampsia.' It can cause headaches and swollen legs but is often symptomless. It creates severe distress during labor and delivery. Women can die from it if their labors go on too long."

A memory washes over me of the scenes I witnessed in the sanatorium. Marguerite's swollen ankles. My mother's birth. Marguerite was in severe distress during labor—the doctor had used a similar word. 'Eclampsia.'

"Mrs. Hill, I'd like to examine you, if you wouldn't mind. You're not looking well, yourself, I must say."

"Of course."

He comes to my side, listens to my heart and lungs, takes my pulse, and examines my eyes, then asks to look at my gums. "Have you been having shortness of breath? Spells of weakness? Fainting?"

"Yes. I just had one yesterday."

"Do you remember when you started your last menstrual cycle?"

"I . . . I don't recall."

"You're severely anemic. It's very likely you're pregnant. I want you to take two full spoonfuls of blackstrap molasses every day and eat as much red meat as possible. If you keep having fainting spells, I'll need to admit you to the hospital for observation."

"Pregnant?" My head spins, on par with the pain.

"Is that a surprise to you?" He smiles. "Many women find themselves in the family way before their first anniversaries, Mrs. Hill. You wouldn't be the only one."

I almost laugh for joy, but then I think of Marguerite, and my mood grows somber. My hand goes to my belly. If I'm expecting, she'll never know this baby. Never meet him or her. Her great-grandchild will grow up never knowing the sound of her laughter. Her stories. Her smile.

I take her hand in mine, tracing the raised network of veins on its back. She's been many things in her lifetime. A daughter. A sister. A lover. I'm not ready to let her go. She's family. My mother's mother. Blood of my blood.

"I'll leave you alone with her," Dr. Gallagher says, his hand resting on my back. "I'll stop by at the end of my rounds to give her more morphia for the night. Make sure she stays warm, comfortable. And talk to her. Sometimes it helps to hear a familiar voice."

"Thank you, Doctor."

He nods and leaves us, shutting the door behind him.

I curl up next to Marguerite, cradling her childlike form, and cry.

Sadie, wake up. You have to wake up. Wake up, Sadie, WAKE UP!

The voice startles me awake, sometime in the middle of the night. Marguerite lies motionless next to me, her breathing shallow. But she's still here. Still alive.

I lie still, my heart hammering, my eyes adjusting to the darkness. And that's when I see Iris, silhouetted in the window. The moonlight shines through her form. She's crying, her sobs soft and muted.

"Iris?" I whisper. "What's wrong?"

We don't have long.

Her voice is a soft rush of wind inside my head. *Hours now. Once she's gone, it will be too late. You must think of the baby.*

"The baby?"

Yes. Come now. Hurry.

She trails past the foot of the bed, her eyes resting on Marguerite. *I must betray you, my love. Only this once.*

I follow Iris's spirit through the hall, down the stairs, past Beckett's sleeping form, his head resting on the dining room table. Iris leads me to the library. I follow her up to the tower. My eyes land on a new painting, perched on an easel between Iris's image and Marguerite's self-portrait. It's me. She's painted *me* over Weston's former portrait, seated in my favorite chair in the library, my head turned toward the window. The paint is still wet. She must have finished it recently, in the past few days.

Iris points to Marguerite's self-portrait, her eyes frantic with urgency.

"You want me to go through here?"

You must hurry, Sadie. You're the only one who can save her. She wouldn't listen to me. Go to Marguerite. Convince her to go back to the sanatorium. Hurry.

Iris's voice rises in pitch inside my head.

If you don't, she'll go into labor tonight, and in her condition, she could die. If that happens, you'll die when she dies. You're already fading. That's what's happening to you. Why you're sick.

"All right. All right. I'll go." I reach out, my head throbbing, my eyes going in and out of focus. I'm too weak to panic. Too tired to think how ridiculously unbelievable this scenario would be to anyone else. But I know Iris is telling the truth. I know I can trust her. So I reach out. I reach out and touch the surface of the painting, falling into Marguerite's past.

Interlude

MARGUERITE

Sadie watches as Marguerite clambers out the window of the sanitorium. She drops her carpetbag on the ground and works her way down the side of the building, using a long trailing vine of Virginia creeper as support. When she reaches the bottom, she's out of breath, her young face reddened by exertion. She picks up the carpetbag and runs, her gait hindered by her swollen belly.

"Stop!" Sadie calls. "Marguerite!"

Marguerite's head jerks toward Sadie. She freezes for a moment, her eyes narrowing in recognition. She turns and hurries down the road. When Sadie catches up to her, she can hear the stridor in Marguerite's breathing.

"Stop, Aunt Marg. Please. I know you can see me."

Marguerite slows but walks on, her jaw set. "Go back, Sadie. I've made sure everyone else got their happy ending. Now I want mine."

"But don't you know what will happen if you leave here?"

Marguerite stops to catch her breath, clutching her belly. "What are you talking about?"

"Your labor. I saw your swollen ankles. Dr. Gallagher told me what that means. You have a condition—something called pre-eclampsia—and if you try to deliver the baby on your own, you might die, and so could Penny."

"How can you know that?"

"I can't. Not for sure. But I'm fading. My memories are full of holes. There's something wrong with me. And there isn't much time left. No time for gambling with these kinds of odds."

"I know I'm dying. I can feel it. My body is trying to pull me back, even now."

Sadie takes her hand. "Aunt Marg, do you trust me? Because I'm afraid if you leave, you'll die in this timeline, too. As a young woman. Penny will die, and I will completely cease to exist."

"But . . . but I could find a doctor to deliver the baby. Somewhere else."

"There isn't time for that, Aunt Marg. You're about to go into labor, and I'm very sorry, but you must deliver Penny tonight, at the sanatorium, and then give her to Florence. It's the only way to make sure I'll be born someday." Sadie's hand rests on her belly. "Doc Gallagher says I'm pregnant. I'm going to have a baby, too. You've tried to make things right, by going to the past, and you have—in some ways. I think you even managed to save Claire. But in this timeline . . . this chronology of events, nothing can change without risking your descendants. Things must remain as they were. Otherwise, there's no guarantee Mama will meet Da. And if they don't meet . . ."

"You won't exist." Marguerite sighs. "Isn't there *some* way I can keep her?"

"It's too risky. We can't take the chance. Once you pass away, we won't be able to change things. It will be too late. We already know Laura will survive and grow up, living with Florence. And I deserve to live, too, Aunt Marg. My baby deserves to live. My brother and *his* children, too. Let me be the one to fix things, going forward. With my children and grandchildren. You've taught me so much about life. About love. About what's most important. I promise I won't take any of that for granted."

Marguerite's lip trembles. "You're asking me to break my own heart again. To give up the most precious thing I've ever loved."

"Yes. I am. But it will also be the most selfless thing you'll ever do. The bravest."

"I was going to find Hugh. Raise Penny with him. We were going to be happy."

"I know. And I'm sorry you didn't get that chance. I'm so sorry."

"Will you find Hugh after I'm gone, and tell him everything?"

"Yes, I promise I'll try my best to find him."

Marguerite smiles at Sadie, squeezes her hand. "I remember it all now, you know. All of the memories I've lost through the years. All of it. And I'm so proud of you, Sadie. So very proud."

"I know," Sadie says, tears streaming down her face. "I know."

The scene shifts, suddenly, and they're in the delivery room once more, the same bald doctor stationed at the end of the bed, Florence at Marguerite's side, clutching her hand. "We have to get this baby out," he says to the nurse. "She's nearing eclamptic distress. Mrs. Knight, you'll need to leave the room."

"But I . . ." Florence protests. "I can't."

"I want my sister," Marguerite says, panting. "Please don't make her leave."

"I'm right here," Florence says, stroking Marguerite's forehead. "I'm not going anywhere, I promise."

Marguerite grips her elder sister's hand. "I'm sorry, Flor."

"It's all right. I'm sorry, too. For everything. Things will be better from now on. I promise."

"Your sister can stay," the doctor says, patting Marguerite's knee. "But please, Mrs. Knight, keep near the head of the bed, out of the way. This may be upsetting for you. Nurses, watch to make sure she doesn't swoon."

The same dutiful nurse from before climbs atop Marguerite, placing both of her hands on Marguerite's stomach. "When the pains come again, push with all you've got, love."

When the contraction comes, Marguerite pushes, and the nurse atop her pushes, too.

"There, that's it!" the doctor exclaims. "One more push should do it."

Marguerite collapses back against the pillows, weak, frightened. She turns her head and looks at Sadie, a weak smile playing on her lips and love in her eyes. "It was all worth it. For you."

"What, dear?" The nurse looks over her shoulder at Marguerite, giving a quizzical look.

"I'm talking to Sadie. There, in the corner."

"There's no one there. She's hallucinating," the doctor says, his voice rising. "We need to get this baby out, nurse. Give it all you've got this time."

Marguerite squeezes her eyes shut as the next contraction sets in, a throttled scream escaping her throat as she bears down. Florence's knuckles blanch white as Marguerite grips her hand. The nurse presses hard on Marguerite's belly, elbows locked.

"Aha!" the doctor exclaims. A thin, reedy cry floats over the excited din. The doctor holds the baby up for Marguerite to see. "A girl. You've done well, Miss Thorne. You've done well."

Marguerite raises herself onto her elbows, her eyes a livid green inside her pale face. "Let me see her. Please."

The nurse clambers off the bed, takes the baby from the doctor, and swaddles her as he clamps and cuts the cord. The baby is red-faced and angry, her bright copper hair contrasting with the linen sheath they've wrapped her in.

"Would you like to hold her?" the nurse asks.

A tear trails from Marguerite's eye. "No. Give her to my sister. She's Florence's now."

Florence eagerly accepts the baby from the nurse, swaying and cooing softly, taking Laura's tiny fingers in her own and kissing them. Marguerite looks across the room at Sadie, one last time, and closes her eyes.

Chapter 40

December 12, 1925

Marguerite is gone by the time I return to her room, as I knew she would be. She rests peacefully in death, still warm, the morning light dancing across her face. I rest my head on her folded hands, my tears running freely. Beckett comes in, his eyes red from crying. "I tried to find you, at the end. Where were you?"

"Right where I needed to be."

Beckett gives me a questioning look, then sits next to Marguerite's body, stroking her hair.

"I'm sorry I've been out of sorts lately," I say, reaching for his hand and lacing my fingers with his. "I love you, Beck. I do."

He raises my hand to his lips, closes his eyes. "And I love you."

The doorbell rings downstairs, echoing through the house.

"That must be Claire," Beckett says, rising.

"I'll get it. If it's Aunt Claire, I should be the one to break the news to her, I think."

I descend the stairs, my nerves jangling. I'm about to meet someone who should be dead, but isn't any longer, for reasons I have no way of explaining.

I ease open the door cautiously, unsure of what to expect. The woman on the porch is petite and compact, her bobbed hair gray now instead of red, but her blue eyes are still as round and wide as they were in her youth. She smiles at me, then pulls me into her arms, kissing both my cheeks. "Sadie. So good to see you again."

"Good to see you, too, Aunt Claire," I say, my head spinning. "How was your trip?"

"Oh, it was fine. You know how the trains are. Tedious. I got here as soon as I could, but I'm already too late, aren't I?"

I duck my head. "Yes. I'm sorry."

"Don't be, child. We can't control these things. Where is she?"

"Upstairs. In her room."

I follow Claire up the stairs but stop short on the landing. One of Marguerite's paintings hangs there—one that wasn't there before. It's the autumnal landscape I saw in my vision of Iris and Marguerite at the gallery. It's eerily realistic, the brilliant, jewellike leaves lit by sunlight, the rolling hillsides drifting like waves into the distance, shifting from gold to deep violet.

"*The Last Light of Autumn.* That's what she called that one," Claire says. "It made her entire career. She bought it back from the Met. She wanted Laura to have it someday. I suppose it's yours now, dear."

"I suppose it is."

Beckett looks up when we enter Marguerite's room. Claire goes to her sister's side, crossing herself as she kneels on the floor. She doesn't cry, only takes Marguerite's limp hand in hers. "What a rich life you had, sister. A full one. May you go easy, knowing you were loved." She kisses the back of Marguerite's hand, then replaces it on her chest with a tidy pat.

The rest of my family descends over the next few days. Louise, accompanied by her husband, Toby, and the children; Pauline; Aunt Grace; Felix, Rosalie, and their boys. Though Harriet is still on strict bed rest, she phones to offer her condolences, with a promise to visit with the new baby in the spring.

Despite my worries, Felix is curiously generous, taking charge of the funeral arrangements and, after meeting with Marguerite's attorney, reassures me he won't interfere with the probate proceedings. Rosalie pulls me aside at the wake and confesses to having smoothed the way on my behalf. "I wasn't going to tell you this, but Felix was gravely ill recently. He and the boys came down with some terrible, sudden anemia—the doctors couldn't figure it out. Things were touch and go for a few days, but they've made a remarkable recovery."

"Oh my." I feel my skin blanch. But of course, it makes sense. I was ill with the same thing. If Marguerite had succeeded in changing the past, I would have ceased to exist, and so would my brother. His boys. We all narrowly avoided annihilation.

"I told Felix he was being selfish, fighting with you over this house. His illness softened him. Made him see that he needs to change."

"I suppose I can't really blame him. Selfishness seems to run in this family. It's our curse, I think."

"Well, we must do better, for our children, mustn't we?" She smiles, eyeing my belly. "Beckett told me your news. Congratulations."

"Thank you. It was unexpected. I don't know that I'm ready to be a mother, but now's just as good of a time as any, I suppose."

"I felt the same way with Leslie and George. But it comes to one naturally. Most of the time." She smiles. "I brought some of your mother's jewelry with us. I'd like you to go through it tonight, pick out whatever you want. It should have been yours to begin with."

"How kind of you."

Rosalie presses my hand into hers. "I'd like us to be sisters, Sadie. I never had a sister, but always wanted one."

"I did, too. I'm sure you can imagine what growing up with two boys was like."

"Oh, I know. Too well." She laughs, then grows somber. "It must be difficult for Aunt Claire, being the only one of her sisters left."

"Yes. I'd imagine so. Although she seems matter-of-fact about it all."

"I suppose as one gets older, the inevitability of death becomes a part of life."

"Perhaps. Although I'm in no rush to find out."

"Nor am I." She squeezes my hand. "I'm glad everything worked out for the best, Sadie. I am. Marguerite was very lucky to have you looking out for her."

"No," I say. "I was the lucky one."

Across the room, I spot my husband chatting animatedly with a new arrival—a glamorous young woman I don't recognize. I go up to them and greet her, smiling. "Hello," I say, "I'm Sadie Hill. I see you know Beckett."

"Sadie, this is Sybil Vaughn. My cousin," Beckett says. "She was Marguerite's companion a few years ago, before you came."

Sybil. "Of course. Beckett's told me so much about you," I say, schooling my face.

"I was so sorry when Beckett phoned me with the news," Sybil says in her crisp English accent. She takes my offered hand, and goose bumps prickle up and down my arms. "I did quite enjoy my time with your aunt. I've just wrapped a movie, so I thought I'd come pay my respects and meet Beck's new wife."

"I'm so, so glad you're here," I say, though she'll never gather the true meaning behind my words. Marguerite did it—she saved Sybil, just as Iris hoped. "I knew your grandmother."

"You did?" She gives me a puzzled look. "How?"

"T-through Beckett and Marguerite's stories," I say, stumbling over my words. "And the portrait she painted. Of Iris."

"Well. Isn't that wonderful? Say, I'm famished, Beck," Sybil says, eyeing me curiously. "Could you show me to the food?"

I take a break in the powder room, splashing my face with cool water to shock myself out of disbelief at meeting my formerly dead aunt Claire and Sybil. It's going to take some time to unravel all the twisted threads of this new reality Marguerite created and I now find myself a part of. There are things that happened in *my* past but never happened to those around me. I'll need to sort my own memories from everyone else's, lest they think me mad. I have no idea how much my own husband remembers about the last few months.

Beckett finds me later, after all our company has gone for the night. It's just the two of us alone now, in this big house. He builds a fire in the library, and we cuddle together on the sofa, my head tucked beneath his chin. "It's not going to be the same house, without her here."

"No," he says. "It never will be. But we'll make it our own, Sadie." His hand rests gently on my belly, and the new life growing there. "Because she wanted us to."

⤜✦⤛

Three days later, Aunt Claire and I linger at Marguerite's graveside after the other mourners have left, the wind frigid despite the warmth of the low December sun. She sits on a stone bench, and I sit next to her, both of us quietly contemplating the small churchyard, speckled with fallen leaves.

"Aunt Claire, there's something I've been meaning to ask you."

"Yes, dear?"

"Did you ever know a man named Weston Chase?"

Her eyebrows draw together. "Weston. Weston. That name *does* sound familiar, but I can't think how."

"He was a writer. Tall, dark headed. Quite striking. She painted a portrait of him. He stayed at your house one summer, in the '70s."

"Oh, yes. I remember him. Papa had all sorts pass through in those days. Mr. Chase was writing a novel, I believe. He stayed with us for a few months."

"Did Grandmother . . . have a fling with him?"

"Florence? A fling?" Claire snorts. "Heavens no. She was too conventional for that sort of thing."

"I don't think she was as conventional as everyone thought," I say quietly. "But Weston was a real person?"

"Of course he was. I believe Marguerite has one of his books in her library, come to think of it. The one about the sisters. He wrote several novels."

"He sounds very charming, from Aunt Marg's recollections. Sort of a ladies' man."

"Oh, he was good-looking, as I remember, but I wasn't interested in men yet. I was much too shy and always had my head in a book. I was a late bloomer. I didn't have a beau until I was in my twenties. You probably don't remember my Harold. He died in 1898. You were very young. Very young." She shakes her head. "We met in California, in 1881, when I was on holiday with Florence and Marguerite. Harold was a stagecoach driver. I scandalized the whole family, marrying him. It was great fun." She titters like a satisfied pigeon.

"Do you ever have strange feelings about the past, Aunt Claire? Like you've been somewhere before. Experienced something before?"

"Only once. The same summer I met Harold. I had recurring dreams the entire month before we left for California. Terrifying ones. I dreamed I fell from a great height, but at the last moment, Marguerite caught my hand and pulled me up over the precipice. On our holiday, we stayed near a bluff on the coast that looked just like the one in my dream. Anytime I went close to that bluff, I had the strangest sensation I'd been there before." She shrugs. "Déjà vu. That's what they call it."

"Yes. I think so." I pause for a moment, thinking. "So, Weston—Mr. Chase—wasn't with you in California?"

"Oh, no. We hadn't seen him for years at that point, and it would have been wildly improper for a man to travel alone with a group of young women in those days, dear. It was only my sisters and I, and Marguerite's friend. Iris." She slaps her knees, standing. "Well, shall we go back to the house? They'll be waiting on us." As we walk away, I cast one final look at Marguerite's grave, wondering how many times she went back to that cliff in California. How many times she tried to save Claire and failed. Until the one time when she succeeded, and brought her sister back from death. As for Weston? I have a feeling I already know the answer—that the peace I feel inside Blackberry Grange is a sign he's moved on and that Marguerite was successful in saving him, just as she saved Sybil and Claire. Marguerite's actions in the past must have shifted things in such a way that Weston never became romantically involved with Grandmother, at least not by the time they were all together in California. If so, he might even still be living, although he'd be an old man by now. I probably wouldn't even recognize him if we passed on the street.

That night, after everyone has gone to bed, I light a lantern and go to the library. I skim my finger over the spines, searching. On a shelf across from the fireplace, I find it—a volume bound in green leather and embossed with gold leaf: *Three Graces* by Weston A. Chase. The frontispiece displays the publication date: 1884. Three years after that cataclysmic day in California—confirmation that he survived.

I sit and open the book, relieved, thumbing through the pages. I pause on a passage that catches my eye.

"And Cecilia was the purest of heart," I read aloud, "though her eyes held an uncommon curiosity her elder sister lacked. Her charms were often disregarded when Felicity was about, but William saw in Cecilia the unrealized potential of the dreamer."

It's the same passage Claire recited from Weston's portfolio in the tête-à-tête in the gazebo I witnessed months ago. I go back and start at the beginning and read straight through, until morning light breaks through the windows. The novel is about three sisters—akin to *Little Women*, in many ways. If there's any similarity between Weston's sisters and those in my family, it's shallow. The sisters go to dances and parties, gossip, marry very different men, and Cecilia—the main character— lives happily ever after with the stalwart and kind William on a farm in Wisconsin. I'm not sure what I was expecting, but it wasn't this. It's an innocent little book. One that would be at home in any child's library.

I stand and stretch, replacing the book on its shelf, content with the sense of closure I feel. I go up to the tower. Marguerite's portrait of me sits on its easel, the likeness filled with as much light as Weston's was with shadow, its colors radiant and fresh. I feel nothing but delight when I draw near to it—no sensation of vertigo, no strange, otherworldly sensations. And then I see the envelope with my name written on it, propped atop the canvas.

I open it and read.

Dearest Sadie,
I hope you like your portrait. I've been sketching you for months now, without your knowing. I thought I'd create one last beautiful thing before I died. Don't be sad. It was my time to go, and I have the peace I've always wanted. I've fulfilled all my promises. To Florence. To Iris. To you. I'm grateful we had our time together. I've lived my life the best way I knew how. Righted all the wrongs I could. And now, you must live. Live well.
I am always with you.
Love, Marguerite

Epilogue

1935

Birchtree Manor is a pleasant-looking place, with walls of red brick surrounded by rustling maples. As I ascend the front steps, I nod at the elderly gentlemen I pass, some in wheelchairs, others as spry and fit as I am. Any one of them might be the man I seek. The man I've come all these miles to see. My heartbeat ratchets higher as I enter the building, the sharp, clean scent of ammonia greeting me. I make my way to the nurses' station and give them my name.

"I called earlier. I'm here to see Mr. Nolan?"

"Yes, ma'am. He's in the dayroom. You'll see it to the right, at the end of the hall—the room with all the windows. He's usually there, sitting in his wheelchair. He likes to watch the birds."

I readjust the paper-wrapped parcel in my arms and walk down the wide hallway and into the dayroom. Just as the nurse said, an elderly gentleman is there, sitting in a pool of sunlight, looking out the bay window, his fine gray hair combed over his freckled scalp. I pull a chair next to him and sit, perching my pocketbook on my lap. "Hello, are you Mr. Nolan?"

"Yes, the very same." He turns toward my voice. "And who might you be, dear?" he asks, his lilting Irish brogue apparent. His smile is so much like my mother's, it's shocking.

"I'm Sadie. Sadie Hill. We've never met, but I've come all the way from Arkansas to meet you."

"My, that's a long way."

"Yes. I've never been to Vermont. It's beautiful here. I've been trying to find you for years."

"Have you, then? And why is that?"

"I think you'll know why, once I show you these pictures." I lift the parcel and unwrap the twine and brown paper. I place the two canvases side by side on the windowsill.

He leans forward in his wheelchair, squinting, and then his eyes suddenly widen in surprise. "Oh, oh my." His hand flies to his mouth. "Is that . . . ? Well, the one on the right is me, as a boy. And the other is . . . no, it can't be."

"It is. I'm Marguerite Thorne's granddaughter." I reach out my hand, and he takes it, clutching it with surprising strength. "And I'm so happy to finally meet you."

"*Really.* I never realized Marguerite had any grandchildren. She must have married, then?"

"No, she never did." I shrug. "You were the only man she ever loved, Mr. Nolan. You're half the reason I'm sitting here today."

Realization dawns on him slowly. "Oh . . . well. I never knew."

"She never told you she was pregnant?"

"No. Never. I knew she was hiding something from me, but not that."

"I didn't know, either," I say. "Not until a month or so before she passed away."

"She's gone, then."

"Yes, I'm afraid so. For almost ten years now."

He nods, his shoulders shaking as he begins to cry, his warm, soft hand in mine. I comfort him as best I can as he remembers. As he grieves. After a few minutes he looks up at me. "And the baby? What happened to her? Or was it a boy?"

"A girl. Marguerite's eldest sister raised her. Her name was Laura."

"Your mother."

"Yes. My mother. Marguerite wanted to find you. She tried, for many years. She even went to Ireland, looking for you."

"Oh, I'm not surprised she didn't find me. I wasn't there long. I met a lass from New York. She and I were married in '81. She was heartsick for home. Didn't like the slow way of life in Kildare, so we came back to the States." He sighs. "But I never forgot Marguerite. How could I? She was my first love. It was hard, how things ended."

"She told me. I'm very sorry."

"Well, in those days, her class of people and mine didn't mix. Things have changed for the better now, but back then . . ." He shakes his head.

"Indeed they have. I married Marguerite's gardener."

"You're happy then?"

"Very." It suddenly occurs to me that I might have a whole family of cousins, aunts, and uncles I've never met. "Did you and your wife have children?"

"Oh yes. Seven of them!"

I smile. "How lucky."

"Yes. Have you any children, my dear?"

"Only two. A boy and a girl. Bridget and Ned. Bridget is the eldest. She's nine." I touch my pocketbook. "I have photos. Would you like to see them?"

"Sure I would."

I draw out the photographs.

He chuckles. "Oh, the girl looks just like Maggie, doesn't she?"

"Maggie?"

"Marguerite. Maggie was what I called her. It suited her."

"Ah, of course." I vaguely remember the riverside scene I witnessed all those years ago, when Hugh had called her that. "My father was Irish, too. Marguerite always had a soft spot for him."

"Yes, I can see the map of Ireland on your face, my dear. We know our own."

We spend the afternoon getting acquainted, until at last the nurse interrupts us. It's nearly dinnertime, and visiting hours are over. "You can show her your room before she goes, if you'd like, Mr. Nolan."

I gather the portraits from the windowsill and follow the nurse as she wheels Hugh to a cozy room tucked into the corner at the end of the hall. Photographs in silver and brass frames sit on his dresser, alongside a shortwave radio set. A double wedding ring quilt covers his narrow bed, a simple wooden crucifix pinned to the wall above the headboard. I gaze at the faces of my distant relatives and at Hugh's wedding photo, given a place of honor at the center, his bride a smiling woman with a headful of unruly curls. I prop Marguerite's self-portrait against the wall and place the painting of Hugh next to it.

"She was such a beauty. This is just how I remember her." He reaches forward, his fingers gently tracing Marguerite's image. I see her eyes flicker, for the briefest second. Hugh pulls his hand back. "Oh my. How queer. I could almost swear she moved."

I smile. "Yes. Her paintings are very special. Remarkably lifelike, aren't they? One almost feels like they could walk right into them. Right into a memory."

He touches his own portrait, and the canvas ripples like water. I bend close, out of earshot of his nurse. "She's right on the other side, Hugh," I whisper. "Waiting for you. Whenever you're ready."

That night, on the last train out of Burlington, as I wind my way south, I'm struck with the impression that time is an invention. A construct of scholars and scientists—a way for us to mark our days, much like the crossties on a railroad mark the miles. But our memories, precious and dear, are beyond time. Eternal. They go on forever. And perhaps, some small part of us goes on, too. It must.

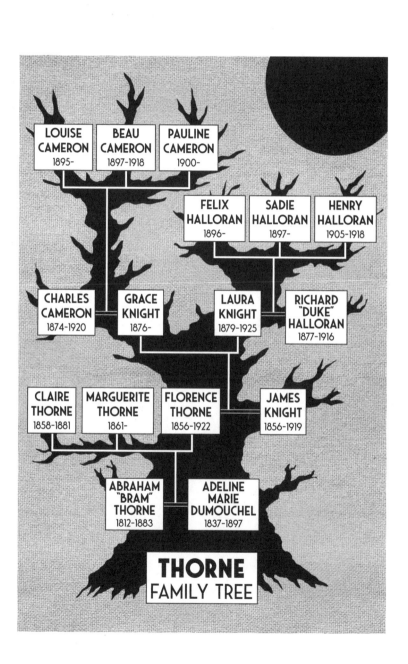

THORNE
FAMILY TREE

AUTHOR'S NOTE

When I first started writing this novel, I intended to tell a very different story. I'd recently returned to California after the death of my mother, whom I cared for during her final year of life in Missouri. I was still grappling with a lot of heavy emotions: grief, trauma, fatigue, and depression.

Unlike Sadie, I went into caregiving fully prepared for the challenges, because I'd also cared for my dad, who died of Alzheimer's disease in 2013. I knew that I was in for sleepless, watchful nights, very little time to myself, and the sometimes critical eye of friends and family members who had never walked a mile in a carer's shoes. But even with its difficulties, becoming a caregiver to someone you love is also an honor and a blessing. It teaches you to slow down. To be present. To be grateful for the time you have left with your loved one. Small breaks in your day, where you can steal away for a cup of coffee or spend time reading a book, become your lifeline and give you just enough air to keep going when things get tough. Being a caregiver humbles you. Makes you live in the moment and realize what's most important.

And so, with this book, I initially wanted to write about the day-to-day experience of being a caregiver to someone with a terminal illness and the empathy, patience, and self-awareness required of someone in this role—and about how much our loved ones teach us about living well and dying well in the process.

While my intended core message can still be found within these pages, Sadie's story is very different from mine in many ways. It's funny how our characters do that—how their voices rise and demand that you tell *their* version of events, despite your best-laid plans. While this is still a story about caregiving, it's also one about generational trauma, and how the echoes of our actions filter down to our descendants. This novel challenged me in many ways. The time-slip elements were especially ambitious, but when Marguerite's voice came to me just as strongly as Sadie's, I knew I had to tell her side of the story as well. Having spent a great deal of time around the elderly, and now edging toward my fifth decade, I've seen for myself how older people are often disregarded and disrespected in modern society, especially those with dementia. Through Marguerite, my aim was to show that our souls and our spirits remain the same, even as our frail bodies, and our minds, begin to betray us.

In the 1920s, memory-related conditions under the dementia umbrella, such as Alzheimer's disease, were just beginning to be named, diagnosed, researched, and treated. And so I concentrated my research on stories of caregivers with loved ones affected by Lewy body dementia (or LBD)—the type of dementia Marguerite would have been diagnosed with, had she lived in the modern era. The symptoms of LBD vary widely and affect people in different ways—making it challenging to diagnose and treat. To inform Marguerite's characterization, I read several memoirs, most notably *I Didn't See it Coming* by Mary Lou Falcone, who detailed her experiences caring for her late husband, the artist and musician Nicky Zann, and *A Caregiver's Guide to Lewy Body Dementia* by Helen Buell Whitworth and James Whitworth. I also relied heavily upon my own memories of caring for my dad, who in the later stages of his disease experienced the rapid mood swings, hallucinations, and paranoia prevalent in LBD, which typically strikes younger patients and has a more rapid progression than other forms of dementia.

For general research on the 1920s, I consulted the excellent *Only Yesterday* by Frederick Lewis Allen, *Anything Goes* by Lucy Moore, and *Bright Young Things* by Alison Maloney. For a better understanding of

Gilded Age and early-twentieth-century Kansas City, I read *Paris of the Plains: Kansas City from Doughboys to Expressways* by John Simonson and *Storied and Scandalous Kansas City* by Karla Deel. I took some liberties with locations and landmarks in the Kansas City area. While there were several speakeasies disguised as tearooms there in the 1920s, the Montpellier Tea Room is my invention. Father Bernard Donnelly, mentioned as Sadie's da's benefactor, was a real person and a celebrated hero in Kansas City. A former stonecutter and civil engineer who became a priest, Father Donnelly sponsored the immigration of hundreds of Irish laborers from Connaught to come to Kansas City in the nineteenth century. Under Father Donnelly's supervision, these Irish laborers carved through the distinctive limestone bluffs along the Missouri and Kaw rivers, creating the city we now know. Father Donnelly also established two orphanages, schools, and several Catholic charities serving the underprivileged.

My experiences as a frequent traveler to Eureka Springs informed the main setting of this novel, but I also consulted excellent resources on the early history of the area, written by local historians and authors: *Eureka Springs: City of Healing Waters* by June Westphal and Kate Cooper, *Eureka Springs Arkansas* by Kay Marnon Danielson, and *Haunted Northwest Arkansas* by Bud Steed. I took certain artistic liberties with locations and geological features. The thermal spring where Sadie and Beckett have their tryst is fictional—while Eureka Springs has an abundance of natural cold-water springs, touted for their healing benefits, thermal springs are a rarity in Arkansas outside of Hot Springs National Park, in the Ouachita Mountains, which is nearly two hundred miles south. Marguerite's house, Blackberry Grange, is loosely based on the privately owned C. W. Terry house, which dates to 1891 and was originally built in Carthage, Missouri, and later moved to Eureka Springs in the 1980s and restored, but is characteristic of the Queen Anne–style of architecture popular during the time Eureka Springs was founded.

Savvy readers will notice my nods to *The Picture of Dorian Gray* by Oscar Wilde, *Wuthering Heights* by Emily Brontë, and *The House on the Strand* by Daphne du Maurier, all of which helped inspire certain aspects of this story.

As always, any historical inaccuracies or oversights are wholly the fault of the author.

ACKNOWLEDGMENTS

Many thanks are due to everyone who played a part in bringing this book to light, beginning with my indomitable agent, Jill Marr, and the rest of the team at Sandra Dijkstra Literary Agency. I am so grateful for the guidance you so graciously impart. I could not have a better team behind me.

I'm equally grateful to the editors of Lake Union, who shepherd and teach and guide my hand until the final product is better than I ever imagined it could be. Tremendous thanks to Danielle Marshall, who took this book on with her characteristic enthusiasm and flexibility. Throughout my career, you've been there as a bit of a guardian angel to my books, and I could not be more grateful for your support. To Jodi Warshaw, developmental editor extraordinaire, whose talent for identifying the bones of a story and the core message behind what I write is unmatched. You inspire my confidence and give me the tools to craft something I can be proud of. And to Erin Adair-Hodges, who originally believed in this story—thank you. To the rest of the team at Lake Union, you are always a joy to work with. I can rest easy, knowing that throughout the process of building a book, from copyedits and proofreading to cover design and marketing, my stories are in expert hands. Special thanks to Rachel Tarlow Gul for her PR prowess, and for her ongoing support for my books long after launch has passed.

A multitude of thanks to my ever-loyal critique partner, Thuy M. Nguyen, who was the first person to read this novel and who flew to

San Diego hours before a hurricane to cheer me on during my first big author event. You dealt with my frazzled nerves and my unhinged California driving with such grace and patience. Some people go an entire lifetime without finding friends like you. You've been there from the start of this journey, and you are precious to me.

To Mansi K. Shah, my treasured friend and fellow author, critique partner, consultant on all things legal, and the main reason I'm willing to drive to the West Side of LA—I am ever grateful for your support, your inspiring presence and resilience, and your outlook on life and wellness. You are the kind of friend who makes me want to be better and do better, and while your ambition and determination are admirable and inspiring, you are always reassuring me that it's okay to rest. Thank you for being you, and for your eagle-eyed review of this manuscript and your admonition that no one can actually "turn on their heel."

To Maria Tureaud, as ever—I would not be here without you. Much love and gratitude for your continuing support and friendship.

To my APub author family, who never fail to support my books and show up for my launches—thank you. My list of author friends has gotten so long I'm afraid of leaving someone out, so suffice it to say: you all know who you are. I love you. Special thanks to my Writer in Motion, WriteHive, and RevPit friends—we're still here, still supporting one another, after all these years! Many, many thanks to Libbie Grant (a.k.a. Olivia Hawker) and our Business Hat chat group, my friends in the gothic/horror fiction community, especially Hester Fox, Kris Waldherr, Dawn Kurtagich, Jess Armstrong, Robert Gwaltney, Constance Sayers, Mary Kendall, Olesya Salnikova Gilmore, and Agatha Andrews. And to the ladies of Blue Sky Book Chat, it's such an honor being in your circle.

To the Bookstagram, BookTok, podcast, and reader communities—thank you for giving of your time by reviewing and supporting my books. It makes me so happy to know that my books have an audience—that I have a community of readers who are eager for whatever I write next. I'll never take you for granted.

To my best friend, Sa'dia, who endures my long silences when I'm on deadline and all my annoying quirks. We've been through a lot together—our friendship has been tested by thousands of miles, the joys and struggles of owning a business, and bracingly cold Mardi Gras winds, but there's no one else I'd trust to hold a twenty-foot ladder for me while I'm at the top. You are my ride or die, and I am yours.

To my sister Lula, who knows me better than anyone. We had a strange childhood. You are the only one who believes *all of it* really happened . . . because you were there, too. Maybe we should write that memoir we've been talking about. It sounds like fun, and Mom and Dad aren't here anymore to be embarrassed.

All my gratitude to my husband, Ryan, who supports my writing and my other aspirations wholeheartedly. Our marriage has survived an abundance of hardships and challenging circumstances. I'm glad we are still laughing, still together, still friends. And finally, to Avery. You are my whole reason, every day, for what I do—and I'm not just talking about the writing. I love you. Thank you for staying.

DISCUSSION QUESTIONS

1. At the beginning of the story, Sadie has qualities that might make her unlikable to some readers. Did you find her to be a sympathetic character? Did your feelings about her shift as the story progressed?

2. One of the themes throughout the book is how the choices we make affect those around us and the generations that follow. Several of the characters make life-altering choices during the novel. Which ones were most relatable to you?

3. The time-slip elements serve to illustrate Marguerite's past and create a frame around the main story and expose the "curse" that plagues the women in the Thorne family. Did you find them to be interesting and effective? Why or why not?

4. Weston represents the "demon lover" often portrayed in dark romance and gothic fiction. How did you feel about Weston? Did you find him at all sympathetic? Was Sadie's ambivalence toward him frustrating, or was it understandable, given her history? Did you think Beckett was a better match for Sadie?

5. The desire to right past wrongs is a major motivation for Marguerite. Can you sympathize with her actions? If you had the chance to go back in time to undo your mistakes and make different choices, would you?

6. Have you ever been a caregiver? If so, discuss your experiences and compare/contrast them with Sadie's.

ABOUT THE AUTHOR

Photo © 2021 Paulette Kennedy

Paulette Kennedy is the bestselling author of *The Devil and Mrs. Davenport,* *The Witch of Tin Mountain,* and *Parting the Veil,* which received the HNS Review Editor's Choice Award. She has had a lifelong obsession with the gothic. As a young girl, she spent her summers among the gravestones in her neighborhood cemetery, imagining all sorts of romantic stories for the people buried there. After her mother introduced her to the Brontës as a teenager, her affinity for fog-covered landscapes and haunted heroines only grew, inspiring her to become a writer. Originally from the Missouri Ozarks, she now lives with her family and a menagerie of rescue pets in sunny Southern California, where sometimes, on the very best days, the mountains are wreathed in fog. For more information, visit www.paulettekennedy.com.